BLOODIN
THE DARK

THIRTEEN TALES OF TERROR

"Blood in the Dark" Short Story first featured in
Doors of Darkness II: Trick or Treat 2024

First paperback edition 2024
Published by Tucker Joneson
450 Jack Sharp Dr.
Seymour, TN 37865
For information email:
tuckerjoneson@gmail.com
Cover Design by Tucker Joneson

ISBN: 979-8-9921655-0-0

Library of Congress Control Number:
2024926058

CONTENTS

INTRODUCTION

Ever since I was a little kid I've always loved writing. Over the years I've scribbled in dozens of notebooks and stashed away flash drives filled with numerous story outlines, partially written novels, and half-finished scripts. After years of tossing around different ideas, I decided that I wanted to create something that combined my talents of drawing and writing. In 2020, I finally self-published my first illustrated children's book, *The Soldier Bear.* This book was inspired by the true story of a brown bear, named Wojtek, that served in the military during World War II. After finishing that book, I had the urge to write something scary.

I have always loved horror. I grew up with it. One of my earliest memories is of watching *Jaws* for the first time with my grandparents when I was four-years-old. Needless to say, it had an affect. I'm still not a fan of the ocean, but more importantly, I love thrilling stories! Those same grandparents are the ones that really got me into writing at an early age. Even some of the earliest stories that I wrote in elementary school were inspired by spooky books and shows like *Goosebumps* and *The*

Twilight Zone. Whenever October came around, I would spend every Halloween decorating the house like a graveyard, dressing up, and working in haunted houses. That's when I learned that there's nothing more addicting than scaring the pants off of people.

Members of my family have even worked on horror projects going back to the early days of Hollywood. Films and shows like the original *Creature From The Black Lagoon, The Lost Boys, Final Destination, Teen Wolf, Maxxxine, Dark Night of the Scarecrow,* and much more. So you could say it's in my blood.

Growing up, it was hard to find books that I liked. For many school projects, I would end up skimming through the assigned books, eager to get them over with. *The Outsiders, Of Mice and Men,* and *Where the Red Fern Grows* were some of the few school books that I actually enjoyed. That struggle ended when I discovered horror! Whenever I found a good scary story, you couldn't get me to put my book down. I grew up reading many books and short stories by R.L. Stine, Edgar Allan Poe, Stephen King, Darren Shan and so many more.

The more I read, the more I wanted to write. With so many different story ideas and directions I wanted to take, I realized I could write something that combined all of them into one book. That's when I decided to create this horror anthology filled with thirteen thrilling tales. A couple of these short stories were originally conceived of years ago, while others I came up with as I was writing this book. Some tales merged into one, while other stories that I had originally planned for this book were shelved. Perhaps I'll release those in a second anthology book in the future.

Whether you like werewolves or vampires, or you prefer ghosts, ghouls, and demons, I'm sure everyone will find stories in here that they are drawn to. Some stories may end in tears, others with cheers. Some of these characters could simply encounter a bump in the night, but perhaps the world will end for others. These thirteen tales can get quite gruesome. For those of you that can be rather squeamish, this was your final warning. I hope you all enjoy reading this book as much as I loved writing it.

TUCKER JONESON

BLOOD IN THE DARK

As the flames in jack-o'-lanterns flickered, children roamed along the sidewalks of a dead-end road. The scent of sweets lingered in the cool night air. A boy dressed as Dracula, with slicked back hair, fake blood dripping from his lips, and a flowing black cape, made his way down the street. The boy carried an old pillowcase filled with candy; the wrappers and small candy boxes crinkled and rattled as he walked along the sidewalk. The boy's two friends were also dressed as classic monsters; The Invisible Man and Frankenstein's Monster. The vampire boy, named Edgar, was currently searching for these two monstrous friends. He'd lost them in the crowd of costumed children earlier that night.

Laughter and screams echoed through the fog-filled streets. As Edgar turned the corner, he was overcome with an odd feeling. There was something different about this street. The boy had no idea of the tricks that were in store for him this Halloween night.

Edgar and the two missing boys, Steve and Joe, were the only ones left in their group of friends that wanted to dress up and celebrate this night. Everyone else their age was either going to parties or out on dates. None of the others were filled with the same passion for horror films and haunted houses that these three shared. It's what bonded them together since the beginning. Despite that, Edgar believed that this would be their last Halloween together. He couldn't ignore the fact that they were all growing up. Eventually they would have to leave behind their beloved childhood like everyone else. For now, Edgar was going to enjoy this night filled with candy, costumes, and creeps.

Aside from collecting sweets, the three thirteen-year-old boys were planning to visit a haunted house. Children would whisper tales of an evil house tucked away on a dead-end road. That week at school, Steve and Joe told Edgar the stories of this creepy place. This house had been standing for nearly a century, and in all that time, the owners had never been seen. There were never any cars seen sitting in the driveway or any lights on inside. The curtains were always drawn and the doors were all locked. No mailmen ever stopped at this house and no gardeners ever mowed its lawn—yet the house always stayed in pristine condition. However, the legends claim that over the years, anyone who dared visit this home would disappear without a trace. Children who knocked at the door never left the front porch, and any animals that went to relieve themselves on the lawn were never seen again. Edgar wasn't sure if he believed in any of this, but he was still curious enough to go investigate with his friends.

Unfortunately, they forgot to mention the address of this deadly home. *If this haunted house was even real in the first place*, Edgar thought. The only thing he could remember hearing was that it was the fourteenth house in the middle cul-de-sac. Somehow Edgar had never heard of the horrors of Pike Street, but Joe and Steve claimed that they were all true. They swore that they were told by this group of high schoolers, who heard it from some other kid, whose friend went missing last year.

Edgar continued trick 'r treating as he searched for the missing monsters. Children ran past him dressed as cowboys, demons, wrestlers, and princesses. Some wore the classic plastic masks while others were covered in makeup. Tired parents struggled to keep up with their sugar-rushed kiddies in the shadows. Unwrapping a chocolate bar from out of his candy bag, Edgar took a bite.

Might as well keep collecting candy, he thought.

The vampire boy turned and made his way across another home's walkway and up onto the front porch. This older wooden structure was a colonial style clapboard house. The two-story house was a ghostly white, with dark burgundy shutters and white columns along its semicircular front porch. The porch was dark and Edgar couldn't see any lights on inside either. Why not give it a shot? He thought as he knocked his fist against the dark red door. The boy's eyes glanced down at his feet to see Steve's plastic Frankenstein mask beside the doormat.

"Steve?" he whispered as he bent down to pick up the monster mask. On the inside of this mask, Edgar spotted a spider sticker stuck along the forehead, confirming that this was his friend's mask. Steve had a booklet of creepy-crawly stickers which he had been applying to his lunchbox and school supplies. As Edgar inspected the mask in his hand, the front door of the large house slowly creaked open.

Had to be a breeze, he told himself. Beyond the red door was nothing but darkness. Edgar wanted nothing more than to turn around and run. Although his gut told him not to step inside, he knew that he needed to find his friends. Edgar reached down into his candy sack, and pulled out a small flashlight. For once, he was thankful for his overbearing parents and their nagging. They made sure that he and his friends took flashlights with them when going out that night.

The small burst of light broke through the wall of dark-ness before him. The house was empty. His eyes scanned the room, noticing that there were no picture frames hung on the walls, no couches, tables, or any other furniture in sight. There was nothing. There wasn't even a hardwood floor. Edgar took his first step, which was farther down than he expected, and stomped down onto a dirt floor. Using his light, he examined the ground, searching for any kind of explanation for this strange place. It felt as if the home was a façade, like the fake structures they build in Hollywood for filmmaking. Edgar had taken a tour of one of those studios on a summer road trip with his family last year. As he thought back to those happy days, his eyes grew wide and his arm froze still. The metal flashlight trembled in his hand. The light was directed down at the center of the dirt floor. A large opening in the earth loomed before him, like a cavity in a rotten tooth. The bright summer time memories faded away. Now there was only moonlight on a gloomy October night.

Edgar slowly walked up to the dark pit, flashlight still gripped in his hand. His knuckles grew white as panic started to seep in. What is this? What's going on here?! Before he could think of any answers, Edgar spotted Joe's faded blue pillowcase hanging limp along the edge of the crater. Noticing that it was nearly empty, most of the candy must have dropped down into the hole below. This gap in the floor must be, at least, five or six feet wide across, Edgar thought to himself as he struggled to make out any visuals amongst the dark descent. Breaking the deafening silence, he called out for his friends. His throat was dry as he whispered, "Steve? Joe? Are you guys down there?"

No response.

He looked around the house once more, realizing that it was getting darker. Edgar turned back to see that the front door was now closed. Before he could move, he began hearing a squeaking noise that was coming from below. Edgar squinted his eyes as he looked on into the dark. His small light did almost nothing to help, until something small appeared. It was fast and jittery as it flew up towards Edgar's face. They flew up and around the boy's head, wings flapping and grazing the boy's skin. He panicked and flung his arms around in the air. As the boy danced, he hoped they wouldn't bite him. He turned to run for the door, but the winged creatures flew back at his face, causing the boy to fling himself back. At that moment, Edgar realized what he had done. The vampire boy fell back into the abyss. The bats shimmered in the moonlight above, for only a moment, before everything went black.

Edgar hit the ground hard.

He choked and gasped as the wind was knocked out of him. Clouds of dust filled the air and coated the boy's lungs as he struggled to inhale. His skull rattled and his vision was blurred. Rolling over, he continued wheezing and coughing, fighting for air. His body ached as he slowly rose to his knees and then to his feet. His left arm and shoulder had taken most of the impact. Tears began to glisten at the corners of his eyes, but he held them back as best as he could. He cautiously raised his arm, bending it and clenching his fist. Weary tendons strained under his pale skin. *At least nothing was broken*, he told himself as his breathing finally settled.

The flashlight blinded him as it rolled back and forth along the cold floor. He clutched the light in his trembling hand. The empty cavern walls stretched out into the infinite darkness—much farther than his weak light could reach. As his eyes adjusted to the large empty space, he began to see strange rock formations peeking out from the dark.

The air was crisp and cold as ice. The rocky floor was harsh and lifeless. The sound of bat wings fluttered in the distance. His staggering footsteps moved across the dusty floor. Every little sound echoed off the dark stone walls. He could even hear his own heart beat. Edgar had descended into another world. He was alone in an ancient cavern hidden just below Pike Street.

Beads of water dripped down from the stalactites above and into puddles on the floor around him. *Or were those stalagmites?* He never remembered which was which, but he did learn how long they took to form in his science class. Based on the size of these formations, he estimated that this cave had to be close to a million years old.

Staring back up at the large gap in the earth, Edgar realized that he had fallen close to eight feet. The boy shambled in circles, searching for something—anything— he could use to climb out of this pit. There was no ladder, no rope, no way back up that he could find. *Why on Earth is a fake house built over this? Who built this house? What is it hiding?*

A chill ran up Edgar's spine as he pondered that last question. The boy was covered in goosebumps and his teeth began to chatter. Edgar could see his breath in the air as he limped forward, shivering. The sound of water droplets falling from above, echoed throughout the cave along with the sound of his shoe dragging across the rubble. Having taken more of the impact than he initially thought, Edgar dragged his left foot across the rubble.

Edgar winced as he rubbed his aching arm and glared up at the empty house above. "Someone help me!" He called out, "Anyone out there!? We fell into this hole! We need hel—" Edgar froze. He was sure he had heard it. A faint, yet audible scream, replaced by silence. He squinted ahead, sure that the scream had come from within the cave and not from above.

"Joe! Steven!" He shouted, "This isn't funny anymore! Where are you?!"

Nothing.

He pressed forward, limping away from the cave's entrance above. "Guys! I'm hurt! Are you okay?" His voice began to tremble. It faintly echoed along the cavern walls before returning to silence. As Edgar stepped forward his flashlight began to highlight the outline of a tunnel entrance. The tunnel floor was littered with Halloween candy. *Like Hansel and Gretel*, Edgar scoffed as he followed the trail of sweets to find his lost friends. He rubbed his sore left arm as he made his way down the dark corridor. Descending deeper into the earth, Edgar watched as the candy trail grew thinner, until finally there was no more. A sharp pain etched across his right arm. "Son of a..." Edgar groaned. Holding the flashlight toward himself, he watched as something trickled down his arm. A jagged rock protruding from the cave wall glistened as his blood met the flashlight's beam. His sleeve was cut, with fabric dangling along his bleeding forearm. He wrapped the material around his arm and applied pressure to stop the bleeding. The short time he spent as a boy scout had taught him a thing or two. *Let's see if they taught me any other skills to survive a creepy bat cave.*

Traveling farther, the caverns would both expand and constrict. At times the rock ceilings would stretch far beyond his reach, endlessly leading up into more dark mysteries. While other times the boy was practically crawling his way through. His Halloween costume was soon covered in layers of dust and mud. He didn't want to go much farther, scared of getting lost himself. He remembered times of exploring historic caves, like Ruby Falls and Carlsbad Caverns, on road trips growing up. However, those were lit and guided.

"Guys! Call out to me, please! We gotta get outta here!"

Dust and rubble fell around the boy, reminding him that this was not the safest place to shout. *What am I doing?! This is crazy!*

The rock walls were beginning to close in on him. He could feel them scraping against his shoulders. He stumbled and tripped as his shoes became caught on crevices along the path. He had to pivot sideways and squeeze his way forward. He kept his flashlight raised to shine ahead, while his other hand gently glided along the rocks behind him. Chilling water droplets rolled down his skin.

This tight path began to bend and turn, not allowing Edgar to see far ahead anymore. Taking his time with his steps, he continued moving forward. The rock walls were beginning to push up against his chest and back as the path became narrower and narrower. Squeezing himself through, he had to keep his head turned to his right, looking ahead. Soon the walls were too close together to move at all. He had to stop, feeling his foot caught between the rocks. He tried to pull at it, but his limbs were now locked in place as well. His chest had begun to burn.

Now knowing that he was stuck, a sense of dread overcame him. His heart raced as beads of sweat dripped down his face. He struggled to breathe. The walls were crushing his lungs. The darkness was closing in. He yanked at his limbs, trying everything he could do to break free. His breathing was short and heavy. "Someone help me! I'm stuck! I'm scared! Please! I—I can't do this!" He yanked his right arm back, loosening it, but cutting the back of his wrist. Pain struck his hand like lightning. His hand twitched and lost hold of his light. The flashlight bounced off the walls, blinding him like a strobe light, before hitting the dirt floor. It rested before him, just out of reach.

"Oh God! No!" He cried as his body shuffled and pulled, desperately trying to free himself. *Calm down! Get it together, Edgar! You are not dying down here! Your friends are not dying down here! They need you! Your family needs you! You will make it home!*

Edgar attempted to slow his breathing. In and out. Closing his eyes, he listened as his heart beat slowed. The boy clenched his fists and began pushing his way forward. The sharp edges of the cave walls scratched his chest and back. A tear ran down his face as he pushed along. Finally, his chest began to feel some relief. His lungs could breathe again. His head was soon able to turn again. He smiled and whispered to himself that he was making it out of here.

Edgar struggled to reach for his fallen light. Trapped between sharp ridges, there wasn't space to kick at it. With no success, he continued forward, watching as the light behind him grew smaller in the distance. It began to flicker and would soon be dead, leaving the boy in total darkness. He had to find his friends soon before they were all lost in the dark forever. The smile faded and Edgar gasped. His eyes panned up from the flashlight to see two glowing dots in the dark. Like cat eyes staring back at him from within the shadows.

At that moment Edgar began to feel weightless. The ground had vanished from beneath him as he fell backwards into the night. The boy flipped and tumbled down a steep hill, hitting rocks and rough formations. He clenched his jaw as his bones were rattled, until finally rolling to a stop along the cold cavern floor. He grabbed his side as he slowly rose to his feet, praying he wouldn't crack his skull on any stalactites or stone walls.

Blind as a bat, Edgar shuffled forward. His arms were outstretched, searching for anything that he could take hold of. His left arm, now covered in dark bruises, ached and quivered. Warm blood ran down his right arm. He imagined the terror and sadness that would overwhelm his parents when he never came home. As well as the pain that the families of his friends would endure. He knew that they—and the police—would spend days, weeks, maybe even years, hopelessly searching for them. No one would ever think to explore the secret, never-ending basement of this cursed house.

We are all making it out of this place, he told himself, unsure if he believed it, but knowing he couldn't afford to give up now.

His bloody hand clasped a chilling round object before him. He stopped and stood in the dark as he tried to make out what it was that he was grasping. It didn't feel like the earth of the cavern. His fingers ran down along its unique curves and texture before feeling smaller rounded pieces. Teeth. His heart stopped the moment he discovered that he was touching a human skull. Edgar leapt back, ready to scream, and crashed into something—someone—who wrapped their arms around him. Before he could shout, a hand clasped his jaw shut. Edgar panicked and fought to get loose.

"Edgar, stop! It's me! Steve!" The voice hissed in his ear. Edgar's heart fluttered as he turned around to see the dark silhouette of his friend.

"Thank God I finally found one of you! Where's Jo—" He started. Steven cut him off and turned his flashlight on, casting devilish shadows across his face.

"Shh! We're not alone in here!"

Now his heart sank. His friend's eyes were wide, his skin was dirty and drenched in sweat. Dark blood ran down his face and arms. The boy in the shredded Frankenstein costume raised his arm and pointed ahead. Edgar noticed that his hand was trembling. He turned around to see that Steve was pointing at the skeletal remains of what looked like an old miner. The bones protruded from mangy black overalls. Beside the body, laid a metal helmet and a rusty pickaxe. The corpse sat on the ground with its back against the wall, staring back at Edgar and Steve with its empty black eyes.

Steve turned his light, pointing right to reveal another miner's body, along with old bags, buckets and crates. He brought the flashlight back and held it under his frightened face.

"There's more bodies in here. Some older and others more recent . . . We need to find a way out!"

"Where's Joe? We can't leave him!"

Steve shook his head, "Something got him."

"There's another person down here? WHERE?"

"*Shhh!* Not a person," Steve whispered. "Something else." His eyes swelled as he slowly exhaled, "When we were exploring one of these caverns—this thing— came out of nowhere and got him. It carried him off into the dark. I tried chasing after them, but at some point I slipped and tumbled down into this pit, hitting my head . . . "

"What are you talking about? What was this thing?" Edgar pleaded.

Steve rubbed his eyes, almost like he was questioning his own vision. "A vampire. I think. It was huge. Not like anything I've ever seen before!" He answered coldly. You really did hit your head, Edgar thought.

"We need to get going and find Joe!" As Edgar stepped by, Steve grabbed his arm.

"He's gone, Edgar. Last thing I heard were his screams, but now . . . it's been dead silent."

Edgar looked into his friend's eyes. He had never seen him like this before. He was horrified. Taking a deep breath, Edgar began limping over to the dead miner's body. He bent down and grabbed the rusty pickaxe. His arms ached as he lifted the heavy cobweb-covered weapon.

"You've got the light. Lead the way."

———

Dracula and Frankenstein, in their tattered, bloody costumes, made their way across the cave. Steve's fading flashlight illuminated the bottom of the steep hill that they had fallen down. "You think there's an easier way to get back up there?" Steve asked. Edgar glanced around the cave for any other paths.

"I don't think—" A large object crashed down next to them. Blood erupted in the air, soaking the boys, as it tumbled along the ground. It was a body. It was Joe.

The wide-eyed boys looked down in horror at their friend's soggy corpse. His throat was slashed open with his head bent so far back that it was almost torn off completely. His suit and bandages were drenched with his dark red blood. Joe's body still pulsed and contorted.

Was he still alive?

The boys, still frozen from shock, turned to look up in unison to see where Joe had come from. Steve lifted his flashlight, illuminating a dark figure above them. Edgar, once again, saw those same glowing cat eyes in the dark, looming over him. The light revealed an enormous bat creature hanging from above. Its eyes were pale white like a corpse. It had crooked clawed feet, patchy gray fur, and a trail of Joe's blood dripping down from its fangs.

It let out an ear-piercing screech. Edgar staggered back as he covered his ears. The unholy creature let go of the cave ceiling, extended its large bat wings, and descended down towards the two trembling boys. Edgar began to run away, and looked back to see Steve still frozen in place. His eyes almost transfixed to the dead eyes of the vampire. The large creature swooped down and grabbed him with its claw-like feet. Edgar was blown over by the force of the wings as they flapped, rolling across the stone floor. Pain shot through his body as he crashed into a boulder. He looked out across the cavern to see his screaming friend rise up into the air.

"No!" Edgar cried as he rose to his feet. The vampire ascended farther, disappearing into the darkness. He chased after them, pickaxe in hand, unable to see anything. He was not ready to lose another friend tonight.

Steve fought back, hitting the creature's feet with his fists and attempting to pull himself free. Its claws dug deeper into the boy's shoulders. He screamed and bit down on the vampire's foot until he drew blood. It was black and thick like tar. It tasted like battery acid and smelled even worse. He didn't stop. He kept biting deeper. The monster's skin was cold and dense. Its icy black blood was freezing his teeth. Steve continued screaming, now gargling on the demon's blood. He kept biting down until finally its grip began to loosen. It roared as it released the boy. The vampire continued to fly away as Steve descended into the black abyss.

Grinding his teeth, Edgar fought through the pain. He staggered over rocky grounds and bounced off jagged walls. Up ahead he could see a light, a tiny beacon in this black hellscape. He slowed to a stop, breathing heavily, and bent down to grab the light. It was Steve's flashlight.

"Steve?" He whispered. A gurgling burst came from the dark. Edgar stepped forward, lifting up the light to reveal his friend. Steve lay sprawled out, impaled by a large stalagmite. Blood was everywhere. His head shook as he spewed more blood from his mouth. He was choking while his hands felt around his stomach. The boy was attempting to push his intestines back inside to no avail. Steve's bloodshot eyes turned to look over at his horrified friend. Edgar stood there, unsure of what he could possibly do, as his friend spat up black blood. He cried and squirmed before finally going limp. His friend was dead. His red eyes still glaring back at him.

The world was silent. All that Edgar could hear was the thud of his own heart beating, "I'm sorr—"

Once more, the vampire let out a blood-curdling scream that boomed off the walls like fireworks. Edgar turned and ran for cover. He could hear the loud swoosh of the bat wings over head. His muscles burned as he sprinted, feeling the weight of the pickaxe that was slowing him down. Up ahead, he could spot the entrance of another tunnel. As he pushed himself harder, the monster was gaining speed and closing in on its prey. Edgar could smell its rancid breath behind him. Reaching the tunnel, he lunged forward, pushing off of the walls and propelling himself farther inside. His knees were scraped and shoulders beaten, but he was still alive.

The vampire crashed into the small tunnel entrance. Its wings flapped wildly as it tried to squeeze inside. Inches away from the boy, it chomped at his feet. Specks of blood and drool scattered across Edgar as he kicked back at the demon's face. Gore and entrails dripped down from its black tongue as its eyes stayed locked onto him, eager for its next meal.

Huffing, Edgar raised his pickaxe and charged at the vampire swinging the blade down into its neck. The beast cried out in pain. Black tar blood spewed from its veins and dripped from its mouth. The piercing screech burst Edgar's eardrums. As Edgar pulled back at the ax, the vampire swung its winged arm, backhanding Edgar and sending the boy crashing into the wall. Feeling something crack, he looked down instantly fearing his bone was broken, only to find the handle of the ax broken off. The head of the ax protruded from the vampire's neck. The metal remained lodged into the staggering vampire's neck.

With the broken ax handle and the nearly dead flashlight in hand, Edgar crawled away from the demon. It bit at the ax before tugging it loose from the pulsating wound. It tossed the bloody chunk of metal away, rattling off the walls like gunshots. The cat-like eyes glowed in the distance watching as the boy ran farther down the dark corridor. Edgar sprinted across the darkness, spotting the way out just ahead. He began his attempt to climb up the steep cavern wall. Desperate to escape, Edgar dug his bleeding fingers into the cavern wall. He heard the thunderous flapping sounds of the creature's wings closing in on him. He was so close. If only he had more time. In an instant, the claws grabbed the boy and he felt the talons pierce his shoulders. His feet dangled kicking for any surface to latch onto.

Edgar fought with the monster, beating at its claws with his broken ax handle. As the bat soared through the underground, the freezing air sent chills down the boy's spine. All he could hear was the deafening screams of the monster and its thunderous wings flapping again and again. The vampire was struggling to fly. Blood continued to run down its hideous figure. Edgar finally raised his broken handle and stabbed the jagged wood into the vampire's clawed foot. It screamed, tightening its grip on him. Edgar cried out as he continued stabbing at the bat's leg. Losing control, the monster crashed into a cavern wall, sending it and the boy tumbling down into the darkness below.

Edgar spat out blood and teeth onto the rocky ground. His broken body struggled to rise up. Pain surged through his limbs as he reached out for his dying light. The boy's stomach churned as he took in the putrid air. It reeked as if the earth itself was rotting. Pointing the light down, he discovered a sea of bones and dried blood coating shredded clothes, shoes, wallets and backpacks from dozens—maybe hundreds—of victims. Bodies of men, women and even children. Skulls, some still coated with bits of rotting skin and hair, littered the cave. They stared back at Edgar as if to welcome him to his final resting place. These corpses wore t-shirts, sports jerseys, torn jeans, suits, and dresses. Some outfits even looked as if they came from another century. *How long has this thing lived down here? How many people have died here?*

Edgar didn't have answers, but he prayed that these victims did not suffer for long. Behind him, laid more bodies of the lost miners. Cobweb coated skeletons were rotting up against the walls, their jaws dropped in eternal screams. Next to these dead men were stacks of wooden crates. Edgar peered inside to see several sticks of dynamite. "Jesus . . . " the boy whispered, as he backed up, nearly tripping over a small duffle bag. He bent down and opened it, revealing emergency flares inside. "I hope these still work . . . " He whispered as he reached inside. His flashlight flickered once more before dying. The world was black.

The cave was silent.

The flare erupted into a blazing red fire. The flickering light illuminated only a portion of this massive space. His head spun as he looked all around him, desperately trying to find any way out. As the light sizzled in his ear, his eyes spotted strange formations hanging from above. These objects were not made of earth or ice, but of flesh. Vampires. Dozens of these creatures hung sleeping throughout the cave. They were all smaller than the beast he had fought off. *Children?*

Edgar's heart was pounding and his lungs wheeze as he struggled to breathe. The blood-soaked boy glanced back over at the miners' wooden crates.

The creatures all remained enveloped in their wings above. Edgar knew he had only so much time before they were all awakened. He rushed over to the crates, counting three—possibly more—filled with ancient dynamite. Edgar cautiously held his blazing flare away from the explosives. Before he could reach into the box, the vampire soared across the hall, tackling Edgar. He kicked and swung his fists at the beast. It was slower and weaker now. Its pale skin and fur were coated in its dark, dead blood. The demon's white eyes glowed with hatred and hunger. Edgar grabbed the monster's bloody neck, jamming his fingers into the wound. The vampire cried and twitched. It caught the boy's bruised arm and flung him across the cave.

Edgar's vision was starting to blur. The crimson flare lay burning on the cavern floor and near it was the jagged wooden handle. Edgar's nerves jolted, scattering pain throughout his body, as he crawled across the icy ground. Muscles in his arms and legs trembled. Dried blood pulled at his skin. The monster let out a chilling war cry that rattled the walls of the demon's dark den. Edgar cover his ears to no avail as the sound echoed in his brain.

The monsters that coated the red ceiling of this hellscape began to awaken.

Their ears twitched, wings had unfolded, and their fangs flickered in the violent light. The vampire charged at Edgar for one final strike. Its claws scraped along the stone floor as it scrambled his way. Edgar rolled over on his back as the devil came down over him. The vampire's fangs and tongue lashed out inches from his face. The putrid smell of death and copper flooded the boy's senses. Its pale eyes blinked in a look of surprise. The bat tilted its head down to discover that Edgar had impaled the monster's chest with his wooden stake.

The vampire squealed as it began to twitch and transform. Its bones cracked and shifted under its skin that tightened and stretched. The creature was shedding its fur and its claws became hands and feet. Edgar noticed that the skin began to rot and peel away. He was aging rapidly as he became more human. It was as if the years were finally catching up to this ancient being. Teeth and fingernails fell out as his skin melted off his bones. His eyes, now a faded green, oozed out from his skull. The gooey remains cascaded down onto the boy until all that was left were bones that had scattered across the ground.

The vampire was no more.

The blood-soaked vampire killer turned and crawled towards his fading flare. His breathing was heavy and uneven. His body was shaking and his head pounding. The fire sparked in his hand like burgundy fireworks in a cloudy night sky. His tired eyes watched as demons crawled along the ancient walls above him. Some had begun to take flight. Dozens of these monsters began charging towards him. They would devour the killer of their father, or perhaps, he was just another nightly meal to them. A smile grew on Edgar's face as he tossed the flare into the crate of dynamite.

———

A broken, bloody figure crawled along the rocky floor. Shredded fabric lingered behind him, dragging along the ground like broken fingers. As midnight grew near, he finally made his way back up to where this nightmare began. Edgar laid back amongst the cold rock and gazed up at the moonlight. Faint beams of light shone down through the open wound of earth above him. The moonlight illuminated the dust that danced through the air like fireflies.

His skin was layered with cuts, gashes, bruises and blood. He could feel his muscles torn, teeth chipped, jagged fingernails and his bones broken. Black blood dripped from his mouth. A tar-like substance covered his body. Specks of dust and rubble coated the tired trick-or-treater. After losing his two friends, he was ready to take out every creature down there, hoping that no one else would have to suffer the same fate. His heart ached, knowing there was nothing else he could have done, but his soul could rest easy knowing that those monsters were banished to the darkness for eternity. His breathing grew faint, his eyes fluttered slowly, as he took one last glance at this Halloween night. For a moment the world was still.

Silence echoed through the cave.

———

Edgar's eyes flashed open. They were pale and empty, glowing like the moon. His body twitched and convulsed as it began its metamorphosis. Bones in his face shifted and hardened, grinding under his skin. His brow sharpened and his eyes were sunken in. His mouth sprang open, revealing ever-growing sharp teeth that descended from under his now flattening nose. The boy was gone and all that remained was monster. Its lungs screamed out into the night sky, rising higher and higher until it sounded human no more. The corpse of Edgar trembled and snapped. Wings formed from skin along the creature's pale arms. Its veins pumped darkness through its black heart.

A vampire was born on Halloween night.

Children laughed as they ran from house to house. Orange and purple lights flickered and fog engulfed lawns. Candy bowls rattled as kids searched for their favorite chocolate bars. The night was bliss, as were the people, unaware of the horrors that lived just below. The door to this horrid home creaked open from a cold October breeze once more, welcoming the world in—or perhaps—letting the darkness out.

SCARECROW

There was a farmer, named Frank Flanagan, who lived on the edge of Midnight, Nebraska. Midnight was a small town that most people had never even heard of, with a population in the double digits. With his family, they took care of their two hundred acre farmland. Mr. Flanagan was a hard worker throughout his whole life. After returning home from the war in Germany, he married his beautiful wife—Theodora. The newly weds bought the land and immediately went to work building the farmhouse and barn. Near the end of construction, they decided the farm needed an extra hand. Out in the field, they assembled a guard for their crops. Stuffing hay inside an old set of clothes, with some stitching and wood framing, their new scarecrow towered over the growing cornfield. Soon after, Theodora was pregnant with twins.

The story goes that Flanagan grew up on a farm, as did his wife. So they always knew the life of growing crops and maintaining the land. Their main produce was corn, but the couple also grew other vegetables, along with raising chickens, and selling the eggs. The two of them were high school sweethearts and they would have been married sooner, if not for the war. They would have been on their sixth or seventh child by this time, as well. Unfortunately, that's where this story takes its dark turn. Theodora died after birthing her two children. Following this tragedy, the farmer began drinking heavily. I don't believe he lived another sober day in his life. However broken, the man was still a loving father to his two kids.

One autumn afternoon—when the twins were about five or six years old—the two of them ran off into the cornfield to play. Meanwhile, their father was still passed out in bed from another late night. Empty bottles littered the counters, filled the trash bins, and were scattered around the man's bedroom. A few hours had passed before he finally woke up. As he wandered around the house, beginning to sober up, he realized just how quiet it was.

The father searched their rooms, the basement, the barn, and the rest of the property after realizing that his babies were missing. He called out for them, louder and louder, but received nothing in return. Jumping into his old beat up truck, the farmer ran into town to continue his search. He spread the word to friends, shop owners, teachers, and of course—the police. Unfortunately, no one around had seen the children. The local police department started a search for the lost twins immediately.

Farmer Flanagan headed back home that evening. As he walked from his truck, back up to the farm house, he heard crows fluttering to his right out in the cornfield. He spotted several large ravens flying in circles far out in the distance. They continued to dive up and down into the cornfield.

He stepped into the cornfield, on his way to investigate—praying that he wouldn't find what he was thinking. The birds cawing grew louder, and louder, as he made his way through the field. He went from walking, to jogging, to running, until finally he reached a clearing. A clearing with a scarecrow hovering above him, hanging off of its wooden frame. The scarecrow that he and his wife had put together all those years ago, was beginning to rot. It was dirty and falling apart. The yarn used to stitch details in its face had come loose and sprung out like wild hairs. Bird droppings and mud were scattered across the coat and pants of the figure. One of its arms had come untied from the frame and pointed its fingers down to what laid at the scarecrow's feet. The birds all scattered, flying up at the farmer's face before disappearing into the dark sky. The farmer looked down to see two mangled bodies on the ground. His twin children lay there dead, covered in flies and maggots. Chunks of skin were torn out of them by the crows. Worst of all—was their eyes—the children's eyes were gone. Gouged out by the crows.

After that night, the farmer drowned himself in alcohol. He would spend days just lying in bed, others out chopping wood with his ax, and screaming into the night. Bringing out his gun, he would shoot and kill any birds that he spotted. He would wander out into the road, praying that someone would hit him. The loss of his family broke him to his core, and he tried everything to fill the empty soul that remained. The drinking, the sleeping, the violence. Nothing solved it. Eventually, he realized that the only way to get his family back—was to take them back himself. Soon after, children around town began to go missing. The small police force did what they could, but were never able to find them. When the cops came up with nothing, that led to the parents taking actions into their own hands.

The parents all knew about Frank Flanagan and what had happened to his family. They believed that if anyone around here had taken their children, it was the drunk widower on the edge of town. Two of the parents— rumor is, that it was Mr. and Mrs. Eggers—were the ones to finally make a move. They were the parents of the first children to go missing. The Eggers had a four-year-old boy and a seven-year-old girl. After they were taken, six other children had gone missing, all of which were no older than eight-years-old. The entire elementary school of Midnight, Nebraska was practically missing before winter. So one night the Eggers parents drive up to the Flanagan farmhouse, where they planned to confront the farmer. They knocked at the door, and shouted when there was no answer, before realizing that the door was unlocked. It looked like nobody was home. The parents wandered through the house, looking for any signs of their children.

The father had brought a small revolver with him and the wife grabbed a knife from the kitchen. They searched both floors, finding nothing but bottles and dust, before turning their attention to the basement. They opened the door revealing a rotting staircase that descended into a dark bottomless pit. It smelled like death. They covered their noses and slowly made their way down. The parents found a light switch at the bottom of the stairs that sparked a dim bulb that illuminated the basement. That's when they found them. The two children were dead, laying in the dirt, their eyes gouged out just like the farmer's twins. They screamed and cried in anguish as their lifeless children's bodies were rotting in the basement of this madman's home.

The distraught parents looked around to see that they were surrounded by bodies. All of the missing children were dead. All of their eyes were gouged out. Intestines and guts were strung out from the bodies and sprawled out along the dirt floor. Gallons of blood soaked the soil and flies buzzed all around them like an overwhelming static. The parents carried their children's corpses out through the house and back to their car. That's when Flanagan stormed out from the barn and attacked the couple. He was a drunk raging mess, screaming that he just wanted his family back. The two fathers fought, slamming each other into the car. The father pulled out his revolver, but Flanagan quickly knocked it out of his hands. It was flung through the air and off into the darkness of the cornfield. Flanagan punched the father repeatedly. Blood erupted from the man's face. Bones cracked and shattered with each punch, until finally the wife stabbed him in the back. Flanagan screamed and punched the woman. She fell back onto the dirt road as the killer ran off into the corn. The bloody parents chased after him as he desperately tried to hide.

They followed his trail of blood through the corn stalks. He cried out, slurring his words and begging for forgiveness, before he stumbled and crashed down into the mud. He forced himself back up as he heard the parents closing in on him. The tracks finally stopped at the base of his scarecrow. Flanagan cried and begged them for mercy, but he knew his fate was sealed. In his final moments, Flanagan cursed them and vowed that he would make them suffer. He promised that he would have his children back—one way or another. Finally, the parents silenced him once and for all, when the father stabbed Flanagan in the gut with his rusty pitchfork. They left his body there in the middle of the field to bleed out under the scarecrow. Just as his children had died before. Soon the crows would come for him just the same.

That night the parents buried their children in their backyard, away from prying eyes. They never told the police or anyone else about what had happened, keeping the truth of that horrible night a secret forever. Before the year was over, the parents moved away and were never seen again. But farmer Flanagan never left that cornfield. Legend says that his soul possesses that scarecrow, and he wanders the cornfield every night—searching for new children to take.

"The legend goes that the scarecrow uses the victims to keep himself alive. He tears the bodies apart, using their guts and flesh to stuff himself, and give him life. Desperate to reunite with his family, but doomed to walk the Earth to pay for his sins. Anyone who dares step foot into his field, never comes out. To this day, no one has ever found any of the bodies. They simply disappear. The scarecrow is doomed to walk the fields 'til the end of time looking for his children, and God help you if you get in his way...The End." A redheaded girl notoriously chuckled as she held a flashlight under her face.

Four high-schoolers sat in a circle around a blazing fire in a rusty, old barrel. It was an unusually hot night in October. Humid and uncomfortable, with a rare breeze that would come and go. Sitting in an empty dirt lot, these kids were surrounded by crumbling brick buildings and large metal silos that made up the town's abandoned, old mill. The sound of crickets chirping echoed across the land. It was the only sound for miles, aside from the crackling of the fire.

Andrew West was the new kid in town. He was slightly taller than the average sixteen-year old, and skinny—but not a toothpick. His dark scruffy hair peaked out from under his old baseball cap, and the wind kept blowing a strand into his eye. The girl sitting across from him had noticed and giggled.

He had just moved to town at the start of the month with his mother, who worked for the government, which meant that they were always on the move. He lost his father when he was only seven-years-old to a drunk driver. His father was standing at the corner of an intersection, waiting for the crosswalk, when a car ran right into him. He was sandwiched between a radiator and the street light. Mom was driving Andrew home from school when they saw the police tape and the crowds. His bulging bloody eyes glared back at his crying son. No matter how hard he closed his eyes, the carnage would never leave his sight. Even in dreams, late at night, he would see his father's eyes staring back at him from the dark recesses of his mind. After that, Andrew vowed he would never pick up a bottle in his life.

Over the years, the boy met hundreds of different class mates, neighbors, and made several friends, some of which he still kept in contact with. He didn't reach out as often as he wanted, but made the occasional phone call. Sometimes they would even visit the old neighborhoods they used to live in. Even after all these years, it still wasn't easy making new friends, knowing that they'd be gone sooner than later.

Andrew wasn't sure about this group, but they were some of the few to reach out and bring him into the fold. Besides, it wasn't like he had many options in a town with a population of just over a thousand and a classroom that barely had twenty kids in it. He thought Midnight was a cool little town that had its charms. However, he'd rather go back to living in places like Fort Worth or Vegas. The boy wasn't sure how long they would be living there in Nebraska. They would stay in some cities for three years, while others barely lasted ten months.

During lunch on his first week at the new high school, one of the kids from this group—the girl—walked over and invited him to sit with them. Leaving his lonesome bench behind, he followed her. Everyone else around him was sitting in their own small cliques, but Andrew didn't mind being alone with his thoughts. He was so used to it by now, especially at the start of a new move.

Someone coming up to him on his first day was a bit odd, but they seemed nice enough. He noticed that they were definitely the cooler kids of the class, which wasn't a bad start, being among them. Although, it also had him on edge, imagining that this could be some kind of hazing. But he liked his chances and agreed to meet them at the old abandoned mill that night.

To his right, sat Raymond Murray, a shorter blonde boy in a plaid shirt and denim jacket. Ray was a bulkier kid—not fat, but solid—who made Andrew look like a twig in comparison. He had a soft voice that didn't seem to match his buzzcut, stern face, and large arms. Ray was a blocker on the football team, and was clearly more brawn than brain, when it came to some classes. Andrew was already helping him out with his Math homework that morning, and by helping, he meant letting him copy his work.

Then there was the 'alpha' of the gang—Charlie Cranston. Charlie stood at six-foot-two, with slicked-back dark hair and a leather jacket. He played the guitar and drove a black nineteen-seventy Chevelle. *His middle name might as well have been, 'Cool.'* Andrew thought, as he noticed a crooked scar that ran along his square jaw. It popped in the light of the flames as he looked over at the final member of the group.

Leslie Caretaker was a tall, slender girl in torn up jeans, with curly red hair that smelled like lavender. She was tough and snarky, and she didn't take anyone's B.S. Even though she was a tomboy, she was still beautiful. Leslie and Charlie had been together for a few months, but she had been friends with Ray since elementary school. Andrew knew right away that Ray had always been interested in Leslie, but never had the guts to make his move. Needless to say, when Charlie entered the group, Ray wasn't exactly ecstatic. He didn't want to upset his friend, so he put on a smile and tried his best to accept the engine-revving, rocker—Charlie.

Andrew was told some of these things, while other parts he figured out for himself. Living a life where you're constantly on the move had taught him how to read people. It didn't hurt that his mom taught him a few things from her job either. Charlie put his arm around Leslie and whispered in her ear. She giggled and squeezed his hand. Andrew was about to speak when she turned to look at them. She leaned in closer to the burning barrel. Ray and Andrew did the same. The radiating glow of the fire illuminated her eyes like burning embers. They all sat there in silent curiosity, until Leslie finally broke the tension with a grin.

"So you wanna go check it out?"

Andrew hesitated to answer.

"Sure, why not. We got nothing else going on around here, anyway." Ray answered, almost sounding bored by the story. Andrew had a feeling that she had recited this story a dozen times before. Who knew if any of it was even true. *This has to be a joke.* He told himself.

Andrew finally spoke, "You guys are just screwing with me, huh?"

"Nope. Dead serious." She replied. "Heard this story for years growing up. Everybody in town's heard the legend of the scarecrow."

"Not sure how many of us believe it, but I bet you most folks from around here steer clear of that farm." Charlie added. Andrew took a breath before responding.

"So do you all believe it? Have you ever gone out there before? Why do—"

"We've passed by the farm before." Leslie answered. "We walked through the corn field once, but never found the scarecrow."

"And that was during the day." Ray added, smiling at Leslie before turning to the new kid, "I believe the story. I believe that the crazy old man killed those kids, but I don't really think the farm is haunted or anything. I just know that a bad man died there, and that the farm's sat empty ever since."

Leslie got up and sat closer to Andrew, "I believe it too…and I want to believe that it's haunted, but I doubt it. We have to find the scarecrow first, though! That is, if it's even really out there!"

"…and you want to go out there now? At night? It's pitch black! If you couldn't find it in broad daylight, what makes you think you could find it now?" Andrew nervously laughed.

"There's a full moon out tonight. Besides, I just got a good feeling, and we got you with us this time. Maybe an outsider will show us the way." Leslie smiled, putting a hand on Andrew's shoulder.

"…Or maybe the scarecrow will sense an outta-towner and kill you for coming onto his property." Charlie chuckled. "I don't believe in ghosts, demons or any of that nonsense, but this town is so boring…not much else to do on a Friday night, ya know? So why not?"

Andrew's eyes darted back and forth between the three new friends he was making. He wasn't much of a believer in the supernatural either, but some part of him, in the back of his mind, was always cautious of it. Just in case.

"We're just messing with you, man. It's gonna be fun, let's do it!" Ray laughed, sounding more aggressive and insistent this time. Andrew's throat was dry and nervous. He didn't think running around in a maze at night was the safest thing to do—ignoring the whole possible killer scarecrow on top of everything. He also didn't want to upset them or be seen as a loser, or a chicken, for the rest of his life. *We get a new start here. Just like mom said. New start. New life.*

"All right. Let's do it."

The four departed their fire. Andrew walked towards his bike and asked, "So where is this place? How are we all getting there? I can follow on my bike…"

"No silly!" Leslie smirked and waved her hand, "Hop in."

The three teens walked up to Charlie's Chevelle. "You don't mind giving Andy a ride, right babe?" She asked Charlie as she leaned against the roof of the car. Charlie looked at her and then over at the new kid.

"Nah, no problem. Get in." He pulled open his door and sat down in the driver's seat. Ray and Andrew hopped in the back as Charlie turned the key. The engine to roared to life. Immediately, the radio came on blasting Creedence Clearwater Revival's "Bad Moon Rising." That song did not help put his mind at ease.

"Here we go!" Leslie cheered as they took off down the road.

———

The Chevelle pulled up to the old Flanagan Farm. Beams of moonlight pierced through cracks in the ancient, wooden barn, shining down like spotlights on the car. Tires crunched over the gravel road. Charlie stopped the car in front of the house and killed the engine. Just like that, the world was dead silent.

The moment Andrew climbed out of the car, he was hit with a feeling of dread that churned in his empty stomach, urging him to turn around and leave. *We shouldn't be here*, he thought. Even the crickets were silent and the wind was now gone. It was as if the world had been put on pause. Something was wrong with this place. They stood around the Chevelle, looking up at the decrepit farmhouse. Andrew could hear the bones of the structure creaking and groaning like a zombie's shuffling corpse.

"Okay, we saw the farm...We should get going now guys." Andrew whispered, but no one seemed to hear him. Leslie pulled out a flashlight and held it just below her chin. The shadows stretched across her face, giving her a demonic demeanor while she whispered.

"Who's ready to go in?"

Andrew and the others slowly approached the edge of the cornfield. The pale moonlight glistened across the endless field that reached out past the horizon. Even though the wind had stopped, the cornstalks jittered and waved as though they were alive.

Leslie finally stepped froward, vanishing into the corn. The others slowly followed. Andrew looked back at the farmhouse and the car parked before it. Part of him believed it was for the last time. The dirt was uneven and bumpy, some parts wet and muddy. They struggled to see where they were going, almost stumbling over each other. Charlie used it as the perfect excuse to hold onto Leslie.

The leaves of the corn scratched Andrew's face and stirred up his allergies. Moments later he was feeling itchy all over.

"Wait...If no one has lived here for almost fifty years...how is this corn still growing?" The new kid asked. "Who's maintaining this?"

"I've wondered the same thing over the years. I've never seen anyone on the property harvesting it or planting seeds. It just comes and goes every year." Leslie answered.

"The Scarecrow must be keeping it going." Charlie snorted. He wrapped his arms around Leslie and pulled her closer.

"What about the scarecrow?" Andrew asked.

"What about him?" Ray responded, irritated as he continued smacking corn stalks away from his face.

"When the corn is gone, and the field is clear for half of the year—doesn't anyone see this scarecrow? Or his post?" Andrew prodded, searching for the logic in this legend. "Anything out there in this dirt field?"

"No." Leslie turned around to face him. "I haven't, at least, but I still think he's out here. If I'm wrong, I'm wrong. But let's just keep looking and have some fun, Andy. Don't stress so much."

Three of the teens continued to venture further into the maze. Andrew stood still. He looked back in the direction of where they parked, but couldn't see the farmhouse anywhere. He turned back to see Leslie's light start to disappear in the darkness of the crops ahead. After a moment of hesitation, Andrew started walking quickly to catch up, afraid to lose his friends in the dark.

―――――

Andrew felt like they had been walking through this field for close to an hour, but when he looked down at his watch it revealed that it hadn't even been twenty minutes yet.

"How much longer do you plan on looking for this thing, guys?" He asked.

"Dude, if you don't want to do this, just get out of here then!" Charlie snapped. He turned around and glared at the new kid. Andrew froze.

"Sorry, just thought I'd ask. It's been twenty minutes already."

"Twenty?" Ray looked down at his watch, "Mine says it's been forty-five minutes since we got here. Look, it's almost midnight!" They looked over at his watch to see that he was right.

This doesn't make any sense.

"What about you guys?" Andrew asked, looking over at Leslie and Charlie. They both shrugged and Charlie answered.

"Don't wear watches."

"Don't you guys think this place is weird, something just doesn't feel right?" Andrew pleaded, trying to stay calm. A moment passed before Ray spoke up.

"Yeah. I'm not loving it here either. We should get going soon if we don't find anything."

"Look! Up there! I see an opening!" Leslie shouted as she quickly made her way forward, pushing corn out of her way. The three boys walked behind her, trying to keep up. Andrew watched as her fiery, red hair bounced in the glow of the moonlight.

Finally, the group reached a clearing, located in the center of the massive cornfield. This was where they were greeted by the large, twisted figure that loomed over them in the dark. The legendary scarecrow. It wore a dusty brown trench coat and faded overalls with a torn red flannel shirt underneath it. Hay, straw—and what looked like hair—poked out from holes in the figure's clothes and gloves. Its head was made from a burlap sack that was stitched up to resemble a human face. It was shrouded by darkness underneath the large, dirty hat that it wore. The scarecrow's arms stretched out, hanging over the wooden supports and its feet hovered a foot above the earth.

Several insects crawled across the scarecrow's weathered body. Maggots were peeking out from under its burlap mask. Andrew noticed that the movement of the bugs made it look like the figure was breathing. Lastly, there was an old rusty pitchfork that was leaning up against the scarecrow's side that glistened in the moonlight. Standing in the shadow of this decrepit thing sent chills down Andrew's spine.

He dropped his head, looking away from the scarecrow's sinister face, and noticed something strange about the old boots that it wore. The scarecrow's faded black boots were coated in what looked like fresh mud. Before Andrew could mention it, Leslie spoke.

"Huh, not as scary as I imagined him to be. The stories always made it seem bigger and ya know, scarier! It just looks like any other normal scarecrow."

"Can't believe we actually found it!" Ray laughed, almost sounding nervous. "Guess you were our lucky charm after all, new kid."

Charlie leaned up close to the scarecrow's lumpy face, "Nasty." He looked back over at Leslie, "Alright, we found your gross, old farmer. Now what, babe?" Leslie grabbed the pitchfork, stealing it away from the scarecrow, before she turned around and waved it at her unsuspecting friends.

"Oooh, watch out!" Leslie laughed, "He's gonna getcha!"

"Watch it!" Andrew jumped back, "That thing is dangerous."

"Yeah, more dangerous than this rag doll." Leslie teased, pointing the farm tool at the scarecrow. She jabbed at its gut with the pitchfork and then at its face. Andrew stood there anxiously watching, wishing he could make her stop. He was done and wanted to go home. This place was creeping him out.

"Well, I'm bored. Let's get outta here. All those stories and this is it? So lame—" Before she could finish, the scarecrow sprung to life, grabbing Leslie by the throat and lifting her up in the air. Her eyes were now inches from the scarecrow's stitched up, rotting face. With its other hand, the scarecrow snatched the rusty pitchfork from her. It slowly moved the tool under the girl's chin as she squirmed. Before any of the boys could move, the scarecrow violently rammed the pitchfork up through her skull. Blood gurgled in Leslie's throat and dripped off her quivering lips.

Frozen in terror, Andrew watched the scarecrow kill his friend. He looked to his right to see that Ray and Charlie had already run off. Turning his head back, he realized the scarecrow was staring right back at him. Andrew couldn't move a muscle as it slowly slid the pitchfork back out of Leslie's skull. Her head wobbled and twitched, before the figure tossed her body to the side. Leslie's lifeless corpse vanished into the cornstalks. The loud thud of her body hitting the dirt was enough to finally snap Andrew out of his trance. Regaining control of his legs, he turned back and ran through the field as fast as he could.

His heart thumped, pumping blood through his veins. Leaves and branches smacked his body as he galloped away from the scarecrow. With Leslie's light gone, he could barely see anything. *Leslie was gone.* He told himself he couldn't think about that. He couldn't afford to think about anything other than survival tonight. He had to get out of this maze. He couldn't remember the exact path that they had taken in, but as long as he kept running straight, he'd eventually reach an opening. He had to. Andrew could hear its booming footsteps pounding in the mud behind him, growing closer with every second.

Stumbling over the uneven dirt, but keeping his balance, Andrew kept on running. His lungs ached and his skin was itchy, covered in scratches from the cornstalks. He pushed through the pain and kept going until he noticed that the scarecrow's footsteps had stopped. He heard a whipping sound cut through the air, hitting cornstalks as it went much faster than anything running. Unsure of what it was, Andrew dropped to the ground. It was the scarecrow's pitchfork that was sent soaring through the air—inches from the boy's skull. The deadly tool flew past him, vanishing into the darkness ahead.

He wouldn't dare turn back to look for the scarecrow. He knew it was gaining on him. Andrew got back to his feet and decided to turn and run in different directions—hoping he could confuse his straw-headed stalker. With no other sense of direction in this maze, he kept his focus on the moon. He knew that if he continued running in that direction it would eventually lead him back to the car and the farmhouse. *We couldn't have traveled much farther in the short time we'd been walking.* He wondered. *I have to be close to the end by now. I have to.*

The scarecrow's footsteps had faded away. Andrew believed he was nearing the edge of the field when he tripped over something that sent him flying through the air. The boy landed hard, scratching his face and twisting his wrist as he braced for impact. Andrew rolled himself over, clenching his jaw in pain. He looked back to see what caused him to fall. It was Ray. He was huddled up in a ball, staring back at Andrew with wide, frantic eyes. He covered his lips with his index finger, telling Andrew to be quiet.

"What are you doing?!" Andrew whispered. "We gotta get outta here, man!"

Ray shook his head as a tear rolled down his face. He slowly raised his arm, pointing at something behind Andrew. He turned around to discover rotting strands of flesh and bloody organs dangling from the cornstalks with dozens of human bones scattered across the ground. They were sitting amongst the remains of the scarecrow's past victims. Flies hummed in the air as they flew over the putrid smelling meats. Dried blood coated the crops and the gory entrails that trailed off into the night.

Andrew attempted to push himself up and get back to his feet when he noticed clumps of hair and teeth stuck in the mud between his fingers. He sprung up, covering his mouth to stop himself from screaming. To his right, Ray remained on the ground unable to move. Andrew limped over to him, stepping over discarded body parts, to help the boy to his feet. Ray struggled to stand, buckling under his limp legs, still paralyzed by the terror.

"I don't want to die, Andy! I don't want to die! That thing killed Leslie! It stabbed her in the freakin' head! She's gone! I don't want to die! I don't want it to get me! I didn't want to come here, Andy! You gotta help me—"

Before Ray could finish, a noose flew out from the shadows and wrapped itself around his throat. Andrew and the boy locked eyes for a moment of silent horror before the rope tightened, and pulled him back onto the dirt floor.

"Help me!" Ray cried, before getting pulled back into the dark. Andrew dived down into the mud and blood to grab hold of his legs. He desperately pulled the boy back, digging his feet into the soil. Ray's screams turned to gurgling as his face darkened to purple. The force taking Ray's body from beyond the darkness was strong and relentless. Andrew held on as they were both dragged through the mud and corn. The rope loosened and stopped its pull for just a moment. Ray gagged, begging for air, before it violently yanked him back again. Andrew lost his hold on Ray's legs and the boy's body was dragged away into the dark field forever. Andrew laid there in the mud, unable to move, until hearing Ray's final screams. He was back up on his feet and running towards the moon when he heard the large footsteps booming behind him once again.

When his lungs were ready to give out, he finally burst through the wall of crops, reaching the end of the endless cornfield. Flanagan's old, rotting red barn stood before him, welcoming the boy inside. He could hear the scarecrow closing in on him and had only moments to hide. With no other choice, he ran for the open doors of the barn. Stumbling inside, he dove into a dark corner behind the farmer's rusty tractor. His lungs burned like fire and his legs were numb as he crawled along the dirt on his hands and knees. He could see the moonlight flow in from the open barn doors before the light was consumed by the ever-growing shadow of the scarecrow.

Andrew covered his mouth to stifle his breathing. It entered the barn slowly. Its disfigured neck and body creaked and moaned as its head rolled on its shoulders. Searching the barn, it shambled forward, flipping over tables and flinging farm tools across the room. Each awkward, heavy step it took rattled the brittle barn around them. His eyes followed the scarecrow until it disappeared around a corner and the barn grew deadly silent. Still holding his breath, the trembling boy pulled at his hair, uncertain of whether he should stay hidden in his dark corner or make a run for the road.

As he sat there, he noticed an itching sensation on his hand. He looked down to find a large spider crawling up his arm. Without thinking, he flung his hand, ridding himself of the spider. Then he felt another crawling up the back of his neck. Before long, he could feel them crawling all over him in the dark. Hundreds of tiny spider legs rapidly spread across his body until he flailed and danced, desperate to clear them all off. As he jumped to his feet, he kicked an old bucket behind him. The clanging rusty metal echoed through the silent farm like cannon fire.

Without hesitating, Andrew scurried across the barn to another dark corner. He could hear the scarecrow coming closer. Crawling under the farmer's rusting workbench, he spotted Flanagan searching the area around the tractor. The scarecrow was silent, but its body trembled as it shuffled, hunched over with clenched fists. It looked angry. The misshapen body appeared to struggle holding itself together between the hay, cloth, skin and whatever else was stuffed inside it. Andrew didn't want to think about it. All he could focus on was finding a way out.

The Scarecrow's limbs cracked and contorted as it bent down, inspecting the bucket, before throwing it across the barn. It knocked over toolboxes, tossed wooden crates, and flung everything else around it—destroying the barn in a fit of rage. Andrew crawled backwards, keeping watch of the monster, when his hand touched something cold in the dirt. It was a lighter. *Looks fairly new.* He thought. *Left behind by another victim of this monster.*

While it continued its rampage of the barn, Andrew slid the lighter down his back pocket and took this as his chance to run. Sticking to the shadows, the boy quickly snuck across the barn. He kept his eyes on the creature, until finally reaching the open barn doors. Andrew took a deep breath and bolted towards the road. His legs ached, sprinting harder than he had ever run before. *Almost there.* He could taste the asphalt. Then something grabbed him. It took him by the arms and flung him against the farmhouse wall. Andrew held back his screams when he realized that it was Charlie! *He was still alive!*

"I thought I was the only one that made it out of there alive!" He smiled with wide eyes. "That psycho got me good! Sliced my leg with that pitchfork! I fought back and ripped his shirt open! Nasty blood and guts covered in hay came falling out of him! Th—that thing is something evil!" Charlie huffed, letting go of the new kid's arms. "I can barely walk, man, but I sure as Hell am getting out of here!"

Andrew looked over at Charlie's Chevelle, still sitting in the gravel driveway. The tires were all flat—slashed by garden sheers that stuck out of from the rear passenger side. The windshield was shattered and Leslie's decapitated head was displayed on top of the hood. A pool of blood painted his black car crimson.

"That son of—!" He started to shout, but Andrew grabbed his arm. Charlie looked back at him with fury in his eyes. Andrew put his finger to his mouth, warning Charlie to stay quiet, and pointed towards the barn. The two turned their heads to witness the scarecrow stepping through the large doorway of the decades-old barn.

Both frozen in shock, they locked eyes with the dark sockets in its bloody burlap face. Steaming intestines hung from a large tear in the scarecrow's gut. The wet carnage was covered in grass and maggots with flies buzzing overhead. Andrew could smell the monster from a mile away. They both turned back to look at each other. Andrew saw the utter terror in his eyes, but he also sensed determination in Charlie. *They still had a chance.*

"Let's get out of here! If we don't make it out, let's at least take this mother out with us!" Andrew rallied, grabbing Charlie's shoulder. Charlie looked at the boy and sighed.

"I'm sorry, but we aren't all making it out of here alive, kid."

Before he could respond, Charlie shoved him back. Andrew stumbled over a rake before falling back through the open cellar doors on the side of the old farmhouse. An eruption of dust filled the air as he crashed down onto the basement floor. The coughing boy choked as he struggled to breathe. Lost in a dark pit, he felt the ground around him as his vision came back into focus and his lungs began to clear. The floor was dirt, but parts of it were wet and mushy. *That doesn't feel like mud.*

Andrew's spine ached as he slowly sat up. He held his ribs, worried that he broke something in the fall. Rising to his feet, he pulled the lighter out his pocket. His heart froze as he illuminated the dark, decrepit hell hole. Decades worth of bodies filled the dank basement. Dusty skeletons and freshly rotting corpses in every direction. Some adults, but most appeared to be children. Every one of the bodies had their eyes gouged out, with blood dripping down their horrified faces. Boney hands clenched into fists, limbs bent in all directions, shredded flesh, and broken jaws locked in eternal screams. The victims' guts were slashed open with their organs stretched out across the ground. Andrew had fallen into the middle of a nightmare.

Breaking from his trance, he looked back up at the opening that he fell through. He climbed the rickety steps towards the moon overhead—the only beacon of light and hope he had left in this world of blood and chaos. He reached the opening when he stopped to listen. Charlie's blood-curdling screams rang out, shaking the weathered house. Peeking his head out, he spotted Charlie on the ground. *He barely made it past his car.*

The scarecrow stood over him, with one foot on the punk's back. It raised the bloody pitchfork up with its right arm. Grabbing it with both hands, Flanagan plunged it down into Charlie's back. His body convulsed, crying in agony. The monster stabbed him again and again, digging the pitchfork deeper into the twitching body. Blood soared through the air, shining in the moonlight as Charlie's body began to sink into a pool of his own fluids.

Then there was silence—Charlie was dead and Andrew was alone. The scarecrow bent over the body and pulled at something. Andrew could hear a tearing sound followed by the sight of more blood. The scarecrow turned to face the moonlight, holding the bloody, disfigured head of Charlie up in the sky. Andrew couldn't move as he watched the monster use its other hand to open up the wound in its gut. Flanagan took the severed head and shoved it inside its gut. Andrew fought the urge to get sick, too scared to make a sound. The farmer crouched down, grabbing scraps of flesh from Charlie's back. The scarecrow was healing, stuffing itself with more body parts, like a Frankenstein's monster from the depths of Hell.

This thing is unstoppable.

Andrew took a deep breath before descending into the basement. He carefully made his way through this hellscape, stepping over soggy corpses and maggot-infested limbs. The smell was unlike anything he ever imagined. A sudden thud from something heavy crashed down in the basement behind him. Andrew jumped and turned back to see what was left of Charlie's body had been thrown down onto the dirt floor. Still holding his breath, he exhaled as he turned back to leave. Then another body was thrown down into the pit. Nearly jumping out of his skin, Andrew ran ahead, not looking back to see if it was Leslie or Ray.

With his small flame, he finally found a set of stairs. He bolted up the steps, careful not to trip. Spiderwebs and dust coated the walls and wrapped around his head as he made it to the door. Ignoring the possibility of spiders, he pressed his ear up against the door, listening for anything that might be waiting for him on the other side. Slowly turning the knob, he entered a relatively normal looking home.

A home that hadn't been touched in decades. Dust coated every surface and spider-webs in every corner. Several empty bottles were scattered across the kitchen counter and dining room table. Water damage had worked its way through the walls and ceiling, leaving a musty smell that coated the house. Down the hall, he could see more doors that he assumed led to bathrooms and bedrooms, but all he cared about was the exit. The floorboards creaked as he crept through the house. They only grew louder with every step as he neared the front door.

The thick dust in the air triggered his throat, but Andrew did everything he could to stifle the cough. Reaching the front door, he peaked out through the window, searching for the scarecrow. Nothing. The farm was just as bare and deserted as when they first arrived. What must have only been a few minutes, had felt like hours on this farm. *But this night was almost over.* He was only a hundred feet away from the road. This was his moment—now or never. Andrew started to run.

His heart was pounding as he sprinted towards the empty road, hoping—praying—for this nightmare to be over. It felt like he had run for miles just to get to the road. He never looked back, fearing that Flanagan's scarecrow would be right behind him. He couldn't hear anything over the rapid booming of his heart and the veins in his skull. Finally making it to the street, it took everything not to collapse right then and there. He looked back and forth down both sides of the dark road.

Nothing.

He couldn't run back to Charlie's car—it was trashed. Losing feeling in his legs, he had no choice but to keep running. Andrew ran to his left—between the road and the cornfield—back towards town. Everything hurt. He could barely breathe, but he knew he would survive this. He told himself he was making it home. With no sign of the scarecrow, he felt a slight sense of relief, but he couldn't slow down—Not until he was miles away from this evil farmland.

That's when he saw a glowing light start to form in the distance. It was a car! *Finally a sign of hope!* He kept on running, now waving his arms and smiling. He was free. He made it. Just a few more moments before he was saved and he'd never have to see this farm again. The nightmare was over. The car grew closer. His smile, wider.

Then Andrew noticed something drop down around him. It was a lasso. Before he could think, it was pulled tight at his ankles, bringing the boy down to the dirt. He slammed his jaw on the road, shattering his teeth and rattling his skull. Blood poured into his mouth as he struggled to scream for help. It just came out as a gurgling mess. Blood and teeth sprayed out from his lips and onto the cold pavement. The Scarecrow had him. He was slowly pulling Andrew back into the madness of the cornfield. He desperately clawed his fingers into the muddy soil, only pulling out grass and weeds.   *I was safe—I made it. I wasn't going to die. I couldn't. Not after everything we'd been through!* He was dragged farther back into the corn as his screams were muffled by the ever-growing pool of blood in his throat. He didn't dare look back at the field. He kept his head straight, reaching out for the road, watching as the car got even closer.

Andrew screamed and threw one arm up to wave for help as he kept the other dug deep into the weeds. He could see the couple inside the car. Their eyes grew wide when they spotted him, slamming down on the breaks as they passed by the blood-soaked boy. Andrew couldn't hold on any longer. The soil gave out and his bruised, aching body was dragged back into the farmer's maze. His final screams echoed across the land. He could hear the couple in the car walking towards the field. They called out for him, asking where he was, as they entered the cornfield. He tried to scream, "No!" He wanted to warn them, make them turn back—anything at all—but they couldn't hear him. The Scarecrow had him, and he was about to have two more...

THE WIDOW

Wednesday, October 14th, 1936

My aching feet kicked up rubble as I sprinted after the train. The ear-piercing whistle rang out from the engine ahead, shattering the silence of the cold, dark night. My messy hair danced in my face as I thrust myself forward. Inches away–I could almost reach the open door of the train car.

"Get back here!" An officer shouted, "I said freeze!"

My heart raced as I heard the cuffs jingling on his belt. Inches from freedom. Inches from jail bars. I knew which way I was headed. My lungs started to wheeze. My body wanted to give out, but I pushed myself even harder. My fingers finally grasped the cold metal of the handle. I kicked myself up off the ground and used the heavy door of the freight train as leverage, swiftly swinging my beaten body up and into the chilly embrace of the car.

"Son of a—" The cop growled as his voice faded away. I sat up, hanging my legs off the ledge, and watched as the middle-aged cop vanished in the foggy distance. The train car rattled and rocked like a boat, gaining speed after leaving the depot. *That was too close.*

My name is Art. It was Arthur something, but I've been on the road for so long—and hit my head more times than I'd like to admit—that I honestly forgot the last name. I'm somewhere in my later thirties and I've been a homeless bum since I was practically a child. I lost my parents in a fire when I was eleven. After barely surviving that, I was tossed into an orphanage, but that life wasn't for me, and I ran away. Since then, I've spent most of my life traveling across this beautiful country hitchhiking, walking, or what I'm currently doing—hopping onto train cars.

A few hours had passed, as I rested my eyes, before the engine started slowing down. Up ahead, I could see that the engine was entering into a train yard. Before passing the gates, I grabbed my bags and hopped out, tumbling across the dirt with my signature hazardous landing. With no sign of police or train engineers spotting me, I rose to my feet, grabbed my gear, and headed for the trees.

I was a thin, but fit man. My hair was dark and scraggly, but I kept it up the best I could. I cut it when I could, and kept my beard trimmed down as well. I wouldn't say that I was the most handsome man out there, but I was certainly better looking than most other homeless guys that I'd encountered over the years. Neither was I a drunk or a drug-addicted hoodlum, like so many others. I was what you'd call a nomad. I grew to love the constant travel. Always on my feet, I'd find short-term jobs and stay at motels or find some empty buildings that I could call home for a few days. I wasn't hurting anyone, and I was staying out of the way—just living my life.

This kind of lifestyle was especially helpful these days with the so-called "Great Depression" going on. Everyone around was starting to look like me. It made finding jobs and food harder than it had already been, but at least I was already used to it in the first place.

One downside to this kind of life was the lack of friends and family—but that's why I'm talking to you. That's right, you! Whoever it is out there reading this journal of mine. I'm sure somebody, somewhere, some day is going to read this notebook I've been carrying around. There's not a whole lot of excitement in my life to write about, but I do this for the exercise—plus it's fun. It keeps me sharp, helps my memory—which is rough enough as it is—and who knows, maybe I was a writer in another life.

There was a light mist in the night air as I walked through the woods. The insects played their music, and even in the dark, the trees were green and vibrant. Bright bolts of lightning crossed the dark sky, followed swiftly by thunder that rattled the Earth below.

I should have stayed in that train car tonight. You can never be too careful, though. I've been caught by security and police before. I've been robbed by other homeless individuals while I slept, as well. One time someone stole my shoe. Not the pair, just one of them. Who steals a single shoe? Anyway, I've learned that it's best to just keep moving, and eventually you'll find some place more private to rest. Hopefully there was an empty room waiting for me in this little town.

As I neared the edge of the woods, I walked along a lone paved road. No cars would be out at this hour, especially with the rain coming down harder. I picked up the pace, walking faster in the storm, when I spotted an old church up ahead. It looked as though it was abandoned. The lot was empty, a stained glass window was shattered, and the roof was starting to collapse in on itself.

Just before the decrepit church, stood a sign declaring:"Welcome to Murrville, Arkansas." I hadn't been to Arkansas in a few years…didn't look like much had changed. Another clash of lightning and thunder overtook the senses. Sleeping in the church tonight seemed like a safe bet. Every inch of my body was drenched under the downpour of the storm, but I'd soon be out of these clothes after hanging them up to dry.

The heavy rain washed out the sounds of crickets and the night life. Under the storm clouds, the wet pavement shimmered and the endless puddles danced in the darkness. Closing in on the church, I made my way across the road. Before I could make it to the other side I noticed a bright light appear to my right. I turned to see what it was, when I was overcome with a sudden shock of pain that rattled through my bones before I faded off to sleep.

––––––––

My head was groggy as I awoke in a soft bed. It felt as if I was resting among the clouds up in heaven, but I was in someone's home. It was clean and organized, the walls were painted a dull pink color, and the trim was white to match the curtains. The calming sound of rain drops tapping came from the window to my right. Outside it was still pouring rain. Lightning struck and the rolling thunder shook the house. When I started to sit up in this soft bed, my body twinged in pain. Looking down, I discovered that I was covered in bruises and bandages. Outside of these injuries, I was clean. I slowly lifted my weak arms to feel that my hair had been cut shorter and my jaw was shaved clean.

What in the world is going on here? I thought, and as if on command: a woman entered the room.

"Oh, hello dear, you're finally awake! Take it easy. I'm sure you're in a lot of pain. I am so, so sorry for hitting you with my car! I couldn't see a thing with all the rain."

The woman was talking so rapidly that I didn't have time to respond, but she had a lovely voice. It matched her beauty. I believed we were about the same age, early-thirties or so. She had blonde hair and green eyes. She was thin and tall, maybe five-nine or ten, and she wore a lovely dark green dress that matched her eyes. This woman made her way over to my bedside as she continued to apologize.

"You've been out for almost two days. Thankfully, I had some medication to give you. I do believe I was able to patch you up the best I could. My husband is... *was* a boxer and I've become accustomed to a man walking through my doors bloody and broken. I would always fix him, and fortunately, I was able to fix you. Again, I am so sorry! I hope..."

"Thank you." I interrupted, "I see you cleaned me up in more ways than one."

Sitting at the foot of the bed, the woman blushed. "I...thought you could use a trim. I wanted to do whatever I could to make it up to you. I also have some of my late husband's clothes for you, since yours were all torn up. I can't believe that my automobile could do such damage."

"Well, I was in rough shape before you even hit me ma'am, so it's not all your fault."

She looked me over, sympathetic to the broken man before her. Then her eyes widened. "Do you have any family?" She rose up from the bed, "A wife or anyone I should contact? They must be worried sick…"

"No, miss. I'm all on my own."

She sighed and sat back down beside me. I started to lose myself in her eyes. "I…I never got your name?"

"Oh, my apologies! My name is Rebecca. Rebecca Marie…and your name?"

I chuckled, "Art. Just Art. Nice to meet you Rebecca." The woman smiled. She looked out into the hallway and then back at me, "I'm just about finished cooking up some supper. Would you care to join me? I made Potato Pancakes. I'm not the best cook, but I do believe these came out pretty well."

I licked my lips, "Sounds perfect."

Rebecca helped me out of bed and to my feet. I was light headed at first. My legs were asleep and most of my body still ached, but the drugs were helping to ease the pain. I hobbled down the hall, following Rebecca to the dining room.

"The door to the right is the powder room, and that door at the end of the hall is my bedroom." She paused as she looked back at me, "…and here on the left is the kitchen and dining room." She waved her arm inviting me to sit down at the table. Silverware was set and the chair was already pulled out for me to sit.

"Thank you again, Rebecca. You really didn't need to do all of this for me. This is the best I've been treated in many years. If I had known getting hit by an old Ford was all it took, I would have started running into traffic years ago!" I chuckled.

She grinned and waved her hand, "Hush now, it's no trouble at all. I'm happy to have the company. My home has been empty for quite a while now. The whole neighborhood as a matter of fact. Not many people left around these parts. Lots of folks moving west. It's practically a ghost town here."

I began to dig into my dinner. The meal was simple, but lovely. I tried to take my time and eat with some manners, even though I felt as if I could eat a whole horse. She sat across from me, smiling and watching as I enjoyed the warm meal.

"This is fantastic, the best supper I've had in a good long time, ma'am."

"Rebecca. There will be no ma'ams around here, *sir*." She said in a stern, but joking manner, "I'm happy you like it."

I gulped down another large bite as I looked around at the warm and welcoming home. This was one of the first houses I'd ever seen with those new electric light bulbs. The soft glow of the house lights revealed photos of Rebecca and her husband that were hung on the walls. Another bolt of lightning painted harsh shadows across the table.

"So, if you don't mind me asking, Rebecca...what happened to your husband? Did you have any children? Or are you all alone here?"

She stared at me for a moment in silence.

"No...no children. My husband, Walter, he...he was sick. Disease took him. It was an awful year, he was in so much pain. I took care of him until his final moments. Unfortunately, there was nothing else anyone could do."

"I am so sorry, Rebecca. I couldn't imagine the pain you endured." I sighed as I reached for her hand. Her eyes softened as she smiled.

"It's alright. God works in mysterious ways. I always say, 'everything happens for a reason.' So...what about you, Art? Have you ever been married?"

I snorted, almost choking on my dinner. "No, not at all. I haven't had any romantic relationships in awhile. I've always been on the move. I don't stay put anywhere long enough to really make any connections like that."

"Oh, I see." Rebecca said gently as she looked down at her plate. After a pause, her eyes looked back up at mine, "Well, for the next few days at least, you're stuck here with me. I don't want you leaving until you are fully healed."

After finishing my dinner, I wiped my mouth with my napkin and argued, "You really don't need to do that. I can be on my way tomorrow morning. I may be a bit sore, but I don't want to take up any more of your time and resources. I know how sparse everything is these days, and a single lady like yourself shouldn't have to take care of a bum like me."

"I'm not taking 'no' for an answer, Art. You're stuck with me." She smiled, "Oh, and by the way, I washed your clothes, although I would toss them in the wastebasket. You have new clothes now. You can take any of my husband's other clothes that fit you as well. They're just here collecting dust."

"I can't do that…" I started.

"Hush. All of your belongings are safe as well. I noticed you had a notebook with you. Is that a journal you've been keeping? I tried my best not to be too nosey."

"Oh yes, ma'am." I nodded, "My little book of adventures across this wonderful country. I've seen Plymouth Rock and been to the big cities like New York and Chicago. I celebrated Mardi Gras in New Orleans, and visited the Alamo in Texas. I've been to most states over the years, but I still need to see some of the newer ones out west. One nice thing about being a homeless bum like me; the whole world becomes your home. If I don't like one area, I move onto the next. Don't like this factory job; I can move on and find a gig in a slaughterhouse or construction. My life may be a mess, but I've had some fun times along the way."

Rebecca's eyes lit up, "Sounds like you have had quite the life, Art. I wish I could go on such adventures." She ran her finger along the rim of her glass. She looked past me, into the sky, thinking of the possibilities. I could see that her troubled past was holding her back. Something was wrong. I wished I could help her.

"—And I will most certainly write a new chapter about the angel that brought me into her home and saved my life!" I concluded, raising my drink up from the table. She laughed as our glasses clinked together.

"I'd love to give that a read when you're done." Finishing her meal, she rose from the table, taking her plate, and grabbing mine as well.

I started to rise, "No, I can take them…"

Before I could finish, she responded, "Nonsense. I'll take these and wash them. You stay put here, I even have some dessert. Hope you like pie! I baked one earlier today, just for you."

The night passed as the two of us sat at the table talking about our lives. She told stories of her childhood and her husband, and I spoke of my travels and misadventures. The ones I could remember, at least. She was a lovely woman. I didn't mind sticking around here for a few days. However, I still felt guilty for putting her through all of this. Fortunately for myself, she wasn't having it any other way.

As we continued talking, I took a closer look at those photos on the walls of her and her husband. Some were from their wedding, others of her as a child, some with family members—I'm assuming—and one of a dog that was long gone. She gently grabbed my bruised hand. Her emerald eyes were mesmerizing.

"So how did you and your husband meet?" I asked, "How long were you two together before...?"

She smiled and took a breath, "Oh, Walt and I met about ten years ago. We bumped into each other at our town's Christmas tree lighting event. We were together for almost a year when he proposed to me. It was right after The Great War had ended that we were married. He was such a brave man. He was shot in battle, but survived to come home and meet me. Like I said before: 'everything happens for a reason.'" Her smile faded as she continued her tale, "But then after those lovely years together it came to a close much sooner than either of us expected. I lost him almost five years ago now, in 'twenty-nine. Such a terrible accident he was in. Sometimes I wish it was me that passed instead of him. Although, he would just be feeling the same as I am now..." She sighed, "But like I said, everything..."

"...Happens for a reason." I said, finishing her sentence. Sitting there, I hesitated for a moment. "That's a lovely story Rebecca...But you said that he was...in an accident? I thought it was a disease that killed him. You told me before that he suffered for a year?"

She sat across the table, staring back at me. For a moment the world was dead silent. Thunder rolled across the land once more.

"Accident? Did I say that? Yes, the disease of course! That's what happened. I don't know what came over me. I must have gotten my wires crossed with another story. Not a silly accident." She smiled, but her eyes weren't happy.

I cleared my throat, "Oh alright. Sorry, I just wanted to make sure I hadn't misheard you, ma'am."

"Now what did I say about ma'am's around here?" She looked down at my empty dessert plate, "Now let me clean all of this up." Rebecca grabbed the two plates and silverware before walking out into the kitchen. "I had a feeling you'd like the pie!" She declared from the other side of the kitchen door.

I sat there, unsure of what to think. My gut was telling me that something was off about this woman. Perhaps it was just my mind trying to conjure up a reason to get out of here and move onto the next town. I was attracted to this woman. I hadn't had any romantic relationships in quite some time. For whatever reason, they never worked out for me. So perhaps this was why I had this sudden urge to leave. Or it was something else. I could hear her footsteps coming closer.

"Rebecca, I know you gave me your answer earlier on the topic, but I really must be going. Thank you so much for everything, but I can not stay…"

"Nonsense!" She exclaimed from behind me.

My body tensed up, surprised.

She giggled, "Didn't mean to spook you, honey!" Rebecca carried a small tray with bottles and boxes of pills. Putting it down on the table, she sat next to me, "Besides, I've got just the right stuff that will make you feel all better!" Her eyes had a look of worry in them as she stared at me, still smiling.

"You go out there in this storm now and you could end up in an even worse state than you are already. Or even find yourself dead and gone. We can't have that! No sir!"

I slowly pushed my chair back away from the table, "I really don't need all this Rebecca. I've used up enough of your time."

She pulled out a syringe from her pile of medications. My heart started to race. A bead of sweat rolled down my face.

"You really need to take your medicine, Art. You can barely walk as it is." I rose up from the chair and went to step forward. My leg erupted in pain and gave out, sending my aching body crashing down onto the floor.

"Oh goodness! What did I just say?" She cried as she knelt down to my side. "Are you alright, darling?"

Breathing slowly, I tried pushing myself up from off of the floor. My arms shook and my skull roared in pain.

"Take it easy, Art!" She wrapped her arm under mine, pulling me up to a sitting position on the floor. Still kneeling beside me, she pushed the syringe up to my arm. Injecting me with some unknown substance. She smiled.

"There we go. You'll be in better shape in no time!"

"What was that?" I muttered.

She ignored my question and began pouring out different pills into her hand.

"Open wide."

Her hand rose to squeeze my nose, holding it shut until I finally opened my mouth. She tossed the pills in and handed me a glass of water to drink. I shook my head. The woman twisted my nose with her sharp fingernails, digging into my skin. Feeling like she was about to break it, I gave in and opened my mouth. She poured the water down my throat until the pills disappeared. I was finally released from her violent grip, choking on remnants of the water that danced down my throat.

"Good man. Now let's get you off to bed!" Biting my lip, I forced myself to my feet. She kept her arms around me as I stumbled along the hallway. Finally reaching the bedroom, she turned me around and sat me down on the mattress. Laying in the dark, I watched her crooked head look me over. Her dark eyes glared into mine, sensing the fear behind them.

"I reeeallry shwould behe goooing…" My words came out slurred and my vision was hazy. She simply grinned as she rested my head back against the pillow. After tucking the bed sheets in around me, she walked over to the doorway.

"You'll be out like a light in just a minute." She said in a cheery voice. Closing the door behind her, she watched me and whispered, "Goodnight, handsome."

I listened as her footsteps slowly grew distant. Laying there in silence, I counted the seconds as time passed. The storm continued to rage on, rattling the house like an earthquake. When I was sure that Rebecca had fallen asleep, I flung the bedsheets off and struggled to my feet. Pushing off of the bed, I shambled across the room. Reaching out for the door handle, I took hold of it, nearly falling. Breathing heavy, I fought back against the effects of the drugs. My eyelids were heavy and my movement had slowed. I denied my body the sleep it desired. The only option I gave myself was leaving this place—and now was my chance. Something was clearly wrong with this broad, and I wasn't sticking around to find out. I'd rather take my chances with mother nature outside.

Turning the handle slowly, I quietly opened the door—just a crack. I could see down the empty hall. There was no movement. The lights had been turned off and her bedroom door was closed. *It's now or never*. I thought to myself, before slowly opening the door further. My aching legs were weak. Stretching my arms out, I used the walls as support. *The front door was around the corner—just ahead.* Lightning flashed once more, followed by earth-shattering thunder. The bright light cut through the home like a shining blade. I could see that the dining room table was cleared off and everything was put away.

The wooden floor creaked. I froze and listened for Rebecca. Nothing. Slowly raising my foot, I stepped forward, trying to avoid any weak points in the flooring. I could feel my heart rate slowing and my muscles giving out. I was almost there. I had to push a little longer. Did I know what I was going to do once I got out of here? No. I just knew that I couldn't stay here any longer.

Losing my balance, I stumbled—twisting my ankle. My hand caught hold of the front door handle, stopping me from falling any further. Biting my tongue, I stayed quiet, restraining my screams from escaping. My nostrils flared as my muscles constricted in agony. A moment of misery passed before I could collect myself. At last, I made it. I was almost free! That was, until the door handle wouldn't turn. It was locked. I scanned the area for any keys, finding nothing. Clenching my fist, I held back the urge to punch through the wall. *Just a momentary setback.* I wasn't stuck. I was getting out of here.

After turning myself around and leaning my back up against the stubborn front door; I surveyed the home in search of my next destination and spotted another door across the living room. I hadn't noticed that one before. It looked different than the other doors. With no better options, I pushed off the wall and stepped forward. One step. Two steps. Another. Then my legs gave out, and I dropped to my knees. The hard impact shot daggers of pain through my damaged legs. My lips trembled with a whimper. Quickly, I clenched my jaw shut, stifling the screams. Tears began to build up in my eyes. I wasn't sure how much longer I could go on. Listening for Rebecca, the house remained silent. I slowly exhaled, relieved that I was safe for now.

My legs were out of steam. There was no way I could get back to my feet tonight. Slowly, I descended to the ground, with no choice but to crawl now. Growing tense, my limbs burned, wanting nothing more than to rest. Scooting across the floor, I inched towards the mysterious door. More lightning flashes painted the house in moments of black and white. A contrast much like the start of this evening, and where I was now.

Reaching the living room, I stopped to rest against the couch. It was soft and smelled like an ashtray. I didn't see any sign of Rebecca smoking. *Perhaps her husband did?* My chest rose and fell as I took deep breaths. At least the pain kept me awake, but the drugs were still working their way through my system. I didn't have much time left. Grabbing hold of the table before me, I felt a newspaper under my fingers. It was laid out on the table, open to page three.

Again, the storm lit the room. That's when my eyes caught something familiar near the bottom of this page. It was a picture of a man. The headline of the article declared: "Husband Still Missing! Boxer, Walt Bigby, last seen six months ago!" It went on to say, "The cold case was closed. Police officials believe they will never find the remains of the beloved husband. He leaves behind his lone wife, Rebecca Marie Bigby." Thunder boomed from above.

"Missing?!" I whispered to myself. *Illness, accidents and now a missing person! I knew something was off about this woman. I can't waste anymore time. I need to leave this place now!* I clawed down into the carpet, pulling myself further along the ground. The door was just ahead. All I had to do was push myself up far enough to reach the door handle. I did, and the door slowly creaked open into a dark void of a room.

A rancid smell, unlike anything I had ever witnessed, assaulted the senses. I gagged as lightning bolts lit up the room before me. What I saw within the darkness was something truly disturbing. A chill ran up my spine. This awful place reminded me of a nightmare. This woman was a monster. Before I could rise to my knees, something hit the backside of my head. An explosion of shock and pain clashed through my skull before the world grew dark once more.

———

Light slowly faded in. My vision was a blur as my eyes struggled to open. Slightly turning my head, my neck spasmed with a sudden aching strike that traveled up to the back of my skull. Gritting my teeth, I laid my head back down.

What on Earth is going on now? I asked myself. As my vision came into focus, I could see that I was back in the bedroom, but now restrained. My arms and legs were each bound to the four corners of the bed frame. I went to scream, only to realize my mouth was gagged with a sheet tied around my head. I shook and moaned, but with the never-ending storm outside, it was a fruitless endeavor to call for help. The woman, Rebecca, entered the room. Her lovely glow was now gone. She was nothing more than a harsh silhouette standing in the doorway, until the lightning flashed, revealing her disappointed grimace.

"You couldn't just play along and be a good man. I cleaned you. I fed you. I clothed you. All for nothing! You had to argue and correct me over the smallest, insignificant, little details. My husband is dead. That's all that matters. I was happy to have a new man in the house, but even someone that's as sweet and as handsome as you can disappoint!"

She clenched her fists and stepped towards me. Her eyes radiated hatred. She pulled the gag loose from my trembling lips. I took a deep breath, ready to beg. Before I could open my mouth, the woman violently slapped me across the face. A bolt of pain jolted through my skull. She raised her arm up, pointing out into the hall and exclaimed.   "Then I find you exploring my home…sticking your nose where it doesn't belong! You just couldn't help yourself! You found my old friends in the base—"

"Lady…I'm sorry if I said anything to upset you, but you have to let me go." I quietly begged, trying my best to stay calm, and to calm her down as well.

"You aren't going anywhere!" She shouted. Her large eyes were bloodshot from crying. Her makeup had run down her face, taking away any softness she once had. Her face was one of rage and insanity. I noticed something was crushed in her hand. Some kind of small bag. It trembled in her fist. She kept her eyes locked on me. They glowed in the darkness that lingered between us. I gently pulled at my restraints as we talked, but she was right—I was not going anywhere.

"Rebecca… I can fix this. I can make it up to you. I'm happy to stay here and spend time with you, but I need you to untie me. Please." She stepped closer, a slight smile grew on her face, but her eyes still shot me daggers.

"I'm sorry for all of this darling, but like I said before, you're not going anywhere. You are going to have a lovely life here with me. There's nothing out there for

you anyway. Nothing you can't have right here with me."
She said as she slowly sat down by my side. Her eyes
never left mine as she dragged her smooth hand across the
side of my face, "You should see just how nice you look
now. You look so much like him." She paused, biting her
lip, "But something is still missing…"

She grabbed my face tightly. I tried to fight, but
her grip on my jaw was stronger than I imagined. She
pulled the cloth away from out my mouth, letting it rest
around my neck. As her eyes were still locked onto mine,
her other hand reached back into a small bag that she had
brought with her. Rebecca pulled out something metal. It
gleamed in the black room when lightning struck once
more. She was holding metal pliers.

My heart was racing as Rebecca brought the tool
closer to my face. I screamed for help and begged her to
stop, but no one could hear me. She slid the cold metal
between my lips as I struggled against her iron grip. The
taste lingered on my tongue, and as it neared the back of
my throat, I fought the urge to vomit.

"I told you that my husband was a boxer. He could
take a real beating, that one. Besides getting his face all
cut up and bashed in, my sweet Walt had some of his teeth
knocked out."

The metal claws latched onto one of my molars.
"Phwease! Irm beggin' you! Don't do dis! Rebec—"

She pulled, grinding the pliers against my teeth.
Screaming in agony, I pulled back, resisting, but she
wasn't giving up. The hand that had gripped my jaw, now
moved down to my throat. The woman choked me as she
continued to pull. I struggled to breathe as she pressed
down on my throat. My head ached and vision became
blurry.

The pliers finally came flying from out of my mouth, as did my bloody tooth. Sparks of pain ruptured in my skull. Blood rapidly overflowed my mouth, dripping down my chin and back into my throat. For a moment she released her grip, letting me breathe.

"See? That wasn't so bad!" She smiled, bringing the tooth closer to my face. "Not too shabby for someone who never went to dentistry school!"

I groaned and rolled my head, fighting back tears. Her soft hand caressed my face once again. "You're looking even better now. Just a few more teeth and you'll look just like my Walt!"

"You're insane!" I barked. Blood splattered across the bedsheets and onto the woman's dress.

"Now that wasn't nice, Mr. Art." She scowled, raising her hand and swinging. My skull rattled as she backhanded my face. More blood spewed out from my mouth across the tidy bedroom.

"Look at this mess! Destroying my home! I never should have welcomed in a dirty vagrant like yourself!"

"Up yours, Lady!" I growled at her, spitting blood at her face. She gasped and rubbed the dripping crimson from her cheek. Her emerald eyes glared back into mine. *How could something so beautiful be so vile?* She was ruthless. She didn't care what she did to me. I was hers and no one could stop her. I had to find a way out of this.

"That was a bad choice. I was going to offer you some of my pain medication, but someone like you needs to suffer."

She clutched the metal pliers in her hand and swung—bashing them against my skull. My ears rang and my vision spun like a kaleidoscope, as excruciating pain rattled through my skull like gunfire. I could feel myself beginning to fade. I welcomed the darkness as sleep grew near. Before it came, Rebecca grabbed my face and crammed the pliers down my throat a second time. Discombobulated, I continued to fight her. With no avail, she pulled out a second tooth. Blood gushed and pooled in my mouth.

"One more to go…Or have you learned your lesson, sweetie?" I choked on my own blood, coughing up the rest. I could barely move. Everything hurt. Before I could give her an answer, my mind started shutting down. I felt the copper liquid dripping down my chin as my eyes rolled back, sending me off to dreamland, once again.

———

Ice cold metal chains jingled as I began to wake. Everything was dark. The air was thick and sour. I gagged as I fought the urge to throw up. The skin on my face was inflamed and bruised. The blood was finally gone, yet the taste of copper still lingered on my tongue. My eyes were nearly swollen shut as I tried to read my surroundings. I rolled to my side and began to push myself up off of the icy stone floor. I wasn't in the soft bed anymore. I was in a dungeon.

A door swung open, slamming against the brick wall. Harsh light punctured the darkness from the open doorway above, illuminating the vile woman walking down the basement stairs. She carried a bag—my bag—with her. A harsh smile stretched across Rebecca's sinister face.

"Hello, darling. You're finally awake! Didn't think a trip to the dentist could knock you out for such a long time. How do you like your new room?"

Glaring daggers back at her, I stayed silent. My jaw began to quiver as the pain rushed back to me. The silhouette of the lady stood a few feet in front of me with her hands on her hips. My blood boiled as she inched near me. I wanted out of this freak show. She was not going to stop me.

Pushing myself up off of the dusty floor, I charged towards her. With my arms outstretched, I was ready to strangle the monster before me. Clunky metal cuffs cut into my shins as I neared her throat, pulling back at my legs and sending my body back down to the ground. As I crashed down onto the concrete floor, my jaw erupted in pain. The bones felt like they shattered. Fresh blood began to pool in my mouth. I rolled to my side, moaning in anguish. All I could hear was ringing, and all I could see was the blurry shadow of the woman ahead of me. Spitting crimson onto the floor, I looked up at her with a look of disgust and disdain across my face.

"What do you want from me!?" I groaned, breaking the silence. Every syllable shot aching pain through my skull as if there were razor blades in my gums. Blood and drool cascaded down my chin.

She reached up and pulled at a light switch. A dim yellow glow filled the room. After a moment, my vision began to clear, revealing a putrid sight. Bloody and beaten bodies surrounding me, filling the basement. They were all men. Men of similar look and age as I. Similar to her husband as well. They were chained to the walls around me. Some were nearly skeletons, while other bodies were freshly rotting.

As Rebecca ascended the staircase, she reached into my bag and grabbed something. With a chuckle, she flung the object through the air. It hit my ribs, bouncing off and landing in front of me.

"Maybe you can write another chapter in your book of adventures…I'd love to see what you write about me!" The slender, dark figure lingered in the doorway, looking like a nightmarish corpse smiling down at me.

Gone were her beautiful eyes and smooth complexion. She was the devil and I was in hell. The door closed behind her, plunging me into a world of darkness. A world of pain and misery.

————

December 1936 or January 1937?

It's cold down here. I can't remember much anymore. I continue to write in this book. I do it to help my mind, to keep me going. I read what has been written before, but I don't remember any of it. Why can't I remember? She's hurt me so much. All of us. The bodies that surround me. The only friends I have in this hell. I hope I can see the light once more. If you are reading this, I hope that you are not suffering the same fate as us. I hope that you are not locked away in this ghastly dungeon as well. Slowly starving to death. Losing your mind. I hope this book can reach the light. I hope these words are free. Unlike me. I hope.

UNMASKED

The floorboards creaked as a man paced in his office. The man wearing a burgundy tie over his sweat-soaked shirt and suspenders was in his forties. His graying hair was receding along his leathery skin. A burning cigarette bounced off his lip. A grim face was hidden behind the continuous puffs of smoke. This man had lived a rough life, experiencing some of the darkest shades of humanity. Surviving the second world war was only the beginning. After joining the police force, he would only descend further down a tunnel which had no light at the end of it. However, he knew that he couldn't walk away. Something inside him was practically addicted to the darker side of reality. He needed answers to the grim mysteries of the world. After everything he had been through, he only wanted to know why. *Was it all for nothing?*

The lights in his office were dim and fading. He kept meaning to go buy some new bulbs, but it was just one of those weeks. Multiple weeks, actually. He couldn't believe how much time had flown by already. He hadn't been sleeping much. His sunken-in, tired eyes could attest to that, and his growling stomach was a reminder that he hadn't eaten enough either. He stopped pacing and looked back over at his desk.

It was still there—staring at him. He could feel those empty black eyes peering deep into his soul. No matter where he walked in this small room, that mask was always watching him. The smell of latex pervaded the office. He hated it. Even engulfed in the scents of tobacco and alcohol, he could still smell that damn mask.

Extinguishing his cigarette in the ashtray on his desk, he slowly exhaled. Smoke slithered from his lips as he walked over to his cabinet and retrieved his bottle of whiskey once more. He refilled his glass until the bottle was finally empty. This man wasn't planning to stop drinking until the sun was up. *I can't sleep anyway, maybe I'll drink myself unconscious.* He chuckled to himself.

This man was Kurt Mahoney, a detective in the Los Angeles Police Department. Mahoney had been heavily drinking for many years, doing whatever he could to rid his mind of the carnage, the vile acts that he witnessed—and everything he took part in. The bottles were never enough to help him forget. Homicides, suicides, watching his men—his friends—torn apart by gunfire and explosives. Burning bodies and burying children. He was practically drowning in blood.

He closed his eyes and took another sip.

The mask was a prime suspect in a long line of murders. Over the last several weeks, numerous bodies had been discovered across the city—all of which, were missing their heads. It was unlike anything he—or any coroner—had ever seen before. The necks of the bodies were melted at the ends, almost like they were burnt or that something acidic had eaten away at the victims' skulls. These were not beheadings performed with a machete, ax, or anything of that nature. These were identical murders that occurred amongst numerous victims. All of which were located within Los Angeles county over the last two months. This earliest case they had on record so far, was the body that was found on the first day of September. Since then, police have discovered fourteen other victims with the same lethal markings. Now it was Halloween night. A night filled with masks. He took another drink.

As his throat burned, Mahoney reached into his pocket and pulled out his lighter. His hands jittered as he lit a new cigarette. The dancing flame glowed in his hands like the jack-o-lanterns outside. During his investigation, Mahoney discovered that the first latex masks were made by a man named Don Post, in nineteen-thirty-eight. So these things had only been around for a little over a decade by this point. However, no masks he's ever seen looked anything like this one. This mask was much more detailed, almost other-worldly looking. Standing near it gave him chills.

The victims were all killed within a few days, sometimes only hours, apart from each other. They were all found headless with strange burn marks along their necks that looked as though they were cauterized. Whoever—or whatever—did this must have used electricity or some kind of chemicals to burn the tissue in order to close the wound. As for the involvement of this strange mask, it appeared in multiple photos from different crime scenes. As far as he could tell this was the only mask of its kind out there. He searched every costume store in town, questioned several shop owners and effects artists, all of which gave him the same answer: They had never seen this mask before.

The detective also spoke with witnesses, friends and family of the victims. Many of them mentioned that they had seen the mask before. Jared Nash, friend of the sixteen-year-old victim, Chris Palmer, who was found dead on October third, stated that he found it on top of a dumpster. Jared gave it to Palmer the night before he was murdered. Witnesses stated that Nash was at the high school football game that night, giving him a solid alibi. Then there was Vikki Nelson, sister of the twenty-seven-year-old victim, Carly Nelson. She was killed September seventh.

"I was on the phone with her that night. Hours before she...was killed. Carly told me about the mask. She found it at her doorstep when she came home from work. She said that it felt so...strange." Vikki whispered, holding back tears. She was out of town with her parents for the weekend on a short camping trip. Mahoney had been maddeningly pacing ever since she left his office earlier that evening.

Nothing made sense. None of these victims were related in any way. The mask was always found in different locations. No one saw it come or go. Everything was just so random. Either way, this mask continued to move on from victim to victim, before somehow disappearing—until now. It was placed into evidence lockup after an officer found it along the train tracks. The most recent victim was strung out alongside it. The victim was a homeless man, appearing to be in his sixties. With no kind of identification on his body, it would take a while before the police would discover his identity. That evening, the detective snagged the mask from lockup and brought it to his office. Mahoney was convinced that this rubber mask somehow killed all of these innocent people. *It must have had something to do with it.*

Looking down from his window, Mahoney spotted the few remaining kids on the street making their way back home. A group of teens lingered by the liquor store below, perhaps waiting for a random drunk to buy them some booze. *Who am I to judge? I'm just another drunk. Up in this room looking down at them instead of doing my job.* Procrastination was a curse that had always plagued him. He clenched his fist before taking another drink.

It's a holiday and I'm up here working. He was alone in his cramped office, when he should have been out there—spending the night with his family. He and his wife were keeping some distance between each other. He was trying his best to make things work. Make it up to her. *She doesn't make it easy, though.* Their daughter had just turned six, and this year she was going out dressed as a witch. *Green makeup and all, just like in the movie.* His daughter was the odd one in the bunch, much like himself, dressing up as the villain instead of a princess or a fairy.

"I guess I might as well dress up for the holiday!" He mocked as he grabbed the rubbery mask up from off of his desk. He raised it up to his face, staring into the dark, empty eye sockets that glared right back at him.

"Screw you." He muttered as he slid the skin-like mask over his face. It was cold and slimy. It felt wrong to wear it. He stumbled and fell back into his chair, almost missing it entirely. The old thing rocked back, almost tipping over, before he caught himself.

"Maybe I should take it easy on the drinks tonight." He grunted. Pushing his chair back, he looked at himself in the mirror. The greenish-blue coloring gave it a slimy, almost fish-like, appearance. The texturing of the mask was also strange. It was soft in areas and rough in others. It was cold at first, but almost instantly began to warm up. The mask seemed smaller in his hands, but now wearing it, he discovered that it fit like a glove.

"Ooga Booga!" He raised his hands like claws and growled at his own reflection. He chuckled and coughed, leaning back into his chair. *What am I thinking? A killer mask? Ridiculous! I can't go saying this to the department, they'll laugh me outta the building. Put me in a straight jacket!* He thought to himself as he adjusted his wrinkled, button-up shirt.

I'm off my rocker! There's gotta be a killer somewhere that connects all of these cases—something I'm missing! Who knows, there could be a hundred of these masks out there! He told himself, even though the evidence pointed elsewhere. After making several calls and visiting every costume shop in town—Mahoney was given the same answer: No one had ever seen or heard of one of these ugly masks before.

He remembered a Mexican kid that was arrested last month in Leimert Park. *He was close to where they found that Dahlia doll all cut up. Nineteen-year-old with a criminal record longer than the Hollywoodland sign!* His eyes scanned across the files from the murder in Leimert. A young girl named Madeline Finch, who was only sixteen, was found without a head, just like the others.

Witnesses spotted this Gomez kid following her the day before she died. Miguel was brought in and interrogated, unfortunately, his alibi checked out. *Right, says here he was on a date with another gal that night.* He tossed the file folder back onto his desk. The detective spent the next few hours going over every last case file again, and again. Eventually there were no more children out trick 'r treating. No delinquents out drinking and speeding. The city was falling asleep, and so was the detective.

His eyes slowly opened. The glow of red neon filled the room. It was still night. *How long was I out for this time?* After rolling over, he attempted to push himself up from the floor, but his one arm was still asleep. Cursing himself, Mahoney got to his knees and with another large breath, rose to his feet. Standing upright, the light-headed Mahoney fell back, crashing into a file cabinet. Catching himself, he leaned up against the wall.

"Jesus, my head hurts. Didn't think I drank that much…"

Once he regained his balance, Kurt brought his attention back to all of the files sprawled across his wooden desk. He shuffled around the office before collapsing into his leather chair. The heavy wooden desk was littered with autopsy forms and crime scene photos. Even though there was no color to these photographs, he could clearly picture the shades of reds and blues of the blood and veins that twisted around the disfigured necks. *This mask had to be what was killing these people.* He raised his hands up to rub his eyes and felt something strange. It felt like his face was numb. It didn't feel like his hands were even touching his skin at all.

Mahoney had almost forgotten that he was still wearing the damned thing. He brought his hands to his neck, feeling for the edges of the mask. At first—he felt nothing. His heart jumped as panic started to set in, believing that his skin and the mask had become one. *Why did you put this mask on, you idiot!?*

A moment later, he found the ridges of the mask. Kurt slowly exhaled and started to chuckle. *I'm letting this thing mess with my mind!* At the base of his neck, he pressed his fingertips along the end of the mask. It was stiff and resilient, not wanting to budge. He pulled harder, attempting to dig his fingers under the latex neck of the mask, but it felt as though it had been glued down to his skin. Rising up from his chair, his breathing grew heavy and his heart raced. Breathing was getting harder as the mask began constricting his throat. The beating of his heart boomed in his skull, echoing throughout the mask. He tried to stay calm as he searched the office for scissors or a knife. He needed to cut this thing off of his face.

Cursing, Mahoney's skin felt like it was burning. His words began to slur. Something was affecting his mind, and it wasn't the alcohol. Losing his balance, he stumbled and crashed into his desk, before collapsing on the floor. The photos that covered his desk were sent flying through the air like confetti, dropping down around him. It was the last thing he saw before his eyes melted down and oozed from out of his mask. He cried and flailed, still fighting the mask. He clenched his teeth as his melting skin began running down his own throat. The mask was turning his skull into soup.

The detective could feel the mask eating away at his skin. He could hear his own flesh sizzle in his ears. The man tried to climb back up to his feet, only making it to his knees. Under the mask, his muscles were bleeding. His face locked up as the mask ate away at his ears and his nose. Soon the mask worked its way down to his bones. Every part of him was slowly consumed by this entity on his face. Mahoney let out one final agonizing scream. Prayers were the final thoughts that crossed his mind before it was lost. His body twitched and convulsed as he gagged and spit blood that dripped down the face of the living mask.

Mahoney fell silent and his body still. The detective was dead. The pain was over. The mask slowly rolled off of Kurt's body and across the office floor. A headless, blood and sweat-soaked corpse laid sprawled out before his desk. His melted neck still sizzled in the dark room, like the sound of the neon sign outside.

The mask began to move on its own. It pulsated and shifted on the floor before tentacles and spider-like legs protruded from within it. The hollow neck birthed several slimy appendages, all of which were the same greenish-blue color of the mask. The creature squealed as it rose up, balancing itself on its many legs. Dark sinister eyes peered out from within the mask's sockets and mouth. Short jagged teeth lined the bottom of the mask's neck, surrounding its numerous legs and tentacles. The thing continued shifting, as if it were breathing, before it jolted to life and skittered across the floor. Its legs ticked and tacked like a crab as it shambled along the creaking floorboards. It left the office and passed down the hall. A moment later, and it skipped out into the street. Searching for its next victim on Halloween night, the creature disappeared into the darkness of a decrepit alleyway—and death followed.

An alien was loose in the City of Angels.

DADDY'S HOME

Years ago in Los Angeles, an average Tuesday evening became the start of something truly supernatural. A family spent their day to day lives in a little home built along the backside of the Hollywood Hills. A young mother in her mid-twenties vacuumed her house. Gwen's head ached as the machine crackled along the carpet. Cutting through the blinds, the warm glow of the sunset filled the home. Gwen was tall and slender with freckles and wavy dark hair. She had a nearly perfect smile, with a gap between two of her lower teeth, and a bad knee from her time playing soccer in school. It always bothered her, but her husband would always say that he loved her little imperfections.

Gwen rubbed her temple as she shut off the vacuum and stashed it in the closet. Ready to make dinner, she scooted over to the kitchen, stepping over a new obstacle course of toys. Her small child sat on the floor with her head inside a now empty toy box. The little girl was named Kayla, after Gwen's grandmother, who unfortunately passed just before the baby was born. She had just turned three-years-old, and was starting to learn new sentences every day, including:

"Daddy's home."

Gwen turned back and stared at her toddler, bewildered, "What was that honey?" The little girl rocked in place as she crudely filled in her coloring book. Gwen went back to searching through the refrigerator. Pulling out a carton of eggs, she carried it over to the stove. Kayla continued her coloring on the floor, until she suddenly stoped. She sat up straight and looked over to her mother in the kitchen.

"Daddy's home, mommy!"

A few seconds later and her husband's dinged-up blue truck pulled into the drive way. The mother walked over to the front door, not taking her eyes off of the little girl. Daddy went to reach for the door handle, but Gwen opened it for him.

"Oh hey, honey! Guess you heard me coming."

"Not exactly…" She muttered, still looking at her daughter in wonder.

"What's wrong?" He asked. His eyes went from her, to his daughter, and back to his wife again. "You're acting stra—"

"Oh, it's nothing, sweetie. Just… our daughter continues to surprise me." She finished with a smile and kissed her husband's cheek. He closed the door behind him and put down his bag. Walking over to his daughter, he picked her up and kissed her chubby cheeks. She giggled as he raised her up in the air and spun around with her.

"Even when you had a day as bad as today, I can always count on coming home to the two of you to make me forget all my troubles." The father joyfully declared.

"I'm sorry you had a bad day." Gwen said as she walked over to him and rubbed his arm.

"Ah, it's the same old nonsense." Don started. He rubbed his eyes and slicked back his blond hair, "This director is a nightmare. He keeps going over time, and not sticking to any of the schedules. He's constantly changing the shot lists and can never decide on where he wants the lighting. He's making everyone's lives a headache. I can't wait for this picture to be done with." She hugged him from behind and rested her head on his back.

"Just a few more weeks and then you'll be back on that horror show. You'll make it through this."

"Yeah, but then it's back to late nights, Gwen. I feel like I barely get to see the two of you as it is. I'm tired of the messy schedules in this business. Plus, I know you could use more help with our little girl. You're already dealing with everything in the house too…"

She held his hand and kissed it, looking up at him, "I'm okay. We will be okay. I love you."

Don kissed his wife and embraced his two girls in a warm hug.

———

As the week went on, Don would return home every night, tired and frustrated. A smile glowed on his face as he was greeted by his two girls. Gwen would spend these days running to the grocery store, the post office and the doctor's office, all while taking care of her baby girl. The following year, Kayla would be heading off to kindergarten. Her mother was preparing for the stress of leaving her little girl alone with strangers for so many hours. She told herself everything would be fine, but even logic couldn't stop her from worrying. She did find some relief in knowing that she finally had some free time to herself. Of course, her conflicted mind was also washed over with guilt. Happy to be rid of her baby. *No wonder my mother smoked like a chimney.* Gwen thought,

Parenting is maddening. At the end of the day, what keeps us all sane is the love we share with our family.

On the evening of a humid Thursday in September, Gwen stood at her stove, stirring a boiling pot filled with spaghetti noodles. The three-year-old Kayla sat on the carpet floor, stacking her blocks into an odd-shaped castle. Gwen was watching her from the corner of her eye as she was close to finishing dinner.

"Daddy's home!"

Gwen turned to look down at her little girl in the next room over. *There it is, again.* She thought. She stepped towards the child, her eyebrows forming a crease on her face. The toddler looked up at her confused mother and smiled. Before Gwen could speak, she spotted her husband's truck pulling into the driveway.

"How did you..." Her eyes focused down on the toddler, "How did you know daddy was home, sweetie?" The little girl continued stacking her blocks and giggling to herself. Don shuffled inside. His white smile gleamed in contrast to his dirty and sweaty face.

"Din... dinner is almost ready, honey." She smiled and kissed his cheek. Wiping her lips, she laughed, "Looks like you need a shower before supper!"

Once Don was cleaned up, the family sat at their dining room table. Kayla had graduated from the high chair and was now sitting upon her booster seat. Mother sat by closely, supervising the girl and her dinner. Gwen's eyes lingered on her. Don put his hand over his wife's slender fingers, "What's the matter? You've barely touched your dinner and you keep looking over at her." Gwen looked back into his eyes. They were soft and curious. He was a sweet man. Logical and hard-working. She knew he was stressed already and didn't want to bother him with something so foolish.

"Nothing's wrong." She gently gripped his hand, "Just worn out from the heat, I guess."

He chuckled, "You're telling me. This heat's been killing us. Apparently one of our actresses passed out today."

"Oh no..." Gwen covered her mouth in shock. He waved his hand, "She's okay.They got her some water and sent her to her trailer. They pushed for sending her to the hospital, but she refused and stuck around to keep working. She was more embarrassed than anything, I bet."

"Wow. Good for her, then. Glad everyone is all right." Gwen released her husband's hand and continued to eat her dinner. Thoughts of her daughter still lingered in the back of her mind.

"I'm just shocked an actor stuck around to work instead of throwing a fit over it. Some of these gals can be so dramatic." Don smirked and rolled his eyes. Little Kayla giggled at her father. Tomato sauce was smeared across her rosy cheeks.

———————

Another week passed by. Gwen continued her regular day-to-day. As she pushed Kayla along the aisle, the girl reached for a box of sweets. Her little fingers could almost reach a box of chocolate bars, when her mother calmly told her no.

"Halloween candy?" She asked with her big blue eyes. Gwen smiled, "It's not even October yet, sweetie. You don't need chocolate right now. Plus, you still have cookies and snack packs back at home."

The toddler pouted, and muttered, "Okay..."

Staring at the rows of candy made Gwen's stomach growl. Time to head home and make lunch. Perhaps today she'd cheat and get some fast food in the drive-thru. After pushing the shopping cart through checkout, they made their way across the parking lot. The sun beat down on them.

"Let's get home and out of this heat!" Gwen said to her daughter. She tossed the couple of paper grocery bags into the back of the Volkswagen Bug, before turning back to her daughter, who still sat in the cart. "Okay, here we go!" She lifted up Kayla and carried her over to the car seat, while whistling like a rocket. Kayla giggled and rolled her head. Gwen buckled the happy girl into her seat and closed the door. The rattling metal cart was pushed back across the lot and placed in front of the store with several others that shoppers had returned.

Climbing into the car, Gwen turned the key and the engine growled to life. She looked in the mirror for any traffic before backing out. Driving in reverse, she noticed her daughter in the back seat who was staring back at her in the reflection.

"Daddy's home."

The car slammed to a halt. The paper bags rattled and rolled over. Gwen turned back to look at the toddler behind her. "What did you just say? Did you say daddy's home? Again?"

The girl smiled, "Yeah, mommy! Daddy's home."

Gwen was puzzled. "But it's…"

A car horn blared. Gwen gasped as she jumped in her seat. Slowly exhaling, she spotted a red Plymouth to her right. She was blocking the road. "Sorry!" She waved as she finished pulling out of the parking spot.

Driving down the side streets, she watched her daughter in the mirror, "Honey, dad can't be home yet. It's too early. It's not even lunchtime yet." The girl just kept smiling. Gwen pushed her foot down onto the pedal, harder than usual. Slightly speeding, she eventually turned left down their road. She gasped. She couldn't believe it. Donald's blue truck was sitting in the driveway.

Gwen pushed through the front door to find Don grabbing a soda can from out of the fridge. Holding Kayla, Gwen gently placed her down on the couch and made her way to the kitchen.

"Hey girls, how are…" Don started. Gwen put her arms around him, hugging him tightly.

"There's something going on with our little girl." She whispered. As she released him, he gave his wife a puzzled look.

"What are you talking about?"

Gwen grabbed his arm and waved to the table, "Sit down and I'll try to explain." Her husband's eyes were locked onto hers with a look of bewilderment, but after a moment he gave in and sat down. Gwen walked over and closed the front door that she had left open. Kayla was still on the couch looking at her coloring book that was left on the arm rest.

"Kayla is…special." She started, struggling to look her husband in the eyes. Gwen tried to think of any logical way to explain away what was happening. Nothing came to her. After sitting there quietly for too long, she finally spoke, "She's supernatural…I know, I know, just hear me out. Our baby is different or at least has…some kind of a paranormal connection." Gwen saw her husband's brow lift. He opened his mouth, ready to ask once again, what was going on. Before he could speak, she continued, "Maybe she's psychic, or she has ESP or a sixth sense! I've been reading up on it. She started doing this a few weeks ago and I can't stop thinking about it—and now with this today—I had to talk to you!"

"What happened today? Sweetie…" He started.

"She's been able to sense you. Sense when you're coming home." She pointed to him and then at the house, "Or in this case, are already home." The couple turned and looked at their daughter. Her big eyes looked lost and in awe, as she inspected the colorful pages in her book.

"Gwen, honey, you gotta fill in these blanks. I'm still lost." He held her hand, "Are you okay?" She took a breath.

"Yes. I know I look a little crazy, but our daughter has told me when you're home before you've even driven down our street. On multiple occasions. Then today at the store, about fifteen minutes ago, she tells me that you're home now."

"Well, kids say weird, random stuff sometimes. I think you're blowing things out of proportion." He explained with a worried look in his eyes. She knew that he was trying his best to not sound condescending.

Gwen continued to explain, "For the last couple of weeks, when I was making dinner, cleaning the house, or out in the garden—she would look at me and say 'daddy's home' just before you pulled in." Don rubbed his chin for a moment, eyes still locked on his wife, before looking over at the stove.

"Well, you were making dinner. She must realize that if you're making dinner, then that just means that daddy will be home soon too." Gwen rubbed her eyes, thinking.

"They were different times of the day, though. One night you came home around five-thirty, while another night was later. I think you made it home just after eight. One day it was still light out, while that other time it was pitch black. That also still doesn't explain how she knew you were home today!" Gwen paused, "Wait, why are you home today?"

"Lead actor got sick and there's a fire near our filming location today. So the whole shoot was canceled until next week. They sent us all home. Thank God it's Friday." He grumbled, "They paid us for a full day, so I don't mind it. I was happy to see you two come in the door, but now you're giving me a headache, darling." Kayla climbed down from the couch and stumbled over to her building blocks. As she began to build a new block fortress, she turned and waved at her parents. Across the room they smiled and watched. Gwen squeezed Don's arm and leaned in closer.

"I'm sorry, but there's something strange about all of this. I've never seen her do anything like this before and I've heard that other children around this age can do similar things. They can sense spirits or know things that no one—especially toddlers—would ever know!" Don shook his head.

"Or it could all be just her imagination. Kids come up with crazy stuff. They see monsters under their beds and are scared of their own shadows sometimes." Gwen sighed. Don rose up and walked over to the little girl. Picking her up and smiling, he added, "She's also still learning how to read and speak. Maybe it's just another term she's getting used to saying." He gently pinched her cheek, making her giggle. "Isn't that right, cupcake? You still learning, Kayla?"

Gwen closed her eyes and rolled her head back, accepting the defeat. She was hoping that he was right and that it was all just a weird coincidence. Kayla was a normal toddler that just said the darndest things. However, part of her still believed. She believed there was something odd happening here. Part of her hoped she could prove him wrong.

That night, after dinner, Don sat on the couch watching the television. Kayla had passed out across her father's lap. He stayed still, afraid of waking her. He noticed Gwen watching him from the kitchen as she was washing the dishes. He smirked at her and shrugged his shoulders. Gwen smiled back and blew soap bubbles his way.

Hours after Donald had fallen asleep, Gwen spent the restless night tossing and turning in bed. She desperately tried to sleep, but couldn't get her mind to rest. All she could think of was her daughter. Finally, she crawled out of bed and tiptoed her way over to Kayla's room. Cracking open the door, she watched as the little girl slept in her small bed. Gwen rubbed her flat stomach, thinking back to the days of carrying her. Was she really just blowing things out of proportion? Letting her imagination get the better of her? She couldn't accept that. Not yet.

The following morning, functioning off of three-and-a-half hours of sleep, Gwen made breakfast for her family. Bacon, scrambled eggs and cinnamon toast. Don read the paper as he bit down into his bacon. Gwen helped feed Kayla her meal. "Make sure to eat all your eggs too, darling."

"I don't like eggs." She frowned.

"Don't like eggs?" Her mother questioned, "You just had eggs last week. Are these ones cold?"

"No. I don't like eggs anymore." The little girl crossed her arms as she chewed on her toast.

"Gotta love toddler logic." Gwen laughed. Don put down his paper and looked over at Kayla's plate, still covered with scrambled eggs.

"Sweetie, you gotta eat your eggs. You can't let them go to waste." Kayla gave her father the cutest grumpy face that he had ever seen. His eyes darted back to his wife, who gave him the look saying, "It's okay." She noticed his eyes were focusing on her now. He must have noticed that she didn't sleep well. "You all right?" He asked.

"Yup. She doesn't like eggs today. It's fine, honey." Changing the topic, Gwen pulled the plate over and scooped up a bite with her fork. "I'll eat them so they don't go to waste."

––––––––

The following week, Don returned to work. It was now October. That afternoon, while he was on stage at the studio, Gwen decided she was going to try some experiments. She needed to see if Kayla truly had something special. After making her daughter some breakfast, she sat her down on the couch. Kayla stared up at her mother while she thought over how she would do this. Finally she smiled and spoke. "Okay, honey. We're going to play a game. I know you like those!"

"Yeah!" Kayla gleefully giggled. Her big blue eyes followed her mother as she held out her hands. She liked her mother's blue sweater. It was bright like the sky.

"All right. So I want you to figure out what I'm doing. Just like how you know when daddy's coming home. Okay?" Kayla nodded while she chewed on her hair. Gwen pulled that out of her mouth and put her hands back down to her sides. "Okay! I'm going to go in the other room, where you can't see me. Then—just like with daddy—I want you to yell out whatever you see me doing. Or if you know when I'm coming back in here to get you. Whatever you see, just shout it out! And if you're right, you win the game, sugar!"

Kayla smiled, while looking somewhat confused. She nodded and told her mother she was ready to play.

Gwen got up and walked down the hall and into her room. She slowly closed the door until it was just open a crack.

"Alright baby, whenever you see something or feel it, just shout it out!" Gwen cheered. As she hid from her daughter in the bedroom, she looked around for items to use. Grabbing a brush off of her cabinet, she began brushing her hair in front of the mirror. A few moments passed before she spoke up, "Anything, Kayla? See what mommy's doing?"

No answer.

"Kayla, sweetie? You hear me?" Gwen hesitated another moment. The silence bothered her and she pushed through the door, out into the hall.

"There you are, mommy!" The little girl laughed. She was still sitting on the couch with a big smile on her face. Gwen bit her lip, somewhat smiling. "I found you!"

"No baby, this isn't like hide and seek. You have to tell me what you see me doing when I'm in the bedroom." Gwen insisted. The toddler made a face.

"I can't see you. The door was closed!" She pouted.

Gwen rubbed the back of her neck. "Think about me like I'm daddy. You know when daddy is coming home from work. So try to tell me what I'm doing before you see me. Does that make sense?" The little girl nodded, once again, although Gwen was beginning to lose hope in this whole idea. She walked back down the hall to her bedroom door. Stopping and taking another glance at her girl, she waved, "Okay, let me know what you see mommy doing in here!" She closed the door behind her. A minute passed. Kayla spoke.

"Daddy fall down."

Gwen dropped her brush. She swung the door open and looked down the hall. The hair brush bounced off the floor, while her eyes stayed locked onto her daughter. Gwen's heart sank. Her smile faded away and dread contorted her face.

"What did you just say?" Kayla stayed silent. She walked over to the toddler and bent down close to her face. Her smile faded as well, as she looked into her mother's eyes. "Kayla. What did you say? What happened to daddy?" Kayla's head dropped down. The girl rose to her feet, legs wobbling, as she carried her toy box over to the closet.

"Kayla, put the toys down. Talk to me." Gwen rose up from the couch. Her heart fluttered as she bit at her nails. She must have heard wrong. She had to be hearing things.

"Daddy fall down." Kayla spoke with a coldness to her voice. Her eyes glazed over as she stared at the empty corner of the room. "...Daddy all gone."

The mother fell back onto the couch. Her legs had given out. She covered her mouth as she felt the tears arriving. Taking a deep breath, she looked down at her daughter, "Where is daddy? What happened to daddy, Kayla?" It took everything to stay calm. Her body wouldn't let her move, just yet. All she could do was sit and beg her daughter to answer her. Kayla dropped her toys. Her lip quivered and her eyes glistened.

The toddler cried and waddled towards her mother. "I'm sorry mommy!"

"You don't have to be sorry, sweetie!" Gwen hugged her baby. She ran her hands through her short curly hair. It smelled like strawberries. Bright and sweet just like her little girl. "Where did daddy go? I'm not mad. I just need to go get him and ...make sure he's all better." Her nose sniffled. She took another deep breath, trying desperately to hold back more tears.

"I don't know, mommy! Lights out. It's all dark!"

Gwen rubbed a tear off of the little girl's red cheek. "It's going to be okay. I'm going to call daddy's work." Rising to her feet, she stepped over to the telephone that hung from the wall. "See if someone knows what happened." She dialed the number of one of their friends, Dallas. He was a special effects guy, and he happened to be working on the same picture as Don. The phone rang.

"C'mon Dal…"

The phone continued to ring.

"Please." She whispered while twisting the phone cord between her nervous fingers.

No answer.

"Damnit!" She slammed the phone back down. Biting her nails, she looked down at her daughter still sitting on the carpet floor. Her face was red but the tears had stopped. Outside the window, she saw her car waiting in the driveway. Gwen grabbed Kayla and ran out of the house, hopped into the Volkswagen, and took off down the road.

Driving just above the speed limit, she darted around slow drivers. Squeezing past yellow lights, she pushed herself as fast as she could. She scanned the roads, watching for any police. She didn't have time for a ticket.

"We're going fast, mommy!" Kayla cheered.

Gwen watched her daughter in the mirror as she put her hands up in the air. The smile on her little girl lifted Gwen's heart. For a moment she felt that everything was okay. A car horn roared and Gwen gripped the steering wheel. Her knuckles were white as she turned the wheel. A city bus flew past her as she veered the bug back across the yellow line. The bug straightened out after almost colliding head on with that bus. Gwen was breathing heavily as she focused on the road ahead. She could still hear Kayla giggling behind her.

Gently stepping onto the breaks, she turned the corner and cut down a side road. The studio was just ahead. Gwen bit her lip as she tried to think happy thoughts. *Donny's all right. He's going to be okay. I'm just over reacting.* The Bug pulled up to the front gate, stopping at the guard booth. A scrawny old man in a security uniform, that appeared to be two sizes too big on him, stepped out from the booth. He hunched, looking down into the car and made a face that seemed like he recognized the mother. Before he could say anything, Gwen started talking. Her voice was shaky as she fought to stay calm.

"My husband, Donny! Donald Johnson! He's hurt... Something happened! We tried calling, but couldn't get answers—" The guard took a step back and raised his fragile hand.

"Ma'am. I don't understand. You're Donald Jameson's wife...?" He leaned his head forward, trying to make sure that he was hearing her right.

"Johnson. Donald Johnson. He's one of the Grips working on the film, *Hide and Shrie*—"

He looked back over his record book, "Okay miss, just let me check out my..."

"I just need to get in and see if he's okay, please!" She clenched her fists around the steering wheel. In the backseat, Kayla looked at the old man in bemusement. Gwen was about ready to simply plow through the security gate and take off down the road to his stage. "He should be on stage fourteen! It's the new Vincent Price movie!"

The old man pushed his glasses down the ridge of his nose as he turned away from his paperwork. "I'm sorry, ma'am, but I don't have any record of you. I can't let you in without a pass—"

Gwen was about to slam her foot down onto the gas pedal. Before she could, Dallas appeared from around the corner. He ran up to the old guard in his booth, "Hey Gus! It's okay! She's with me! Her husband had an accident."

Gwen's heart plummeted. She couldn't breathe. The confirmation horrified her. *What happened to him? Please tell me he's still alive! How does my baby girl know this! What's wrong with my baby!?* Dallas waved his arm, inviting her into the backlot. The old security guard, Gus, opened the gate and tipped his hat towards her, "Sorry about the confusion, ma'am. Hope Donald is okay!" She forced a smile as she drove forward. Dal walked alongside her car.

"How'd you get here so fast? I was just running to call your house, but then I heard you shouting, and I ran over to the gate!" Dal was in his late thirties, that she and Donald had met years ago on another picture. Dallas was shorter and bulky. He had a buzzed head and a flat nose, with round glasses. His eyes looked nervous and his buttoned up shirt was stained with sweat. She thought that he pulled off the jock and nerd looks all at once.

"Don't worry about it—what happened to Donny?" Gwen fought back tears.

"He fell. Fell off of his ladder and hit his head. He was knocked out and taken to the studio's medical building." Gwen gasped. She pulled over and stopped the Bug in a no parking zone. She rapidly rose out of the car and then bent down to get her little girl unbuckled. Dallas watched the road for any oncoming traffic. Fortunately, it was a slower day at the studio. Gwen pulled her out and held Kayla in her arms.

"Is he... What kind of shape is he..." She started. Dallas grabbed her arm gently, pointing ahead of him, "He's down this road, up ahead. Let's go." Her arms grew tired, as they walked, realizing that Kayla was getting too big to carry anymore. The three quickly made their way over to the medical building and pushed through the door. A heavy woman in snug scrubs was standing at the front desk. She turned around to face the new arrivals while she arranged a stack of forms and files.

"Hello, how can I help you?"

Gwen set her daughter down and repeated herself, "My husband, Donald Johnson. He's been in an accident. We wanted to see him—"

"Shoot." The nurse set her forms down on the desk, "You three just missed him. We patched him up here, but sent him off to the hospital. Saint Joseph's across town." Gwen cursed under her breath, before picking her daughter up again. "Don't repeat that, Kayla. Those are adult words." Kayla giggled and repeated the curse words. Gwen, exhausted, closed her eyes and shook her head.

Gwen and Dallas made their way back towards the Volkswagen. "Hand me the keys, I can drive you there!" Dallas volunteered as he neared the driver door. Gwen tossed him the set of keys and climbed into the passenger seat. He turned the ignition and the engine rumbled to life once more. Dallas gave Gus the security guard a nod as he drove the bug out through the front gates.

About ten minutes later, the car pulled up to the front doors of the hospital. "You take Kayla and go find him! I'll park the car and meet you in there!" Dallas exclaimed. Gwen tapped his arm and nodded, thanking him. She turned to the backseat to unbuckle little Kayla.

"C'mon sweetie! Let's go find daddy!"

After talking to a woman at the front desk, they finally pointed her the way to go. "Mr. Johnson is going to be recovering in room five-two-six." The young nurse smiled. Gwen and Kayla quickly walked over to the elevators. They were told that the doctors were running some imaging tests on him after he had his concussion. From what little she was told, it seemed like Donald was going to be all right, but she couldn't know for sure until she finally held him in her arms. *Please be okay, baby!*

After pushing the up button, the old elevator took its time descending down its shaft. Kayla watched as her mother nervously tapped her foot. Soon she followed, although her body wobbled and her tapping was not as consistent as Gwen's. Her mother noticed and smiled. *Ding.* The doors finally opened and she rushed inside. A moment passed before the doors began to shut. Before they fully closed a hand cut in, stopping the doors. *C'mon!* Gwen thought to herself. An overweight man in a suit and tie squeezed in next to Gwen. He was sweating and his nose whistled as he inhaled, "Four, please."

Gwen blinked and looked over at him. He pointed to the buttons, "Fourth floor, please."

She raised her brows, "Oh, yes. Sorry." She pushed down on the button labeled four, now matching the illuminated number five button. The doors finally closed and the elevator began to rise. The heavy man smelled like tobacco and there was no way to avoid it in such a small space. He coughed into a handkerchief. Gwen kept her distance. Catching a cold was the last thing either of them needed.

"Or was it three...?" Gwen heard the man whispering to himself. "Sorry, can you push the button for the third floor as well?" The man politely asked.

Gwen—frustrated—smiled, "Of course." She pressed down on the level three button. Her hands rested on her little girl's shoulders. She played with Kayla's hair as she continued her nervous foot tapping. Soon the elevator doors opened to level three. The big man in the suit peeked his head out. He was taking his time looking down both hallways, still appearing to be lost and confused. Gwen stood there, biting her tongue.

Eventually, he decided to step back into the elevator, "Must have been the fourth floor after all. My mistake." The sick man harshly coughed again through a throat filled with phlegm. Gwen simply nodded and held her child close. After reaching the fourth floor, the man made his way down the hall, muttering, "This has to be the right place." The elevator doors closed once more, and did not open again until they finally arrived on the fifth floor. Gwen and Kayla rushed out of the small box and down the hall to the nurse's station.

"Hi, I'm looking for my husband. Johnson, Donald Johnson—"

An older man with white hair and a mustache, wearing a matching doctor's coat, greeted her from the hallway to her left. "Hello, Mrs. Johnson, your husband is right down this way." He calmly spoke as he led her to room five-two-six. Gwen and Kayla were greeted by a smiling Donald as they stepped into the room. He sat up in his bed, with bandages wrapped around his head.

"Hey, there's my girls!" He smiled. The three held each other close in a group hug.

"I'm so happy you're okay, Donny!" She kissed her husband. Don grabbed his little girl and pulled her up to sit in bed with him.

"Wee! Hi, daddy!"

"Hey there, darling!" He smirked and pinched her cheek, before looking over at Gwen. "How'd you two get here so fast?" She looked at Kayla and then back to him.

"Our little girl."

"What?" Don questioned. Gwen took his hand, looking into his eyes.

"She knew. Instead of just knowing when you were coming home, today she said that you fell down. That you were all gone! It scared me, and we drove straight to the studio! By the time we were finally let in, we bumped into Dallas, but then we were told you were taken here and—"

"Whoa, whoa. Hold on, honey. Start over for me. Are you still freaking out over Kayla's imagination?" Donny turned, dropping his legs off the side of the bed. He started to climb out when Gwen stopped him.

"Listen Donny, please! This isn't her imagination. She knew that you fell down! She knew you were taken away to the hospital!"

"Okay, okay. What should we do about this? She isn't hurting anyone. I say keep an eye on her, but don't go telling everyone in town about it. I'm just so happy you're here. I'm fine, you're both safe." He wrapped his arms around the two of them. He smiled at his wife and she gently caressed his bandaged head. She wanted to say so much, but it was no use. Not today, at least. Don turned back to his little girl, "Now let's get out of here and head home!"

"You should probably wait for the docs to say when you're good to go. You got your noggin rocked." Dallas laughed as he walked into the hospital room, "Don't want any bits of your brains spilling out of your ears on the drive home!"

"Well, at least I still got some brains, unlike you!" Don winked and laughed.

The four of them spent the next hour sitting in that hospital room talking about their day and what the production was doing after this accident. Dallas said they went right back to filming after Don was taken away in the ambulance. Don rolled his eyes, "Of course... Can't wait for the cards and balloons from the producers!"

"You hit your head, buddy. Don't go acting like you lost an arm and a leg!" Dallas chuckled and smacked the side of Don's arm, "I think you'll pull through!"

"You keep abusing me and I'm gonna need to take off more sick days!" Don smirked.

Soon after, the doctor walked back into the room and spoke with the family. Dallas waved goodbye and made his way down to the lobby. Gwen offered to drive him back to the studios, but Dallas told her that one of the teamsters was waiting out front to give him a ride. The doctor with the white mustache told the Johnson family that they were free to go.

Once Donald was dressed, a nurse with a wheelchair wheeled him through the hospital halls. The four of them rode the elevator down, Gwen chatted with the nurse, discussed the injury, and thanked her. Although, deep down Gwen couldn't stop thinking about her little girl. She looked down at her husband in the chair. Kayla sat in his lap and giggled as he tickled her. Gwen told herself that there were other times to discuss what was going on. For now, she was just thrilled that her husband was safe and happy.

———

The days went on like normal. Donald was ready to go back to work the following week. Kayla had been quiet when it came to premonitions. Days turned into weeks and life carried on.

One weekend in November, as they closed in on Thanksgiving, the family spent the afternoon in the backyard. Gwen showed Kayla how to pick out the vegetables from their small garden. Meanwhile, Don washed his truck in the driveway as he kept an eye on his two ladies. Gwen pulled potatoes out from the soil and tossed them into her basket. Kayla played with one of them in her small hands. The potatoes, along with their home-grown lettuce and corn, were going to help make up their Thanksgiving dinner in a few days.

"Whew. I'm all dirty. You two keep playing, I'm going to head in and shower." Gwen stood up and tossed her gloves aside. She lifted up her heavy baskets and walked towards the back door. Don was using the hose and swerved the water towards her, teasing his wife. She held up her fist and winked. Don turned the faucet off and rolled up the hose.

After she stepped inside the back door, she walked over to the kitchen and placed the baskets on the counter. Gwen hesitated at the window for a moment, watching the two play outside. Don stomped around the backyard, playing hide-and-go-seek with little Kayla. Even in the autumn afternoons, the weather in Burbank was perfect. The sky was red and warm like a hug. Crickets started chirping and and a soft breeze swayed the trees. Gwen felt at ease, there was a comfort in the air. Perhaps the worst was finally over for them. Life had settled back down and the three of them were happier than ever. She smiled and walked down the hall to her bedroom.

Donald found Kayla attempting to hide behind one of the bushes. She had her hands over her eyes, thinking he couldn't possibly see her. "Gotcha!" He laughed and tickled her before pulling her up into the air. She giggled and squirmed in his arms. Don placed her back down on the grass and asked, "Alright, am I hiding now or do you want to go hide again, sweetie?" Kayla stood frozen, staring off into the distance. Her giggles had stopped and her smile faded as the little girl watched the sunset.

"Mommy fall down."

Donald's smile faded, "What was that, honey? What happened?" The toddler waddled off towards the garden again. Don followed, now nervous. "What did you say about mommy?" Kayla sat down on the grass. Her hands were still stained with dirt. Donald noticed that his daughter wasn't acting like herself. Something was wrong. He looked over at the back door, then back down at his daughter's empty eyes. His heart raced as he ran for the door. Searching the home, he called out for his wife, but Gwen never answered. Kayla sat on the grass, playing with the soil in the garden. A scream could be heard from inside the house. It was her father. Donald cried out in agony. His screams shook the house and rang out through the windows, off into the neighborhood.

Soon after, police sirens joined in. The flashing red and blue lights bounced off the walls and Kayla's face. Donald held her in his lap. They sat on the front porch of their small home, while Donald spoke with two officers. They quietly discussed the accidental death of his wife. Gwen had fallen in the shower and cracked open her skull in the tub. A gurney with a black body bag rolled down the driveway and into the ambulance. Kayla watched as it passed. The little girl's eyes appeared confused, but aware. She was right, once again. She looked up at her daddy and he looked back down at her. She told her daddy,

"Mommy all gone."

<u>MONSTER</u>

A little girl squirmed while she hid under her bed. The wind roared outside as tree branches scratched along the house walls, like boney fingers and razorblades. Rain poured down against the window just above her bed, yet she still managed to hear the faint sound of footsteps in the hallway. Wet boots squealed down the hall with every step as the figure drew nearer. The stomping stopped just outside her door. For those eternal few seconds, the little girl held her breath.

Her lungs burned as she fought the urge for oxygen. Turning red, she clenched the carpet in her small fists. Then the footsteps began again—now heading further down the hall. Unlocking her lips, she took in a large breath. Her racing heart began to slow and just when the little girl felt safe—she could hear another door in the house slowly creak open. She knew just where the monster was and wished that she could do something, anything at all to stop it—but the child's body was frozen still.

A young boy's chilling scream rattled throughout the house. The girl's muscles tightened up. She felt so small hiding under her bed. Silence overtook the dark house. Her eyes went wide as she watched the door in front of her. It remained open, just a crack, allowing the weak moonlight to pass through the gap. Suddenly something large passed by, blocking what little light came through, replacing it with an endless darkness. This massive figure stood just outside of her room. She could hear it sniffing the air like an animal. Something primal was out there. It did this for a moment, before it continued walking down the hall.

The child let out a sigh of relief. The monster was gone and she was safe, for now, at least. She looked back over her shoulder, searching for the small flashlight that she brought with her. Under the bed, she reached out, desperate for the safety of the light. Seconds felt like hours as her fingers scratched along the soft carpet. As hope slipped away, she felt the sudden chill of the cold metal at the tips of her fingers. The child grabbed hold of it, quickly bringing it close to her face and turning it on. The bright light revealed a gruesome, smiling face inches from her own under the foot of the bed. She screamed as the large hands came towards her. In an instant, the monster grabbed the girl and pulled her out from under the bed. It raised her high in the air above the dark figure's face.

"I got you!" the monster growled, before turning on the nearby lamp. He chuckled and tickled the little girl. She giggled and shook as he put her back down on the bed.

"You got me grandpa!" She cheered. The bright light filled the room, revealing her grandfather who played the grumbling monster. He was a tall, lanky man in his early sixties, with combed back graying hair and glasses. The grandpa's kind, blue eyes rested over his crooked smile.

"You finally found her!" the girl's brother shouted as he barged into the room, "How does he always find me first?"

The sister laughed and said, "I guess I'm just a better hider! Or it's because I don't make loud farts all the time like you do!" The girl and her papa chuckled. Her brother pouted before also joining in on the laughter.

"Yes, the smell of the farts attracts the monster right away!" Grandpa snarled, with his fingers outstretched like claws, as he pretended to attack the brother. The boy laughed, tensing up and doing his best to dodge the inevitable tickling. A moment later, the grandfather cleared his throat and stood up straight. "Alright, it's time for bed now, kids. Teddy, make sure to brush your teeth first."

"But can't we play monster again?" The boy, Teddy, begged, "Or what about watching another scary movie? What about *The Lost Boys* or uh, *The Thing*...or *The Blob*?"

"Or *The Wolf Man*!" the sister added and howled at the moon. Grandpa smiled and shook his head.

"It's already way past your bedtimes, and we can't have you two screaming and waking up all the neighbors. So Teddy get brushing, and Sam, you too." Sam and Teddy reluctantly nodded their heads and made their way to the bathroom.

After finishing brushing their teeth, and getting into their pajamas, the twins jumped into bed, where their grandpa was waiting to tuck them in. He gave them goodnight kisses on their foreheads and werewolf bites on their arms. The two children giggled and squirmed under the covers of the large guest room bed. Their grandpa stood smiling in the doorframe, before turning the light off and heading to his room.

The twins stayed up late discussing old scary movies and their favorite thing to play with grandpa—*the monster game*. They had been playing it for years. It was a game where they would run through the house and find somewhere to hide, much like hide and seek, except the seeker was their grandpa who acted like his favorite movie monster—the wolf man.

He would creep through the home, hunched over, like Lon Chaney Jr. Raising his hands up before him, and twisting his fingers like they were claws, he growled and howled at the moon in search of the children. Sometimes the twins would take turns as the monster too, but it was never quite as fun for them. *No one could play the wolf man better than grandpa.*

Sam and Teddy would spend many of their weekends at their grandpa's house. They would watch all kinds of scary movies while consuming endless amounts of pizza and candy—all of which they never told their mom about. The twins loved their weekends with grandpa and wished that those nights would never end.

As the years went on, and they all grew older, their lives only got busier. In a flash, ten years had passed by, and the twins were now high school seniors. Sam and Ted sat in their living room, both on their phones as *Army of Darkness* played on the television. Ted was playing games on his phone. He sat hunched over intently as the match was coming to a close, on the verge of winning another round.

Sam laid back on the couch scrolling through college websites. It was her time to pick out schools and prepare for the applications. Her long blonde hair hung off the edge of the couch. Her feet rolled back and forth, anxiously dancing on the arm rest beyond her torn jeans and the worn out Dracula shirt she wore. Her nails were painted a dark blue like her eyes that were reflected in the cracked glass of her phone screen. She thought of all the times when Teddy would tease her. Scolding her for always leaving her phone behind—and when she did have it—she would drop it. *All those brains and you can never remember that phone,* he would say.

Her brother stood a foot taller than her, with dark, scruffy hair that crawled out from under his blue baseball cap. He shuffled in his red flannel shirt, laying his head back against the couch and tossing his phone down with a sigh, "Stupid game anyways."

"Lost again? Doesn't matter, you'll be back to playing again in no time." Sam muttered without looking away from her own cracked screen.

"Oh, ha ha." He mocked. Rubbing his eyes, he sat there, fidgeting. Teddy glared at the device laying face down on the table. A moment later, he snatched his phone back up to start a new match. Behind the twins, their mother entered the living room. She looked up at the TV then down to Ted and Sam and sighed, "Always on those screens."

"Unlike someone, I'm looking at schools to apply to, mom." replied Sam.

"I'm gonna get to it. Just don't know where I wanna go yet…" The mumbling Teddy trailed off.

Their mom shook her head, and smirked, "It's fine. I could just use some help in the kitchen. By the way, did either of you give grandpa a call?" The siblings sat there quietly, glancing over at each other.

"No. Not yet," Sam started, "I forgot, but I'll—"

"You two need to pick up the phone. He misses you. You guys used to live there with him on the weekends, but once you started growing up and getting so wrapped up in school… he hasn't seen you or heard from you in ages."

"He can see our posts and stuff online." Ted said.

"That's not the same, Teddy." Mom remarked, her arms resting on her hips. She could see the guilt in his eyes when he looked up at her.

"I know. I'm sorry, I'll text him now." He promised, sitting up straight on the couch.

"I understand that you guys are busy, but you have to make time for family, especially him. He misses you both a lot. I was just on the phone with him this morning and he was wondering when we'd be visiting again." She stepped closer, resting her hands on the back of the couch. The mother looked down at both of her children. They finally put away their phones and focused on her. *Nearly adults, and I still have to treat them like toddlers some days.*

"I was thinking, maybe you two could spend the weekend up there. One last time before you both go off to college and everything. He would love it. Order a pizza, maybe make some popcorn and watch some old movies together. You guys could play some board games or you could even show him some of the games on your phone, Teddy." She gestured to her son. "Anything to get you guys out of the house and spend some time with your grandpa. He's not getting any younger either…"

The twins looked at each other, realizing just how long it had been. Nodding, they turned back to their mother and spoke.

"Okay mom. That sounds good. We can go up this weekend." Sam rose up from the couch and walked over to their mom, "I'll call him after dinner. What are we making tonight?"

———

That Friday afternoon the twins stepped out into their driveway and tossed their bags into the car, one after the other.

"You're staying for the weekend, not a month long adventure!" Their mom sarcastically exclaimed, "What do you need all that for?"

"I tossed some water bottles in my bags. All grandpa ever drinks is black coffee and off-brand sodas that are terrible. I can't survive on that." Sam replied. Her brother chuckled and closed the trunk door.

"I can survive off the beers he keeps in the garage fridge."

Before his mother uttered a single word, he knew everything she had to say from her grumpy glare.

The children hugged their mother and climbed into the suburban. Sam drove while Teddy rode shotgun. After driving for only a few minutes, Teddy retrieved his phone from out of his pocket and started playing one of his games, just as Sam predicted.

Sam pressed down on the brake, harder than usual, when they neared a stop sign. The car stopped with a sudden jerk and Teddy choked on his seatbelt.

"What the he—!?"

"Just making sure you're paying attention." She smirked and pulled forward.

A few blocks further, and the twins merged onto the freeway, leaving their home town behind. Sam made sure they left the house early enough that they only had a two hour drive ahead of them. She did not want to be stuck in a car with her stinky brother any longer than she had to. Sam groaned as her brother passed gas the moment they drove onto the freeway. *Every single time. He is so gross!*

Orange and yellow trees remained scattered along the sea of dying trees. Boney wooden fingers, outstretched towards the sky, waiting for spring time to return. November had passed, it was the first week of December and the air was bitter and cold. As they drove further up the mountain, houses were few and far between. Many of which were empty and locked up for the winter. So many of the residents were already in the skies or on the road, headed to see family in warmer destinations.

Sam watched a family packing their trailer in their driveway as they passed by. A little boy, only five or six years old, carried a box of toys with him. A space alien and a cowboy figurine hung out over the ledge of the container. The boy's scruffy blonde hair and little brown eyes peaked out over the box as he shuffled towards the family's trailer. He was on his own little adventure. Somewhere far away from this mountain.

Sam pulled up to the long gravel driveway of their grandpa's cabin. It was a larger two-story wooden structure, much older than the twins. The car dipped and bumped up the hill and pulled to the side, next to the old man's beat up truck. The bed of the truck was filled with all kinds of junk. Grandpa was a collector of all things rusty. His backyard was filled with shells of antique cars, parts of old gas pumps, metal signs and anything else Americana he would find on his adventures. The old man was a mechanic, carpenter and man of all traits. He could do anything with his hands, but the years were catching up to him and he wasn't as limber as he used to be. Not quite retired, he still tinkered with things every day, but the imprint in his recliner had grown more worn out since they last stayed the night.

Sam put the car in park and turned off the engine. Teddy closed up his game and slid his phone back in his pocket.

"This is gonna be fun." Sam said to her brother. "Haven't spent the weekend here in a long time. Be nice to feel like little kids again."

"Yeah, one last trip through memory lane. I missed coming up here too. Maybe I'll go wander the junkyard out back and find a body this time." He joked.

"Would be fitting with the movies we're watching tonight." Sam smiled.

They climbed out of their suburban and opened the trunk. Teddy grabbed his bags and handed his sister hers when grandpa walked out through the front door.

"Hey kiddos! So glad you made it! How was the drive out here?" He gleamed.

The twins met him at the steps of the house and hugged him. He didn't want to let go.

"It was fine." Sam smiled. "Longer than we remembered it being, but its nice out with the fall leaves and the gray skies."

"Oh yeah, best time of year." Grandpa chuckled, "I want my summer back. Give me ninety degrees any day."

"Nasty. You can have it!" Teddy grimaced. "I'll take the cold and the rain anytime."

"Doesn't bother you when it just gives you an excuse to stay inside and play your games." Sam jabbed.

"Hey, those are things are fun. I've seen some of the gals in those things." Granda winked. "Just the type of entertainment a growing boy needs."

"Gross." Sam hid her red face in her hands.

"Let me help you with those bags and get you two situated." The old man said as he picked up Sam's duffle bag. "Heavy. You planning on moving in?"

Grandpa walked them through the house, and brought them to the two guest rooms that were located across from each other. His master bedroom remained at the end of the hallway. Not much had changed over the years from what Sam could remember. He even kept some of their old drawings framed and hung up on the walls next to their baby pictures and photos of the whole family together around the Christmas tree.

"Looks like you are all set!" The old man declared as the twins placed their bags down in each room. "You need a drink or anything? I've still got some pop in the fridge!"

"I'll just get some water later, thanks." Sam answered while going through her bag. She dug out her phone charger and plugged it into the wall, along with her book she placed on the nightstand. It was a sleazy romance novel her aunt had gotten her for her birthday. Sam knew it wasn't great, yet she couldn't seem to put it down.

"Any beer?" Teddy asked with a smirk.

"You're only fifteen, mister." Grandpa crossed his arms.

"Seventeen. We graduate in six months, gramps."

"Ooh, seventeen, right. Big difference." He scratched his scruffy white chin. "Sure, why not."

"Really?" Teddy jumped up from his bed.

"No." Grandpa answered sternly, but he couldn't hide his grin. "Maybe later...But your mother never heard about this!"

———

Sam and Teddy wandered the junkyard out back. They listened to the crickets and the birds sing as the sun was slowly descending across the horizon. The last of the Autumn leaves were falling around them. Sam took a deep breath. The air here was crisp and softer. It really felt like they were living up amongst the clouds. She forgot how much she missed coming up to their grandpa's cabin.

"Oh hey, that reminds me!" A smile grew on Teddy's rosy face. "Our time capsule! Do you remember the metal lunchbox we buried here?"

"Woah, yeah! We left it somewhere along the horse trail, right?" Sam asked as her eyes lit up with excitement.

"Yeah! I mean, I think so." Teddy shrugged, "Let's go look for it! I can't remember half the stuff we buried. Been close to a decade now!"

"It's getting kind of dark…" Sam began, rubbing her arm and looking up at the sky. With winter on the way, the sun was down before it was even time for dinner.

"Yeah, but we got time! Let's go dig it up!" Teddy gleamed and skipped off towards the trail.

"Alright, hold on, dork!" Sam giggled, "Just let me talk to grandpa first!" Turning back to the cabin, she headed for the back door. Pulling the screen door open, she found grandpa cooking in the kitchen. Lettuce, ketchup, mayo, onions and beef patties laid sprawled out across the counter.

"Making burgers?" She asked. Grandpa looked over at her with his crooked smile.

"Yup! Pulling all the ingredients out now, sweetheart. And don't worry, I remember just how you like 'em!" He pointed at her with his spatula. "Extra pickles!"

"I hate pickles!" She replied, crinkling her brow.

"I'm just pulling your leg!" He chuckled and turned back to the grill. "…but how you don't like pickles is beyond me, girl."

"Hey grandpa, while you finish up dinner, we wanted to go on a quick walk along the old horse trail, if that's alright with you?" Sam asked with her best puppy-dog eyes. "…But I'm happy to stay and help you cook dinner, too!"

"We're gonna go explore the woods a little before the sun goes down!" Teddy shouted from across the yard. "Did you want to join us, grandpa?"

"Oh, no that's okay. I've seen enough of these trees as it is! You two go ahead." He answered. "Just be careful! Watch out for wild animals and traps. The trail itself should be clear, but you can't be too careful."

"Will do!" Teddy smiled. "We're still watching the newest *Evil Dead* movie after dinner, right?"

"We could watch that, or that new one with the blind lady in the haunted castle." Sam added.

"Both sound good to me. Why not make it a double feature!" Grandpa laughed, "Unless you don't want me to keep you two up past your bedtimes."

"Hope you can keep up with us, gramps! Sorry we had to interrupt your bingo night with the old ladies!"

The old man chuckled and flipped his grandson the bird.

Teddy laughed and ran down the hill, "Love you too!"

"I'll make sure to help you with the cleanup after dinner!" She waved back at him while she skipped across the field after her brother. "We'll be right back!"

―――――

The twins had followed the dirt path up and over the hill, venturing out into the woods. Grandpa owned several acres, giving them more than enough land to explore growing up. The old trail brought back childhood memories for the twins. Sam remembered bird watching and jumping into piles of fall leaves. Teddy thought back to the times of collecting bugs and climbing the tallest trees he could find. Together they would play their monster game and chase each other around the woods. Sam would be Little Red Riding Hood, while Teddy chased her as the Big Bad Wolf.

"Hey, right here! These trees...This looks like the spot!" Teddy exclaimed as he jogged ahead. Sam giggled as she followed him. Leaves crunched under their shoes and a raven called out overhead. Teddy crouched down and dragged his fingers along the dirt, searching for the spot.

"I know we didn't bury it too deep." Sam said as she scanned the area around her brother. "Can't be too hard to find..."

"Yeah, just give me a minute. I think it's right around here." Teddy started. Sam's smile faded. She wasn't looking at her brother anymore. Her eyes focused on something in the distance. Teddy kept talking, smiling as he searched for their buried treasure.

"Hey, Sam! Aren't you gonna help me dig?" He asked, looking back over his shoulder, now aware of his nervous sister. "Hey, what's going on? You're freaking me out..."

She didn't speak and she didn't blink. Sam raised her arm, pointing ahead of her. Teddy turned to look. Beyond the bushes and through the trees, he spotted what she had seen. It was a house. One of their grandpa's closest neighbors. They couldn't remember her name, but she was an older lady, close to his age. Teddy remember her flirting with grandpa last time they had been up at the cabin.

"Jesus…" Teddy muttered. The twins now stood at their feet, eyes wide and jaws dropped. Their brows crinkled their nervous faces. The neighbor's cabin was destroyed. *Vandalized? A robbery? Something worse?*

The twins silently left the trail, cutting through the trees and shrubbery. Their hearts beat harder as they neared the home. The brisk night air had begun to blow in as the sun set in the distance, leaving an orange and purple sky above.

The windows were shattered. Shards of glass littered the carpet and the front steps of the home. A trail of blood drops ran inside the house. The twins turned to look at each other. Unsure of what to do. Scared to go further. But they knew they had to investigate. Someone could be hurt inside.

"Hello?" Sam called out nervously.

Silence.

"Is anyone in there? Are you…okay?"

There was still no answer.

"We gotta get outta here, Sam. We need to—" Teddy cautiously followed her.

"We have to check inside. We can't leave yet." Sam whispered, "The neighbor might need help in there. We need to know what we're dealing with."

"Dealing with?" Teddy exclaimed, "We aren't dealing with this, we need to call the cops and get out of here! Especially the latter!"

Sam stepped forward, through the broken door frame. Bits of glass crinkled under her shoes. The home was dark. The only light came from the setting sun that passed through the windows. Sam neared the closest light switch on the wall. With a flick of her finger, nothing happened. She tried another switch. Nothing.

The power was out.

The trail of blood continued further into the house, disappearing down a dark hallway.

"This wasn't just some robbery. We shouldn't be here. This isn't safe." Ted hissed as he stood back in the doorway.

Sam continued further into the derelict cabin. Her mind was screaming at her to turn around, yet her body kept moving forward. A part of her would not leave until she knew exactly what had happened here. She wasn't sure if she would find answers. She feared what she would discover, imagining the worst thing she could. Pushing those thoughts aside, she kept on stepping.

The furniture inside the house was flipped over and torn apart. Cabinets were pushed in front of doorways and lightbulbs were shattered. The TV was cracked on the carpet floor and the landline was seen torn from the wall. Four large cuts ran down through the back of the couch. *An animal couldn't have done all of this damage. Could it?* She prayed it was just a wild animal. She prayed this violence was not done by a man. *A man still lurking in the woods around us.*

"Sam! Let's get out of here! Now!" Teddy begged.

That's when Sam noticed something in the dark ahead of her. It was looming at the end of the hallway in the bedroom doorway—something misshapen and harsh. The rancid smell hit her first. As she stepped closer she began to gag. Her stomach churned as her senses were assaulted. The taste of copper and rotting meat filled the air. It was a body. A body ravaged by some kind of beast. The old woman's blood painted the walls of her home. Shredded-flesh from her severed leg rested against the wall. Half of the woman's skull laid upside down on the dark red carpet. A blood-red eye ball still sat inside its socket, staring back at the young girl.

Trembling, her legs nearly gave out as she backed up, stumbling against the wall. A rush of emotions overtook her body. Her mind spiraled, unsure of what to do, what to say.

"What is it?" Teddy nervously asked, his voice shaky as he stepped inside the cabin. "What happened—Are you okay?" Sam, still silent, staggered out of the house, nearly knocking her brother over.

"Phone! Where's a phone?" She blurted out. Her mind was clouded, unsure of herself as she tried to rationalize what was happening. Ted stared at her, even more concerned, after seeing the look on her pale face.

"What is—" He started.

"Stop! Don't go any closer!" Sam panicked, ordering her brother, "Go back outside!" Rapidly searching the house, she finally found a landline near the kitchen counter. With shaking hands, she picked the decade old phone up from off of its charging base. Before she could dial nine-one-one, her ear was greeted with the sound of nothing. The line was dead. Whatever did this, must have taken out the phones and the power. *But this had to be an animal. Animals don't do that. Only people can, but this can't be a person. I hope it isn't.*

"What?" He whined.

"I said get out now, Teddy!" She barked. Her panicked eyes locked with his. Truly scared, he stepped back, but before he was out, he spotted something in the distance. The body.

"Oh my God…"

"Call the police! Call someone, anyone!" She cried. Ted reached his hand down into his right pocket, clasping onto the plastic protective case. Pulling it out, his brow creased as his eyes read of failure. *Of course*, he thought, scolding himself.

"My phone's dead!" Teddy groaned.

"Dammit! You and your phone—" Sam exclaimed, her chest burning as the dread began coursing through her veins.

"Stop it! What about you?! Where's your phone?!" He interrupted, clenching his fists.

"…I think I left it in the car again." She shrugged, frustrated with herself.

"Awesome." He burst. Sarcasm quickly turned to concern, "What do we do then?" His sister stood there, her eyes glazed over as she stared down at the trail of blood.

"Sam!?" Her brother called.

After a moment of hesitation, she cleared her throat and spoke with a hush, "We need to get out of here. Now."

"Why are you whispering?" Tilting his head left and right, he scanned his surroundings. She finally looked up, locking eyes with her brother.

"…because whatever did this is probably still out here." Sam took one look back at the elderly woman's decimated corpse and took in a deep breath.

"We need to get back to grandpa right now."

The siblings sprinted through the woods as fast as they could. The sun was nearly gone as the full moon hovered over them. The dark blue sky and its stars sprinkled through the atmosphere were beautiful, and on any other night would be a wonder to watch, but this was a night that the twins wished was over as soon as it began.

Sam did her best to keep up with her brother. Neither of them had any flashlights with them. They struggled to read the ground as they rapidly soared between the trees. One wrong move and they could wipe out. Teddy had broken his leg and fingers over the years, but Sam was lucky, only ever spraining her ankle. She prayed to avoid even that on this night. They were getting close to their grandpa's cabin. *Only a little further,* she told herself. *We didn't walk that far, did we?*

The booming howl of some creature cut through the crisp night air. The owls, the bugs, everything else went silent. The kids came to a stop, frozen in place.

"What was that?" Ted whispered, struggling to refrain himself from shouting.

"Had to be a dog." She lied. Sam knew it was something much bigger. "We just need to keep moving."

"Did it come from behind us? It almost sounded like it was up ahead..." He started, digging his jittering nails into his palm. They glanced back and forth, left and right, scanning the woods that surrounded them. Everything looked the same in the dark. Too busy running straight for the cabin, they lost track of the dirt trail.

"Where's the cabin? Did we pass it?" Sam started to panic. "Did we go the wrong way?!"

"No, we should be close now" Teddy began, sounding unsure of himself.

"You better not have led us the wrong way!"

The chilling howl of the beast rang out from the darkness of the woods once more. Goosebumps scattered across their skin as their hearts sank in their chests. *It's getting closer.*

Without saying another word, the two took off, heading in the same direction forward. As their shoes smacked down against the dirt and dead grass, the sound of something else moving in the shadows grew near. She could hear something crashing through bushes and shrubbery. Then came a faint growling in the distance, but it was getting louder, and closer. Whatever the creature was, it sounded like it was right behind them.

"There it is!" Teddy screamed with a bit of joy in his shaking voice. Sam felt a tinge of relief and a small smile formed on her face. *Almost there*. Their lungs ached as sweat dripped down their faces. Teddy pushed the thought of a cramp in his leg away as they started the steeper incline up the hill that their cabin stood on. Sam soon caught up, passing by her brother.

"C'mon! Don't stop!" She shouted, noticing that he was slowing down. He nodded his head, and gritted his teeth, "I got it!"

Sam's legs felt like they were on fire, ready to melt and break off of her body. They neared the top of the peak as the back door of the cabin came into view, only a few dozen feet away. The twins pushed their bodies to the limit as the roars of the beast were even closer. Teddy thought he could feel the warmth of its breath on the back of his legs.

Please don't be locked, Sam nervously prayed. They leapt over the steps of the back porch and nearly crashed into the wall. Rapidly turning the handle, Sam swung open the door. Teddy jumped into the kitchen, sliding across the floor and crashing into the cabinets. Sam slammed the door shut and locked it. Turning to her right, she started pulling at the fridge.

"Help me with this!" She screamed at her brother who still laid sprawled out on the kitchen floor, heaving and sweating. Teddy stumbled to his feet and grabbed hold of the other side of the fridge. They twisted and turned it as glasses clinked and other items danced inside it. In seconds they pressed the heavy fridge up against the back door. Struggling to get their breath, Sam stepped closer to the kitchen window to look outside.

"Stay away from the windows!" Ted nervously hissed. Sam nodded as she leaned her head forward, trying to see through the blinds and the glare of the house lights.

"Get the light." She ordered. Teddy skipped to the other side of the room and flicked the switch. Now everything was dark and silent. She couldn't see anything out back besides trees and bushes. The kitchen smelled like burnt meat and onions. The ingredients of the burgers still littered the counter and the burnt patties were now smashed on the floor alongside the hot pan. *What happened here? Where's grandpa?*

"The front door!" Teddy jumped. Sam followed him through the mostly dark house. Some lamps throughout the house and in the corner by grandpa's recliner still lingered on. Teddy skipped ahead, grabbing a cabinet in the hall and shoving it up against the front door. It was already locked, he noticed with a heavy sigh of relief.

"Doesn't look like anyone broke in...but where's grandpa?! Teddy cried. Sam swiftly stepped towards the house phone and grabbed it off the counter, raising it to her ear. *Yes! Still works!* After dialing the police she looked back over at her brother.

"I'm calling the cops. Let's look for grandpa."

The line rang in her ear. She slowly followed Teddy through the house. Sliding his hand along the wooden wall, he kept his head on a swivel, searching for danger in the dark. He flicked on the next light switch, illuminating the empty hallway. They noticed several large claw marks that were engraved along the wood flooring. Looking closer, Sam spotted a trail of blood drops that ran down the hall. The phone rang twice. They stepped further down the hall to the bathroom with its door half open. He flicked the light on and flung the door open to find that no one was there. The phone rang a third time. Click.

"Hello, nine-one-one, what is your emergency?"

A sigh of relief burst out from Sam. "Oh, thank God! We need help! There was a woman killed! Sh—She was torn apart! Some kind of animal was chasing us and —and our grandfather is missing! We're securing the house, but we don't know what's going on—"

"Okay, ma'am. Slow down, please. What is your name and location?"

"I—I'm Samantha. My brother, Ted, and I are staying at our grandfather's cabin in the mountains. The address is nineteen-forty-eight, Shudder Road, in—"

The bedroom door crashed open as a figure stumbled out of the dark room. The twins screamed until they realized what it was.

"Grandpa!" A wide smile beamed across Sam's face for only a moment before it quickly faded away. The old man was covered in blood. A large gash sliced across his cheek, coating his gray beard with dark red blood. His lungs wheezed as he held his hunting rifle in his shaking boney hands.

"Kids! Thank God you're alright!" He choked, wrapping his arms around the twins. She hugged the old man, with a brief sense of relief, until she felt the gun against her back. Grandpa stepped back and gripped his rifle tight. "I was worried...that *thing*...got you two—"

"Ma'am, are you still there? What's going on?" The woman on the phone asked. Her voice remained calm and almost robotic. *She must have dealt with countless phone calls like this. Heard stories of so many murders.*

Listened to hundreds of people crying. Experiencing their agony alongside the victims. Sam hesitated for half-a-second before answering, "Yes! Sorry, I'm still here. We found our grandfather, but he's badly injured! We need police and an ambul—"

The power shut off, and the line went dead, plunging the family into darkness. Their only light came from the full moon and the stars above.

"Get behind me kids." Their grandpa ordered quietly, shielding the two with his arm and guiding them behind him. Terrified, the three continued walking down the hall. The pale moonlight pierced through the windows and the shadows of the twisted tree branches outside stretched across the floor like fingers reaching for the children.

"What is that thing, grandpa?" Teddy asked.

"Did it attack you?" Sam added.

"Shh…Yes. I called both of your phones and neither answered. Then I walked out back to call out for you two. That's when this thing came charging out of the bushes and slashed my face with its claws."

"We're sorry we didn't answer." Sam apologized.

"It's okay, sweetheart…When it charged at me, I turned and ran for the door. I didn't have a chance to lock the door behind me when it burst through. I stabbed it in the ribs with a knife in the kitchen…but it kept on coming." Grandpa hissed in pain as he shifted. The older man put his hand at his side, revealing more gashes under his ribs. The lower back of his shirt was shredded and soaked with his blood. He coughed, clearing his gravelly throat, while giving the kids a knowing look.

"I turned the corner and ran into my bedroom, locking the door behind me." He coughed. "I grabbed my rifle and started to load it when I heard all this commotion outside and I opened my door…to find you two standing here."

Sam started to open her mouth when her grandpa added, "Don't look at me like that, I'm alright. Been through worse." He tapped the bill of his Vietnam veterans hat. "Are you two okay? Did it get you at all?"

"We're okay!" Teddy answered, "What the hell was that thing?!"

"Looks like a damn werewolf to me, kids." He shrugged, holding the wounds at his side again. The twins stood there emotionless, unsure if he was being sarcastic.

"You're joking, right?" Teddy asked through a forced chuckle.

Grandpa looked back at him, "I don't know, but it's big and it's pissed off." He stepped over to a small cabinet by the dining room and opened a drawer. First, the old man pulled out a flashlight. It sparked to life with all the power of the sun in such vivid darkness. With a subtle grin, he pulled out a revolver and tossed it to the boy.

The old man filled his pockets with more bullets after he finished loading his .30-.30 lever-action Winchester Rifle, while Teddy admired the Smith & Wesson .44 Magnum in his hands. He pulled out ammo and handed a box to each of the kids to stash in their pockets.

"Here. You know how to load it, right?" Grandpa asked.

Teddy nodded, releasing the cylinder. The metal was ice cold in his hands. It had been years since they went shooting with their grandpa, and it was only ever at the range. Teddy and Sam weren't hunters like their old man. They had never shot at something living before.

"I know it's been awhile, but you'll be okay. Most likely you won't even have to fire it. I've got you two covered and it sounds like the cops should be on their way. Twenty minutes—maybe less. It's a bit of a drive from here to the sheriff's department." He explained as he peered out the different windows in the house.

He hadn't seen any movement yet, but he knew it was still out there. Watching them. He looked back at the twins, noticing the terror in their eyes. He rubbed Sam's arm and gave them a warm smile. "Just be careful. We're gonna make it out of this."

The white glow of the moonlight faded as dark clouds passed overhead. Like the jaws of the dark wolf, they consumed the light.

"Follow me. I've got a few more guns stashed in my safe downstairs." Grandpa whispered. The children quietly kept close as they followed him across the cabin. When they reached the basement door, the old man turned the handle and slowly swung the door open. Somehow, the basement appeared even darker than the rest of the dead house. With a nod to each other, they followed the old man down the stairs.

Dust danced in the shadows as grandpa's flashlight cut through the dark. Focused on the lack of vision, they almost didn't hear the noise coming from the other side of the room. It was a low bellowing sound that rumbled off the walls and it was coming closer. Grandpa realized what it was. It was a growl. His wide eyes shot across the room to find golden wolf eyes staring back at him. *It was inside.*

"It's here!" He whispered. "Run!"

Teddy and Sam turned around and hastily ran back up the creaky wooden stairs with the creature coming up behind. His wavering flashlight gave the twins glimpses of a hound from hell, foaming at the mouth as it bit at their ankles, just beyond its reach.

"Damn!" Grandpa gasped, slamming the door behind him. "We need to get out of here! The cabin isn't safe!" He shuffled back with his rifle still aimed at the door, waving the kids ahead of him, "That way! Garage door!"

The beast rammed into the locked basement door, shaking the house with every hit. Its deadly claws dug into the door as cracks splintered across the wood. The family didn't have much longer. Grandpa caught up to the kids as they creeped through the house and into the kitchen. Next to the fridge, they swung the garage door open to find their grandma's dusty car still sitting inside. Five years since she passed and he never had the heart to sell it. He barely even drove it, but today he had no choice.

Grandpa pulled the keys out from the visor of the older Volkswagen sedan and started the engine. Meanwhile, Teddy flicked the switch to open the garage door and ran for the car. The old door creaked and rattled as it rolled. Dust sprinkled down from the ceiling. Christmas lights dangled from their box that lingered on the edge of the storage loft above.

Teddy jumped into the backseat while Sam sat shotgun. Grandpa pressed down the pedal and peeled out of the garage. For a moment the three of them felt weightless as hope burned in their chests. They saw the driveway and the road ran down to up ahead. *Almost free.*

The wolf pounced out from the shadows, colliding with the car, shattering the driver's glass window. Grandpa reached for his rifle, but as he raised it up, the strap was caught on something below. Teddy nervously raised the revolver up, aiming it at the wolf's head.

"Grandpa, get down!"

Without question, he covered his head and leaned down to the center divider. The raging wolf sliced at the old man's back with his claws, but before he could do worse, Teddy pulled the trigger. The bullet scrapped across the wolf's skill and sliced through its ear. The wolf cried and flung its head back, away from the car. Its dark ear dangled along its neck, hanging on by a strand of its burnt flesh.

The wolf bit at the tire, shredding it with a loud pop. The car instantly sank to the ground. The wolf didn't hesitate before it lunged forward, slashing the back tire with its drooling sharp teeth. Teddy fired the gun again, this time missing the beast.

"Damn! We're screwed!" Grandpa shouted, punching the wheel. "Get back to the hou—!" The werewolf slammed down onto the hood of the car. Its massive weight dented the hood as it stepped forward, biting at the windshield. One of the passenger tires popped and then the final one gave out once the wolf was on top. It scratched at the window with its claws and teeth, desperate to get in.

Grandpa pulled his rifle out, loosening it from the seat and bringing it to his shoulder. He fired, shattering the windshield. The bullet went down the wolf's open throat, causing it to gag and cry as it vomited blood. Teddy went to fire, but the chamber was empty. He hastily dug through his pockets searching for more bullets, while Sam climbed into the back seat with him, searching for an escape.

The wolf smashed its face through the windshield, inching closer to grandpa's face. He could feel its hot breath on his face and grimaced from the rancid smell of death and bile on its tongue With wolf blood oozing into his lap, grandpa fired again. The wolf shook its head, knocking the gun away.

Sam took the gun from his hand and swung it at the back window. After a few hits the glass shattered and she ran the metal of the gun along the edges, clearing it out. Sam tossed it back to Teddy and started crawling over the broken glass and out through the back window.

Grandpa swung the gun back at the monster's head, hitting its clenched sharp teeth. It whimpered and backed off for only a moment. Just enough time for grandpa to crawl over into the back of the car. With his legs dangling in the air behind him, still stuck between the seats, the wolf dove through the windshield, biting at his feet. It got hold of one of his shoes and pulled him back towards the front seat. Teddy grabbed the old man's arm and pulled him forward with all his might. Teddy laid halfway through the back window, with his head still in the car. He pulled his grandpa up towards him. With a final tug, grandpa swiftly slipped out of the broken back window.

The wolf was caught on the jagged glass. Its head whimpered inside the car as it sliced against its neck and shoulder blades.

"Get back in the cabin!" Grandpa ordered, limping behind the two grandchildren. Grandma's destroyed car shook behind them as the werewolf fought for freedom. Teddy pressed the garage door switch just before grandpa made it inside. Slow and clunky, it rolled back down. That was when the beast flung its body back, breaking loose of the car and rolling down onto the dirt road.

The door was only halfway down when the beast rose to its feet. *Crap.* Grandpa reloaded his rifle and raised it to his eye.

"Get inside, kids! I'm making sure he doesn't!" Before the children could argue, he fired another shot, passing through the wolf's ribs. *How is this thing not going down!?*

Before the door could touch the ground, the wolf snuck its head and front legs through the gap. Grandpa kicked down on the door, slamming it over the wolf's head. It hissed and howled at the old man. Grandpa fired another bullet through the wolf's neck and it pulled back, leaving a trail of blood behind. He pushed down on the garage door again, now slamming down onto the wolf's leg. It hit the concrete floor with a bang, cracking the bones in the wolf's leg.

It screamed and slammed its body up against the other side of the metal rolling door. The old man brought his foot down on the mangled paw, smashing it again and again before the wolf retrieved it, limping and crying as it ran off into the shadows of the night. Grandpa locked down the garage door and ran back inside his cabin.

Sam and Teddy had been running around the cabin locking every door. Teddy pushed cabinets over, blocking each window and barricading the doors. Sam found an old hammer in grandpa's tool box and ran around nailing down the windows. Without saying a word, grandpa joined in, securing his wooden home. The beast was gone for now, but he believed it would be back. That thing wasn't dead. He just made it angry.

"This wolf is smart. The cars are totaled. We can't escape…We have no choice but to stay and kill it." Grandpa said, leaning back against the wall. He rubbed at his bruised arm and winched when he rolled his aching neck back. "Or at least survive the night 'til it's gone."

"That thing looks like something out of *An American Werewolf In London*!" Teddy pleaded, "Do you have any silver we can use? If it really is a werewolf, that should kill it, right!"

"I don't know, kid. I don't have any silver bullets on me. There's some silverware I'm sure, but we gotta get close enough to stab that thing. I don't want you taking that risk."

"Well, the bullets don't seem to be working." Sam added. "What other choice do we have? Should we pour a salt circle down around us?"

"No, that's for ghosts and demons. Not werewolves." Teddy reminded her, peering through the curtain of the dining room window. Still no sign of the monster. The woods were deadly still.

"Oh, right." She sighed. "Sorry, not really thinking straight right now. Didn't think we'd be hunting werewolves this weekend."

"Well, you always said werewolves were your favorite monsters, grandpa." Teddy nudged the old man as he passed him, checking the front door again.

"Yeah, I like werewolves in the movies. Not when they're knocking at my door—"

Suddenly the wolf crashed through the dining room window. Glass shards erupted, twinkling in the air, as the beast crashed into the nearby wall with such a thunderous impact that picture frames were flung off the wall. They shattered along the floor by Sam, who the wolf had missed by only a few inches. She felt one of its razor-sharp claws slice by her head. Blood dripped down the side of her face from the gash along the top of her burning right ear. She jumped to her feet and bolted over to her brother.

Grandpa and Teddy shielded her, firing their guns back at the imposing monster. It ignored the metal tearing through its flesh. Blood dripped down from its dark fur.

Its sharp dirty fangs protruded from its snarling snout. The beast was done playing with its food and charged towards the family. Grandpa pushed the twins away from him and fired off another shot.

"Go, hide in there!" He ordered, pointing them to the bathroom door. "I'll lead it out of here!" The kids wanted to argue, but nodded and shut the door.

"This way, you stupid mutt!" He shouted.

A gunshot from the rifle rang out. Then another. The monster roared, chasing after their grandpa through the old cabin. They could hear him screaming, but couldn't make out the words. Teddy's knuckles grew white, as the wolf's beastly growls rattled the walls. *God, I hope he's okay.*

Then everything went silent.

Not even the old wooden floorboards creaked. Teddy placed his ear against the door. He listened for his grandpa, the wolf, anything. There was a thud. It was followed by more banging sounds. It was the wolf coming back their way.

Sam and Teddy covered their mouths, listening as the large wolf stomped down the hall. It brushed up against the bathroom door, rattling the handle. Teddy wrapped his hands around the doorknob, keeping it pulled closed. For a moment it sounded like the wolf stopped. Sam bit her lip and Teddy held his breath.

The wolf charged the door, slamming its body into it. It growled as it scratched the wood with its long claws. The twins pushed back at the door, desperately trying to keep it closed. The wolf wouldn't stop. It kept charging and clawing, determined to kill the surviving twins.

Sam looked over her shoulder at the narrow bathroom window. With no other options, she turned back to her brother and whispered, "The window! Go now, Teddy!"

"You first!" He argued.

With a frustrated huff, she nodded and turned her attention to the window.

Teddy pressed harder, kicking against the sink for leverage, as the big bad wolf crashed into the door. The wood creaked and snapped with every impact. They didn't have much longer. Sam rolled the small window open and started to crawl through. *Teddy won't fit through this.* She panicked. Sam made it outside of the window and landed on the grass below. Before she could say a word, Teddy lunged forward through the open window. His broad shoulders caught on the small frame.

Sam rushed to pull on her brother as she shimmied, wrestling with the narrow window. A loud crash boomed behind him. The wolf was breaking through the fractured door. Sam kept on pulling. Inch by inch his arms made it through. Finally, Teddy used his hands to press against the outside of the house, pushing his hips through the gap.

Another loud crash came from the bathroom. The wolf was inside. Sam pressed her foot against the house as she yanked her brother by his shirt. The walls dug at his skin, scratching him. He ignored the pain feeling the warmth of the beast's breath on his heels. Teddy kicked and flailed his legs before finally falling free of the window, crashing into the dirt below. The wolf's massive snout and fangs bit at the window, too small for it to fit through. It howled and roared into the sky as the kids got to their feet. Drool and blood cascaded down from its foaming mouth, dripping along the twins' heads. With looks of disgust, they gripped each other's hands and ran.

"What are we doing? What do we do now?" Teddy whispered.

Sam answered, "We look for grandpa and if we can't find him—we hide. We can't outrun that thing in the dark."

They jogged along the side of the house headed to the backyard. Sam looked around at the outside of the cabin for any sign of their grandpa, while Teddy cautiously searched through the junkyard for any kinds of weapons or working vehicles. Outside of shattered windows and claw marks along the walls of the cabin, Sam couldn't find anything useful. She desperately wanted to call out for him, to scream at the top of her lungs, but she held it in. *I can scream later. Cry when this is all over. I need to stay strong. Keep a level head. I panic and we all die.*

Teddy violently dropped to the ground with a snap. It rang out like a gunshot or a broken bone. Sam's heart stopped. Teddy screamed and twitched, pulling his leg back from whatever had a hold of it. It burned as it tore through his skin. Under the leaves and shrubbery was an old rusty bear trap.

Fighting back tears, Teddy slowly slid his fingers around the metal jaws and pulled back at the trap. Stands of flesh and muscle dangled from the cold, steel claws. Sam ran to him, gasping at the carnage. She looked at the trap, searching for any way to release him. Her numb fingers trembled in the winter chill as she wrapped her fingers around it. Together they pulled.

In agony, Teddy screamed, swearing at the dark sky. He flung his body back and laid crying in the field. He looked up at the moon still overhead and clenched his fists in the grass. The sun was nearly peaking over the horizon. Its warm glow burned in the distance. *This isn't fair. We're so close.*

"You need to get out of here! Leave me behind!" Teddy ordered her.

"No way! I'm not letting you die!"

"You've got your whole life ahead of you! You got it all planned out. I don't know what I'm doing, where I'm going. Don't let me be the reason you throw it all away!" He cried.

"I'm not leaving your side." She answered. "You're stuck with me!"

Sam joined him, pulling back with all her strength. Cursing and crying, Teddy slowly slid the rest of his disfigured leg through the metal jaws of the bear trap. The flesh was shredded like paper and strands dangled from his crimson shin. Remaining bits of muscle and tissue clung to the jagged edges of the trap. Teddy felt light headed as his face grew pale. He could barely sit up as Sam struggled to lift him. She wrapped his arm around her shoulder and pushed.

"C'mon baby brother. I know it hurts! I know, but we gotta go!" She whispered, stumbling to her knees as Teddy's good leg gave out.

He roared in anguish as waves of excruciating pain shot through his tender limb. Blood soaked the soil around them. He didn't have long. He knew it when he heard a rustling in the woods. It was coming closer. Out of options, Sam struggled to drag her brother across the field.

The enormous dark figure erupted from within the trees. Its sharp teeth shined under the layers of dark blood that oozed from its mouth. The creature was on all fours as it made its way towards the kids. It reeked like burnt hair and bile. They would have covered their noses if they could, but they didn't dare move a muscle. Its golden eyes never blinked as it stared them down. The monster's distorted muscles warped and convulsed underneath its thin patches of hair. Its ears folded back against its skull as the monster growled. The hound's harsh face was one of hatred and carnage. The woods were dead silent around them. Every living thing had fled or died at the feet of this wolf. The blades that were its claws carved into the soil as it started to circle the helpless siblings.

Terrified, Sam held her brother close. She bit her lip as her legs began to tremble. Teddy's vision began to blur as he struggled to focus on the wolf among them. The pain had consumed him and his body felt limp. The wolf could smell the copper in the air from the boy's oozing red leg. Sam rested her head against her brother's and closed her eyes, accepting their fate. The wolf stepped closer. She could feel its hot breath blowing against her clammy skin and through her tangled hair.

"Run kids! Go!" Grandpa screamed, firing another shot into the wolf's boney spine. "I love you both!"

The wolf shrieked and stumbled back away from the twins. Sam opened her eyes and in a flash the wolf charged across the field. It galloped up onto the deck of the cabin nearing grandpa as he sent another bullet slicing across its shoulder blade. Matted with blood and remains, its dark, scruffy fur smelled like something that crawled out from the depths of Hell.

The massive hound tackled grandpa, sending them both flying back through the kitchen. Grandpa and the wolf slammed into the stove and cabinets. His rifle fired off in his hand before it was sent sliding across the wooden floor. *Out of ammo.* With a crack in his beaten back, grandpa rolled over and started to crawl away from the creature.

Sam grabbed her brother's gun. She dug for the last bullet they had in her back pocket. Sam took control of her jittering hands, took a breath and loaded the revolver. Raising the gun over her bleeding brother, she fired at the wolf. The bullet soared through the air, hitting the wolf's head and slicing through its right eye. The beast roared and flung its head in rage. Blood dripped from its shredded yellow eye.

Bloody and broken, grandpa shuffled across the floor. He didn't have time to think about the pain. He didn't have time to worry about the blood he was losing. He had to save his grandkids. He had to stop the monster.

It rubbed its mangy paw against its screeching face. Grandpa only had so much time before it would heal. He had to act fast. He heard the hissing sound grow louder. *The gas line!* Nearing the stove, he struggled to his knees, pulling himself up by grabbing onto the counter. Now at his wobbling feet, he pulled the stove further from the wall with a violent tug. He pulled again and again until the line was broken. The gas was rapidly filling the room as the wolf rose to its feet. Its yellow eye was already reforming inside the black, mucky socket. Grandpa shuffled through the drawers behind him, searching for a weapon.

The wolf lurched forward biting down on his arm, still in the cabinet. Grandpa cried out as the wolf tugged his body, whipping him around. The old man stabbed at the wolf's face with a small knife he pulled from the drawer. He brought the blade down again and again into the beast's snout. It cried through closed teeth as it bit down harder on the old man. It shook its head, launching grandpa across the room. He hit his head against the fridge sending shockwaves through his skull. In his other hand, he held something small, bunched up under white knuckles. Blood soaked the old man's clothes and stuck to his pale skin. He didn't have much longer.

The werewolf staggered against the wall before it climbed on top of grandpa. Blood trailed behind it as its legs wobbled and its lungs wheezed.

"I hope you choke on it!" The old man said before it brought its long fangs down into his stomach. It tore and chewed at his flesh. Intestines and chunks of muscle spilled out from the grandfather's gut. The wolf pressed its face deeper down into his torso, eating away at his insides. With grandpa's final breaths, he opened his hand, revealing a lighter. He flicked the spark wheel.

Nothing.

He flicked again. Unknown bolts of agony charged through the man's system. He spasmed and convulsed as the wolf ate away. He could hear the gas still hissing over the sounds of his carnage. He flicked it again. Nothing. Grandpa looked out at his kids crying in the dirt. Sam screamed as Teddy sat there frozen. They didn't know what to do. They couldn't do anything. But *he* could. Grandpa gave them a final lingering wave with his broken, bleeding arm. A tear ran down his face as he flicked the lighter on.

"I Love you."

The house erupted in a massive ball of fire. The blaze soared through every inch of the wooden cabin. Glass windows blown out sending shards into the woods. Chunks of wooden beams and boards soared through the air. Sparks flew as sizzling cables and wiring flung like whips across the house. The flames consumed the monster and their grandfather. In an instant they were gone. As debris descended from the sky, littering the woods around them, the world fell silent. For only a moment. Car alarms rattled to life. Hundreds of birds took to the skies from the dead branches below.

The sun rose over the flame infested home. Sam and Teddy laid in the grass, surrounded by remains of their cabin. A burnt picture of the family fluttered in the wind, passing over them. They were only a few years old in the photo, with their awkward smiles hidden away under specks of blood and ash. Everything was gone. Grandpa was gone.

Sniffling, Sam wiped her face and rose to her feet. She put her hand out and her brother took hold of it. Together they got him to his feet. He wrapped his arm around her shoulders, resting some of his weight on her. Now balanced, they stepped forward, down the long driveway of their grandpa's roasting home.

Birds chirped as the sun went overhead. The sky was shades of orange and gold, like the leaves all around them. The warmth of the day passed over them, soothing their bleeding skin. The twins made it down to the road when they heard sirens in the distance. Police cars were making their way up the winding roads of the mountain. The brother and sister held each other close and kept on walking. They made it. The monster was gone.

THE MAD HOUSE

Brittle orange leaves flew up from the warm pavement and into the air as a boy sprinted down the street. His heart was pounding and his muscles strained as he forced himself to keep running. The boy's severe asthma caused his lungs to ache and wheeze. This pudgy, freckled, sweat-soaked fourteen-year-old boy was Joey Nelson. Joey wasn't exactly the most athletic kid. He would often be seen with his nose in a book or found wandering the local museums. He was a freshman at King High School and for the last two months he had endured the daily festivities of his welcoming committee. That committee was made up of three seniors; Jacob, Daniel and Trent. This autumn afternoon Joey was in for a whole new kind of hell.

The three—nearly adult—males, were members of the high school football team. Trent Lindhagen was the typical bulky, blonde rich kid who seemed like he had his whole life planned out for him. He was the quarterback of the team and leader of this gang. Sitting next to Trent, was his best friend, Jacob. The running back of the team. He was a not-so-rich kid that enjoyed riding along in Trent's blue nineteen seventy-eight Pontiac Firebird. They were practically lifelong friends, who always had each other's backs. The two combined barely made one functioning brain. Jacob was ever so slightly smarter than Trent, and would always help him out with his homework. Rounding out this trinity, in the back of the car, was Daniel. He was a drop out at their high school as well as their longtime drug dealer. One night after a game, his locker was discovered to be filled with his merchandise. He was then swiftly booted off the team and out of the school. However, that didn't stop Daniel from hanging out with his pals and carving out some time to terrorize the fresh meat; Joey Nelson.

The Pontiac's engine roared as it flew down the road. Joey could hear the monstrous muscle car gaining ground behind him. He knew he couldn't run for much longer. A gust of wind sent dozens more fall leaves cascading from the sky and across the road. The neighborhood was a fiery copper blaze with endless orange and yellow shards across the horizon. Beyond the leaves in the distance, the boy found an exit. Two houses down, Joey spotted a gap in a wooden fence. Pushing himself harder, he made a run for it. After sliding across the grass, barely squeezing between the wooden beams, the boy gained some distance between himself and the trio.

These guys had been bullying him since day one of high school. Joey thought of them as predators on the hunt during the first week of classes. They were scouting for the weakest links in the sea of new awkward students. Occasionally, they would go after George Peters. He was a fatter freshman with red hair. They would steal his books and toss them in the trash. Sometimes they would steal his lunch and eat it themselves. Other days they simply tossed it on the ground while making sure to tease the poor kid about his weight.

They had also given Norman Lancer his weekly swirlies in the gym bathroom after discovering that he joined the chess club. However, they seemed to heavily focus on Joey for some reason. Perhaps they sensed that this kid would put up more of a fight, and that enticed them. They would go on to break into Joey's locker and steal everything inside it. One day they poured a chocolate milk carton over his head at lunch. Then there were the occasional beatings after school. They never had a reason for any of this. Joey thought that they were just bored and needed to take out their anger on something.

Joey had taken this again and again for weeks until today. He was tired of being the punching bag. It was October now, and the constant stress was beginning to take its toll. As soon as the bell rang and the school day was over, he decided to strike back. As he walked out front of school, he spotted Trent's baby sitting across the street. Its bright blue paint glistened in the sun, as if calling out to Joey. The freshman was ready to give Trent a little taste of the hell they had been putting him through.

Nearing the car, he pulled his house key from out of his pocket. Looking left and right, his head was on a swivel, searching for any sign of the bullies. The key shined in his hand like a silver bullet. He clenched it in his fist before carving into the sparkling blue paint. He dragged his key from the front bumper to the back of the Pontiac and across the trunk. One long silver line along the body before engraving the word, "MONSTERS" in bold letters across the trunk of the car.

For a moment, Joey stood back under the shade of the trees, appreciating the work he had done. Looking up from the car, he spotted one of the senior football players across the road. Frozen in shock, his wide eyes locked onto Joey, before turning back and running inside the building. It was only a matter of time until the all-star quarterback was alerted of what just happened. Joey took a deep breath and began to run.

———

Fifteen minutes later, Joey was starting to regret his decision. Beads of sweat dripped down his face as he ran through backyards and hopped over fences. If the jocks didn't kill him, a heart attack would. After cutting across a few blocks, the boy finally came to a halt on the sidewalk to breathe. As his lungs wheezed he looked around, noting that this was a road he did not recognize. In the corner of his eye, he caught the street sign labeled, "Stoker Street." Before he could give it another thought, he heard the rumbling engine of the Firebird growing near. Searching for a place to hide, he continued down this road. Joey was drenched in sweat and breathing heavily. He could feel his lungs shutting down. The boy needed his inhaler, but had no time to search for it in his bag. Not until he was somewhere safe.

He slowed to a stop as he realized that this road led to a dead-end up ahead. *Of course!* He thought to himself, *What a perfect place for these jerks to kill me.*

Joey knew what Trent and his buddies were capable of. They had beaten him until he could barely walk, and that was on their good days. After what Joey had done today, he was prepared to end up in the hospital. The boy stood in the road, wanting nothing more than to collapse, as his eyes scanned the homes of this cul-de-sac. His eyes finally settled on the home that lingered behind him. He stood before an old decrepit house that looked as if it had been left to rot for decades. The ancient wooden structure was cracked and deteriorating, coated in layers of faded off-white paint.

Among the rest of the homes, it stood out like a corpse on this dead-end block. That's when the boy realized where he was standing. He had heard the legends of this house. It was cursed or haunted. They say that there was something evil about this place. He recalled the stories of, "The Mad House on Stoker Street." The door appeared to be locked and the windows were boarded up. Much of the glass had been cracked or shattered from kids tossing rocks at it. The front porch was littered with stains from thrown eggs and dusty spider webs that covered every corner of the home. Clearly, no one had stepped foot inside this place for years, yet Joey still had this feeling that someone was watching him from within.

Before he could search for any other place to hide, the Firebird furiously turned the corner onto Stoker Street. Tires screeched and the engine roared as it hurtled his way. Joey wasn't sure if the jocks had seen him, but he knew that they would if he didn't start moving soon. The freshmen turned back to the Mad House in front of him, noticing that the front door was now wide open. The house was practically inviting him inside. *Was that open before?* No time to think. He only had two choices now; hide in the haunted house or stay outside and get beaten to death.

Joey ran up the front porch and into the house before slamming the door behind him. He prayed that the three men didn't see him. The air was stale and filled with dust, causing the boy to choke and cough. His lungs were burning and his throat had locked up. He frantically dug through his backpack as the Pontiac came to a screeching halt outside. Finally grasping the inhaler, Joey shook it as he raised it to his mouth before finally pressing down on the button. He spent the next minute slowly breathing, attempting to relax his tense body, and bring his heart rate down.

Sitting on the ground, with his back against the old front door, Joey pressed his ear up to it, listening for the bullies outside. The Pontiac could be heard idling out on the road. Joey continued to slow his breathing, hoping that they would give up their search and turn around. He wasn't sure if they would come inside this house. Everyone in town knew of the legends of The Mad House. He prayed that the three were too scared to step foot in this place.

Joey rose to his feet and creeped over to one of the front windows. The wooden floorboards creaked with every move he made. The house moaned, almost whispering to the boy. He could hear it and sense something was off, but he was too focused on the jocks to think about the house at the moment. Joey wasn't much of a believer in the supernatural. He enjoyed hearing ghost stories and watching scary movies, but he didn't take much of it too seriously. The boy would always try to look at everything through a scientific and logical perspective.

Joey could see Daniel and Jacob sitting in the car looking around at all of the neighboring homes. Then he locked eyes with Trent who was staring directly back at Joey inside the house. He dropped down to the ground and out of sight from the window. *Oh please, tell me he didn't see me!* Joey stayed down on his hands and knees listening for their voices. He could hear the three of them arguing.

"Screw this!" Trent barked.

Joey peaked his head up to watch as the Pontiac roared down Stoker Street, away from him and this haunted house. Letting out a sigh of relief, he slumped back down onto the ground. His inhaler was still clenched in his right hand. The temperature of the house rapidly dropped and the sweat soaked boy shivered from the chill.

Thinking back to the stories that he heard over the years, he remembered most of it, maybe forgetting some minor details. The legend of this house began back in the nineteen-twenties when it was built. The architect and owner of the home was named, H.T. Sevier. He was described as a mad man, an occultist who worshiped ancient creatures and gods from other worlds. He was an older man in his late-fifties who lived here alone. Sevier was the sole beneficiary of a large inheritance, most of which he spent on researching and worshiping these gods. No one knew exactly where this strange man was from. Some say he had a foreign accent, while others claimed that he came from the New England area. When Sevier came to town, he built this house from the ground up. What people did not know at the time, was that this home was supposedly built with all kinds of ancient spells and symbols carved into the wood and foundation. There were secret rooms, passages, and who knows what else. It was a death trap built for murder by a man that was said to be as evil as the Devil himself.

After construction was completed, Sevier would lure his innocent neighbors over for dinner. People claimed that he always appeared friendly and courteous when out in public, but mostly kept to himself. He would have his neighbors over once or twice for a normal dinner, showing them that he was, indeed, just another normal man in town. Then, once they felt comfortable, he would finally strike. He drugged their meals and dragged their unconscious bodies down into the basement. Sevier would then don his sacrificial robes, after the victims were tied down and bound to his stone altar.

The basement was dark, lit only by the dozens of candles scattered throughout the space. Sevier had sculpted and constructed this altar, along with large statues of his deities surrounding it. By now, the victims had usually awoken from their sleep, just in time to see their neighbor holding a large dagger over them. Sevier would cut his hand, dripping blood down onto their faces, while he chanted ancient psalms. His horrified victims would try to scream through dirty rags that gagged them. Pulling at their restraints, fighting for their lives, the victims prayed for some way to escape. Unfortunately for all of them, there was no escape, and the dagger was brought down into their beating hearts.

That was until the night where his final victim, Mary-Anne Cooper, escaped! She was drugged, much like the others, however she wasn't a neighbor. She was a young woman, hitchhiking on the side of the road, that Mr. Sevier had picked up and taken back home. She had just turned eighteen and decided to run away from her family. She was perfect, Sevier thought, as he dragged her body down the stairs. She was a clean slate, a perfect victim, unlike the victims of his neighborhood, whose disappearances were starting to become noticeable.

The first victim, John Tyler, was a veteran who had just come back from World War One. He was still setting up his new life. He was single and far from his childhood home town. If anyone were to ask where John had gone, Sevier could easily say that he moved away. The Morrisons, an elderly couple down the road, were the next to be slaughtered. He killed the husband the first night, and kept the wife alive to watch, before killing her the following night. They also had no children, no family, and no one to look for them. Sevier would take the victims' cars and drive them far away, ditching them in the woods. He killed a few more people on the neighboring streets to spread out his victims. As time progressed, his surviving neighbors were beginning to talk and question things.

On November thirteenth, nineteen twenty-three, Mary-Anne awoke from her slumber and broke free from her restraints before he had completed tying her down to the altar. The two tussled in the basement. She kicked her attacker back into some of the candles, causing his coat to erupt into flames. This gave her enough time to run upstairs and towards the front door. He tore his coat off and ran after her. He screamed out in rage, not caring about the noise he was making. If anyone heard them, he would kill them too. He would kill them all, he thought, anything to appease his gods.

Mary burst through the front door, screaming at the top of her lungs. It was nearly midnight, but neighbors awoke, turning their porch lights on and coming outside to see what the commotion was all about. They spotted the scared woman and her attacker, both bruised and covered in blood. Sevier was wielding his dagger, screaming and cursing as he chased her. She made it to the arms of one man standing near. She collapsed, crying and shaking as Sevier froze in his tracks. He realized just how many people were out on the street watching him. Several neighbors began to shout and charge Sevier. One neighbor shot off his gun, hitting the killer in the arm. Sevier finally dropped his knife, before turning and running off into the darkness, never to be seen again.

The house sat empty for over twenty years after that night. Then in nineteen forty-seven, a newlywed couple with a child on the way moved in. James and

Chelsea Skinner were married soon after he returned from the second world war. After the honeymoon, the couple moved into town to buy their first home. They were told the stories of what had happened here before, but the basement had been cleared out and cleaned. Now it was simply a hollow concrete room below the floorboards. No altars, no statues of gods and no bodies. The real estate agent, who sold the couple the home stated that he even had a priest bless the house before he even stepped inside himself.

Unlike the real estate agent, The Skinners were not strong believers of the supernatural. They saw this house and the neighborhood as a nice place to raise their child. The baby was due in three months, but unfortunately the massacre occurred only one month after moving in. There were nights where Chelsea would wake up around three in the morning and notice that her husband was missing. She assumed that he was just in the bathroom, before turning over and going back to sleep.

However, after noticing that this had become a pattern over the next few weeks, she finally climbed out of bed and walked over to the bathroom door. She knocked, but there was no answer. Opening the door, she discovered that the small room was empty. Chelsea called out for him. Nothing.

She continued to search throughout the entire house before ultimately reaching the basement. This was where she found her husband. The man was naked— kneeling on the ground—as if he was praying. His body was pointed towards the dark, empty corner of the basement. She was trembling as she slowly stepped closer to him. Chelsea could barely hear his voice as he whispered in the dark. He was praying, but the words didn't even sound human to her.

She gently called out her husband's name, "Please... James." Before she could finish, his body jolted to life. He stood up straight and turned to face his wife. Towering over her small stature, she slowly raised her hand towards him.

"James. Sweetie, it's Chelsea. What's wrong?" His eyes were cold and lifeless as he lunged forward, grabbing her throat. She tried to scream, but the figure had the strength of a hundred men in the palm of his hand.

The police were eventually called to search the home after getting calls from some of the neighbors. They stated that they hadn't seen the couple in weeks. They were worried. Police found Chelsea's dead body on the basement floor. The body was sprawled out right where the altar had once stood. Her heart was impaled with a knife and her baby was cut out of her. The officers would go on to state that this was the most gruesome crime that this small town had ever seen. The husband, James Skinner—much like Sevier—went missing and was never seen again.

Almost two decades later, the next owners of this cursed home arrived. It was another young couple named Michael and Kate Morgan. The Morgans had moved to town from New Jersey in nineteen sixty-three. The couple was also told the history of this home. Sadly, they didn't have much money between them, and this was the best place that they could find. They were fond of the neighborhood and this small town that they were about to call home. They had just gotten married and wanted to eventually start a family. Kate was an artist and Mike was a mailman.

Once again, after only a few weeks in the home, the couple started to notice odd things. Mike was awakened, drenched in sweat, from an intense nightmare.

He couldn't remember exactly what it was about, but visions of gore, torture, and pain were etched into his mind. It was the middle of the night and as he looked over to his wife, he realized that she was not there. Already anxious, he pushed himself out of bed and went to look for her. He too searched the entire home, before finding her in the dusty, dark basement. Just like Skinner, she was naked and praying in the dark corner of the room.

One week later, the police arrived after getting calls from neighbors. These officers had heard the legends of the past murders in this house, and were preparing themselves for the worst. They found Michael Morgan's corpse in the center of the basement. Like the other past victims, a dagger was brought down into his chest. A pool of blood—now dry and sticky—surrounded the dead man. Kate Morgan was now missing, and she too, was never seen again.

All these years later, Joey now stood alone inside this house. After hearing all of the gruesome stories and watching kids double-dog-dare each other to go inside— or to even step foot on the front porch—he felt that it was a bit underwhelming.

"This place doesn't seem so bad." He muttered.

It was old and rotting, much like the outside. The paint was faded, wood was dry and cracked, and everything was covered in dust. The strangest part of the house was that most of the furniture, from whoever lived there last, was still sitting inside. Photos of the happy couple were hung up on the walls, dirty dishes were left in the kitchen sink, and even the placemats were set at the dining room table. The photos and furnishing all looked to be from the late nineteen-fifties or early sixties. Joey took a closer look at one of the faded colored photos. It was a man and a woman dancing. The woman's smile was bright against her thick, dark hair. The man was thin and tall, with long slicked back hair and a sharp jawline.

"So you two must be the Morgans." Joey whispered.

The soft sound of music hummed through the halls of the old home. Joey could hear it coming from somewhere upstairs. He thought against going up there, but couldn't stop himself. It felt as if he was hypnotized. Knowing he shouldn't be walking up those crusty creaking steps, the music continued to call to him. As he made his way closer to the door at the end of the hallway he began to make out the lyrics of the song. It was "All I Have To Do Is Dream," by The Everly Brothers. Closing in on the door, he slowly reached for the handle.

All he wanted was to turn back, run down stairs, and leave this place forever, but he couldn't. When he swung the door open, the music took over, as if welcoming him in like a warm hug. The room was pristine with fresh paint. The windows were no longer shattered and the carpet was clean. Looking outside, he noticed that it was suddenly night time. The moon and the stars twinkled in the sky above as he stood alone in this small, dark bedroom. The only light illuminating the room was a small lamp at the side of the bed. The bed sheets were tossed to the side while clothes laid sprawled out on the floor. Across the room—shattered on the floor—was the old radio that continued playing the song that echoed through the house. The music was soothing. Joey felt like he was floating, almost forgetting that there was clearly something wrong here.

"Kate!?" A man's voice shouted from behind Joey, who jolted up and flew back against the wall. Breathing heavy, Joey covered his beating heart. It was Mike Morgan. He stood out in the hallway holding a flashlight.

Joey realized he was looking for his wife. Somehow he had traveled back to the past, reliving that nefarious night in nineteen sixty-three. The man began descending the stairs of his home. Not knowing what else to do, the boy followed him. The entire house was now clean and tidy. The paint smelled fresh and the air was clear of dust and mold.

"Hey, mister! You really don't want to go down there!" Joey called out.

Mr. Morgan continued walking as if the kid didn't exist. Frantically waving his arms, Joey continued yelling to no avail. He finally reached forward and grabbed Michael's shoulder. The man stopped and slowly turned his head around, locking eyes with Joey. Without a sliver of emotion he spoke,

"Don't."

His voice turned deep and cold. Turning his head back, he resumed his search of the house.

"Kate!? Honey, where are you!?" The ghostly man began walking faster, wide-eyed and sweating. Unlike a moment ago, his voice was shaky and filled with dread. Joey believed that something was controlling this memory. *The Mad House.* It wanted Joey to see this, and it did not want any interruptions. As the two neared the basement doorway, another voice called out.

"James? Sweetheart, where are you?"

It was Chelsea Skinner. She stood near the top of the stairs in her off-white nightgown. The lantern she held illuminated her worried face. She, too, was searching the home for her missing partner.

The two lost spirits eventually met downstairs, where they faced the door to the basement below. Opening the creaking wooden door sent ghostly echoes down into the dark. They could hear the whispers of ancient dark prayers coming back up from the depths below.

Joey followed Michael and Chelsea as they made their way down the dark steps. The temperature was dropping an unnatural amount, as if they were stepping into a walk-in freezer. Whispers came from the darkness in all directions, surrounding the frightened boy. The basement was pitch black outside of one single lightbulb hanging in the center of the room. Illuminated below, was the stone altar that Sevier had crafted all those years ago. Large stone statues of ancient gods stood around this stage of death. Dozens of candles instantly burst to life. The flames surrounded the glowing altar. Amongst all of the candles, were the two naked bodies of Kate Campbell and James Skinner. Pale and shivering, they knelt on the ground. Their lips frantically whispered their sinister prayers. The two partners stood there in horror with their lights, calling out to the loved ones.

"...James?" Chelsea cried as Michael stuttered, "K-Kate?!"

The praying bodies turned to look back at them. Their eyes were dull and empty without any sign of love or humanity. The bodies rose to their feet. Chelsea and Michael pleaded with them. They were silent. Joey stepped back. Goosebumps rose across his skin as he prayed to leave this nightmare. The bodies screamed as they charged at the three witnesses. The murders had begun. Joey turned and ran for the stairs. He climbed the creaking steps, unable to hear the wooden boards over the howls of agony behind him. Reaching out for the door handle, he looked back one last time. Kate and James were hunched over their partners as they tore them apart. Blood glittered red in the light as it flew through the air. Behind them—at the altar—stood H.T. Sevier. The thin, old man was wearing his dark red ritualistic cloak. This killer held a large dagger that glistened in the shadows. He was staring directly into Joey's eyes as to say, "You're next!"

The boy's heart sank. He turned back to exit, leaping through the doorway, and slamming the basement door shut behind him. The house rattled, and with it, the boy's skeleton. Then everything went still. All Joey could hear was the thunderous thumping of his heart. He looked around at the empty—now decaying—home, praying that it was all over. At the end of the hall, stood the front door. He was so close. Hesitating for a moment, he listened for any movement below, but the house lay silent. Finally ready, he made a run for the door.

Rotting corpse hands burst out from the floorboards below. They grabbed Joey by the ankles. The boy fell forward, slamming his jaw down onto the ground. Pain rattled throughout his skull. The taste of copper flooded in his mouth. He didn't have much time left as the boney claws pulled him back across the floor. Just out of reach, he tried to grab at any furniture or the walls around him. He glanced back to see zombified corpses of the two killers pulling at his legs. James Skinner and Kate Morgan were gaunt with pale, decaying skin, and eyes dark as midnight. Their hair was receding and falling out, with mouths opened wide, moaning as they pulled the boy back into the basement. Joey kicked at James's head, sending his skull back with a loud crack. Even as his head was now bent back upside down, the body continued pulling. Joey kept kicking until the two lost their grip on his legs. Shambling to his feet, the boy ran for the front door.

The decrepit corpse of Sevier twisted around the corner, grabbing the boy, and slamming him up against the wall. His robes were now ripped and tattered. His skin was torn and cut up and his breath reeked like a moldy grave as he roared in Joey's face. Tired of this place, Joey punched the dead man, breaking his brittle jaw. This only made the corpse angrier, tightening its grip on the boy's throat. Kicking aimlessly, he fought to breathe. Joey clawed at the old man's face, stabbing his fingers into— and rupturing—Sevier's soggy eyes.

The corpse screamed and released the boy. Collapsing onto the wood floor, he rubbed at his throat, still struggling to breathe as his asthma was worsening. Joey spotted the other two corpses closing in on him. They were blocking his path to the front door. The only opening he had left was to the stairs. He didn't have time to think. He had to move or die. Joey ran up the steps once again, as the killers followed closely behind him. The bones of the stairway rattled, barely holding itself together.

Reaching the top of the stairs, he saw a large bookcase across the hallway. He skipped over and took hold of the heavy cabinet, before pushing it back toward the stairs. Like everything else in this nightmare, it creaked and wobbled, somehow staying in one piece. Sevier appeared from behind the boy, grabbing his shirt and throwing him across the hall. Joey crashed against the wall. His teeth chattered as the wall cracked, and debris sprinkled the floor. The rotting old man shambled across the hall toward the beaten and bloody boy.

Joey, knowing he didn't have much time left, pushed himself back up to his feet. He charged towards the ghostly corpse and rammed his shoulder into Sevier. The old man was sent crashing back into the bookcase. Sevier clung onto the wall as the bookcase behind him was sent hurtling down the rickety stairs. The bookcase came to a halt at the bottom of the stairs, after crushing the corpse of Kate Morgan up against the wall. The undead James was knocked off of the stairs, crashing through the rotted railing, before getting knocked out on the hard-wood floor below.

Joey ran back into the bedroom where the visions of James began earlier. It had felt like a lifetime since this all started. It was still dark out—like before—but now the music was gone and the lively bedroom was filthy and coated with cobwebs. Sevier slammed the door open behind Joey, cornering him in the room.

"There is nowhere else to go, boy! You will be sacrificed like all of the others! I will make sure you suffer! My God will feast on your blood!" The evil man's voice boomed, shaking the house to its core. A warm gust of wind blew through the home. The curtains waved and the old man's messy long hair danced in the darkness. Sevier came charging with his arms out like claws—ready to kill. Behind the attacking corpse, Joey spotted a cracked glass window across the room.

With no more time to think, he pushed himself off of the wall, sprinting toward the towering corpse once more. He prayed that this would work, otherwise he was as good as dead. With all of the power he could muster, Joey slammed his shoulder into the rattling ribs of the killer. Sevier let out a ghostly moan as the two hurdled towards the window. It shattered, sending glass shards flying through the air. They glittered like fireflies under the moonlight. The body soared out of the house and back down into the earth. There was a loud crack as the man's skull hit the pavement out front of the old home.

Joey stepped forward and looked down through the shattered window. Expecting to see the corpse of Sevier below, he found someone else instead. Down on the pavement was his bully, Trent. The jock was dead, laying in a pool of his own blood. His bloodshot eyes glared back up at Joey.

A man screamed from within the house. "What did you do!?" He screamed once more, his cries ached with misery. Joey ran back to the top of the stairs to find another one of the bullies down below. It was Trent's friend, Jacob. He was looking down at what remained of his friend, Daniel, who was crushed under the massive book case. His body was bent and contorted from the fall. Blood leaked from his nose and mouth as his hand still twitched like a bug in a web. Jacob was bleeding from a large cut on his forehead. His eyes radiated red from tears and terror. He glared at Joey Nelson above, who was just as startled as him.

"You! You did this! How could you kill...!?" Jacob fell silent as he saw something in the distance. Outside of the front door, which was now wide open, he could see the blood-soaked corpse of his friend Trent.

Jacob ran outside to the front of the house. He knelt over Trent's body screaming for help. Front porches lit up across the street as people came shuffling out of their houses. They saw the crying boy screaming for help and ran over to the front yard.

"This kid...J-Jo...Joey Nelson! H-He killed my friends! He tried to kill me! He went insane in that house! The Mad House is haunted! That crazy kid killed them! He killed my friends! H-He did it!"

Joey stood frozen at the top of the stairs of The Mad House. He couldn't believe what was happening. *This couldn't be real!* He thought, *I couldn't have killed them. I was fighting off the ghosts of the killers!* As he said that, Joey realized just how crazy he really sounded. He was a monster, whether he believed it or not. The house drove him to murder. The scared boy looked down at the basement door below. The door was wide open and hidden deep in the shadows was H.T. Sevier. The old man stood in the dark smiling back at the boy. A moment later he was gone.

Joey didn't know what he could believe anymore. He fell to his knees as tears filled his eyes. He only had two options now. He could stay in that house, wait for the police to arrive and accept his fate. Or he could just keep running. Like the other survivors of this Mad House on Stoker Street, Joey Nelson ran off into the cold and bitter autumn night. Blood on his hands and madness in his mind, the boy was wanted for murder. He couldn't go home. He couldn't explain this away. No one would believe him. That house was truly evil and nothing could stop it. He had to get as far away as he could from Stoker Street. Away from The Mad House. After that night, Joey was never seen again.

BLOODY EGGNOG

T'was the night before Christmas Eve and all through town, several creatures were stirring, even ol' Saint Nick. Although, this Nicholas was no saint. Something unholy hid behind that holly-jolly disguise. Standing on a busy street corner in downtown Knoxville, he rang his bell. His dark eyes darted as he watched the people pass him by along the crowded sidewalks. He wasn't searching for any donations, or charity—he was hunting. This Santa Claus wasn't human. He was something else. His eyes—with a slight crimson glow—followed the dozens of shoppers walking by, searching for just the right victim. Late into the nights, he would linger out on the streets, following any stragglers who were still out on their own.

As time passed on, most people had wandered home. The snow was beginning to come down at a much faster rate. The weatherman stated that there wouldn't be any more snow until Christmas Eve. Looks like he lied. A tall, thin man with graying stubble along his rugged jawline, and clad in black with a white collar, walked down the road. He noticed this Santa standing in the distance. He was one of the few people left on this dark, quiet street. The tall priest's name was Father Roderick Campbell. In his late-fifties, he had short dark hair and weathered features, giving the kind-hearted man a rough exterior. The priest served his little church downtown for nearly thirty years. With such a history, he practically knew everyone in town. However, he had never seen this Santa Claus before.

A young woman dressed in white, with blazing red hair, passed by the Santa. The priest recognized her. Becky Keele. She always attended church with her family when she was a child, but it had been years since she last appeared at mass. She looked to be in her early-twenties now. As she glided by, the Santa's gaze followed her. He left his charity bucket behind and slowly stalked the woman. Father Campbell curiously followed the pair.

Violent winds of winter came soaring through the downtown buildings, screaming like vile banshees in the night. The shivering priest pushed through the harsh winds. Picking up pace, Becky headed towards the park. Campbell watched as the stalking Santa followed. The snow was hard and slick under his boots. He squinted to see through the snowfall, watching his step as he crossed the icy ground.

Up ahead, he spotted her cutting across the street and the man in red followed. She vanished when she turned the corner. Moving faster, the stranger turned down that same street. Campbell started running, desperate to catch up. The preacher's teeth chattered as he shuffled through the bitter snow. He had always loved the winter time, but his age was beginning to disagree with him.

He turned the corner onto a one-way road where he was greeted with nothing. The street was empty. The preacher was the only living soul left in sight on this chilly December night. *They were just here! Where could they have gone?!*

A bloodcurdling scream erupted from the dark, bouncing off of the tall buildings and into the sky. It sent chills down the priest's spine as he began running toward the cries for help. Charging through the snow-covered roads, he discovered faint tracks that Santa and the young woman left behind. Following the trail, it led him down a narrow alleyway between storefronts. Halfway down the alley, he discovered the gruesome body that laid before him. The preacher came to a stop, standing over the bloody white clothes that covered the—now dead—Becky Keele.

A crimson pool surrounded the silent young victim. Her eyes looked as if they were about to pop out from her skull. Her face contorted into a horrified grimace when she died. The priest couldn't imagine what terrible thing could have happened to the poor woman in such a short time. He looked down at her neck to see it had been torn open, as if a wild animal had attacked her. Her skin was shredded like paper, with dangling strands of flesh strewn across her face and chest. Snow continued to fall, now melting in the pools of red blood. Breaking from his trance, the priest looked up and surveyed his surroundings. There was no one. Nothing around at all. *What could have done this? Was this the work of that jolly Saint Nick?*

The red and blue lights of the police cars lit up the alleyway. Cameras flashed as officers took photos of the scene. Campbell watched the officers as they set down yellow number markers around the body and rolled out their police tape, blocking anyone from entering the alley. The priest sat on a cold, metal bench at the curb. Looking down at a puddle of snow in the gutter, his dark reflection glared back at him. He looked tired, and as old as he felt.

A firm hand grabbed Campbell's shoulder. The fingers felt like claws, giving him a shock. He turned back to see that it was just one of the officers. His name was Detective Mark Thomas. Mark was a fit man, in his mid-thirties, with a buzzed head and stern brow. From what Campbell knew of him, he was a good cop, a man that would always try to do his best. *Not a regular at the church, but he always came in around the holidays*. Campbell let out a sigh of relief, his breath danced in the frosty air.

"Sorry to frighten you, father. I just wanted to let you know that you can go home. Don't need you out here freezing to death on us."

———

It was nearly two in the morning when Campbell made it to his front door. He didn't realize just how numb his body felt until he stepped inside and turned on the heater. The shivering man stripped out of his damp and frosty clothes before crawling into his warm bed. Restless, he tossed and turned throughout the rest of that night. He couldn't stop thinking about the incident. He needed to know what really happened. The police were on the look out for this killer Santa Claus. Even though it sounded ridiculous, the officers believed the tired preacher. They suspected that the killer used a knife, but this wasn't some random mugging or attack. This monster wanted to tear her apart.

It couldn't have been any animal in the middle of downtown. There were no other tracks anywhere to be found. The strangest part of all, was that the Santa's footprints immediately disappeared after Becky was killed. He didn't backtrack or climb up any walls. There was nowhere for him to go in that alleyway without leaving more tracks behind. This was not normal. *It was supernatural.* Everything was beginning to add up in the priest's mind. He didn't want to believe it. He wasn't sure if these even existed. The torn throat, the body drained of blood, the killer's disappearing tracks.

Father Campbell was beginning to believe that this was the work of a vampire.

He was not a believer of all the things that go bump in the night, but he knew the rules of the supernatural. Over the years he'd seen dozens of the classic monster films, television shows, and even read some of the books. However, he never thought in a million years that they could be real.

Five years ago, Campbell was called to perform an exorcism on a young girl in Seymour, Tennessee. The poor child barely survived, and what she had done over those few weeks—of supposedly being possessed—were things that no human could ever do. Campbell began the exorcism just like he had been instructed by his superiors. He entered the girl's home. It was small and run down. Her father had passed and her mother was struggling to take care of her. The walls of the house were covered in crosses and crucifixes. The mother had a rosary clenched so tightly in her hand that her palm was bleeding.

The preacher entered her bedroom. She sat on the floor next to her bed. Her sheets were torn and flung across the floor. Feathers from her shredded pillows lingered throughout the room. Her walls were etched with markings. Some with ink, and others with her fingernails and blood. The child appeared to be beaten and starved. Her face was pale and sunken in, but her eyes still sparkled like only a child's eyes could. He saw what she once was, and his heart sank seeing what had become of her.

He knelt down and introduced himself to the little girl. Her voice was rough and gravely from screaming. Her sobbing mother helped Campbell place the child into her bed, restraining her arms and legs. He began instructing the girl to repeat after him:

"Jesus, I repent for any sin I committed against you. Please cleanse me of my sins. Through the blood of Jesus, I claim salvation and am pure." He then shook a few drops of oil, which were from the Holy Land, onto his thumb. With that, he drew a cross on her forehead.

"I anoint you in the name of the Father, the Son, and the Holy Spirit." The little girl whimpered, holding back tears. She was in pain—and it was only going to get worse. He stared into her eyes and whispered, "Demon, tell us your name."

The child rolled her head and bit at her tongue. She was fighting the darkness inside her. Her limbs tugged at the restraints as she flung her body left and right. The tears soon ran down her pale cheeks. She was weak. Campbell was glad he came when he did. She didn't have much fight left in her. Then she went still. The sparkle in her eyes had vanished. The little girl was gone.

He repeated, "Demon, tell us your name. In the name of Jesus Christ, I demand you tell me your name!"

The child groaned, "Demoriel."

Exorcisms performed by the church are extremely rare, and typically not as dramatic as the movies make them out to be. Even he was hesitant to believe that a demon really was controlling the girl. That was, until he saw her break her own arms and legs with a hammer. The child broke free from her restraints, nearly killing her mother, before harming herself. She laughed while she did it, her eyes rolled back up into her skull until they were nothing but white.

That painstaking event had stuck with the priest ever since. Memories of the girl would flash through his mind, keeping him up countless nights. It took three days for him to finally exorcise the demon from her. It took a toll on both of them. Eventually, after three months in the hospital, she had fully recovered. Fortunately, by the grace of God, she couldn't remember a single thing—but unfortunately for the priest, he remembered everything.

———

It was almost six in the morning, when the sun was just beginning to peak over the horizon, that the priest climbed out of his bed. Barely resting, Campbell shuffled through his home and into the kitchen. Tossing bread in the toaster and starting his coffee, he watched the sunrise through his kitchen window.

The sweet aromas of breakfast filled the house, awakening the tired man's senses. For just a moment, it erased the smell of the bloody crime scene from his mind. Campbell stepped over to the front door and opened it. Out on the lawn he spotted the newspaper of the day. He quickly scampered across the icy yard and ran back inside, with the wind nearly slamming the door shut behind him.

He grabbed the toast as it popped up from the toaster, sliding butter over it, and cutting the slices on his plate. Sitting down on the sunken cushions of his old couch, he raised the crinkled newspaper paper up to his face. The front page exclaimed, "Young woman brutally slain downtown! Suspect Santa at large!" Two photos filled the page; one was of the dark alleyway and the other was a recent photo of Becky with her bright red hair and even brighter smile. The preacher still couldn't believe what he had seen. Nothing like this had ever happened here in his lifetime—especially around Christmas time!

Turning the pages he spotted another obituary. It was a young man, only twenty-three. Heath Fitch. Murder victim, brutally attacked at the World's Fair Park, just last week. Drained of blood. At the bottom of the page listed another victim: Jennie Tyler. Forty-two. Mother of three found dead behind the Tennessee Theatre in Downtown Knox. Again, the body was brutalized and drained of blood.

Campbell tried desperately to prove himself wrong or to find some other reasoning for what he had witnessed. He recognized these names and faces from around town. He was upset he didn't know of these murders sooner. With the constant snowfall this unusually harsh December, he had missed some of the papers. These deaths couldn't just be a coincidence. *Something evil was here.* It was hunting them.

The priest tossed the newspaper aside and dropped his dirty plate into the sink. Rubbing his eyes, he shambled over to the bedside to grab his bible. He knelt down beside his bed and began to pray.

"Heavenly Father, I ask for your guidance. My followers and neighbors are dying. I must help them, I must stop this evil. If it truly is a creature of supernatural powers give me a sign. Shall I destroy this monster with the power of your love my God? I don't believe anyone else can help me. These people need protection, my lord." He paused, opening his eyes and looking out the window at the rising sun. "Lord, forgive me for what I must do. Amen."

———

Dressed in his priest attire, and bundled up under a heavy coat, Campbell began his walk to church. Fortunately for him, it was only a few blocks down from his home. The wind roared between buildings, rattling the glass windows. Goosebumps scattered across the old man's skin like fireworks. He rubbed his arms with his gloved hands, attempting to stay warm. Turning the corner, he spotted his church up ahead. However, something was different. A large object hung from the steeple.

"Oh, sweet Jesus..."

He muttered, looking up in utter horror. Campbell staggered and fell to his knees on the sidewalk as a body hung upside down from his church steeple. The butchered body belonged to Ezekiel Peyton. He was a kind old man who had attended this church longer than Campbell had even been alive. Ezekiel was sliced open—gutted like a pig—his intestines dangled down from his bloody belly. The old man was drenched in gallons of dark blood that glimmered under the bright, blinking Christmas lights that were wrapped around his lifeless corpse.

Campbell was frozen in anguish. *Only an unholy creature—a vampire—could do such a thing.* He knew now what had to be done. The priest turned around and hastily walked back home. A woman's blood-curdling scream erupted across the intersection behind him.

I don't have time to deal with the police again. I don't have time to mourn. He had to stop this monster before it killed again. The creature knew that the priest was on to him. This was a warning. The next dead body in this town could be his own.

Entering his home, Campbell's keys rattled between his trembling fingers. His eyes darted left and right, searching for any kinds of weapons. Clenching his fist around his keys, he finally put an end to the shaking. He urgently stormed through his house, grabbing hold of anything he could think of that could fend off this demon. He loaded an old duffle bag with knives, crosses, his bible, and water from the sink that he blessed himself. This was a good start, but he needed more.

———

Campbell's rapid footsteps tapped along the tile floor of the colorful supermarket aisles. Elevator music lightly played overhead as he strolled down each row. The rattling metal shopping cart was filled to the brim with supplies. He had picked up bags of garlic, several more crosses, a dozen boxes of ammo and a good old fashioned shotgun.

Fortunately for him, the store was rather quiet, and he didn't have to worry about bumping into any locals. Campbell let out a sigh of relief, knowing that he wouldn't have to conjure up some kind of excuse for this cart full of vampire-killing surplus. The lady working the cash register scanned his items with an almost emotionless face. It was still early in the morning, the store had just opened, and she did not seem mentally prepared to deal with something like this. Her hair was a dark purple and piercings littered her ears and nose. The aroma of roses filled the space. It was a cheap perfume, but effective. Campbell noticed her name, Lucy, was written on her badge.

Lucy Bram? Was this the same small child that came to every church Sunday all those years ago?

It didn't matter, he didn't have time for small talk. He wanted to get in and out of there without drawing too much attention. The scanner continued beeping. The noise was sharp like a dagger in the priest's ears. The cashier kept her head down as she bagged his items. The priest's eyes darted from her, down to the guns and garlic, and back up to her. He was nervous, but too tired to lie.

"Hunting vampires."

A silent moment filled the air. The cashier looked up at the priest. Her heavy makeup lingered over her tired eyes.

"Father, I've seen a lot of wild stuff here. This is just another Tuesday."

Campbell nodded as he handed her his cash, "Keep the change." He pushed the heavy cart ahead while she printed out his receipt. Handing him the paper, she watched as he walked away with a cart full of heavenly defense.

"God be with you." She called out.

The father smiled as he exited the store.

———

The bell chimed in the swinging arm of the Santa Claus standing in the market square. The thin Saint Nick lingered in the corner, near the park as the crowds died down later in the night. Slowly, all of the shops and restaurants turned off their lights and locked up for the night. Footsteps crinkled in the thin snow that remained scattered across the ground. A woman's breath puffed in the brisk winter night air. Turning her key, she locked the front doors of her small bar and walked away. Her heels clicked along the pavement, all alone on this silent night.

The Santa's eyes narrowed as his eyes stalked her movements. He was the only other person out at this time, and she was coming his way. Rubbing her gloved hands together, she let out a squeak of a sneeze and sniffled. *The sick ones are never as sweet. The blood is weak and riddled with the bitter taste of medications.* But the vampire was too hungry to care tonight.

"Ho ho ho! Good evening, ma'am." He greeted her with a lopsided grin. Her frizzy short hair peaked out from under her beanie and covered her pierced ears. A swarm of butterflies were tattooed along the side of her narrow neck, precisely where the vampire had desired to bite.

Soon the flesh would tear and blood would rain down her body. The sweet taste of life and death cascading down my lips. Only a moment longer before she is mine.

"Care to donate…"

The vampire started. Then he froze. His eyes danced as he sensed something near. He quickly turned his head to spot the priest coming up behind him. The old man pulled something from out of his coat and swung his arm at the vampire. The Santa screamed in pain as something sizzled across his face. A shape he knew too well. A shape of death. *The cross.*

Campbell pressed the crucifix further, melting through the dead man's skin. His legs wobbled, almost giving out as he cried. The monster extending his arms, slamming his skeletal fingers into the father's chest. Campbell was sent flying back ten feet through the air before crashing along the icy pavement.

The woman from the bar screamed as she watched the chaos unfold in front of her. The Santa's face was melting as it contorted into a devilish glare. Human features shifted as the evil took form. Spitting black blood into the snow, the vampire scowled at the woman, and then back at the priest who struggled to his feet. The bar owner wanted to run. She wanted to call for help. She wanted to do anything other than scream, but her body was locked. Her eyes were transfixed by the monster before her. Its hateful gaze rushed closer as he slashed his claws through the air.

A moment later and blood oozed down from her shredded neck. The butterflies were buried under layers of red and dangling flesh. The vampire licked his fingers before taking off. In a flash, the vile figure vanished into darkness as the dying woman dropped to her knees. Campbell ran over, gently laying her back on the cold ground. The blood quickly pooled around her as she struggled to breathe.

"I'm so sorry...I was too slow. I should have saved you!" The father painstakingly spoke. Holding her hand, he looked into her terrified eyes.

"You will soon be greeted by our heavenly father. Your pain will be gone and you will be surrounded by loved ones. I pray for you, my dear. I will avenge your death and the death of countless others. We will pray for your soul... I'm sorry." He whispered as the life had left her eyes. Softly, his fingers slid her eyelids closed over the blank stare of the young woman.

"God help me, the demon dies tonight!"

Prepared for battle, the preacher chased after the monster. Stomping through the snow-covered alleyway, he recited Psalm 140: "Who devise evil plans in their hearts and stir up war every day. Keep me, O Lord, from the hands of the wicked; protect me from men of violence who plan to trip my feet. O Lord, I say to you, "You are my God." Hear, O Lord, my cry for mercy."

The father followed the satanic Santa's trail of blood to the doors of an old abandoned toy store. The doors swung open and closed from the bone-chilling wind of the night. Checking that his shotgun was loaded, Campbell took a deep breath and entered the empty building. Inside, it was as dark as this vampire's soul. The priest turned on the flashlight that he had taped to the barrel of his weapon. *It didn't do much, but it was better than nothing*, he thought. That was when he heard the crackling of a record player come to life from the far end of the toy shop. Bing Crosby's voice echoed across the walls as he sang his rendition of "O Holy Night."

The priest swiveled his body back and forth, inspecting every dark corner, ready for this monster to appear. He heard a switch click and Christmas lights flickered on and off, illuminating the large shop. The walls glowed red and green, as did the empty shelves and aisles. Graffiti littered the walls, as did blood. Victims of the vampire were strung up in these lights across the store surrounding our father. He recognized a homeless man who he had given money to a few weeks ago, along with two other vagrants he didn't recognize. All of their throats were torn open, strands of skin dangling in the breeze. Their eyes wide and blood shot, with gaping mouths, like every other victim. Dead faces, forever frozen in horror and agony.

"I thought I'd make your death a festive one." The vampire's voice boomed from the shadows, "After all, you've given me the Christmas gift of a challenging hunt. I haven't been discovered in several decades, and the last time I had a meal that actually put up a fight was before your petty Civil War. Too bad someone else got to your president before I could, he looked like a delicious meal. Most politicians taste bitter…"

"Come out and face me, you devilish coward!" The priest demanded.

"I will kill you when I want to—not a moment sooner. It is more fun to drag your misery out. I'm not bored of you just yet." The Santa retorted like a cat playing with a mouse.

"I made you bleed! I hurt you—and I will kill you!" Campbell's head still rang after hitting the icy concrete. "You've hurt enough innocent people! God will forgive me for what I do here tonight. He will judge you and I both, but your day of reckoning is now!"

The vampire laughed, "What you've done has merely given me a paper cut. I'm already healing as we speak. These vagrants gave me the boost I needed. They were disease-ridden. Their blood was coated with the vile sting of drugs and alcohol, but beggars can't be choosers at times like these."

"Those were people! Lost, yes, but they could have been saved! Turned in the right direction! Now they are gone!" Campbell shouted, his voice trembling with anger and sadness.

"They were rats like the rest of you. Rodents like these spread disease and sickness. I was putting them out of their misery. I don't want them poisoning the rest of my food supply." The Santa said with a coldness in his voice that made even the harsh winter outside feel warm.

Campbell was listening to the vampire's voice as it traveled in the darkness. He continued walking down each aisle, with his gun at the ready. Every time he spoke, he could hear him coming closer. He could smell the scent of copper growing stronger. The song that cracked through the store's aging speakers faded away before the voice of Elvis Presley began singing of a blue Christmas. In that brief moment of transitional silence, he could hear the rapid tapping of footsteps coming up from behind him. Campbell swung his body around and fired.

There was nothing there, but an empty aisle.

Then came the sound of water slowly dripping. *Where was that coming from?* His heart skipped a beat when a drop of a dark liquid hit his shoulder. Then another dripped down the back of his neck. It was warm. The father's eyes rolled up to find the blood-soaked Santa clinging to the ceiling above him. Blood fell from his smiling lips down onto the priest's forehead. Quickly, he raised the gun to fire off another round at the ceiling, but the vampire was already on him, knocking the weapon away. His flashlight hit the ground with a crack, spinning along the filthy floor and illuminating the deadly Santa like a haunted house strobe light.

Campbell reached into his jacket, frantically searching for something. The vampire's mouth opened wide, revealing his gore-stained fangs. Nearly biting him, Campbell yanked a flask of holy water from out of his coat, dousing the monster with the heavenly liquid. The vampire hissed and screamed as the water boiled his pale skin like acid. As it stumbled back into a shelf, the priest went for his gun. Before he could reach it, the furious vampire threw a chunk of the shelf at the priest—striking him in the back. Stumbling to the ground, bolts of pain shot through his body. Groaning through gritted teeth, he slowly crawled towards the shotgun.

"You are beginning to bore me, old man." The Santa growled, stepping towards the priest that shuffled on the floor.

With his left hand, Campbell took hold of his gun, but the vampire's icy leather boot slammed down on top of it. Campbell roared in agony as the bones in his hand were crushed. His fingers cracked and shifted beneath the vampire's relentlessly twisting boot, scraping his hand along the cold floor. The monster finally stopped, leaning down close to the priest's ear.

"This is only the beginning of the pain that you will experience tonight. You have succeeded in pissing me off, father. Now I will show your God just how cruel his creations can be." He whispered sadistically.

"Our lord did not create something as vile and repulsive as you. When I'm done with you, you'll meet your maker in Hell."

The priest glared into the monster's red eyes as he spoke. Eyes of the devil. The vampire chuckled in amusement while the father subtly reached his right hand under his coat. In a flash, he pulled out a wooden crucifix. The bottom of the cross had been sharpened into a wooden stake. Campbell violently swung this cross into the vampire's throat. Blood splashed across the aisle and the monster shrieked in agony like something otherworldly. The creature fell back against the wall, trying to pull the cross out of his throat. When he took hold, the crucifix burned the creature's pale hand.

Hearing the beast's sizzling skin, the priest got to his feet and grabbed his shotgun—aiming it at the monster's head. As he pulled the trigger, the vampire violently kicked at the priest's shin, shattering the bone in an instant. The gun fired off to the side of his target, yet some of the pellets still speckled across the left half of the creature's face. Campbell's bullets were individually blessed and packed with garlic powder. While not lethal, the shards embedded themselves deep inside the monster's skin, roasting its flesh.

The screams were ear-piercing as it flew up from the ground and latched onto the ceiling. Limping and moaning, it scattered across the roof like a dying spider. Trails of blood dripped across the store as the vampire vanished into the darkness once more. A moment later, Campbell could hear the sound of the crucifix falling to the floor in the distance. The priest rolled onto his back and inspected his leg. It was   layered in dark shades of purple as it began to swell. *Hurts like hell, but I can't let this stop me.* He was ready to die fighting this night if it meant sending that vile creature back to Hell.

The priest limped down the walkway, aiming his light along the ceiling, in search of the evil. He recited segments of the Bible as he hunted the creature, shouting his prayers in defiance to anger—and possibly—weaken this monster. The crimson Santa came sprinting around the corner and tackled the priest, sending them both flying into a pile of boxes and debris. The priest grimaced and shouted in pain. The vampire smiled and grabbed his broken leg, squeezing as hard as he could. Campbell screamed in horror.

The vampire laughed, "So weak, old man! I am going to…" Before he could finish, the priest swung his shotgun into the vampire's jaw, sending him flying back. The priest didn't hesitate. He jumped to his feet, screaming his way through the pain, and grabbed the Santa Claus by the coat, throwing him against the wall.

Campbell grabbed his flask and crammed it into the vampire's wound. Holy water flowed down the bloody gash in the monster's neck. Before the beast could react, Campbell backed up and shot the vampire in the knee cap. The Santa fell to the ground heaving. He pulled the flask out of his neck and tossed it across the room. The priest struggled to reload his gun as the evil Santa flew across the room. He grabbed the priest and threw him over the counter at the front of the store. Both men collapsed to the cold tile floor, bleeding and moaning. Catching his breath behind the counter, Campbell prepared his aching body to continue the fight.

"I have never had…such a worthy opponent before, priest. Maybe your God really is on your side. Or perhaps I'm just getting old." Coughing up blood and resetting his shattered knee, he slowly rose to his feet. "This was fun, but now it's time for you to die."

"Will you shut the hell up already?!" Campbell groaned as he reloaded his shotgun.

There were only two shots left. His coat pocket was torn open and the other bullets were now gone. He frantically checked his other pockets for supplies. Another flask of holy water, and a cross that had broken in his pocket were all that he had left. His eyes darted around the store, searching for anything else he could use. Eyeing the flickering Christmas lights on the walls, he debated using those to strangle or restrain the vampire. That's when he spotted a Christmas tree sitting in the corner of the shop. *I could do some damage with that.*

Campbell crawled along the floor, hiding behind broken shelves and debris, closing in on the tree. It was a metal artificial tree, heavy and sturdy. Ignoring the burning daggers of pain that shot through his limbs, the priest rose to his feet and limped over to the tree. He detached the top third of the tree and held it like a sword. The father pulled out his flask and poured the rest of his holy water onto the tree.

He tossed the flask to the side, and with his broken cross in one hand, and a Christmas tree doused with holy water in the other, he stood ready for the final act of battle. Campbell's head was on a swivel, scanning every dark corner around him. The place was dead silent.

"Let's get this over with!" He coughed. Blood dripped from his nose, his lungs ached and his mind was fuzzy. The priest came to a stop when he noticed two red eyes watching from the shadows of the manager's office.

"The power of Christ compel—" He started, before the vampire soared through the air, grabbing the father and slamming him up into the ceiling tiles. The monster held him there—face to face—against the ceiling.

"This is it, old man! You aren't much, but I'm starving!"

The vampire's jaws extended wide open like a snake. It's large fangs protruding from his skull. The putrid breath of a thousand deaths blew in the priest's face. Father Campbell had never seen anything as truly horrifying as this creature. He was ready to send it back to Hell. Still holding the cross between his white knuckles, Campbell shoved it down the monster's throat. The vampire gagged. It attempted to scream as they began to descend. Its body was flailing and panicking. Campbell knew he had only moments left to attack. He raised the Christmas tree up over his head as the Santa kept howling. With one final thrust, he violently swung the tree down—impaling the vampire's black heart!

Gravity brought the two bodies crashing down onto the tile floor. The vampire Claus let out an ancient, demonic scream that rattled the Earth. Thick, dark blood erupted from its lips. The beast's legs and arms twitched. The sharp nails of his hands clawed at the floor. Campbell, still on top of the monster, rose to his feet. He looked down at the shrieking evil and it looked back up at him. Its eyes blazed like an inferno.

The father grabbed hold of the bloody Christmas tree and pressed it down, deeper into the vampire's heart until the metal finally cut through its back, colliding with the floor. Gallons of blood spattered up from out of the wound. The monster's movements began to slow, and the screams turned to whimpers. The two kept their eyes locked on each other. The priest watched as those hateful crimson eyes relaxed and finally faded.

The vampire was no more.

Campbell looked over the body of this monster, not realizing just how much it had transformed throughout their battle. The once human hands had turned to razor sharp claws. Veins that ran all across the body were pronounced, glowing blue and red. The bone structure had also transformed. Its shoulders had become broader as the limbs had stretched to inhuman lengths. Lastly, he looked at its blood-soaked face. The now dim red eyes were sunken in, surrounded by darkness. His white hair and beard were scraggly, thinning, and beginning to fall out. A new set of sharper teeth had descended from the gums above his human teeth. This creature was truly a work of evil. *Only God knows how long it had lived, and how many innocent people it had murdered.*

The priest dragged the dead creature's corpse outside of the empty—and now destroyed—toy store. He brought it out back to an open space in the snow-covered lot. Not a soul was around. Everyone was home tucked in bed waiting for Santa Claus to come. It was almost dawn on this bizarre Christmas Day. *Perfect time for a yule log*, the preacher thought. He lit a match and said a prayer before tossing it down onto the corpse. The evil Saint Nick ignited into a blue burst of fire. The priest sat down against the brick wall of the store, holding his bleeding wounds.

"Thank you, Lord. I did what had to be done to save these people. I know that the violence I have committed was wrong, but I ask for forgiveness. If we confess our sins, he is faithful and just to forgive us our sins and to cleanse us from all unrighteousness. Amen."

As Father Campbell prayed, he sat there in the snow watching the evil burn away. The fire kept him warm. He wasn't sure if he would make it to see the sun rise on this Holy day. He had lost much blood in this battle. His body was tarnished with cuts and bruises. His chances of survival were thin, however this was a time of miracles. What mattered most was that he protected his people. His job was done. Now he could rest.

THE CRIMSON CANVAS

Five strangers dressed in black sat in a white van that drove down winding back roads along the mountains of Wyoming. The sun was setting on a gray and cloudy day. Flickers of orange and red radiated through the clouds. The strangers listened as their leader went over the plans one last time. These five strangers had all just met for the first time last night. Their names and any and all information was kept secret. The mysterious man who organized this whole operation instructed everyone to go by code names, which included himself. These specialists were given names based on famous artists, which only made sense seeing as they were hired to steal an infamous piece of art.

The leader of the mission was called Picasso. He was in his late forties with rugged skin and graying hair. The man had a commanding, stern brow and a rugged jawline that had seen its fair share of right hooks. The moment he entered a room, everyone simply knew that he was a figure that demanded respect—if you wanted to keep all of your teeth, that is. The other members of the team knew nothing about the man, yet looking at him told them everything they needed to know. As long as they followed orders and didn't mess up, they knew they'd make it through this in one piece.

Driving this van—was Dali—the old man of the group. He was the weapons specialist and the team's lookout. He carried a bolt action sniper rifle fitted with a night vision telescopic sight, and a high-ballistic performance centerfire cartridge. Dali had a shaved head with a white beard. A long scar made its way down the side of his face and over his left eye, which was legally blind. Only one eye, yet he was still the best shot on the east coast.

The hulking figure sitting behind him was Warhol. He was the brawn of this mission. Warhol's eyes were dark, and his glare was enough to scare the devil himself. His dark skin was covered in scars and ink, and a chunk of his right ear was missing—most likely from a bullet. Warhol was a man of few words, but when he did speak, his words were buried under some kind of South American accent. The bulky man's dark clothes strained to cover his massive limbs. His arms alone were wider than the next member of this group—Frida.

She was the only woman on the crew. Frida was the tech specialist who could hack anything you put in front of her. She was quiet and mostly kept to herself, standing in the corner of any room. Her pale face was nearly shrouded by her wavy dark hair. Even dressed in layers of black, you knew she was the kind of girl that was covered in tattoos. Making up for her small size, she had studied different martial arts over the years and knew her way around a gun. Just like the other men, Frida was capable of many things, and God help anyone who got in her way.

Finally, sitting in the back of the van, was Monet. He was the youngest of the crew—outside of perhaps, Frida. Monet was the locksmith of the crew and the art historian. He knew how to handle and preserve anything they were tasked with acquiring. Some thieves would go through all the trouble of stealing a sculpture or a canvas, only for it to end up scratched, dented, torn or melted. Some of the pieces that he had stolen over the years were centuries old and worth more than his life doubled. Monet had a modest criminal record, having been arrested a few times growing up. Breaking and entering, stealing basic things like TVs or silverware. He didn't have much growing up and was forced to find alternative ways to support himself and his family. He knew there were better ways to make cash, but this was faster, and he was good at it. Monet never did too well in school either—but the one thing that always fascinated him was history and art.

Monet wasn't much of an artist himself, but he loved the craft. He admired all of the hard work that no one saw when studying a work of art. Famous names like Van Gogh or Francisco Goya—with dark and tortured souls—fought their demons off with brushes and oils. Or perhaps they let them win. Perhaps that was what really brought out their hidden talents. No one really knows the lives that these men lived. Most could never understand their struggles to bring to life these things that burned inside their hearts and minds for others to see. Not to mention the fact that these creations outlived their creators and survive to this day. Centuries later, these artists continue to inspire people across the globe. Art is a magical thing. It has the power to leave its mark on history, to survive generations, watch civilizations rise and fall. Art embeds itself within our hearts and minds.

Most people don't realize or even think of these things. Monet was sure that the men and woman around him didn't give a damn about what they were stealing—or anything else that they had snagged in the past. They just saw dollar signs where Monet would see history etched into stone and canvas.

Monet had stolen paintings, sculptures, and other works, because he knew that if he didn't—others would—and that put these historical items at risk. He knew what it took to preserve these works for so many years and he was sure that he could keep them safe. With that being said, Monet never claimed to be any kind of saint. He knew that what he was doing was wrong, but he was good at it, and it kept him sane. This kept the young man working, and put food on the table for his family. They never knew what he really did—and it would kill them to find out—but they didn't have to, because this was it! After this heist, Monet told himself that he was finished. While on his honeymoon last year, he realized that he had to make a choice. He wanted a new life with his wife and newborn baby. This job was his little boy's college fund. With all of the money he earned from his past jobs—they were financially secure for years to come.

None of them knew what they were stealing yet. They were only briefed that it was a very rare and unique painting. This canvas was locked inside a secure metal casing. Something that they needed Monet to break into. What was left of the sun hiding behind the storm clouds was setting on the horizon. The gray sky grew dark as they all prepared for the long night ahead of them.

The five of them met the night before inside a restaurant called, *última parada,* outside of Idaho Falls. The business appeared to have been shut down years ago. Tables sat empty, occupied only by dust. The empty building was drenched in darkness, except for the glow of the kitchen in the back. The five criminals made their way back, eyes darting back and forth, unsure of each other or this location. Walking through the swinging kitchen doors, they spotted an old man standing under the light at the other end of the room.

This man that hired them went by Munch—named after another artist, famous for his painting, "The Scream." Munch was an older Englishman with sunken blue eyes that pierced through anything they glared at. He stood behind the table smoking a cigar, with an impatient look on his face, as if they were all running late. "Good evening, everyone. I assume that you all received your personal instructions on why I've brought you here tonight, as well as your code names…"

They nodded, still unsure of each other. Picasso kept looking over at Monet suspiciously. Monet was lanky and young. Not like the other three men in the room. He thought to himself that he stood out like a sore thumb. Frida kept to herself on the other side of the room. Warhol stood with his large arms crossed, locking eyes with Munch, while Dali scanned around for cameras or other soldiers. The air was tense.

"This isn't like the typical crews I work with. My men are always the best of the best. Ex-military. Who are these people?" Picasso waved to the others, not taking his eyes off of Munch.

"These people… are the best, Mr. Picasso." Munch said sternly.

"You ever worked with any of these people before? I sure haven't." Dali questioned Munch, with a raspy voice that sounded like three decades of smoking. "Why should we trust you? How do we know that your money is any good?"

"Oh, I know all about your little escapades. For instance…" Munch turned to the woman known as Frida, "I know you can handle the security on this mission. After what you pulled off at the Gardner Museum in Boston two years ago, I'm sure you can handle anything else that comes your way."

Frida stepped back in shock. "How did you know I was part of that!? No one knows who stole those paintings!"

"We do now." Munch smiled. Everyone else's eyes nervously darted around the room. "Thirteen paintings. Millions of dollars worth of art. Well done." He softly clapped his hands, before turning his attention to the others. "Like I said, I chose all of you for your special skills and experience. You all have quite the resumes." Munch glared up at Picasso who stood across the table from him. "Your fearless leader on this little adventure." He started, pointing at him, "A decorated veteran of multiple wars. A proud American patriot. That was until he turned his back on this country for better pay as a mercenary. That's the American dream, right there."

Picasso clenched his fists. Munch noticed. He stepped to his right, tilting his head back to lock eyes with the giant man in the corner.

"I don't think you even want to hear about the shenanigans that this large chap, Warhol here, has been involved in. Quite the resume indeed."

"Alright, get to it. We don't need to sit back and watch you analyze us all night." Picasso grumbled. Monet glared back at the man. After a silent pause, Munch shrugged.

"I have spent a good amount of time and money on tracking down this object. I've been planning this heist for years. Finally, after all of this time, I've located it. It's on the move, and will be delivered to a large mansion tomorrow night. It's just east of us and over the border, in Jackson Hole, Wyoming."

"What exactly are we stealing?" Picasso questioned.

"It's a canvas painting. The dimensions are twenty-nine inches by thirty-six inches. As for safe-cracking and the handling of this artwork—I selected Monet for that. You just need to focus on getting everyone inside and out of that building. Understand?" The old man waited for Picasso to finally nod. "I will rendezvous with you at this location." He pointed down to a small private air strip on the map. "There, I will take the painting off of your hands and give you all the rest of your money. Half tonight and the rest tomorrow."

His eyes scanned each member of the team, "If any of you are to be apprehended, or worst case—killed, your profits will be divided up to the remaining members. However, I believe you will all take this heist in stride. Deadly force is not required, but if there are no other options…do what you must to complete the task at hand. Do we understand?"

————

They parked the van off of the main road as they approached the mansion. They could see it in the distance. A long narrow road snaked its way through the woods that surrounded the rich man's home. Dali remained in the driver seat, as the other four stepped out. Once they commenced their plan, Dali would find his vantage point and watch over the team. Brisk winds blew across the land. Frida and Monet zipped up their jackets. Originally, it was going to be a nice day out, but a sudden storm appeared to be headed their way. Picasso appreciated the surprise as it would help cover them and drown out the noise of fighting and gunshots.

Monet never killed anyone before, but as far as he could tell, the team wouldn't need to. They were only to shoot as a last resort. Dali was their backup if something were to go wrong as they took out the security team with their tasers—or in Warhol's case—his bare fists. No one needed to die on a mission like this. There was a minimal security force and several cameras that Frida could easily disarm. Their mission would be short and simple. As far as Picasso was concerned, he believed that they'd be in and out in less than thirty minutes.

The team got into position where they waited in silence amongst the bushes and trees for the package to arrive. At eight twenty-eight that night, an armored car made its way down the road, passing the team, before pulling up to the front door of the mansion. The buyer, Mr. James McGavin, stood on the front steps with two of his armed security guards, ready to escort the men with the painting inside.

"You're clear for now." Dali's harsh voice whispered in their ear pieces. Squatting ahead of Monet and the others, was Picasso, who waved his hand forward, "Let's go." The four of them made their way through the trees, shrouded by the shadows, as they inched closer to the mansion. Dali remained hidden a few acres behind them at the front of the property. The clouds had fully covered the skies now and rain began to fall. At first it was gentle, but the closer they moved to the mansion, the harder it came down.

Picasso held up a fist, "Hold." They stopped, making sure to stay hidden by the nature around them. The two armored car guards walked back out of the manor's front door. They quickly shuffled towards the armored car, attempting to stay dry. McGavin stood in the doorway and waved them goodbye, with a martini in his other hand. James McGavin was a spoiled rich kid, in his late twenties, wearing a robe and silk pajamas that surely cost more than most people's cars. He was a lone child who inherited his family's riches when his parents died in a helicopter crash two years ago. He was the only remaining descendant of his great grandfather who owned oil rigs across the nation.

This young man was not involved with the actions of the company that his family had built. He simply enjoyed the constant flow of money that rolled in, and boy, did he love to spend that money. He was a collector of things. Not because he loved these things, or desired them, but because he could. Because he knew that others desired them. He wanted to feel special and appear more sophisticated than he actually was. James McGavin lived all alone in this big empty house and surrounded himself with things that had more meaning than his own life.

The armored car took off, back down the road, unaware of the guests that hid beside the road. McGavin watched the car ride off into the night, before turning back and staggering through his doorway. Picasso pointed to his left, up at the cameras installed at each of the corners of the manor, "Frida, get to work." She ran to the corner of the building, making sure to avoid being seen. Meanwhile Picasso pointed to his right, "Warhol. Take him." A single guard stood by the front door with his gun holstered, as he looked back at the mansion. Warhol slipped out from the shrubbery and grabbed the man with his giant hands, putting the guard into a choke hold. A few moments later the man was unconscious.

Monet was watching the team's handy work in awe when Picasso whispered to him, "C'mon kid, we're going in." Bringing the young man's mind back into focus, he jolted to his feet and followed the leader. The two thieves scurried across the driveway and slid inside the front door that was left cracked open.

Monet pulled out his taser and followed Picasso across the larger-than-life foyer that greeted the crew inside. The sound of the storm faded as they walked further into the home. The two men could hear music coming from somewhere deeper inside the estate. Fortunately, it aided in drowning out the sound of their wet footsteps that bounced off the sleek hardwood floors. Poking his head through one of the many doors in the hall, Monet found himself inside a bedroom where he spotted the record player blaring Mozart. *How much more cliche could this guy get?* Monet scoffed.

"Cameras and Comms are down." Frida stated, "Making my way inside."

Picasso adjusted his ear piece, "Copy that. Keep an eye out, we still have hostiles inside. Warhol, where are you?" There was a pause. Picasso slowed to a stop before peeking around a corner and down another hallway. The house was dark and rich, made of mahogany and marble. They pushed past a heavy wooden door that welcomed them into the study of the manor. Surrounding the two thieves were classical paintings that hung from the walls and shelves filled to the brim with books of all kinds. Regal leather chairs and ancient lamps were staged in corners as the aroma of cigars lingered in the air.

"Took out a second hostile around back." Warhol grunted. "Once we're clear, I'll tie the men up inside."

"There should only be two more guards inside the building, along with the buyer." Dali responded.

"Copy." Picasso whispered, "Remember team, we need the buyer conscious. He's the only one that knows the combination."

Picasso moved forward through the next door way. As he pushed the door open, he spotted another guard up ahead and backed away from the door immediately. Picasso and Monet swung their bodies back against the bookshelves with the doorway between them. The guard, noticing the swinging study door, quickly stepped towards it. The door creaked as he slowly pulled it open. He peered inside, not noticing the hiding thieves as he passed them.

Sweat mixed with rain as it ran down Monet's neck. He slowly raised his hand to his hip, searching for his taser. The guard scanned the room before turning and locking eyes with Monet. As the guard began to shout and raise his gun, Picasso soared off the wall and tackled him. The two men crashed down onto the floor. Monet stood frozen in place as he watched the struggle. Picasso had his hand over the guard's mouth as muffled screams came out. The guard fought back, elbowing Picasso in the ribs. They continued to roll across the floor when Monet heard another guard's footsteps coming down the hall. The guard reached for his pistol on the carpet while Picasso struggled to put him in a headlock. Monet kicked the gun away before finally shooting the man with his taser.

Picasso kept his arms wrapped tightly around the guard's neck as he slowly fell asleep. As his eyes were closing, a second guard burst through the other door into the study. Before either of them could react, the guard seized and collapsed on the floor in front of them. Frida stood in the doorway holding her taser as it continued to electrocute the unfortunate guard.

"All hostiles down...Now we find the buyer." Picasso stated with a heavy breath. Monet put his hand out and helped the older man up. Picasso gave him a look and muttered, "Next time, shoot the guy a little sooner."

The three of them left the study and continued making their way through the mansion. The sound of rainfall tapped along the large windows. Lightning bolts flashed and the stark shadows brought to life the masks that hung from the walls. Some of them grimaced as others screamed. With the wind blowing outside, Monet could almost hear the masks whispering to him in the dark. Knights stood shining in the halls, looming over the uninvited guests. A plethora of enormous stuffed beasts filled the center of this grand hall. Deer heads, antlers, and elephant tusks lined the walls above. "This place is like a museum." He whispered to himself.

"I got movement in the west wing." Dali called over the radio.

"Copy. Headed there now." Picasso responded.

Monet took note of the paintings that lined the halls. Tribal masks, sculptures and pottery, dinosaur bones, and even ancient weapons filled every room of this illustrious castle. Monet thought to himself, *If this wasn't my last job, I'd come back here and steal a whole lot more than just one painting.* Which made him wonder—what was in the armored car that was more valuable than anything else in the mansion?

Picasso stopped, pressing himself against the wall before the final door that loomed at the end of the long hall. With his hand up, he signaled to the others to hold position. Frida aimed her taser back down the hall behind them. Monet kept his head on a swivel, ready for anything to come around the corner. A beam of warm light passed through the gap, illuminating half of the older man's face, as he peered inside the room. With a smile, Picasso waved on Frida and Monet to come closer, finally locating McGavin standing in his enormous library.

Bookshelves lined the walls, stretching twenty feet up towards the curved ceiling. It was built like a chapel. A large model of the globe stood near large leather chairs and old oak tables. More tribal masks and weapons were displayed in glass cabinets and mounted on walls throughout the library. All of which lead to a grand fireplace crackling at the other end of the room, with the pompous man they were after standing before it.

Picasso slowly pushed the heavy wooden door open and slid inside. Frida followed him with Monet behind her. They stayed hunched over, attempting to hide behind what little furniture could give them cover. Blinding sparks of lightning shot through the long windows of the tall room, followed by an eruption of thunder from the wicked storm outside. The crew noticed that it was only getting worse out there. They needed to act fast. McGavin threw his head back, finishing the rich drink in his hand. He turned away from the crackling fireplace to place his glass on the table. The three of them veered left, but it was too late.

"Who the hell are you people?!" McGavin shouted. "Get out of my hou—" Frida went for her taser while Picasso ran at the man to take him down. Seeing this, McGavin screamed and ran for the door, but Picasso turned and kept up with him. McGavin grabbed a lamp and tossed it back at Picasso, slowing him down for only a moment. The rich man grabbed hold of the nearby door and swung it open, revealing a giant man on the other side.

Warhol squeezed through the door frame, lowering his head as he entered the library. Before McGavin could scream again, Warhol swung his right fist into the smaller man's face. He crushed his nose with an eruption of blood that shot through the air. McGavin stumbled backwards, crashing into a table, and knocking himself out. Picasso slowed to a stop, looking down at the bleeding man.

"Son of a—What did I say about needing him conscious?!" Picasso barked at Warhol. Perhaps, the only man not afraid to speak this way to the giant.

"He was running. My instinct was to stop him. I did." Warhol shrugged. Picasso shook his head as the large man walked over and grabbed hold of McGavin, dragging the unconscious body by the collar of his robe. He dropped him in front of the fireplace, where the bleeding man's head hit the ground with a thump. Monet turned his eyes from them over to the container that withheld their prize. He walked up to it, investigating the object. While he worked, Picasso spoke into his earpiece.

"Location secure. We have the target. All hostiles incapacitated."

"Copy that." Dali responded, somewhat disappointed that he didn't get to kill anyone yet. The rain poured all around him. The sniper had worked in much worse conditions before, however he was thankful for the cover the trees provided. *If I'm gonna get a cold from this, I better at least get to shoot somebody.*

Warhol went around grabbing all of the unconscious guards and dragging them back into the library to join their boss. Frida began to zip tie their wrists and ankles while Picasso collected all of their guns. The leader tossed them all into a bag, while he slid one pistol down the back of his pants. He walked over to Monet who was looking over the locked container.

"We're in the library of the mansion—south west wing. Gathering and restraining all hostiles. Keep your eye out for any other unwelcome guests, Dali."

"Copy that. Repositioning now." Dali grunted as he got to his feet. He grabbed his belongings and moved across the hill, searching for a better vantage point.

"This slime ball doesn't wanna wake up." Picasso groaned as he smacked the rich boy's bloody cheek.

"Give me some pliers. I can wake him up." Warhol grinned. The hairs on the back of Monet's neck stood up seeing the large man smile.

"Throw some water on him or something." Frida suggested.

"It's fine. I got it." Monet answered, confident of his skills. He wouldn't admit it, but deep down he wanted to come off as cool as the rest of his crew. "Probably easier doing it myself than trying to squeeze an answer out of that weasel, anyways."

Monet fidgeted with the large container. He noted it was made from impact-resistant polycarbonate. Tough and durable, with rubber over molding. Armed with duel four-digit locks and a finger print scanner.

"Haven't seen this exact model before, but just give me a few minutes and I'll be in." Monet reported. "Keep McGavin close by, I'll need a hand."

The crew stood over Monet's shoulders, watching intently as he unlocked their treasure. More lightning flashed outside followed by the growling thunder above. Outside, Dali laid hidden under the trees, watching the team at work through the large library windows. He kept his eye on the restrained guards and their whimpering client in the corner. The old man's trigger finger was itching for an excuse. He couldn't stand obnoxious elites like McGavin. A world with less of those people was a better world in his mind.

After unlocking the container, they removed a smaller wooden crate from within it. Gently using a crowbar, Monet cracked the crate open. It was filled with styrofoam packing. Underneath it all, was the painting wrapped in bubble wrap. The corners of the package were reinforced with cardboard. Monet let out a sigh of relief after discovering that the painting was wrapped in bubble wrap with the bubbles facing away from, rather than against, the surface.

There were many precautions that must be made in order to protect and preserve these historical artworks. Peering through the wrappings, Monet could see shades of red hidden beneath. A sudden ill feeling took over him. He felt light headed. Monet closed his eyes and took in a long breath. Exhaling slowly, the art thief pushed through the dizziness. His eyelids fluttered while a bead of sweat dripped from his forehead.

Peeling back the wrappings, Monet could faintly smell copper in the air. He was even beginning to taste it. Blood. In his eyes, he believed for only a moment that the reds of the canvas radiated in the dark. It felt alive. He felt alive. He slid his knife along the wrappings. It slowly sliced through, careful not to harm the item. It was nearly free of its packaging. It was almost unleashed.

"Wait! You can't do this!" McGavin pleaded. A look of terror trembled behind those eyes. "This is the Carnage Cramoisi! Don't you know of the curse?! Do you know just how deadly this thing can be?!"

Monet froze in place. *La Carnage Cramoisi?!* He had heard the stories—the legends—of this piece. Most historians believed that it was simply that. A story. Monet wasn't sure if he even believed that it was real, but here it was, in his hands. A chill spread up through his arms from the evil at his fingertips.

"What are you doing? Keep going!" Picasso ordered. His arms were crossed as he stood over Monet's shoulder. Heat radiated off of the grizzled man. Monet turned back to look at McGavin. The rich kid was laying on his side over a million dollar rug. His eyes bulged out in panic.

"Believe me, this thing can not be unleashed. It must stay confined!"

Monet looked back down at the object in his hands.

"This is ridiculous! You believe in this nonsense, Monet?" Picasso growled. Frida stood back, watching the men argue. Warhol stood over McGavin, ready to knock him back out.

"I...I have heard of *La Carnage Cramoisi*. It's French, which loosely translates to 'The Crimson Carnage.' Supposedly...it's an evil painting." Monet stuttered, "Most historians didn't even believe in it. I was never sure if I believed the legends myself."

"What's so evil about this canvas?" Picasso indulged them.

"It's made of—" McGavin started, before Picasso kicked at him on the floor.

"Shut up! Not you! I'm asking him!"

Monet's eyes rolled from the rich kid on the floor to his impatient commander. He swallowed, trying to free his dry throat.

"The canvas is said to have been made of human skin. The paint itself was blood and other human fluids. The...artist...who created it was a mad man. A serial killer, before the term even existed. The canvas dates back to the sixteenth century, possibly much older than that.

The name of the artist is unknown. Historians that do believe in the legend, believe that he killed dozens, perhaps hundreds of people." Monet looked back down at the canvas in front of him. The red peering through the wrappings.

"There have been other paintings found throughout history that scholars try to tie back to him. Nothing anyone has found has ever been as twisted and unholy as this piece. They believe this was his Mona Lisa, his finest work, where the artist found his direction and his style. After torturing his victims, he was said to have skinned them. He would use the skin, the bones and other parts of them, to create furniture, decorations and anything else his demented mind could conjure up." The team stood in awe, watching as Monet continued his story. McGavin gulped, still cowering on the floor.

"The artist was a monster. He targeted anyone and everyone that he could isolate and abduct, including children. He would torture these people for days. He stored them underground. Somewhere that no one would ever hear them or find them. The artist would scalp them, gouge out their eyes, break their limbs, and much more. He knew how to keep them alive for as long as possible. Some believe he was a man of science and medical knowledge. What he committed were some of the worst acts of violence in recorded human history." Monet felt a warmth radiate at his fingertips. He looked down at the canvas that was still in his hands. It was welcoming him in, like a warm hug. He didn't want to let it go.

"As for the canvas itself, it was deadlier than the mortal man ever was. This canvas was an ancient evil. The legend goes that there is a curse tied to this art. Those who gaze upon the painting will descend into madness. The viewers would turn sick and hateful. They would lose their minds and become tools of the devil. These unlucky victims would be overcome with violent urges and pain. They would become just as sinister as the artist himself. Death would erupt from within the canvas, and there would be no survivors left in sight. This explained why the work was lost to time. That being said, it's never been proven. It's simply been a myth—a scary story—told over campfires and spread throughout books and history lessons. Nothing more. Unless, what I'm holding truly is it. *La Carnage Cramoisi.*"

A wave of silence passed over the room. The team stood breathless, their eyes on the object in Monet's hands. Picasso broke the silence, "Lovely story, but we're here to do a job. Finish unwrapping it or step aside and let me do your job for you!

Monet hesitated, "I—I can't. This isn't meant to be seen." He took his hands off of the object, already feeling better. Picasso pushed him aside and grabbed onto the canvas. His meaty hands pressed harder, gripping it with fists of frustration, unlike Monet's cautious and gentle care. He tore at the protective wrapping, like a kid on Christmas, sending Monet's stomach down into his feet.

"Stop! I'll do it! Just…be careful!" Monet pleaded.

After cautiously removing the last of the plastic wrapping, Monet spotted the final layer of protection. It was safely wrapped in a protective layer of nylon material and more cardboard. This helped with preventing condensation for art pieces. Monet slowly backed away to the side of the library, with the canvas out of view.

"I really think we should just wrap it back up and get out of here! Munch can look at it all he wants, we don't need to take this risk!" Monet begged. Frida was starting to worry. She saw the fear in McGavin and Monet's eyes. Something wasn't right here.

"Oh, give it a rest, kid! It's all a bunch of superstitious bull. We need to confirm that we acquired our target anyway. I'm not wrapping this up and heading home, only to unveil the wrong painting to our benefactor." Picasso ordered, out of patience. His knuckles grew white as he clenched his scarred and beaten fists. "So I'll need you to come out from your corner and get back here to look this over!"

Monet exhaled and stepped forward. He picked the painting up once more, and began to peel away at the final layers. Monet turned the painting around and kept his eyes aimed above it, only getting glimpses of the framing of the canvas. Supernatural or not, he wasn't taking any chances. A tense and silent minute passed before it was done. The canvas painting was finally uncovered for all to see.

"No no no!" McGavin squirmed to his feet and ran for the door. On his way, he grabbed hold of an Edgar Allan Poe bust that stood on one shelf. Knocking it over, he revealed a red button below. McGavin slammed his hand down onto it and continued running. Warhol and Picasso were right behind him. An alarm began roaring throughout the castle. The lights had shut off, leaving only red emergency lights, drowning the world of the mansion into a sea of crimson. Metal doors and barricades came rolling down across all the windows. Every door was automatically locked. That panic button was locking down every inch of the mansion.

McGavin nearly took hold of the door handle when Picasso grabbed a knight's shield and flung across the room at the screaming rich man. It violently crashed into the man's back, sending him tumbling to the floor, just before the door. He winched and cried as he continued to crawl, but Warhol walked over and pulled the man up by his collar with ease. His broken nose was still bleeding, as was a large cut on the back of his neck.

"Frida, find a way to turn that off!" Picasso demanded while the sirens still blared. The room matched the redness in his face. This mission was turning out to be a real mess. He was better than this. He worked with better teams than this before. After he returned with the painting, he never wanted to see that old Brit's face again. *He can hire someone else next time.*

"I'm the only one that can disarm the mansion!" McGavin declared as blood dripped down his quivering chin. "If you want out of here, you'll have to do what I say!"

Picasso walked up to the bloody man that Warhol was still holding by the neck. Their eyes met and Picasso never blinked, while McGavin shrunk into himself. "You're going to do exactly as I say. If you do not—you die. You have no leverage here."

"But the police will be on their way…" McGavin started. Picasso laughed.

"We took out your whole security team. You think we can't handle a few cops?" Picasso bluffed. He knew they were in a vulnerable position. He still had the upper hand in fear tactics. He knew what kind of man McGavin was. He'd be putty in his hands if he even threatened the man with another punch to his pretty rich face.

"What's going on in there?! The mansion has been totally locked down—I have no visual! Have the authorities been called?" Dali's voice came through their earpieces, grainy and loud.

Picasso winched, adjusting his ear piece. "We've got it under control. Just keep an eye out on the roads. We should be out with the target in ten minutes."

While the team was dealing with McGavin, one of his guards had woken up. He was sitting on the floor with his back against the wall, surrounded by the other four guards. Their wrists and ankles were all zip tied. This guard, who's name was Michael, looked up at the mysterious canvas that they had unveiled. He knew nothing of this shipment either, only that it was a serious item that required their protection that day. He couldn't believe that a simple painting required such firepower. Yet, once his eyes landed on the canvas, he couldn't look away. He was locked in a kind of trance, completely unaware of the blaring sirens and red lights. He was gone.

Warhol slammed McGavin down into one of his fancy leather chairs. Picasso stood over him and demanded the code. Before McGavin could answer, the guard—known as Michael—began screaming. The crew looked over at the guard who was frantically shaking on the floor. He began growling and pulling at his restraints. His body bent and rolled, yet his eyes strayed locked onto the painting. The plastic ties cut into the man's skin at his wrists and ankles. He wasn't stopping. Picasso and his team watched in horror and confusion. His eyes grew red with rage as drool dripped down from out of his mouth. His gaze finally broke free of the art, turning his attention back at the crew.

While he continued to growl and lunge like a rabid dog, the rest of the guards began to wake up. They were just as horrified as the others. The men screamed and struggled against their restraints, attempting to get away from their deadly friend. The insane guard finally broke free of his restraints as chunks of his skin were peeled off of his hands and legs. Michael got to his feet and sprinted towards Picasso.

Picasso drew the pistol from his back, shooting the mad man in the chest. Nothing. He kept on running. Picasso fired off another two round into the man's gut. Then Frida raised her weapon and fired into his leg, but the guard kept coming. The guard leapt through the air, tackling Picasso. The two tumbled into a bookshelf. The rabid guard clawed and scratched at the older man like a zombie. He even tried to bite at Picasso's arms as he pushed him back. Warhol grabbed the guard and flung him across the room. Hitting a smaller bookshelf, it toppled over crashing down onto him. He still tried to crawl free from under it, before Picasso stumbled over, aimed the gun and put a bullet in his brain. Michael, the guard, was silenced once and for all.

The team was breathing heavily as they looked around at each other. McGavin's mouth hung wide open and his eyes glazed over. Whatever sanity he had left, it wasn't much. The other guards still sat on the floor in disbelief of what they had witnessed. Picasso's bulky arms were covered in blood and scratch marks. He reloaded his gun as he stomped towards the rich man.

"What the hell was that!?" Picasso demanded, pointing the gun at McGavin.

McGavin looked up at him, his jaw still dropped. Picasso, tired of these games, pressed the pistol up to McGavin's forehead. He sat there in silent awe, unable to construct an answer. His eyes said it all.

"The curse is real." Monet whispered, "Everything… It's all real!"

"How is that even possible?" Frida asked, "Paintings can't do that! Art can't… possess people!" Rubbing her fingers against her temples, she looked down at the dead guard on the floor. A pool of blood formed around the fallen bookshelf.

Monet stepped towards the canvas, only looking at the backside of it. Praying it couldn't affect him. He noticed something strange. Something red was dripping from it. It looked as if the painting was bleeding. He reached out with his gloved hand and pressed into the red puddle below. It was blood. *This can't be happening! This can't be real!*

"Picasso, guys...we need to get out of here right —" Monet began before another ear piercing scream rang out from across the room. It was another guard. He too, had gone mad. His eyes grew dark and his veins bulged under his pale skin. "You're all dead!" The guard harshly screamed. Blood dripped out from his nose and ears as he fought the restraints. The other guards pulled away from the manic man, attempting to break themselves loose.

"I'm gonna tear every single one of you apart! I will bathe in your blood and feed the canvas! La Carnage Cramoisi will be nourished! It demands it! The world will run red as the artist prophesized!" The man proclaimed. He licked his lips as he scratched and cut at his own wrists. Breaking loose—he charged the team. Warhol grabbed the guard and slammed him down onto the ground. The mad man wasn't fazed, and continued to attack. He bit down onto Warhol's meaty arm until blood spewed out from his flesh. Warhol flung back in pain, crashing against a table, before kicking the guard in the chest and sending him flying into the wall.

The psycho got to his feet. His right ankle was now broken, and bone protruded from his leg as he limped forward. The possessed man turned to attack one of the other restrained guards. He violently bit into his neck, tearing through skin and sending crimson through the air. The restrained guard let out a gurgling scream of agony as this monster bit down deeper into his victim's throat. The monster flung his head back, pulling strands of meat and tissue from the guard's neck with him. The victim's screams turned to choking and puking before growing silent. Another man was dead.

He howled with laughter, spitting out chunks of gore onto the floor. Frida fired her taser at him, making the guard jitter and dance. He chuckled, *"Tickles."* She reached for another weapon, but the maniac was already leaping towards her through the air. Picasso quickly grabbed an ax off the wall, running towards the attacker. As he pummeled Frida against the wall, Picasso came up from behind. He brought the ax down into the man's shoulder. Blood soared across the library as he tore through the flesh at the base of his neck. Dropping to the ground, he coughed up black blood. He laughed again, looking up at Frida and Picasso.

"We're just getting started!"

Picasso didn't hesitate. He fired two more bullets through the bloody man's face. The body jittered for a moment, before finally resting still. He was finally dead.

"Thanks." Frida coughed. "Can I get one of those guns?"

Looking for only a moment, Monet watched in horror as the canvas pulsated and stretched. Only witnessing the backside, he didn't dare risk viewing the front of the painting. The painting continued to bleed. Puddles of red formed on the table and the floor around it. Monet glanced up at Warhol who lingered in the corner. His body swayed as his face was locked onto the target resting on the table. The large man's eyes were turning red as he glared at the painting.

"Frida! Picasso! Don't look at the painting! Whatever you do, do not look at it!" He turned back to warn them. "Watch out, Warhol might be compromised! He could—"

A heavy wooden desk was sent flying through the air. Monet caught it in the corner of his eye and dropped to the ground, barely missing the table as it crashed into the wall behind him. Warhol roared, shaking the foundation. He punched at his own head and clawed at his skin.

"We're all dead! Just wait and see! The crimson demands the carnage! The canvas will be fed!" Warhol screamed as he grabbed hold of one of the tribal spears on display. Chucking it through the air, Frida and Monet leapt out of its path, before it impacted Picasso's shoulder. The force of the spear knocked Picasso off his feet, sending him crashing back into the wall. He cried in agony as the large spear mounted him onto the mansion wall. Picasso grabbed onto it and squirmed, trying to break it loose. It pulled and tore at his muscles and tissue. The leader grit his teeth, his hands were covered in his blood as he continued to fight with no avail.

Monet looked up to see Warhol charging at him. The behemoth roared like a beast, knocking tables and statues aside with ease. Monet jumped to his feet, taking off to his right. The raging bull of a man pivoted, locking onto Monet as he ran away.

"Picasso! Where'd you put the guns?!" Frida shouted, keeping her distance from the wild Warhol.

"In a...duffle bag! Over by the fire...place!" Picasso groaned. The two dodged Warhol as Picasso struggled to break free of the tribal weapon. Warhol continued crashing through shelves, flipping chairs and tearing items off of the walls. Frida ran towards the fireplace, eyes darting around the room, desperate to find that bag.

"It's not here! I can't find it!" She shouted to her leader. A sinister laugh burst from Warhol's bleeding lips. She turned to see the mammoth of a man holding the duffle bag. He spit at the woman and flung it into the fireplace.

"No!" She cried. In an instant the mad man crossed the room, swinging his arm, and backhanding Frida. Her body was sent crashing back into a large bookshelf. Pages cascaded around her as her head was rattled and vision blurred.

As the intensity of the rain began to settle, Dali could hear the sounds of chaos coming from within the mansion. The bag of roasting pistols in the fireplace sparked to life. Bullets fired off in all directions, soaring through the large room. Frida and Monet dropped to the floor, covering their heads. Two bullets crashed through the wall, inches from Picasso.

"Jesus Christ!" He screamed, helpless as he watched for more incoming gunfire.

One bullet sliced through Warhol's hand. What remained of his pinky dangled from a strand of flesh. The beast roared out in fury.

Dali watched as cracks began to form in the library's barricaded windows. He peered through his scope, trying to figure out just what in the world was going on in there. In an eruption of glass and debris, a large table came crashing through one of the large windows. The table tumbled down into the grass field, dispersing chunks of soil and flowers all around. Hundreds of frightened birds burst into flight.

Dali heard the bone-chilling roars of the possessed Warhol inside. Before he could peek inside the shattered window, the sniper heard sirens in the distance. The police were on their way. Dali had to take care of them, or it was game over for everyone.

The old man jumped to his feet and ran to a better vantage point along the hillside. Getting back down to the ground, behind some cover, he spotted a single police car coming down the road.

"Sorry buddy, nothing personal." He muttered as he pulled the trigger.

The bullet soared through the air, hitting the front tire of the police car. The tire erupted with a bang and the car swerved. The officer driving gripped the wheel, fighting for control. Dali pulled the trigger again, firing off another shot. This sent a bullet through the cop's shoulder. A flesh wound. The cop tensed up in pain before the police car veered out of control. It twisted and flipped, rolling several times down the road. Bright sparks and shards of glass and metal erupted like fireworks around the crumbling car. It tumbled down the hill and into a ditch along the road before finally coming to a stop.

Dali kept an eye on the vehicle through his scope, watching for the officer. The crash was a rough one, but he should have survived it. Dali hoped he did. Another loud crash boomed across the hills from behind. Dali turned back to see more destruction at the mansion. He looked through the scope spotting Warhol, bloody and disheveled, chasing after the other members of the team. He spoke into his ear piece.

"Police car down. You're clear out here, but what in God's name is going on in there!?" Radio silence. He called again, but heard nothing outside of Warhol's guttural screams. Turning his head back, he noticed a fire was starting to grow on the underside of the crunched police car.

"Damn." He whispered. Dali had killed before, but it was always criminals. The guilty, not the innocent. He thought of running down the hill. He wanted to pull the unconscious cop from the wreckage before it was too late.

"Dali! We need help! Warhol has gone AWOL! Take him out!" Picasso growled. He was still lodged into the wall. Blood and spit dripped down his chin. The exhausted leader was soaked in sweat, still pulling at the spear, but he had to be careful. He couldn't afford to lose any more blood.

Dali peered through his scope again, searching for the other team members amongst the ruins of the grand library. That's when he noticed something strange. In the center of the library, untouched amongst the wreckage, stood a canvas. *The* canvas. It was a vibrant red. Bright like the sun, calling out to him. Dali noticed it was surrounded by a puddle of crimson. The canvas appeared to be bleeding, and it was moving—like it was breathing.

The sniper was disgusted, but fascinated. The old man couldn't look away. His good eye slowly began to turn bloodshot red. He twitched and groaned., unsure of what was happening. His head rattled in pain. He could hear the blood pumping through his skull. His bones ached as his muscles twisted and contorted under his skin. Blood dripped down from his nose and out of his ears. His grip tightened on the rifle. He was ready to kill.

Looking down into the library, Dali spotted Frida hiding behind a broken table. He fired off a shot, smiling with quivering lips. The bullet tore through the woman's shoulder, shredding skin and muscle, and chipping away at the bone. She cried and fell to her side. Blood splashed across the rug.

"Frida!" Monet called out, running towards her. "Are you alright?!" He crouched down to help her, dragging her back behind the flipped over table.

"You okay?" He asked her, pressing down on the bleeding wound. Breathing through gritted teeth she answered.

"Yeah, stings like a mother, but I'll be alright."

Looking over the table and back up at the shattered window, he screamed at the sniper. "What are you doing!? You hit Frida!"

"Whoops." Dali chuckled. *"I missed. I was aiming for her head."*

Their hearts froze. Another member of their team was corrupted. Warhol was busy stomping the dead guards' bodies into red paste along the floor. Dali found the large man in his scope and prepared for the shot. Then a fiery explosion combusted behind him. It was the police car. Dali watched the fire cook the car and the man inside. His wavering smile still spread along his face. He bit at his inner cheek like gum, tearing his insides apart. His pulsating hands still held the sniper, white knuckled, ready for more destruction. The end was here—and he was ready to deliver it.

Bullets rang through the shattered glass, slicing through curtains and bookshelves, knocking over vases and armor on display. Frida leapt to her left, toward Picasso as Monet ran to the right. He soared through the air, crashing behind a leather couch drenched in blood and bile.

"What the hell is wrong with him?!" Picasso shouted, still impaled on the wall. Frida crouched behind an overturned oak table, staying clear of Dali's sight. Another bullet tore through the display case only inches behind her head.

"The painting! He must have seen it through his scope. I didn't think it could corrupt someone from such a distance..." Frida answered him, shocked by her own response.

"This is ridiculous!" He growled, "I didn't sign up for this supernatural bull—"

"Shut up! Let's get you off this wall!" She ordered.

He grinned, "About damn time!"

While Monet crawled away from the open windows, he spotted McGavin in the corner by the fireplace. He was searching through the bookshelf for something. Another gun shot rang out and a bullet zipped by Monet's head, ricocheting off the knight's armor that stood behind him. He quickly dropped his head down, uncertain where the bullet went next.

"Jesus...that was too close." Looking ahead, he watched as McGavin pulled back at a small book on the shelf. Suddenly, that entire bookshelf popped out of place, tilting back into an opening in the wall—revealing a secret doorway.

"Sneaky rich boy." Monet muttered.

McGavin snuck through the gap and closed the door behind him. Warhol let out a bone-chilling shriek, flinging a stuffed bear across the room. Monet laid frozen on the ground, but it was too late. The monster had locked eyes with him.

"Crap." He whispered, frantically searching the room around him. Under rubble and shredded leather-bound books, he spotted a medieval shield that laid against the wall. *Now or never.*

The thief jolted to his feet, running towards the fireplace with the shield in hand. Gunshots boomed as bullets went flying. One hit the shield, sending sparks through the air. Monet nearly stumbled, but kept moving.

Warhol started to charge, until another bullet tore through his leg. The possessed Warhol screamed and turned his attention to the sniper outside of the mansion.

Nearly colliding into the wall, Monet dropped the shield to his side and hastily dragged his fingers along the rows of texts. He scanned through the shelves, rapidly pulling back at every book that remained, until finally discovering the switch. A small hardcover copy of *The Invisible Man* by H. G. Wells. *How fitting.*

Monet pulled back the book, and with a click, the bookshelf slowly rolled back, revealing a hidden room behind it. A dim lightbulb illuminated part of the narrow hallway as it stretched off into darkness. Monet pulled out his flashlight and stepped forward into the unknown.

The enraged Warhol heard Picasso's cries from across the room. Together he and Frida pulled at the spear. Again and again until it finally came loose. Picasso roared in pain and fell to his knees. He pressed his hand down on the wound as blood rained down from his shoulder. Before he could breathe, Warhol was closing in, ready to kill.

Frida grabbed Picasso's gun shooting the large man in the chest, but Warhol kept coming. The mad man's eyes were bloodshot. His arms and legs were shredded like paper from so much destruction. His blood coated the walls and floors. His breathing was heavy. Teeth were shattered and missing. His dislocated left arm hung limp, and several of his ribs were broken under his bruising purple flesh. Frida fired off four more shots until the clip was empty. She kept pulling the trigger as the gun clicked, hopelessly trying to stop him. Dark blood poured from the several bullet holes in his chest. Yet he still kept on coming. This man was going to kill everything in sight until he was dead. There was no reasoning. No stopping him. He was gone.

Another bullet cut through the air as the sniper pulled his trigger. In a flash, Warhol's bloody face shattered into hunks of brain and bone. His fierce eyes had vanished in the carnage as his nose was nearly pulverized by the bullet that tore through his skull. A mist of spit and blood rained from his limp lips. His arms and legs jittered before the body loosened up, slowing to a stop. The mammoth-sized man crumbled to his knees, before completely dropping down onto what was left of his face. More blood and gore splattered the walls and floor around him. Specks of Warhol's flesh and teeth clung to Frida's horrified face. The beast was no more.

Dali laughed. He listened to the crackling fire behind him and took in a deep breath, savoring the smell of gasoline and burning flesh. The smile faded. His muscles jittered as if he was fighting the laughter. He bit down on his lip as he loaded another bullet. Struggling to act against the curse, the shooter slammed his head against the weapon. He struck it again. And again. Blood dripped from the gash across his forehead. The old man held the rifle in his trembling hands. A tear dripped down his cheek.

"Sorry I...couldn't do more." He whispered. Pulling the trigger, Dali sent a bullet tearing through his skull. The thunderous gunshot rang out across the land, echoing amongst the clouds, until finally fading to a haunting silence. The sniper was dead.

"Thank God our sniper at least had some live ammo to take care of him! These tasers ain't done nothing for us!" Picasso spat blood onto the floor. "Sounds like Dali is out of the picture now, too. Poor bastard." He shuffled forward, maneuvering through the chaotic library. Books were everywhere, pages torn and blowing through the air. Chunks of the windows were busted open, allowing beams of the setting sun's light to pass through.

"Where the hell is McGavin!?"

Around the bend, Monet came in contact with his target. The rich boy turned and panicked in the bright glow of his flashlight. "Oh God, I'm sorry!" He pleaded, cowering against the wall on his knees. "Don't kill me, please! I don't want to die!"

"Shut up! Get to your feet! Hands where I can see them!" Monet ordered, wielding his taser. The pathetic millionaire started to weep. Monet was losing his patience.

"Let's go!" Monet interrupted, pushing forward. He didn't care about this mission anymore. He wanted out before they were all turned into red paste in the carpet.

"Please! Please—Let me go! There's a secret tunnel under the mansion that can get us out of here. It's not on any blueprints! You can follow me out! Let me do this and we can all survive! Just please let me go!" McGavin begged on his knees.

Monet hesitated, "Okay."

"You promise you won't hurt me? You'll let me go free after this?" The rich boy nervously got to his feet. His legs were quivering under his blood-soaked designer pants.

"Yes! Just make it fast!" Monet ordered.

McGavin turned back to the knight armor and opened the helmet, revealing a hand scanner and keypad for a code. While he began unlocking the secret room, Monet heard a creak in the floorboards behind him. There, he was greeted by Picasso standing behind Frida with a medieval dagger pressed against her throat. It shimmered in the shadows as the old man's dark eyes glared back at Monet. For a moment everyone froze. Before Monet could reach for the taser at his side, Picasso raised his other arm—wielding an ancient crossbow. The trigger was pulled, sending an arrow slicing through the back of McGavin's skull. The rich blood drenched the ancient armor and the fresh corpse laying at its feet. A corpse that wasn't able to finish the code—locking the surviving members inside the burning building.

"Noo! Why!? Why Picasso, you idiot! Wh—" Monet screamed, but stopped himself when he saw Picasso press the blade deeper into her soft neck. The possessed leader grinned, tossing the crossbow aside.

"Drop your weapon now." He ordered, slowly retrieving a second blade from his pocket. It was a personal weapon of his, a sleek militaristic knife that was now pointed at Monet's face. Frida held her breath. *"I said drop it. I ask you again and she dies."* Monet bit his lip, begrudgingly casting his only weapon off into the shadows.

"We're not going anywhere. We stay with the canvas. We are apart of the canvas. You'll see." Picasso spoke coldly. Any sign of humanity and warmth had left his voice and what remained was cold and harsh. The undead spoke through him. He was as much a corpse as the men turned to paste that stained the library rugs.

Picasso tilted his head, gesturing for the two to walk. *"Lead the way, kid. Stay right where I can see you. I'm keeping my arm around the lady. Got her nice and close. You try anything and I'll drink every drop of blood her corpse has to offer."* He spoke in such a calm and nonchalant tone that frightened Monet more than any of the barbaric acts he had witnessed this evening.

As they made their way back, the hallway appeared to be moving. Almost as though it was breathing. Monet shut his eyes and told himself he was just seeing things. *You're tired.* Monet thought, shaking his head. *Or you're going crazy.* His body was sore, his mind numb. He was exhausted, but after going through what they had seen—everything they survived this evening—he wasn't sure what to believe anymore.

Entering the desecrated library, the three stepped towards the canvas. It faced the crackling fireplace at the end of the room. A trail of dark fluid dripped down from the painting. The warm light of the flames bounced off the thick substance. Closing in on the cursed art, Monet bit at his lip, debating what to do next. He could feel the cold tip of the metal blade press against the back of his neck. He had to think fast.

With no other options, Monet swung his leg to kick the table. It rattled the heavy wood desk, sending the painting flying forward, closer to the fire.

"No!" Picasso shouted, loosening his grip on Frida for only a moment. She elbowed the man's bleeding shoulder as her other hand pushed away at his arm wrapped around her. Picasso staggered back, losing his hold on the woman. Monet charged the older man and wrapped his arms around him, "I got him!" Monet shouted, "But not for long!"

Prying the blade loose from his hand, Frida reached for the other. Picasso frantically swung his arm, slicing through Monet's right leg. Monet screamed out and loosened his grip on the leader enough for Picasso to break free.

In a flash, he elbowed Monet's face, breaking his nose. Monet flailed as he stumbled backwards, knocking over a chair and collapsing on the floor. The heat from the fireplace radiated before him. He spat blood on the floor and gently touched at his nose. Pain shot through his skull like a hot fire poker. He bit his lip, refraining from screaming. Looking to his side, he saw the chair he knocked over had fallen into the fireplace. A blaze overtook it as the fire was quickly spreading. He got to his knees when he remembered the canvas. It was behind him. He could feel it.

Monet slowly rose to his feet, careful to avoid the art. Its presence churned his stomach. The growing fire soon spread to the curtains. The flames traveled up and across the room, destroying the countless books on endless shelves. All while Frida was fighting the possessed Picasso. Monet stepped backwards, keeping the canvas out of his gaze. He could hear Frida struggling behind him. Picasso had to be stopped. This painting had to be stopped. *It needed to be destroyed.*

Picasso had his hands around her throat, pressed up against one of the display cabinets. The glass cracked behind her as her attacker pressed harder. His dark eyes flickered as flames spread around him.

"You heretics! Blasphemous in the presence of our most sacred artifact." Picasso spat, with a brutal voice that sounded like a shovel dragged through gravel. Frida was beaten and slashed, with cuts that bled across her cheek and another over her brow. Her eye was nearly swollen shut. Picasso threw her to the ground like a rag doll. As she struggled to crawl away, the mad man retrieved the old spear that rested in a puddle of blood. Rolling on her back, she kicked at him and spat as he grew closer.

"Go ahead, you psycho! I hope you burn in Hell!" She screamed before he brought the spear down, slicing through her stomach and impaling her to the floor. He twisted the wooden weapon in his hand as it mangled the guts under her ribs.

Monet roared, charging at the older man, but he was too fast. Picasso threw his left arm out, grabbing Monet by the throat. Picasso's grip pressed down tight until he could barely breathe. The laughing mad man pulled him closer to his face that was layered in gashes, dark blood and bruises. He grinned menacingly, revealing two missing teeth. Gore dripped from his lips as he spat in Monet's face.

"I was finished playing with her anyway." He chuckled. With his other hand, Picasso punched the young man's face. Pain shuddered Monet's body as his muscles spasmed and bones cracked. Again, the possessed man punched Monet. Harder this time. Monet couldn't feel his nose. All he could smell was copper. He scratched and pulled at Picasso's arms, but there was no chance of escape. It was over. The painting won.

The Library was burning all around them. Growing bored of the art thief, Picasso flung his limp body to the floor. Monet violently slid across the wet wood and stopped just before the painting. The canvas loomed at the center of the room, oozing guts and black bile. Radiating hatred. Pulsating and contorting in the glow of the fire. *It was alive.*

Picasso lumbered over to Monet, pressing his boot to his neck. The crazed leader pulled an ancient viking ax from a shattered display case and raised it over his head, ready to lodge it through the younger man's skull. Monet could barely breathe as the boot pressed down harder. His fingers pulled hopelessly at the shoe, too weak, as his vision began to fade. He accepted his fate. The older man smiled with blood and sweat cascading down his face. His eyes were wide with pupils nearly consuming the sockets with darkness.

"Part of the canvas! Part of the legacy! We are the blood! We are the—"

A tribal spear erupted from the man's bleeding chest. He looked down in disbelief as the stone tore through muscles and ligaments. Coughing, he began choking on his own blood. It driveled from his stuttering chin. Behind him, stood Frida, wielding the same spear he used to stab her. Gritting her teeth, she forced the spear further through the mad man's torso. Guts poured out from his chest as he roared, raising the ax once more—determined to kill them. She raised her leg and kicked the back of the man's knees with all of her force. He dropped to the floor next to Monet. The pool of blood splashed around his knees as he loosened his grip on the ax. He looked over at Monet, and Monet glared back. He watched as the darkness left his eyes, and for only a moment, his humanity was back, before dropping down, face first into the bloody floor. A few bubbles rose to the surface, until there were none.

Frida followed, by collapsing at Monet's side. The blood seeped into their clothes like wet sand. The two were left exhausted, struggling to move under the thickness of the crimson pool they resided in. The heat from the growing fire radiated around them. The two criminals looked at each other, unsure of what to say.

"You need to get out of here, before it's too late!" Frida muttered, her face as pale as the moon rising in the distance.

"I—I can't leave you here. We need to get—" Monet argued, coughing and wheezing as he slowly rolled onto his side.

"I'm not leaving this place. Looks like it's curtains for me too." She paused and then smiled, "At least I wrapped things up with one hell of a heist."

"We can still get out..." Monet started, pushing himself up from the dense lake of bloodshed. He spit as the taste of copper infected his mouth. Rising to his feet, he looked back to her, "Frida..."

He locked eyes with her once more, but she was gone. A burning beam broke free of the ceiling and came crashing down, landing directly onto Picasso's corpse. It crushed his body with a symphony of crunching bones.

Blood and chunks of skin splattered across the floor as the flames grew higher, now spreading to what was left of the man's dead body. Dodging the beam, Monet leapt out of the way, landing on his injured leg. There was a crunch and a twist. He bit his tongue as he stumbled over a busted chair and debris, crashing down into the blood once again.

Monet laid there, his blood pooling with the rest. He was dying. He knew it. There was no saving him. He didn't want to be saved. He had to stop this madness. *The evil dies here, and I die with it.* The thief rolled over and started to crawl. His fingers dug into the soggy red carpet. It squished and bled like a raw steak as his body was dragged over it. The mansion walls were just as red as the bleeding canvas of gore. Looking around him, he thought: *this must be Hell.*

Monet gripped the crimson canvas in his hands. Like the artwork, he was buried under layers of blood and guts. The room reeked like a rotting slaughterhouse. The historian coughed harshly as black smoke filled the room. Soon the fire would engulf the library, followed by the entirety of the mansion—if they were lucky. Monet wasn't taking any chances. He needed to end this. There were stories of this painting, stretching back centuries. All rumors. All legends. Until tonight, he believed they were nothing but scary stories to tell around the campfire. Stories of villages where the people would turn on each other. Towns eating themselves from the inside out. Massacres of innocent women and children. Bodies torn apart. Corpses displayed like works of art. Cannibalism. Sacrifices. Madness. All of it was true.

He couldn't fight it anymore. His eyes were lost in the depths of the painting. He could feel it taking over. Infecting his blood like a virus. Everything started to hurt.

Everything started to burn. Monet could feel his soul on fire.

It was splatters of paint, shades of reds, browns and blacks. It was nothing, yet something and then everything all at once. The longer you looked at it, the more you could see within it. Faces, symbols, stories and history, worlds of life and death. Was it really there? Was it like a Rorschach test, where we saw what we wanted to see or was it all actually there? Faces stared back at me. Admiring me like I was the art. The faces in the blood— dark, empty, bottomless voids where their eyes would be. They would glare into the core of your being. You could feel them crawling under your skin. Deeper inside you. Scratching at your brain. At first all I could feel was fear and confusion, but that soon faded away until finally I felt nothing at all. It was as if I was falling asleep. However, I was truly waking up for the first time. Something was coming to life within me. A new life. A new purpose. Now I felt rage. I felt anger. I felt the need to kill. The need to bleed.

Blood was rapidly dripping down from his nose and ears. His vision was blurry and his eyes ached. It was an intense feeling of pressure. Enough pressure to crush them. Monet kept his grip tight on the painting as he stepped forward. His muscles tensed and ached, fighting his motion, begging him to stop. The painting had its deadly fingers in his brain. Monet pushed harder. Inching his way closer to the flames. It ended tonight. No more bloodshed. No more pain. Screams escaped the mansion as fire consumed it. Smoke and ash were all that remained.

DARK RIDE

The sun was setting on the Santa Cruz Boardwalk as a tired ride attendant baked in the heat. The ocean breeze chilled the beads of sweat on his neck. Goosebumps rapidly spread along his sunburnt skin. This scrawny twenty-two-year-old employee, with shaggy dirty blonde hair, was Derek Weston. A few weeks had passed since he began his summer job on the tourist trap boardwalk, and tonight was his first time closing. It was late July, and the boardwalk was unusually dead that evening. Raising his sweaty arm, he checked his watch. *Just a few more minutes 'till closing and I can finally head home*. Derek remembered, once again, that he still had to pack for his trip to Vegas with friends for the weekend. His parents were not aware of this trip and he intended to keep it that way.

Derek knew that he didn't have the money to go on an adventure like this, but he hoped to win some cash at the poker tables. After burning endless amounts of money in college before dropping out, he thought to himself, *how could things be any worse gambling?* He chuckled as he day dreamed of slot machines and shuffled card decks. Derek was lost in life. After returning home from school, he started this lousy job to keep his parents happy—and himself occupied. They weren't fans of the gang of friends he was traveling with either. More reasons not to tell them. After all of the arguments he had with his parents this Summer, he needed a break from the house. Just for a few days.

Derek watched as the food stands, carnival games, and rides along the boardwalk turned off their lights and locked up their doors. Employees—and the handful of guests still there—shuffled their way towards their parked cars, and away from the setting sun. It was three minutes before closing, when one kid stumbled through the turnstile and into the queue for this haunted attraction.

"Of course!" Derek grumbled under his breath. He worked as a ride attendant at a cheap, haunted dark ride attraction. It was a dollar bin haunted mansion that the house of mouse would scoff at. The kid—who looked too young to be here on his own—waddled up to Derek, excited to board the ride just before closing. He was short and pudgy with scattered freckles, curly dark hair, and what looked like a chocolate stain on his shirt. Derek hoped that it was chocolate. He was not cleaning up another mess after that O'Doyle family puked on the ride two weeks ago. Derek could still smell the stench they left throughout the ride. It nearly took all afternoon to clean through the whole ride.

Derek sighed and let the kid onto the ride. It was a two seater buggy with a metal lap bar that he lowered down onto the child. He did this while reciting the usual safety spiel that he had memorized. The child was giddy as Derek pushed the start button. Two large metal doors with a spooky skeleton face spray painted on them opened wide. In a flash, the kid in the buggy was consumed by the shadows of the dark ride.

Alright, about two minutes and that kid should be back, and then I'll be out of here! He muttered to himself, "Just two more minutes…"

Those two minutes passed. Nothing. The only person left on the boardwalk was Derek and that child who was somewhere in the bowels of the haunted house. He checked his watch once more for the time. It was just after eight—closing time—and the kid should have been back out by now. Derek waited another moment, just in case his time was somehow off. He had only loaded a couple thousand kids onto this ride over the last few weeks. *I should know the timing of this ride by now*, he thought. Another two minutes had passed and Derek was starting to get nervous.

"Something must be wrong with the ride." He whispered as he pushed another button, stopping all ride vehicles in place. Derek then stepped out from behind the controls and walked over to a maintenance door near the exit. He entered the dark ride, eager to find the kid and get out of there as quickly as possible. All he wanted was to go home, but this night had something different in store for him.

As Derek wandered the old tracks of the dark ride, he thought back to the stories his coworkers had told him since he started this job. Apparently this attraction was haunted. He wasn't much of a believer when it came to these things, but he let them tell their stories anyways. Nearly a decade ago, when this attraction was a little nicer than it was now—but still an old piece of junk—a woman died on the ride. Her name was supposedly Judy, although he heard one guy call her Jane. She was tall and thin, with dark hair and tan skin. No last name, no other info as far as he knew. She was a drunken mess and climbed out of the buggy. The lady, who some say was in her early twenties, others say thirties, was running around on the tracks. Somehow she tripped and fell back, causing her hair to get caught in some of the gears, tearing her scalp off.

But that's not all! Blood splattered everywhere as she was screaming, and another one of the ride cars came her way, crushing what skull she had left. It was a brutal scene and the ride was shut down for months. It was almost torn down, before someone decided to re-open it by simply re-branding the attraction. The new owners didn't change much, just a new sign, a couple of new animatronics and a new paint job. A cheap combover to hide the dirty secret underneath. When anyone asked about the mysterious woman's death, employees were told by management to clarify to the people that that story took place at another attraction. Anywhere but there. Which technically was correct, since this was a new attraction—but it still felt wrong. Luckily, Derek hadn't been asked about it yet. Even if he didn't believe the ghost stories, he couldn't go along with lying to people about something like that.

"Hey Kid!" Derek called out as his flashlight cut through the darkness. The building was silent besides the occasional animatronic that would scream or shout out cheesy dialogue. When they didn't speak, their gears and bolts would cry and moan in desperate need of maintenance. The emergency button he had pushed stopped the ride vehicles from moving, but the rest of the attraction still operated like normal. Derek continued to call out for the child again and again as he made his way further into the depths of the dark ride.

Robotic skeletons and ghosts would pop out and howl as the worker passed them. The screams vibrated off the halls drowning out Derek's shouting in his desperate search for the lone child. Slowing to a stop, he realized that he should have been back to the loading zone by now. This track seemed much longer than he remembered. He noticed rooms and scenes in this dark ride that he had never seen before.

"What's going on here?!" He whispered. Derek started walking again—much faster now—as he called out for the boy. He noticed that he was passing things that he had already seen. He already walked through the graveyard scene of this ride, yet he was back here again. Somehow he looped back around without ever passing the loading zone or ever turning back on this path.

This wasn't making sense. Was he losing his mind?

"Kid! Where are you!? If you're playing hide and seek or something, this isn't funny! We need to get out of here!"

A woman's chilling scream came from behind. Derek's legs gave out as he dropped to the floor. He looked back up to see an old and deteriorating ghost bride animatronic leaning over him. Brushing himself off as he rose back to his feet, he glared at the bride for a moment before walking off into the dark. Behind him, this robotic figure's head turned—its eyes followed the young worker. The once hot and stuffy air had dropped to a chilling cold. Derek rubbed his arms as chills spread across his body.

"What the hell is going on here?" He asked, looking at the decrepit walls that surrounded him. Webs covered every corner of the rickety haunted house. Wooden beams stretched across the room with old black and white ghostly photos nailed to the walls. The riders were presented with a never ending fictional family of spirits that haunted the cursed grounds. Derek came to a stop when he noticed something odd out of the corner of his eye. One of these photos was strange, stranger than all of the other spooky images framed along the halls. He walked up to the circular wooden frame, wiping layers of dust off of the glass to reveal himself. It was a photo of Derek, dressed in an old suit with a cane standing in front of an old house. He couldn't believe what he was seeing. This had to be a prank put on by some of his coworkers. Derek told himself that they could have easily cut out and placed his face over an old photo—maybe this kid was in on the joke too. *Maybe the kid was a younger sibling of theirs? Maybe they paid some random kid to hide in here!? They're making me walk around in the dark like an idiot. Now they're just waiting for the perfect moment to pop out and scare me.* Derek, now angry and exhausted, spun in circles looking around the dark room.

"Good job, but this isn't funny anymore! All of you come out now! I'm done playing this game and I want to go home!"

Silence. No one responded. All that he could hear was the groaning mechanisms and the ride's looping horror music that echoed through the dark hallways. Derek continued down the hall, looking for any kind of maintenance door or emergency exits. He had no luck. He didn't recognize where he was anymore. The sets and locations had become more detailed and life-like. He waved his arms ahead of him as he walked through spider-webs, choking on dust.

Coughing, he looked down at the ground to realize that the ride's track was gone. Derek looked back over his shoulder and then forward down the dark hall. The ride track was missing in all directions. He wasn't in the ride anymore—he was in an old derelict haunted house. Lightning flashed from outside, blinding him in the darkness. Derek jumped out of his skin from the sudden loud roar of thunder that blared through the house. The creaking house rattled in the storm. Derek reached out to a wall for support. His vision was still strobing from the fierce lightning as his eyes struggled to adjust to the dark once more. The aged wallpaper crinkled and disintegrated in his hands. The wall was damp and moldy, bending under the pressure of his hand.

He kept moving forward. He didn't like this. Not one bit. Screw the kid, he had to find an exit. He needed out now. The thunder rattled the building. Hinges creaked and wind rushed through the corridors. He kept coughing. His throat was as dry as a desert and his coughing only got worse. It became more and more persistent. He couldn't stop coughing. He looked down at his hand. It was wet. Light flashed through the curtains. His hand was red. It was covered in blood. He could taste it on his lips. His head was spinning. Derek finally stopped and leaned against the wall. He struggled to slow down his breathing. His lungs wheezed and his throat burned. He needed to wake up from this nightmare soon. He feared it may already be too late.

Water came rushing down his back. It was warm and thick like syrup. He felt the resistance of it clinging to his shirt. Stepping back, he watched as the walls oozed blood. Gallons of dark crimson dripped out from holes in the walls like open wounds. Derek fought the urge to puke. His stomach churned and the smell of copper relentlessly coated the air and his senses. Gallons of the dark liquid started to cover the floors around him. Closing in on the young man like hungry sharks. He skipped forward, searching for a way out. He couldn't find another door in sight. The halls just went on forever. He started screaming for help. Banging on the walls, desperate for safety. He was losing his mind. This couldn't be real.

Behind him, stood a figure. It was gaunt and twitched like a rag doll in the wind. The moaning winds of the storm outside caused the shredded curtains to dance. The house was nearly pitch black, with only the beams of moonlight piercing through the broken windows and crumbling walls. The shadowy woman glided down the empty hall towards the young man. He could feel the temperature plummet, now seeing his breath.

Turning around, he flinched as the woman reached out at him. Her boney rotting fingers gripped his throat. Her exposed ribs rattled as she screamed. Her pale eyes stared deeply into his. He couldn't breathe. Then everything went black. The house—or the ride—was shut off. It was silent.

Power surged. A loud bang and bright lights flashed on. He threw up his arm and squinted his eyes, fighting to see ahead of him. Now he was somewhere else. The lights, now dim and flickering, hung along the ceiling going down this never-ending tunnel. He was in a hallway with lockers. He knew this place. It was his high school. He slowly inhaled and exhaled, rubbing his neck now that he couldn't feel the boney fingers pressed around his throat.

"What the heck is going on...?" He mumbled. His head was aching. Someone crashed into his shoulder from behind. Derek caught himself from falling, watching that student continue walking on by. She looked familiar. Another student, a large boy with a buzzed head and thick brows, walked by on his right. He remembered him. That was Frankie Santoro—or was it Santagato? Derek had some classes with him and knew he was on the football team. Frankie was the biggest kid on campus. He was even larger than most teachers. Derek felt bad for anyone tackled by him. Must have felt like getting hit by a cement truck. Slowly more and more students faded in. He saw banners for prom hung on the walls and heard teachers talking in their classrooms. It felt like he was fading into a dream. But this was a memory.

"Zack!" Derek whispered. One of his best friends from school ran down the hall. This was sophomore year when he was still growing out his luscious dark locks. After graduation he joined the marines and buzzed it all off. Derek hadn't seen him since. He gained control of his numb legs and skipped forward, chasing after his friend.

Running down the long hallway, he saw Ms. Master's class and passed by Mr. Hiatt's English class. *This was so weird!* Not paying attention, he crashed into the back of someone. They spilled papers all over the floor. Turning back—annoyed—it was Mr. Carman glaring at him. He was the principle that Derek had come to know all too well over the years. The boy was constantly getting into trouble and screwing around with the wrong crowds. Derek could remember nearly having monthly lunch detentions outside of his office.

"Sorry." Derek muttered. His voice sounded strange. Something was off. The principal's frown changed to a smile and a nod before bending over to pick up his papers. *Why did he smile? That old man hated his guts!* Derek almost forgot about his friend. He glanced down at his angry principle and shrugged before taking off down the hall and turning the corner. Suddenly he was outside, in the blazing sunlight, behind the cafeteria. Zack was still on the run. Derek finally caught up to him, when he heard someone shout, "Now!"

A wave of chills rushed through his body as a cold, thick substance crashed down over his head. Squinting his eyes open, we could see that he was drenched in blood. A rumbling noise came from all sides.

The world was a high pitch hum as he looked down at his crimson stained arms and clothing. But it wasn't him. It wasn't Derek's body. The rumbling came into focus. It was laughter. Crowds of students circled around him laughing and cheering. Derek titled his head back, spotting two more students laughing on the stairwell above him. The student holding the bloody bucket was familiar. It was Derek. He was cackling and pointing down at the bloody mess below. Whoever this was, that he and his friends were laughing at, was overcome with rage. Derek's head ached violently as the vision became blurry. Then everything went black.

Derek remembered that day. He and his friends pranked their old English teacher, cranky Ms. Luther. She was always bitter and they were convinced she despised all children. Derek came up with the idea of their prank after she refused to let him do his report on a horror novel. She looked down at genre writers like King and Lovecraft as inferior, second-rate authors. Derek wasn't the best in school, but he finally found something he was passionate for. Luther didn't care. That was the final straw for the group of friends. That was when Derek decided to pour a bucket of fake blood onto the cold-hearted teacher. Just like his favorite book *Carrie*, things did not end well for the pranksters. She stood there, fuming, watching as all of the ungrateful students laughed at her. Mocked her. She had enough.

After the prank—she just snapped. Attacking Zack right in front of everyone on campus. She gave the boy a black eye before she was arrested. Luther was fired and they never saw her again after that.

Derek wasn't around the night that Luther walked the boardwalk. After losing her job and being blacklisted from the education system, Luther went out with some of her friends to the Santa Cruz pier. They had some drinks and went on some of the rides. Luther, however, had continued drinking far more than the others. They tried to talk her down and get their friend to stop for the night, but Luther was relentless. Eventually the group parted ways. One friend stayed behind, urging Luther to let her drive them home. Luther proclaimed that she was fine and would find herself a cab.

"Right after …I go on the sca—scary ride!" She blurted. Luther stumbled forward, her heels awkwardly dancing along the boardwalk. The friend, whoever she was, waited outside of the ride for Luther to return. But that was the last time she would see her again.

Derek was bombarded with flashes of that night. Luther staggering out of the ride car and crumbling onto the cold metal of the tracks sent chills through his limbs. He felt the seasick motions of the drunk. His stomach churned and his head rattled. She laughed and crashed into one of the moaning ghosts animatronics. Swinging her small purse, Luther snapped the head of a skeleton back, flying through the air. Derek stumbled in the dark. His mind felt as if it was being torn to shreds in a blender. Whispers of the angry woman cut through his skull like daggers.

"Look what you did!" Her voice boomed. Derek folded, dropping to the floor. The vengeful words pierced his ears. Derek's fingers dug into his temples. Fighting the pain, praying it would go away. He saw the drunken teacher trip over the track. He felt the same blow to his skull. Her bleeding head rolled back and forth. She rubbed her eyes, before rolling over to vomit. Derek fell forward on his hands and knees, puking into a dingy corner of the dark ride. Then his head was pulled back. A burning pain coated his skull as he could feel her hair getting pulled into the ride's machinery. Both of their bodies were dragged back along the tracks.

"You killed me! You ungrateful brat!" She screamed. He begged for silence. Her cries rattled out, echoing through the endless hallways. A phantom pain that has lingered in these depths for years. Derek rolled over to his hands and knees, pushing forward, struggling to leave this place. He couldn't take it anymore. He couldn't stand the pain. He couldn't stand the guilt. He wanted out.

"You're not leaving this place! You're trapped, just like me! You're a dead man walking you rotten imbecile!" Luther roared as if she was inside the boy's throat. He vomited once more, now blood and bile dripped down from the young man's chin. Her body grew nearer to the machine as her hair was tangled up in the burning gears. Her cries were soon stifled like a flame as the metal cut through her skin and skull. Blood was everywhere. The woman was nearly dead, when in her fading vision, she saw the ride car coming her way. It jittered along the metal tracks, vibrating under the woman's neck. Her bones chattered and her tired lungs burned. The car crashed into Luther's skull, shattering her teeth. Her nose was crushed inward along with the rest of her skull. Blood and bones coated the broken ride buggy. Luther's nearly headless body twitched and convulsed in the dark room.

Screams of horror and agony erupted around Derek. Every fiber of him burned and ached. He cried out in pain, begging her to stop this. He couldn't take it anymore. She didn't care. She was just getting started. The young man saw a light ahead of him. He crawled through a dark void with no end in sight. He couldn't tell what was reality anymore. Was he even still alive? Was this Hell? From the light came a figure. A corpse covered in blood. Its boney hands were outstretched coming for him. He was too weak to fight it. He could barely move. With a flash he was stumbling along the warm pavement of his school yard. He heard the laughter coming from all around him. He saw his friends pointing and laughing. He saw himself holding the bucket. Standing over him was the rotting corpse of Luther. She kicked him in the ribs, sending his body rolling and the wind out from him.

Instantly Derek was transported back into the dark ride. He was backed into a corner. The screaming corpse of the woman had her hands on him. Her pale hair danced in the air like she was under water. The corpse's mangled face was hidden in the shadows. Her rancid breath burned his senses. He pulled at her arms and kicked at her legs. The small skeletal figure was not budging. Her decaying fingers dug into his throat. Derek screamed as blood dripped down his chest. She pushed the boy down to the ground, knocking what wind he had left out of him. Derek gasped for air as she dragged him along the floor until slamming his neck down onto the ride 's metal tracks. The vibrating metal jittered on the back side of his neck. His head rested between the rusty rails. Her pale eyes glowed like flames in the dark. A crooked smile spread across her rotting face, revealing missing teeth and torn lips.

Lights flashed across her face, giving Derek glimpses of her disfigured face. Her skin was dry and peeling. Chunks were missing and segments of her skull were showing. One of her eyes had sunken in from the crushed skull. Dark, dried blood ran down her pale face. Maggots crawled out from crevices slowly eating away at her face. Behind all the gore and horror, he finally saw who she really was. She was the crazy teacher from high school. The one they pranked. The one that got fired. She was the drunk that died here that year. Her body disfigured and skull crushed in by the metal cars of the dark ride.

"I'm sorry! I'm so sorry!" He shouted. Her breath was rancid, leaking out from behind her yellow rotting teeth of her crooked smile. "Please! I'll do anything! Let me go!" His voice was raspy and dry. He could feel her nails digging deeper into his flesh. Her body twitched as a sinister cackle creaked out from her throat. Tears dripped down from his eyes. He clenched his jaw, holding back the screams. His head was throbbing and his chest burned.

Derek tried turning his head to the right, his eyes straining to see something coming his way. It was one of the dark ride cars. His gut sank, realizing what a monster he had been. Maybe he did deserve this. Light danced off of it as it danced in the dark. The winding tracks dipped and turned between prop skeletons and tombstones— coming ever closer to the young ride operator. He could see blood splattered across the car. Pieces of skin and hair stuck to its bumper. A body flopped around inside of it. It was mangled and melted, barely holding itself together under the safety bar. Derek caught a glimpse of its face in the flashing lights. It was him. It was his fate—and it was on time.

"I know I'm a bad person! I didn't mean for this to happen! I'm sorry! I wish—" CRACK!

———

The sun had risen. Surfers ran to the sea as cars filled the parking lots and children rushed to the attractions along the pier. Business was booming on another warm, summer day. An employee in a matching uniform to Derek's walked down the pier and turned the corner. She had short dirty blonde hair that shined like gold in the sunlight. Her eyes were soft like honey. Derek had liked this girl for a while now. He always meant to get around to asking her out. Her name was Jackie.

Jackie entered through the employee gate and walked over to the controls. Turning on the machine, she looked at the monitors and watched for the buggies to come through the loading zone. As the crowds grew, the line of families extended out from the queue. Jackie loaded her first group, a young brother and sister, into the car. Pushing the start button, the buggy took off and turned into the dark entrance of the ride. Another empty buggy approached as the safety bar was raised. Now a mother and her daughter were escorted into the car. Again, the red control button sent the pair off into the darkness.

A few moments later the first car with the siblings came crashing out through the doors. The sounds of screams and church bells roared across the structure, before being stifled by the automatic closing doors. The two children were crying. The little girl held onto her slightly older brother. Her face was buried into him. His eyes were closed and he was breathing rapidly, waiting for the car to finally stop.

"Hey kids, the ride is over! It's okay!" Jackie sympathetically called out. The two finally opened their eyes, both red from tears. The bar was raised and they quickly got to their feet. Stepping out through the exit, the little girl yelled out, "That wasn't fun! Too scary!" Jackie shrugged, used to the endless amounts of crying children exiting the ride. The look in their eyes realizing that they were not ready for such an adventure. Warning signs were posted, yet families still took the risk. Soon after the mother and her daughter came around the corner in their small buggy. The little girl, too, was sobbing. She held onto her mother's shirt and screamed into her arm. Her mother had a stone-like face, eyes filled with shock and anger. *Oh boy.* Jackie thought, H*ere we go.* The mother stood up from the car, still holding onto her girl and attempting to exit.

"That was disgusting! This ride is too intense for the families here!" The mother exclaimed, shooting daggers into Jackie's soul. The mother's dark hair blew in the ocean breeze. Her face was red and flustered. The small child still held onto her mom's leg, crying into her snot-coated shirt. "You people are sick!"

"It's gonna be one of those days, huh?" Jackie muttered as the woman and her child stormed off into the crowds of the boardwalk. A few more groups, mostly children, were placed into the ride vehicles and taken off into a dark adventure. All of which came out sobbing or in shock from the horrors.

"That was gross! It smelled awful! The ride wasn't like that before! Why'd you do that!?" A grandfather called out as he took his grandson off of the car. The old man was shaky as he used his cane to walk away. The six-year-old boy followed closely behind, wiping his nose and tear drops away with his sleeve.

Changes? When did we add smells? Jackie pondered. The day had started off in a strange direction. Just then, she looked down at the ground along the track, noticing something red. There were thin trails of what looked like dark red paint along the ground. *That wasn't there before—was it?* She glanced back over at the monitors at her control station. Everything appeared to be fine. She had to investigate. Something was wrong here. Before the next group of middle school boys could board, she put up a chain blocking them. A look of defeat came upon their faces. Annoyance came next.

"I'm sorry everyone! I need to do a routine exception of the attraction! It shouldn't be too long!" The rows of irritated tourists in line glared at her. She bit her lip, anxiously. "Not long at all!"

With that, she entered the attraction, just like Derek had the night before. Stepping through the first set of doors on this ride, she flicked the maintenance lights on, seeing things much clearer than he ever did. Ghosts screamed, gears groaned, the lifeless faces of mannequins stared creepily into her eyes. Everything was normal. She pushed through another one of the painted doorways on the track. Spider webs dangled from the black ceiling. This room was made to look like a decrepit chapel from long ago. Fake moss and weeds had taken over the pews and a raven sat atop the damaged cross falling loose from the back wall. A cheesy old animatronic of a zombie would appear reaching out at the guests from between two of the pews. It was slow and creaked. The lights of its glowing red eyes were faded and blinking. The ride was a dump, but in this case, everything still appeared normal.

She eventually found herself in one of the final rooms. A graveyard with ghouls and zombie animatronics attacking the riders from all sides. She could see that they all moved and moaned like they should, but her eyes were focused on the cart ahead. It was sitting in the middle of the scene, jolting on the track, but not moving forward. She stepped closer, hearing something wet. She felt resistance under her shoe like she stepped in something sticky. It was a red fluid that coated the floor. Her eyes followed the trail of it that led to the ride buggy. Slowly walking ahead, attempting to step around the red floor, she wandered over to the front side of the cart. It stopped twitching on the tracks—as if it noticed her standing there. More crimson stains were splattered across the small car. *It looked like a crime scene in here.* She thought, her heart rate beginning to rise.

Something shifted in the shadows. It lingered over the broken cart, moving back and forth. A zombie's putrid corpse was animated behind a large tombstone. She didn't remember the ride having any scents in it. She certainly would have remembered how awful this room smelled. *Must be something new maintenance added over the weekend.* She shrugged.

Then she looked closer. Her eyes scrolled up this animatronic. It didn't look familiar either. The same crimson fluids on the floor and the car, all oozed out from this thing. Its arms waved, reaching out at the cart. The latex skin looked so life-like. It was pale and she could see blue veins and bone structure underneath. The torso of this figure wore a shredded uniform. Intestines and gore dangled out from his gut. She couldn't believe how good it looked, but asked herself why was it wearing an employee uniform?

That's when her eyes locked with the brown eyes of the corpse. The shaggy hair hung down over his face. The skin was torn and shredded. Bits of hair and teeth dangled from the shattered skull. Even in all of this carnage she knew—it was Derek.

The dark ride burst to life. The lights went out and the cart took off—grazing Jackie's legs. Ghostly moans echoed through the dark ride. Ravens squawked and doorknobs rattled. Legs trembling, and blood pumping, Jackie started screaming out in the darkness. The buggies kept on driving by as she fell to the ground in tears. Children could be heard laughing from outside. Or were they here inside with her? Flashing strobes and black lights gave the mangled corpse a sinister glow as it looked down at her. The bully was on full display for the world to see. A gut wrenching act for one—entertainment for the rest.

MINES OF MADNESS

The rapid clicking sounds of a keyboard jittered through the small room. A young woman sat at her desk, hunched over her laptop. It was an older one, beat up, and covered in stickers from horror films and albums. The typing woman was in her early-thirties. Black wavy hair ran down her back, over the dark red tank top she wore with matching lipstick that made her icy blue eyes pop. She was a slender girl, covered in tattoos, with a nice smile that had a slight gap between the center teeth. Much like the rest of her, it was something unique that made her stick out from the other girls.

She continued to click and clack, repeatedly refreshing the window of the website, checking the channel's views and subscriber count. Again, she discovered that it still had not risen, and in fact—had been declining. Clicking over to another tab on the site revealed charts illustrating the ever-dropping revenue and viewership numbers.

The phone rang, jolting the woman out of her distressed daze. She pulled the buzzing cell out of her pocket. It was Henry. *He must have seen the numbers too.* She thought as she raised the phone to her ear.

"Hey Steph! Did Rob call you yet? He just talked to me. He's really amped up. I...don't know about this one."

"No. What are you talking about? What's he up to now?" She questioned, shutting her laptop. A loud thud boomed at her apartment door behind her. Stephanie leapt out of her chair, nearly tripping over her own feet.

"Hey, Steph, it's me. I gotta talk to you!" It was Rob's muffled voice behind the door.

"Steph? You there?" Henry asked, still on the phone. His voice was grainy and hard to hear through the cracked cell's small speaker.

"Yeah, I'm here." She exhaled. "So is Rob. I gotta go." She tapped her screen, hanging up on Henry, and walked over to the door.

Right away, Rob had Stephanie sit down on the couch as he began his pitch. "So I know you know the site's been dead lately. I know Henry and the others have been losing hope and all. But I don't think we're done just yet! I was thinking of this last night...I've got something that should—no, it absolutely will—help boost the channel back to its glory days! Get us back on the map, ya know?!"

Steph tilted her head, "What's the plan this time, oh fearless leader?"

"I'm getting to it. Don't worry. Have you ever heard about the haunted Wilson Mines in East Tennessee?"

"The Wil...wait—wasn't that the one with the cave-in that killed dozens of miners?"

"Yes! Almost a century ago!" He lit up with excitement. "Actually, the one hundred year anniversary is coming up next weekend!"

"Alright, go on..." She nodded, indulging her friend.

"I say we go there! Get the team packed up, get a hotel like we used to. We can get up bright and early and hike out there, since it's not exactly the easiest place to get to. Give our audience something no one else has ever seen. No other ghost hunters that I know of, have ever gone there before. None of the pros on TV or anyone online like us!"

"Yeah, because it's dangerous!" She answered, rising up from the couch. "For one, that place is buried away in the woods, falling apart. I remember reading that the structure was walled off by the city. Then there was another cave-in years back when that freak earthquake struck, only making it worse! That mine buried itself away long ago and the city threw the key away."

"I know. I know. We'll be as safe as we can, and bring all the hardware we need. This is what will make us huge! Bigger than we ever were! No one has entered those mines in decades. No one knows what's in there! There has to be tons of paranormal activity inside!" There was a long pause. The two stared at each other as she softly shook her head.

"But if you don't want to do it...just say the word, Steph." Her eyes rolled as she thought about the project. She knew that this would be their last chance, if not, it was all over. Everyone would part ways, and that left her with the option of going back to working at a damn coffee shop, or as an office assistant. Mind-numbing days spent answering calls and organizing the never-ending lists of meetings. Some of which would be meetings just to discuss other upcoming meetings. She wanted to gag.

"Sure...Let's do it." The two friends reached forward and shook hands. "But if I die. I'm haunting your ass!"

———

Three days later, the five friends that made up this film crew were driving along the winding roads of the Great Smoky Mountains. Several bags filled with ghost-hunting gear, helmets, lights, cameras, reflective vests, knee pads, and any other survival gear that they needed for this endeavor were packed away in the team's gray van.

Stephanie and Henry were the co-hosts of their paranormal investigation series. Stephanie was a strong believer in the supernatural and was fascinated by conspiracy theories. She wasn't one to claim that the Earth was flat or that Elvis faked his death, although there was an argument for the second one.

Her co-host, Henry—the skeptic, sat next to her. He was lean, with long legs and a large Adam's apple that dribbled along his neck. Behind the round glasses that framed his dark eyes, he was a very logical and analytical person that, at times, would drive Steph crazy. Henry enjoyed his role on the crew, giving him the opportunity to point out the mundane and scientific reasonings for so-called ghost sightings, hauntings, and more. There were always creaks in the floorboards and rattling pipes for him to find. In the nicest way he could, Henry would shrug off witnesses and believers, claiming that many of them were sleep deprived or stressed. He believed most people sought after the fame that came with spotting a ghost in the basement or Bigfoot in their backyard. Even when he wasn't very popular amongst the crowds of believers,

Steph respected that he remained respectful. *And tried his best to not come off as a complete asshat*, she thought.

Robert, the producer and director of the series, sat behind the steering wheel, taking them through the woods of the Appalachians. He handled the business side of things and guided the group's career over the years. Rob gave Stephanie a look through the rear-view mirror. She locked eyes with him for only a moment, before darting back down to her feet. She could feel her warm skin turning red. The two had grown distant over time. With this possibly being their last hurrah, Rob hoped to rekindle their colorful history on this trip. If he was losing everything else, at least he could have her back. His chest swarmed with a heat that danced like fire. He looked back at her in the mirror again, but she was looking out her window at the road and passing trees.

"Lookout!" She shouted. Her eyes shot open as she flung her hand, pointing ahead. Rob's eyes flashed down from the mirror, spotting a large buck galloping along the small road. Instantly, Rob brought his boot crashing down onto the brake pedal. The tires skid, and the car swerved as he fought to stop their van. There was a sharp breaking sound that chattered like teeth. Rob was swarmed by a cascading wave of water bottles, bags, and loose papers that all came rushing to the front of the car. The crew braced themselves between the chairs, closing their eyes and preparing for the worst. A second later and the car finally came to a halt. The deer was gone. That sharp clashing sound was the glass windshield that shattered in the corner by the passenger seat. No blood, no fur, just the sign of a baseball—sized impact.

Breathing heavily, they all sat stiff in their seats, silently glancing at each other. "Everyone okay?" Rob quietly asked. The four pale faces all slowly nodded.

"Just need a new pair of pants." Jack muttered with a laugh. The others giggled while Rob ran his fingers through his hair. "Good to know." He responded, turning his head back from the others to face the cracked windshield before him. "At least we're in better shape than that deer."

With a slow exhale, Rob pressed down on the gas pedal, and took them further up the twisting backroads. Jack was the camera man for their series. He was a large man, with a bushy beard and messy hair, that towered over everyone around him. His glasses rested along his pudgy nose, just below his beady eyes. Many of his weekends were spent partying hard, but he always remained responsible when it came to his work. Unsure of his beliefs in the supernatural, he always kept an open mind.

Without hesitation, Jack agreed to this trip. He loved being part of this team, and wanted to keep the gang together. Without a girlfriend or much of a family to go home to, like the others, this job was the best thing he had going on in his life.

Lastly, there was Hannah who was the Sound Operator of the film crew. Ironically, the sound girl was the quiet one of the group. She was thin and short, usually wearing jeans and a sweater. She was the shy little church girl that moved out to Hollywood from a tiny town in Kentucky. Like Steph, she was a believer of the supernatural.

After finishing school, and a few years of working with her friends, she decided to move back home. Her soon-to-be-husband waited for her back in Kentucky. With only a few more months until the wedding, the couple still had much to arrange. Hannah hadn't said anything to the others yet, but she was ready to leave the team after this final adventure and move on to the next chapter of her life.

"Alright, here we are!" An excited Rob announced. Just beyond the van, stood a battered chain-link fence. The old, faded road, lined with potholes and cracks had ended, becoming nothing but a dusty, old dirt road that continued off into the distance. Rob jumped out of the driver's seat and skipped over to the metal fencing.

"Is he doing what I think he's doing?" Hannah asked.

"Yup." Henry sighed, "Those are bolt-cutters in his hands."

Stephanie shook her head. *He's going to get himself arrested one of these days.* Rob looked around before snapping the chain loose and pushing the rusty fence open.

"Open sesame!" Rob whispered to himself with a smile. He scanned the area as he returned to the van, spotting no signs of humanity in sight. They were in the middle of nowhere, surrounded by nothing but trees and wildlife high up in the mountains. Rob hopped back inside the van and pulled forward, following the ancient dirt road up the mountainside.

"Glad we're committing more crimes, boss." Steph side-eyed him in the mirror.

"Hey, it's not like we haven't done this kind of thing before!" Rob replied. The van carried the team up another few miles before the road finally came to an end. A small trail still lingered between the thick branches of the trees ahead. *There it is!*

Swinging the van door open, the crew was bombarded by the brightness and heat of the sun overhead. The air was thick with humidity. Insects buzzed as they flew through the air and the bushes rattled with the songs of cicadas.

An old rusty sign hung on the barbed wire fencing that blocked the path ahead. "Danger! Do not enter!" It warned, "Hazardous environment! Trespassers will be prosecuted!"

"I know it says that it's not safe for people to explore the mines, however, that is a warning to the common folk. It doesn't apply to professionals, like ourselves." He smiled, as the others shrugged. A chill ran down Hannah's spine, already feeling uncertain of this endeavor. *We could still turn back and leave*, she thought, but no one else around her had spoken up. Not wanting to be the only person to quit the job, she quietly, and begrudgingly, followed her team over the fencing.

The air was the thickest in this part of the woods, yet the pestering bugs had vanished. There were no more birds in the sky or any squirrels amongst the trees. Hannah could barely hear the cicadas in the distance. It felt as though even the animal kingdom was banned from entering this haunted place.

The trail went on for a few hundred feet, before finally reaching the entrance of the old mine. Surrounded by trees and shrubbery, the entrance of the tunnel was framed with large wooden beams that dug into the side of the mountain. Beneath the overgrown weeds and branches, the mine was boarded up, littered with several more posted warning signs. Now that they stood before the century-old ruins, members of the crew began to feel uncertain of this adventure they were about to begin.

"Don't worry guys, I got this." The sarcastic producer smirked.

Rob pulled a crowbar from out of his bag. The metal shimmered in the sunlight as he stepped towards the barrier. The crowbar crashed against the wood with a loud bang. The producer struggled as he pushed the bar underneath the old plank. It slowly rose, creaking and snapping. With one final push, the heavy board broke loose, falling at his feet. Dust billowed in the air as more boards were pulled away. The crew held their breath, waving the clouds away until the tunnel cleared.

The entrance to the mine was opened for the first time in decades. A bone-chilling breeze came blowing out from within, sending shivers down the spines of each member. The first tunnel stretched off into the endless darkness before them.

Before going any further, Steph and Henry readied their gear. The two hosts wore helmets, not just for safety against the hard rock walls of the caverns, but the gear was modified with a headlight and go-pro cameras on the sides and front. These would record every angle possible. Viewers were able to see the path they walked, along with the reactions of the host's face as they explored. The other three members of the crew wore their own helmets with lights and go pros facing forward to film the hosts ahead. Each member of this crew also slid on their own reflective safety vests.

"Everybody ready?" Rob called out, as if preparing at the crowds of a pep rally.

"Yes." Henry responded. Hannah nodded, as did Steph before Jack barked, "Hell yeah!"

"C'mon guys, this is gonna be our big break! No one has explored this place in decades! We're in uncharted territory!" He licked his lip and smiled as his eyes darted between the members of his crew. "I said…is everybody ready?!"

Together, the five of them shouted and clapped, "Hell yeah we are!" A few high fives later and they stepped into formation. Steph and Henry stood side by side in front of the entrance to the mine. Jack held his camera with Rob watching over his shoulder. Hannah listened to her gear, checking the mics clipped to the vests of each of the hosts.

"Alright!" Rob smiled, looking around at his team. "Sound ready? Cameras rolling? Everyone good? Great! Action!"

"Hey everyone, welcome back to *Spectral Spectators!* Been a minute since you've seen our faces!" Stephanie started, with an enthusiastic smile. "We have a very special adventure for you all to see today! We are about to explore the infamously haunted Wilson Mines located deep in the Appalachian Mountains!"

She leaned back as Henry stepped towards the camera, "The Wilson Mines were opened by Logan D. Wilson in eighteen-sixty-six. This was around the same time that the boomtown of Ore Knob was forming on the other side of the mountains, in Ashe County, North Carolina. Both Knob and Wilson ran successful copper mining operations. At that time, Copper was selling for about eight cents per pound."

Taking a breath and looking back at the dark tunnel, Henry continued, "The Wilson mine expanded over the years, digging five new adits, each of which were nearly four-hundred feet long, with twelve tunnels branching off from those."

Stephanie stepped forward, taking over telling the tale, "In those first five years of operation, the mine produced over four-hundred-thousand pounds of copper. As time went on, six more mine openings were documented at this site. While in operation, it produced hundreds of millions pounds of copper worth billions today! This is one of the deepest abandoned mines in the nation, filled with an endless amount of underground tunnels, and over twenty sub-levels, with depths deeper than twenty-two-hundred feet."

Henry added, "Twenty years ago, there were survey assessments taken that documented two mine openings, the main hoist base, a boiler tank, and the winch. That was the last time anyone stepped foot on this site." He paused, looking down at his notes, "They say that to this day several of the walls and foundations of these mines are visible, even after the tragedies that occurred in these tunnels…"

'Which brings us here today!" She interjected. "Today is actually the one-hundred-year anniversary of the tragedy that befell this mine!" Stephanie exclaimed, both somberly and excited. "Fifty-three men were found dead, along with twenty-two more missing bodies that were never recovered. This tragic loss was due to a sudden and massive cave-in. Explosives rattled the foundations of the mountain, sending everything into utter chaos. It was a bloodbath, the likes of which no other cave in America has ever seen."

Taking a breath, Steph concluded, "Today we hope to explore and discover secrets of this historic cursed place and perhaps, even capture footage of the spirits that loom the tunnels of this mysterious mine!"

"There's also legend of a secret gold mine buried away in these caves! Around the start of the Civil War, it's believed an old blacksmith discovered gold somewhere deep in this mountain. This was back before the mine was fully operational. Even the owner of the mine knew of the tale and searched for it himself." Henry concluded with a whisper and a smile. "To this day no one has been able to track down the legendary gold of the cursed Wilson Mines."

"Who knows, besides hunting ghosts, maybe we'll find ourselves some gold in these hills too!" Steph laughed.

Rob turned his attention to his cameraman, "Jack, get some B-roll footage of the cave entrance and the woods around us." Then he looked over at Hannah, "Need some wild sound, too."

"On it." She replied. Jack gave him a nod and a grumbly 'mhmm' as he chewed on his gum.

Henry pulled out his flashlight, flicking the switch on. The small beam traveled as far as it could before it was overtaken by the shadows of the earth.

"Guess I'll go first." He said hesitantly, giving the group a weary smile. Steph and Jack followed with Rob and Hannah taking up the rear.

"Oh, wait." Henry warned, crouching down to inspect a puddle that took up much of the pathway. The dark, murky water was still, churning the host's anxious stomach. He slowly stood up and turned back to the others.

"I read that if there's stagnant water in a cave like this, that it can be very dangerous. If there's moving water in the cave, then it's safe...But stepping in dank, stagnant water could possibly release hazardous chemicals into the air. Things in the water that could harm—or even kill us!" Henry warned. "I don't think we should go in there."

The group stood in silence, for only a moment, before their producer stepped forward. A dashing smile gleamed on the jaw of their fearless leader.

"It's alright, we'll play it safe for you. We can step around the puddles." Rob said, placing his hand on the shoulder of the nervous host. "Besides, we aren't turning back after making the trek all the way here. This is gonna blow up, man. No one else has dared to come here. It's ours for the taking!" Rob pushed past Henry, stepping over the large puddle and venturing further into the tunnel.

Jack held the camera with one hand as his other was crammed into his pants pocket. The large man shuffled for a moment before pulling out his lighter. Holding it between his thick fingers, he flicked it on. The small flame flickered and danced in the dark before he released the switch and the darkness returned.

"What was that for?" Stephanie asked him as he stashed the lighter to his back pocket.

"Some caves can trick you. If you enter a cave with a lighter or a torch, and the flame dies out immediately—that means there's no oxygen. Even in wide open caves where it doesn't make sense." Jack shrugged, standing in the entrance of the mine tunnel, "But it looks like we're safe." Stephanie smirked with a curious look on her face.

"I didn't know you were such a smarty pants, Jack. Thought you were busy partying. Rock 'n roll, right?"

Jack returned the look with a chuckle, "Saw it on the history channel or something one night…And I am the party guy! Don't go around telling people I'm smart and ruining my reputation."

The cavern was a cold and empty space that seemed to carry on for miles. The sounds of water dripping from the rocks above rang off the walls like choirs in a cathedral. The air was crisp and cool. Already, the team's fingers and noses began to numb. Traveling deeper into the dark cave tunnels, the crew began to hear something. It was a rustling in the distance. *That isn't wind. It's something else.*

"What is that?" Hannah asked.

"Water!" Henry answered, stepping forward with his dim headlight spotting a calm river of water traveling along the smooth stone floor, descending deeper into the earth. "Thank goodness."

"Looks like we're safe after all, huh?" Rob jabbed at Henry's side. Henry glared as he passed him by and let out a sigh of relief. He didn't want to admit it, but he was hoping that the still water would force them to turn back. Henry didn't feel right about this adventure. This trip picked at the back of his mind like a tick. Something was wrong here.

The team passed by several tunnels that ran in all directions. Rusty metal tracks for mine cars ran off into the unknown. Dusty, rotting ropes hung from metal hinges lodged into the Earth.

"Feels like stepping back in time." Stephanie gleamed, "Every time we go on these trips. It never gets old."

"No, it does not." Henry smiled, pointing ahead with his light. He looked through his notes and pulled out his map. "If my memory serves me right, that tunnel to the left is the original tunnel they first dug. Those to the right were added a few years later. Around the corner, that other section must have been added in the early twenties, after the first World War."

"Just before the cave-ins." Stephanie Concluded.

"One more fun fact, biologists have determined that these mines contain some of the largest known hibernating colonies of Rafinesque's big-eared bats in the United States! Guess we should have brought some garlic with us on this adventure too!" Stephanie added with a smile and a wink.

"And watch out for lots of bat sh—hhiiiiiittttttttt!" Jack screamed as the ground gave out from under him.

The large man descended into darkness as the floor around them began to rattle and collapse. In an instant, the others all tumbled down, following their friend into the black unknown. A sharp rock sliced at Stephanie's arm, a boulder cracked Jack's back, pebbles scrapped along the skin of Hannah's back. The five members rolled and flopped along the harsh surroundings of the cavern walls before stopping in the cold dirt below.

"Everyone okay?" Rob coughed. The others groaned as they all rolled onto their backs, coughing dust clouds into the air. They waved their arms, clearing the dust in the air.

"I got some nasty cuts on my lower back." Hannah winched, raising her shirt up. Blood seeped through the thin fabric of her shredded top and coated the inside of her coat.

"My left hand is pretty screwed up." Henry added, feeling the painful numbness of spraining his wrist as he tried to sit up. A warm sensation ran down his forearm. He slowly rolled up his sleeve to discover a bleeding gash had sliced through his skin from elbow to palm.

"My leg is cut up and my pants are torn to shreds." Stephanie groaned.

"I feel like crap, but at least I'm not bleeding." Jack spoke with a raspy voice, harshly coughing as he cleared the dust from his throat. "Externally, at least."

"Who's got the first aid kit with them?" Rob asked.

"I got it…somewhere. Anyone got an extra flashlight? I can't see nothing." Jack called out, huffing as he stumbled to his feet.

"Here." Hannah waved and tossed him a small metal light. The members all rose to their feet as their lights danced in the dark. Stephanie looked around, unable to spot any walls ahead. Turning her head back, she spotted the caved-in floor that they fell through, and the slope that they gracefully rolled down. *Lucky we didn't break our necks.*

"Damn…" Jack muttered, digging through all of his bags a second time over. "I had it…but I can't find it."

"What? You lost it!?" Rob scolded his cameraman.

"It's alright, let's just look around for it." Stephanie stepped in front of the producer, attempting to calm his hot head. Her leg stung with every step as strands of material dangled from her bloody knee.

"I got nothing over here." Henry called out, holding his aching hand. The others stumbled in the dark, waving their lights in hope of finding anything useful. They were surrounded by dark stone and earth. Land that hadn't seen the light in centuries. The air only grew colder the longer they wandered.

"Jeez, I'm sorry guys." Jack started, limping towards the others holding his now broken camera in his burly hands, "I screwed up."

"You stupid—" Rob stormed towards the larger man.

"This isn't his fault!" Stephanie interrupted. She looked back up at the hole above, "We all fell through the floor. We all got hurt and broke equipment. My headlight is busted! Henry lost his mic. This whole thing is a mess."

"This was not a safe location to film at." Henry added. "We've gone to some sketchy places before, but nothing like this."

"Your back looks pretty bad." Stephanie said, tearing the bottom of her right pant leg off. She walked across the dark space and handed it to Hannah, "Here, wrap this around you. Until we find the first aid kit, this is the best we can do."

"Thanks, Steph." Hannah held her hand for a moment before taking the material and wrapping it tight around her, covering the carnage on her slender back.

As they all got to their feet, taking care of their injuries, Henry wandered the dark cave, in search of a way out. He looked up at where the floor gave out and followed the trail of debris with his light until he stopped at the bottom of the cave where they stood. The only other path he could spot was headed in the other direction.

"That's too steep of a climb for any of us to make. We have no internet, no phone service. Our best bet is to follow this trail and see where it takes us." Henry pointed from the hole above and turned to the darkness ahead. "I'm sure this was some abandoned section of the mine they stopped using before the rest of the cave-ins. There's gotta be another way back up there."

"Everyone, just be careful where you step. Clearly, this place isn't stable. Let's take things slow. Not hurt ourselves anymore than we have to." Stephanie concluded, "Lead the way, partner." She pointed her light at Henry.

The team of five steadily made their way deeper into the dark. Stalagmites hung from above and bats chirped in the distance. The caverns only grew colder, the deeper they traveled. Steph clenched her fists inside her pockets as her teeth wanted to chatter.

The narrow tunnel ended, opening into a much larger cavern. Henry stopped in place as his jaw dropped open.

"Oh my God."

Steph looked over at him, confused, "What is it?"

Henry's face stayed locked onto something in the dark. He simply reached out his hand and touched the side of her head, turning her in the same direction. Her jaw dropped next.

The team looked on in awe as they discovered an enormous doorway carved into the stone. It was over fifty feet tall and nearly as wide. *Who would make something so elaborate in these caves in the mountains? How old was this place?*

There were carvings etched into the archway and the rock walls around them. No one could figure out what they were or what they meant.

"This isn't any language I have ever seen before..." Henry said as he squinted at the markings that trailed off into the darkness above. "This entire structure has to be centuries old and taken decades to carve. The lettering and design is so precise for something so ancient and primitive...This doesn't make sense."

"Jack, use your spotlights. Get whatever shots you can of this! This is unbelievable!" He smiled. Looking over at Henry, he asked, "Ever seen anything like this before?"

"No." Henry answered, dumbfounded. His mind was at a loss for words.

"Not even on TV." Jack added. "This is nuts, dude."

"What do we do now? Keep going?" Steph asked, unsure of what lies ahead.

"Nothing else we can do." Rob answered. "Keep rolling guys, this is incredible! When we get out of here, we're gonna be superstars! This is gonna blow the world away!"

"This can't be real." Hannah whispered. "It feels like we're descending into Hell." She stuck close behind Jack, reluctantly inching her way forward.

The group hesitantly stepped forward, passing under the massive gateway. There was a shift in the air. The pressure seemed to intensify. The hairs on Jack's arm rose. Goosebumps ran down Steph's back. Everyone felt it. Something was different. With no other choice, they moved onward, further into the darkness. Deeper inside the earth. Further from humanity, as though they were in a new world. A darker world. A colder world.

"What is that?" Steph asked, optimistic, but nervous. Up ahead they spotted a light. It was a cold, bluish glow. She quickly stepped towards it. Her curious co-host followed behind along with the rest of the crew.

"It's a torch!" Henry answered, nearing the blue blaze. The metal torch hung from a decorative hook fastened to the stone wall. "The design in the metalwork is beautiful. Looks like something out of the medieval era."

"That's cool and all, but how is there a torch lit down here?" Jack asked as he zoomed his camera in on the flame.

"Must mean someone else is down here right!?" Hannah said with excitement.

"That's great!" Rob added.

"I don't know." Henry stopped. "Depends on who it is that's down here with us…"

"Ooh spooky!" Rob chuckled. "I'm sure it's some kind of touristy spot I missed doing my research."

"I don't know of anything like that around here." Henry doubted.

"There's all kinds of things like that here in the Smokies! I bet there's even a gift shop down that way!" Rob pointed. "Let's go!"

Cautiously, Henry continued forward down the dimly lit tunnel. Steph was right behind him, unsure of the situation as well. Everyone's lights stayed on, as did their cameras.

"Another one!" Steph called out, spotting another blue torch at the end of the hall.

Blue. Why are the flames blue? Henry pondered.

Turning the corner, they were welcomed by something none of them had expected. It was an altar. Some kind of religious structure. Several blue torches lined the walls of the circular cave giving it a deathly cold glow. The walls were smoother here. Carved away at, with etchings in the stone. The team found themselves in a place that felt as though they were in Hell itself.

"Are those...bodies?" Steph asked, spotting thirteen shadowy figures surrounding the altar.

"Jesus." Henry gasped. "I think they are..." Henry gasped, nervously inching towards the strange bodies. The four other members cautiously followed him, entering the harsh cavern cathedral.

The thirteen strangers knelt on the ground in a circle, all facing the stone altar. They wore dark tattered clothing that appeared to be centuries old, much older than these mines. Under their dusty black robes, Henry could see pale shriveled up skin and exposed brittle bone.

He raised his flashlight, looking at their faces. They all wore pale white masks, possibly made from clay. They had smooth blank faces with round eye holes and an arched brow that ran down into their sharp sculpted noses. They almost looked like owls in the shadows.

"Wow...They must be hundreds of years old!" Henry exclaimed in awe as he continued inspecting the bodies. The host gingerly grabbed onto the chin of the one figure's mask, slowly pulling it up to reveal his face. Henry backed off, repulsed by the bitter smell and expression on the corpse's face.

"Jesus…" He whispered.

"What is it?" Steph asked, stepping up behind her co-host, curious in their discovery. He walked over to the next body and pulled back its mask. Underneath was the same smell. The same type of face.

"Fascinating…" Henry whispered. Hannah and Jack lingered behind, keeping their distance from the bodies. Rob stepped closer to the altar, watching as his two hosts investigated the corpses. "What do you see?" He turned his head back to Jack, gesturing to get a close up of Henry.

Without taking his eyes off of the figure's decrepit face, he replied, "Every one of them. Their faces…what's left of them…are frozen in horrid expressions of fear and agony."

"Guess that's why they got the masks on." Rob coldly joked. After a silent response he asked him, "Who are these guys? What is this place?"

Still crouched down with the corpse, he put the mask back over its face and rose to his feet. Henry stroked his chin. "They appear to be…some kind of religious cult. Something ancient."

"Know what religion?" Steph asked, staying close to her co-host.

"I don't know. I don't recognize these odd markings or whatever language that is." He looked over at the altar, spotting something displayed before it. It was a book. "But I bet that might contain some answers."

Henry outstretched his hands toward the dust-covered leather book. The hair on his arm rose as a tingle of electricity passed through his bones. The air shifted, almost getting warmer as his fingers grasped the edges of the book. It was thick and heavier than he predicted as he raised it up in his hands. Blowing away decades of dust,

Henry revealed the book's cover, embedded with the text of the ancient language.

Liber Orbium Aliorum

"The Book of...Other Worlds." Henry whispered to himself. He looked up at the others who stood tentatively over him with their lights and cameras. "It's Latin."

"Are you sure?" Rob asked. He thought for a moment and snapped with a followup question, now filled with excitement. "Can you read the rest of it? See what this is all about?"

"I took some classes on Latin. I can read a handful of languages, but we'll see how well I can do with...this." He muttered doubtfully.

The hundreds of yellow pages crinkled as he slowly opened it. Inside, were pages filled to the brim with writings, and some with illustrations. Many pages were written in Latin, like the cover, but others were in strange lettering that not even Henry had recognized. "Wow...this book has to be centuries old. Some of these illustrations look medieval. Others, even older. It's not only in Latin, either. I see pages in German and others in Spanish. Scribbles and notes on pages in French and... Italian, I believe. This is insane." Henry gasped, enthralled by the history that he was holding. He backed up, never taking his eyes off the pages, and sat down on the stone step before the altar.

The four friends hovered over him, now deep into translating the prehistoric book. Stephanie's non-injured leg anxiously tapped away as she was ready to get moving. She didn't like this place. Something about it felt wrong. *We shouldn't be here.*

"From what I can decipher, it looks like this ancient religion served some larger than life God-like being." Henry looked up from the dusty wrinkled pages of the large book. Stephanie noticed something in his eyes. It was fear. Her co-host cleared his throat and continued, "A being that demanded...sacrifices for the people to feel its mercy."

"They must have used this dagger for the sacrifices!" Rob exclaimed, pointing at the golden blade ahead of him. He stood over it, entranced like a kid on Christmas morning.

Henry turned the book around to show the others, "There are illustrations here, depicting the followers that they would kill and how they did it. It was anything but peaceful. It sounds like your worst nightmare. This... God...wanted them to suffer." He ran his fingers along an image of a figure being disemboweled, cultists under masks tearing intestines and other organs from out of a woman's bloody body. Her face was forever frozen in anguish.

"The pain and suffering they must have felt...My God." Stephanie gasped.

"It says they would keep their victims alive while they scooped their eyes from out of their skulls. They would cut off their tongues and tear off each and every finger and toe. Their god wanted the human sacrifice to be as vulnerable and miserable as humanly possible. I can go on, but I think we all get the picture." Henry exhaled.

"You're all getting this right?" Rob asked, looking over at Jack, and then the others. "Everyone's cameras still rolling?"

They nodded.

"Great. This is great!" The producer smiled. Henry closed the ancient book and placed it back on the altar. It was laid back in the dust outline from where he had taken it from. He stepped back from the altar, a chill ran down his spine as his fingers trembled. Stephanie stepped closer to her co-host, with the slight feeling of something watching them in the shadows.

"Make sure you guys get some close up shots of these bodies and the altar! Don't forget the dagger too!" Rob added as he stepped closer to the golden blade. "Steph, Henry, we gotta get some shots of you two walking up to this thing and picking it up! It'll look awesome! Let's set up some more light!"

"Will do, man." Jack nodded and lowered his bag off his back, searching for some of their portable spotlights. His ribs ached as he hunched over his gear.

"Do you know what these bodies are doing here?" Steph asked her co-host. "I mean, like, why they all died here. Kneeling in this circle around the altar. Something... must have happened to them?"

"From what I could read...It seems like they were performing some kind of ritual." Henry looked over one of the rotting bodies. Something was different about these people. He had seen photos and videos of other human remains over the years from criminology classes and his own morbid interest in true crime. *Something was different here. Something wrong.* He turned back to Steph, "I think whatever they did...something...went wrong. Something bad. It killed them where they stood."

"Something like what?" Hannah panicked, attempting to control her breathing as she felt the dark rock walls closing in around her. She slowly backed away from the altar, sweat dripping down her temple. She gestured the sign of the cross as her eyes pivoted back to the exit.

"I have no idea." Henry sighed, "...and I don't think I want to."

"Guys, we need to get out of here. Now." Hannah pleaded. "This place is…it's evil. I don't want to be here."

"Yeah, I don't think this is safe. This is just too much, Rob." Stephanie added.

"I agree. We need to go." Henry stated and Jack grunted in agreement with the others.

Rob looked at his team, irritated with them all. "What are you guys saying? Look at where we are! Look at all of this! This is groundbreaking stuff! We didn't *just* explore an abandoned haunted mine. We found an ancient sacrificial cult's lair hidden within the mine! This is huge! We can't run away with our tails between our legs! Not now!"

The team stood there in silence. Four of them stood close together—inching towards the exit, while Rob stood alone, looming over them at the ancient altar.

"You're all a bunch of cowards! You know how much work I put into this? The money I spent and the resources I used to get us here! I sacrificed a lot for you all. For this!"

"I understand your frustration, Rob." Henry spoke, stepping ahead of the others. "I get it. This didn't go how we planned it would…but we need to get out of here."

Rob stood there, fuming, Stephanie could see in his eyes that he was slowly accepting their decision. "If we're leaving…" He reached his hands out toward the dagger that rested on the stone altar. It glittered in the light, almost as if it was beckoning him. "…I'm at least taking something for my troubles."

The cold flesh of his fingers gripped onto the golden sacrificial blade. The metal was warm, as if someone was just holding it. Hannah looked back at one of the cult figures that glared in her direction. The pale eyes sent chills through her bones. It looked too real.

Then she leaned closer. It was real. She reached out her hand, gently brushing the figure's face. It was brittle and flaked like old paper. The figure's dead skin fell to the floor and underneath revealed the cheekbone of its skull. This was real.

The dagger felt good in Rob's hands. He gripped it tighter, with a smile. "This thing is gonna be a nice payday. Maybe I can finally get that new car I've been wa —"

A gust of bone-chilling wind came rushing through the cave, blowing dust and debris all around them. The bright blue torches were swiftly extinguished. Entrenched in smoke and chaos, all of their lights flickered, dying out, plunging them all into utter darkness.

"What's going on?" Stephanie cried, stumbling in the dark. She bumped into something warm and before she could react, a large hand grabbed her arm. She screamed, but then heard a voice.

"Steph, it's me!" Jack said, trying to calm his friend down. "Jack! Don't let me go!" She exhaled, relieved. "Henry, grab my hand!"

Stephanie felt something graze her arm. A body. It was cold. She knew that it wasn't one of her friends. It felt different. She could smell it. The five of them desperately shook their flashlights and fidgeted with their cameras. All of their tech had gone haywire when the torches went out. As the lights flickered back to life, they saw movement in the blackness around them. Then they heard rumbling. It was growling. The decrepit bodies of cultists emerged from the dark, moving and breathing, somehow alive. They staggered towards the crew, hissing and moaning. Their boney fingers shot out like daggers, clawing at the trespassers.

Henry screamed as a sharp pain shot through his left arm. He jerked back, aiming his light towards the pain. Within the shadows, a rotting figure had latched itself onto him, biting down into his shoulder. Dark blood ran down his arm, dripping from his trembling finger tips. The thing was dusty and covered in mold, hidden under shredded robes. It's skin was dry and peeled off the bone. The smell of the rotting corpse sizzled his senses.

As the members stumbled back in the black cave, the figures came at them faster. Hannah tripped over a crack in the floor, sending her flying back, hitting her head on the stone wall. The monsters growled with delight, quickly surrounding her. In an instant their hands were on her, tearing at her arms and others at her legs. One demon had its boney fingers wrapped around her throat. Her screams were quickly drowned out as one figure shoved its hand down her throat. Stephanie could hear them tugging at her limbs. She could hear the skin tearing and the blood dripping down onto the cold stone floor. She could hear as Hannah was torn apart by these monsters in the bitter darkness. Her final cries were in muffled agony.

The others took off, struggling to block out the sounds of their friend being ripped apart in the distance. Rob was farthest ahead, sprinting over the rubble of the uneven dirt floor. Henry and Steph tried to keep up as Jack struggled in the rear.

"That way!" Rob shouted, pointing off to the right. "I see another tunnel!" The three pivoted, following the producer down a narrower path. The jagged cave ceiling came down closer to them, forcing the team to slow down. Hunched over, they quickly kept moving. It was only a matter of time before those things came for them. *What were they? Are there more of them?!* Stephanie's gut tightened under her ribs as a cold sweat ran down her neck.

"There's a door!" Henry called out, spotting it at the end of the dark corridor. It was a thick carved wooden door with hinges that looked older than the mountains themselves. Without hesitation, Rob pushed forward. Whatever was behind it, couldn't have been worse than what they were fleeing from.

Henry tried to decipher the text etched into the stone walls around them, but they did not want to stop moving. He kept up behind Rob as they passed through the ancient doorway. They were welcomed in by the chilling air. Thick with moisture, like a storm was on the way. The wheezing, sweaty camera man shuffled through the doorway. Jack frantically turned back and slammed the wooden door shut behind him. There was no lock or latch to seal it. He kept his body pressed back against it as he fought to catch his breath.

The others panted, leaning against the icy walls. Rob cleared his throat, "I...I think we're safe for now—"

"What the hell just happened!?" Stephanie cried. "Hannah...She...She's gone. Just like that! Those things...Wha—what are we gonna do?" She slowly dropped to the ground with her face in her hands. Henry stepped towards her, placing his hand on her shoulder.

"I don't know what's going on, but we're going to get out of here."

"Right. We need to keep moving. We can discuss Hannah later." Rob spoke with authority. He saw the look on his friends' faces. Through her red eye glare and clenched fists in front of her face, Steph looked ready to punch the producer. He paused, then spoke with more care in his voice. "My mind doesn't want to accept what happened either. I—we lost our friend. But if we don't push forward and fight on, we could be lost too."

"Wait…do you hear that?" Henry asked, tilting his head to listen. A low humming sound slowly filled the dark stone room. The team looked around to see what it was. Still blocking the door, Jack pressed his ear to the wood. It was coming from the other side. It was them. The moaning creatures' deathly voices rang off the cold walls like an unholy choir. They were coming.

"Oh God…" Henry whispered as sweat ran down his pale face. His green eyes glowed against the dark circles of his sockets. "They're coming."

"Yeah…we need to go." Rob added.

Jack, still catching his breath, sighed, "Well, shit."

The producer spotted an old wooden beam leaning against the cavern wall. Nearby was some rope and a shattered old wooden crate. *Some of the old miners must have come down here at some point. But did they ever make it back out?* Rob shook his head, pushing that thought away as he took hold of the beam. Heavier than it looked, he dragged it along the ground. "C'mon, give me a hand with this guys!" He called out.

Jack and Henry awkwardly took hold of the beam, carrying it to the door. A splinter shot through Jack's finger as it slipped from his grip. He bit his lip and kept going, now hearing the moans of the corpses growing louder.

Henry winched as a bolt of pain shot through his arm. The bite burned like acid. He let go of the beam and stumbled backwards into the wall. He went to touch his shoulder, gently applying pressure. Black blood and bile oozed out from the flabby flesh wound. He hissed, covering the wound with his jacket. *Need to get this cleaned and bandaged as soon as possible. Who know's what kind of infection this could...Not the time to worry about this.* Henry told himself.

"You okay?" Steph asked him.

"Yeah...I'll be fine." He answered her, rubbing his arm. He forced a smile across his grimacing face. "Thanks, Steph."

Rob and Jack rolled a nearby boulder up against the door, praying it would stop them from coming in. Sweat ran down the mens' red faces. Their wide white eyes glowed in the shadows as they searched for anything else to use. Then came the pounding. The monsters slammed their fists against the door, demanding to come in. They growled and cried, speaking tongues of old that they couldn't understand. Again and again they beat against the door. The sounds only grew louder and the door shook harder.

"Oh crap!" Jack yelled, backing away from the rattling door. With every impact, the cave wall shook. The world around them started to rumble. Pebbles descended the rocky walls, clicking as they bounced along the ground.

"Get moving!" Rob shouted at his team, "We got another cave-in!" As he screamed, the stone floor cracked, splitting and folding in on itself. Jack pressed himself against the wall, avoiding the forming canyon. Henry tripped, skidding his knee on the jagged rocks while Rob jumped out of the way. Steph slipped over rubble, falling and slamming her face against the cold rock floor. A large chunk of the earth teetered up, slowly dipping into the black crater. Steph clawed her fingers into the soil and kicked her feet, desperate for traction. Sliding down helplessly, her skin was dragged along the gravel. Before descending into the darkness below, a hand reached out and grabbed her. It was Jack.

The large man groaned as he yanked her back up. She finally grasped at an edge, pulling herself higher. She wrapped her one leg over the ledge and finished pulling herself up to safety. Jack kept his hands on her, trying to keep themselves stable in the quaking cavern. When they both got to their feet, they ran without hesitation. Off into the dark. With nowhere else to go.

Rob kept a tight grip on the dagger as he ran. He could feel the warmth radiate from it against his ribs. Henry was coming up behind him. He felt a change in the air. A smell. He looked over his producer, and for just a moment, he swore that the golden blade seemed to glow in the dark. Before Henry could say something, a small boulder came crashing down to the right of him. Another fell behind Jack, shattering the ground. The four of them wanted to stop, but their legs kept on running. The herd of monsters continued to follow them, growing closer with every step.

Henry pressed himself harder, catching back up to his producer. Jack struggled behind them, still limping from his injuries. His lungs wheezed and coughed as the large man's body shuddered, slowing down with every step. Steph grabbed his arm, attempting to help him run with her. She pulled at him, shouting, "C'mon man, we gotta keep going!" Her leg burned as his weight pressed down on her.

"I'm trying, Steph. I—it hurts." Jack staggered with her under his arm. He grit his teeth as jolts of pain shot through his body. More stones, dust and debris rained down around them. She could feel bits of rock and dead weeds cascade down her back and get caught in her hair. Gone were the two friends who ran ahead. The air was getting thicker with dust as they coughed, struggling to breathe. The only thing keeping them moving was the sounds of the moaning bodies moving in close behind them.

"Dammit. C'mon, let's go, Jack! Keep walking!" She cried, urging her aching leg to keep stepping. A sharp stone collided with her knuckles that rested on Jack's sweaty back. The rock sliced through her dirt-covered hand, burning like blisters on her flesh. She clenched her hand and bit her tongue, pushing Jack further down the rumbling tunnel.

There was the sound of a snap before the ceiling of the cavern tunnel ruptured in an explosion of earth. The room had caved-in, building a barrier between Jack and Steph and the others up ahead.

"Up there!" Jack pointed. "There's a small gap you can fit through! I'll boost you up!" She stepped towards him, a weight lifting off her chest for only a moment.

"But wait, what about you?"

"I'll figure something out." He argued, pushing her worries away.

"There's nowhere for you to go!" Steph argued, still pulling back at the unmoving rubble. There was no way of clearing this wall. Not in the short time they had.

"Just go! Don't worry about me! I'll be alright!" He choked, ignoring her resisting cries. He grabbed her arms and started pushing her up the wall of debris. The creatures were now only a few feet behind them. Their outstretched boney fingers danced in the air as their decrepit boots dragged along the dirt.

She wiped dust from her eyes as tears ran down her cheeks, "No! There has to be a way! This isn't fair!" The cultist dead gripped down onto Jack's dirt and sweat-soaked shirt. He winced as they pulled and pinched, slicing into his skin.

"Get going now, Steph! Find our friends! Go!" He pushed her forward, heaving her through the small gap. She quickly lost footing as nothing was under her, tumbling and hitting rock as she rolled down to the dirt floor.

Her head rang as she wobbled up onto her hands and knees. More blood ran down her leg, joined by a new cut across her temple. The ringing faded as the sounds of screams took over. Steph got to her feet, searching for an opening. She dug and pulled at the boulders, scratching her fingertips on the jagged debris. She listened as her friend was overpowered by the monsters. Bones snapped like gunshots. The figures hissed and whispered as they pulled at his flesh. An ancient language she couldn't understand. The voices hushed in rhythm like chants or songs, perhaps, prayers from Hell. She heard his moans fade as the sound of Jack choking on his own blood took over. Then there was nothing but the sound of the skeletal creatures shuffling along the ground. Steph pressed her ear closer. It sounded like the monsters were dragging his body away. A sloshy sound of wet clothes and flesh slapping and dragging against the stone. They were taking her friend away in pieces.

"I'm so sorry, Jack!" She sobbed, dropping to her knees. She rested her head against the boulder, praying that her friend was at peace.

Rapidly running down another decrepit tunnel, Rob and Henry slowed to walking, and then finally stopping. As the dust settled around them, they both stood hunched over, hands on their knees, as they took deep breaths. Rob spat at the ground and stood back up, wiping the dust off of his clothes. The muscles in his neck were still tense from their fall. The pain had expanded from the back of his neck, up and around to his temples, now thumping at his brain.

"You were right! We need to get out of here right now!" Rob declared with sweat dripping down his rattled face.

"We can't just leave Steph and Jack behind!" Henry argued.

"If they weren't killed in the cave-in, those... *things*...have them by now! I'm sorry, but they're gone! We need to survive!" Rob barked anxiously. "If we die too, then this was all for nothing! No one will know what we did! What happened to us!"

"Are you still worried about our video? This trip? Who cares!?" Rob went to rebuke, but Henry kept going, "Hannah, our friend, was just torn apart by these—these things—I—I don't know what to call them! They were dead. Still as marble statues and then just magically came to life. None of this makes sense! Those things were monsters! Zombie-fied cultists! Henry pulled at his hair, feeling like he was losing his mind.

"I never believed in any of that stuff! I can't! But after today...How else would you explain this sh...It doesn't matter. Only one thing matters. We need to make sure that no one else dies here today!"

"You just said it, man! You can't explain what we saw! This is something groundbreaking, no, it's earth shattering!" Rob exclaimed, stepping closer to the skeptic host. Henry looked down at the shining golden blade in his hands. Rob's white knuckles were tightly wrapped around his treasure. Their eyes were both wide and frantic. The world felt as if it was turning in on itself. The ground had stopped shaking, but Henry kept his hand on the wall beside him. His legs trembled, ready to give out. Rob grabbed his friend's shoulder.

"Ancient religions, sacrificial cults...and now *zombies*! All hidden within a haunted mine in the Smoky Mountains! We're living proof of miracles! Sick, twisted miracles, but what matters is that we get out of here and share this story! We need to go!"

Henry backed away from his producer. His eyes twitched back and forth, focusing on the caverns behind them and the man holding the golden dagger before him.

"I'm sorry. I can't leave my friends." Henry stood, with a defiant, but sorrowful glare. "You can run off, but I'm going back."

"You're an idiot." With a chuckle, he sighed, stepping further into the next narrow tunnel. Rob stopped himself and turned back to his host. "But...good luck." With a nod, the producer ran off into the dark with his light, leaving Henry behind. Alone.

————

Scanning the walls of the drab cavern tunnels, Rob dragged his hands along the stone, feeling for something —anything. Then there was a gap. He turned his headlight to see where his hand was placed. It was a small opening buried between boulders. In a jolt of excitement, Rob pulled away at the weeds and rubble hanging loosely over the hidden gap. It was the start of another tunnel. It was small, like an air vent, only a few feet wide. He aimed his headlight down the tunnel, finding no end in sight. Cobwebs dangled from the sharp rocks that lined the roof of the tunnel. *This isn't gonna be fun.* He groaned, but with a shrug, he got down on his knees and began the trek forward.

Rob crawled deeper through the narrow tunnel. Sharp stone scratched at his flesh as webs caught in his hair. Rob bit his tongue and kept pushing on forward. Slowly, the walls began to close in on him. They pressed down, scratching his shoulders and back like needles. The bulky golden dagger that he stuffed down the back of his pants was catching on the rocks. He shifted and bent his body, but it kept on catching. The jagged stones shredded through his jacket and pants. As he inched forward they sliced through his trembling skin. Rob screamed, swearing into the dark. He couldn't move any further. The dagger was wedged into the wall. He tried to crawl backwards, but the producer was stuck.

"Damnit!" He growled. The walls were getting closer. The darkness was taking over. *Was this real or am I losing it?!* He panicked as his lungs struggled to breathe. With a groan, he reached his hand back to grab onto the dagger. His wrist was sliced as his fingertips neared the gold handle. After a struggle, he pulled it loose, tossing it back behind his legs, praying that would work. Slowly shifting his shoulders and hips, Rob was able to squeeze further through the narrow tunnel. *Forget about the gold. We can come back for it after this story blows.* He argued, wanting to kick himself in the head for leaving the valuable artifact behind.

The producer was almost through. He could finally see some kind of opening ahead. *I'm not dying here!* He told himself, pressing his bleeding shoulders forward as the rocks dug deeper into his skin. Warm blood trickled down his arms as he screamed through clenched teeth.

Finally, he pressed his head through the open gap of the next small cavern. Breathing heavy, he nudged his body forward, loosening up as he further broke free of the tight tunnel. His body fell to the floor with a thud. Rob laid there as the dust settled, rubbing his bleeding arms. Several burning cuts lined his limbs and his back. Bruises began turning darker on his dirt-soaked skin. *Still alive.*

Tilting his head back, he noticed something across the way. Rob rolled over and got to his feet, his eyes locked onto the shape in the shadows. His cracked flashlight flickered with every small step he took. *Please God, don't be more dead things.*

Another inch forward and the strange object came to light. Henry chuckled with relief when he realized it was another door. This was a larger stone doorway with carvings down each side. His light was too dim to read exactly what it said. From what he could see, it wasn't any language he recognized. *A door like this must mean some kind of pathway.* He urged himself to think positive. *Perhaps, I finally found an exit.*

He pressed his hands against the cold rock. The ancient door weighed an unfathomable amount, sunken into the soil after centuries of stagnation. Sweat dripped down Rob's back as he used every muscle he had to push. Inch by inch it scratched against the dust-covered ground. Just when he thought he was making progress, a twinge in Rob's back caused him to lock up and stumble back.

"No no no! Damn!" He spat. Letting go of the door and rubbing his burning lower back. He was close. He could have made it. Frustrated, he kicked at the floor, which only caused the aching muscles in his back to spasm more. Rob groaned through clenched teeth as he brought his fist down against the rock wall. Then he heard something in the distance. A voice. It was soft. Human. It was Steph!

"Henry…? Rob?" She whimpered. "Guys? Are you out there?" The slender woman shuffled down the dark tunnel. Tears stained her dusty face. Rob saw her dim light dance in the dark and ran towards her, ignoring the pain that shot through his spine.

"Steph! It's me!" He cheered. "I'm so happy I found you!"

She smiled, limping faster towards him. "Thank God! I was so scared…alone in this damn place."

"I know, me too! I never should have brought us here, Steph!"

"Have you seen Henry?" She asked, out of breath. "We got separated. I'm not sure if he made it out." Rob lied. "Jack?"

"No." Steph dropped her head with a somber whisper. "He sacrificed himself to save me."

"I'm sorry, Steph…He was a good guy. He knew to do the right thing." Rob comforted her, rubbing her arm. "We won't forget him." She pushed forward, embracing her friend with a strained hug. Their bodies ached, but the warmth of her heart soothed their beaten bones.

After a quiet moment, she pulled back and looked up at him. "We have to get out of here. There's gotta be some way back to the surface!"

"I think I found something." He turned and pointed behind them, "There's a heavy door, back down that way. I couldn't get it open myself, but maybe together we can pull it open."

———

Henry limped down an endless dark cavern, searching for a way out. He wanted to call out for his friends, but was too scared to make a sound. Those things were still out there—hunting them. *Who knows what else lurks in the shadows. More monsters like those dead things. Maybe something worse. It really does feel like we're in Hell.* He thought, nervously looking over his shoulder. *I just hope I find them before anything else does.*

The bite on Henry's shoulder suddenly shot lightning bolts of fiery pain throughout his body. He cried, nearly collapsing to his knees. Hastily, he ripped off his jacket, throwing it to the ground, and aimed his light at his blood-soaked shoulder. It burned as it continued to eat away at his flesh like acid. Henry pressed at his shoulder, clenching his fingers around the wound, desperate to make the pain stop. Thick black blood dripped down his arm from the pulsating gash. The blackness glowed as it expanded under his skin. He watched as an alien substance bled into his veins. It sizzled as it traveled through his body, like every nerve was on fire.

What's happening to me?! He panicked. Soon his muscles flexed and contorted. He could feel his body shutting down. He wasn't sure if he was dying. He could feel a metamorphosis in his atoms.

That's when he heard it. A voice. It was inside him. He could feel it rattling inside the back of his skull. The language. It must have been what was written on the walls. It wasn't human. That voice was otherworldly. If it even was a voice. *Maybe I'm just going mad?*

Henry cried as his legs gave out. His knees came crashing down onto the stone floor. "Jesus!" His skin crawled. His hair stood up and his eyes watered. He could feel drool pooling out from his mouth. Henry was losing all control of his body. Whatever was inside him was taking over. *How much longer until there isn't any of me left? What will happen then?*

He ripped off his shirt as his body continued to burn. Sweat dripped down his face and back. Rashes, different shades of reds and purples, popped up across his body. Struggling back to his feet, he noticed blisters forming around his fingers. He could feel pressure building in his ears. His right leg began to swell around his knee. It sloshed like a water balloon, he wanted desperately to pop. He pushed through the pain, stepping down the dark tunnel. Without light, without hope, he couldn't stop—he had to keep going.

Ironic, the skeptic...becomes the supernatural. Henry pushed that thought away, still in denial of his fate. He was going to survive. He was going to see the sun again. *Feel the wind. Smell the rotting corpses at my feet. Taste the blood on my lips. Savor the agony—What!?*

The host's misshapen body shifted and inflated. He collapsed in a dark corner of a cavern. Henry had no idea where he was, but he didn't care. Through the blurry vision of his one eye, he spotted something shining in the darkness. It twinkled like the north star in the black void of space. He reached out for it, and felt something cold.

It was gold!

Henry laughed. *Looks like I finally found it!* He snorted. *All it took was me getting lost!* He started to cry, unable to stop the laughter. He rolled on the ground in tears. His ballooning stomach twitched and his lungs ached. He felt a warm melting sensation behind his lips. Then he tasted blood. He felt the crunch of bones at the back of his throat. Slowly his teeth began to fall out. Choking on them, he kept laughing. His swollen eye began to leak a bluish fluid as his other eye could barely see. The hair on his head littered the ground around him. Henry's body was falling apart, and his mind wasn't close behind. This was it. He truly was lost.

Rob led Steph back to the heavy stone door. They both shuffled quickly, ready to leave this damned place for good.

"Woah." She muttered, placing her palm against the   cold rock structure. "That is a big door. Why would they make a doorway out of such a heavy stone?"

"Yeah, not very practical." Rob replied sarcastically, attempting to push against the door again. "Maybe you can ask them before we leave."

Steph joined him, ignoring the comment. The two struggled as her feet slid across the ground and the muscles in his back constricted.

The skeletal cultists poured in from the narrow tunnel. Numerous bodies unnaturally crawling across the rocky floor, headed right for the survivors.

"C'mon!" He spat, grinding his teeth. Strands of his messy hair stuck to his sweat-soaked face. "Keep pushing!"

"I'm trying!" She cried.

The corpses shambled closer. Dislocated jaws dangled from their skulls as they moaned, like siren songs of death in the dark abyss of the mountains. Time to go! Rob pressed himself against the narrow open gap. He held his breath, sucking in his gut and pushed forward. The jagged stone scrapped across his cheek and his back, leaving bits of flesh and blood along the frame of the door. Steph pushed harder, fighting the returning stone. There was only so much time until it closed once again.

As Rob inched his way forward, he looked ahead of him at the other side of the door. It was a dark room with no features that he could find. He didn't have time to scan the room with the door now slowly rolling back towards him, putting more pressure on his ribs. He dug his nails into the rock and pushed the door back with all of his strength. Steph tried to move forward behind her producer, towards the gap in the doorway, but something stopped her.

Rob looked back over his shoulder, spotting the skeletal creatures shuffling towards them. Their outstretched rotting hands were inches from Stephanie. "I'm almost loose!" She claimed, tearing at her jacket. The tight space was too narrow to shimmy out of it. Leaving her with only one option—tear it apart. The material slowly gave away, each thread slowly ripping. *There's not enough time.* Rob realized as he finally squeezed his body through the narrow gap. He looked down at her one last time, before pushing back at the heavy door.

"What are you doing!? Robert! Stop!" She screamed. He couldn't look at her. He shut his eyes as he pushed the stone against her. His fingers bled as the gravel dug into his flesh. "Damn you! You coward!" With that, the door was pushed shut. Crashing like thunder against the cold rock walls. *I had no choice.* He told himself.

Rotting fingers pulled at her hair as she squirmed and pushed away from the corpses. They pulled her headset loose, taking away her light. Shattering as it hit the ground, Steph descended into complete darkness. With no other choice, she sprinted down the dark cavern, her hands out, desperately feeling for walls. Her heart raced as cold beads of sweat ran down her skin. Her legs burned and her teeth chattered. A trail of her blood dripped along the icy dirt floor, followed by an army of the undead. Stephanie prayed, knowing she didn't have much longer. *There has to be a way out! There has to be a way out!*

Brushing the cobwebs off his shoulders, Rob kept limping forward. He didn't have time to think about his team. He didn't have time to think about closing that door. The only thing he could do now was keep moving forward. *I have to survive.* The light on his helmet was fading, flickering more frequently in the empty black tomb. *Where am I now?!* The producer huffed.

With his next step, the floor vanished from under him. In an instant the producer was rolling down a cliff. Jagged rocks sliced at his skin. Dust and debris clung to his eyes. The man coughed and groaned as his body was beaten by the sudden impacts. Finally, his trip ended clashing into a pile of rocks below. Rob's head ached, his skin burned. He wanted to vomit. *This nightmare has to end.* He pleaded. Then he noticed something about the rocks. They were long and narrow. The textures felt different. He wrapped his fingers around one of them in the dark. Then he saw it.

Rob was laying in a massive pit of human remains. He screamed as he rocked in a sea of skeletons and tattered clothing. The pit reeked of rotten flesh and urine. Thousands of bodies filled this dark pool in the cavern. Rob's heartbeat thumped in his skull as his stomach sank. Shaking his head, he saw nothing but endless skulls and bones in every direction. The cliff that he descended stretched off into the dark heavens above, with no hope of climbing to his escape.

Something moved in the pit. It was quick. Then he heard something else behind him. He flipped and swayed his head, looking all around him. There was something rustling under the bones. A sharp claw clenched onto his right arm. Rob screamed and pulled away. It was a skeletal hand. The boney fingers fidgeted in the dim flickering light, tightening its grip on the man's pale wrist.

Another skeleton came up from behind him and pulled at his shoulders. He could feel fingers like talons, scratching at his legs. He was surrounded. Overpowered. Rob couldn't move. Everything hurt as the skeletal digits dug into his skin. He mashed his teeth, crying as they pulled at him. His muscles cramped and his limbs gave out. Warm blood trickled down his cold flesh.

Then he heard it. A voice. Booming in his head. It felt like his skull was ready to rupture. Something so powerful, surging through every nerve in his brain. He couldn't understand the language, but he knew what it was saying. He knew what it was. The God. The thing that those rotting living corpses worshipped. It was here.

Rob stood shaking before an enormous beast, something so vile it could only have come from Hell itself. A creature as old as time. Older. It had scales like a reptile, that protruded from human-like skin, covering the being in a shiny dark armor. It had feathers protrude off its shoulders and behind what appeared to be its skull. The being had several eyes that radiated in the darkness. All of which seemed to have focused down onto the little man. His legs trembled, nearly giving out. He couldn't look away from the monster. Even if he could spare a glance around, he knew that there was no escape. He struggled to form a prayer on his tongue, but his mind began to unravel. The colorful eyes that had locked onto him, seemed to transverse his thoughts.

He saw many things. Everything. The past, the future, his and others. The beginning days of humans. The evolution of beings across the globe. Things on other worlds. Other galaxies and dimensions. The eyes burned into his chest. His soul seemed to be slipping away from him. In these rapidly flashing images he saw the earliest of days as well as the last. Fire. Death. Destruction. Countless screams. Voices of anguish and misery, blaring in his skull. Bodies and blood painting his world. A world that was no more. Those final days were nearly the present. He knew that—and he knew that it was his fault.

Something as simple as exploring a cave, looking to boost his business and make some money, something that seemed so mediocre in the grand scheme of things truly was the pivotal point of his life and every other life on Earth. The fires were started. The death was here. The screams would grow and the blood would soak the soil. It was time.

The end was here.

But first, he would end. His demise was merely a whimper of mercy shown by this beast. He prayed to be taken first. He couldn't live to see what he had done to everyone. He prayed it wouldn't hurt. Those were the last thoughts to pass through Robert's mind. As the images turned to blurry colors, his body grew limp. Urine trailed down his legs, soaking his socks as drool and snot cascaded down his chin. His eyes rolled listlessly as he collapsed to the rocky floor. Nothing more than a vegetable, the man laid there as the beast rushed towards him. Its mouths opened wide, revealing the hundreds of dagger-like teeth. Dark tongues that were shades of purples and greens, flopped out from the throats that reeked of otherworldly stenches. Vomit spilled out from Robert's drooling limp lips. Then the beast clamped its jaws down and the man was gone.

Stephanie pulled at weeds and dirt as she crawled deeper through a narrow tunnel. With no light or visibility at all, she kept moving forward, praying for an opening—an escape from this hell. She pushed on, gritting her teeth as rocks and debris cut through her skin. She could feel insects crawling through her hair, along the back of her neck, and up her legs. Thousands of little legs trickled across her skin. Fighting back the tears, she dug her nails into the cold Earth, desperately keeping her mind focused on survival.

The world around her rumbled. Pebbles and dust rained down on her. She rolled back and forth like a ship lost at sea. Then came a harsh drop, jolting her body like lightning in the dark. *An Earthquake? They don't get those here!* She thought. Then a thick gulp ran down her throat as she began to imagine what else it could have been. What else could create such a displacement in these mountains. What else had that kind of power. She prayed it was only an earthquake. She prayed it wasn't due to their actions. She had to escape this dream. This horrible nightmare that laid shrouded in the darkness of the Smokies.

Stop panicking. Get moving! She scolded herself. She didn't have much time left. She had to get out.

The gravel was lighter. The soil moved and loosened up until an overpowering beam of light pierced through the dark earth. Stephanie could barely breathe after her lungs gave out such a sigh of relief. Her muscles nearly shut down as she was so close to the sanctuary of sunlight. *So close.* Stephanie cut through the earth, pulling herself forward by the roots that dangled over her head. Another set of wooden beams boarded up the small entrance of this caved-in tunnel. She pushed and pulled at the brittle wood. It cracked and creaked under the pressure of her bleeding fingers.

C'mon, almost there! She told herself as the boards finally broke free—filling the dark tunnel with the glow of the blinding sunlight. Rolling and twisting her beaten body, she crawled out from the dark dirt coffin and out into the open world. The sun blessed her skin with its warm presence. She laid sprawled out across the dirt road that hugged the edge of this mountain. Stephenie slowly took in a deep breath. *Fresh air. Thank God. It's over. I made it. I made—*

Stopping that thought, she looked around at her surroundings. She was in a completely different area than where they had entered the mines. The sun was now setting. *How long were we in that hell hole?!* Endless lists of questions rushed through her mind, but there was only one thing she wanted to know at that moment: *What was that noise?*

The sounds of cicadas and the songs of singing birds were still missing as they were that morning. However the world was not silent. Something strange and almost alien rang out around her. It was faint in the distance, but she had a feeling she knew just what it was.

Screams.

She could hear the constant screams of thousands in the distance. Deep in the woods of the smokies, she couldn't see much, but trees. Rising to her feet, she climbed in search of the horizon. The screams never stopped. The crowds only grew louder.

Her blood stained fingers clenched onto the rocky wall of the mountain. With every last bit of energy she had, she pulled herself up onto the ledge. Slowly breathing in and out, she rolled over and sat up, looking out at the horizon.

"Dear God…" She uttered in shock. Her tired eyes had widened over her dropping jaw. The world was on fire. Flames danced across the horizon. Smoke billowed across the skies and a red sun was setting in the distance. Soon darkness would consume her world. The fires had destroyed hundreds of acres of the Smokies and weren't stopping anytime soon. The blaring cries of ambulances and car alarms chattered across the land amongst the sounds of chaos and panic.

DESPERATE TIMES

"Happy Birthday to you!" Two smiling parents sang. The mother leaned in close to her daughter, "Now make a wish and blow out the candles, baby!" The little girl smiled with gaps in her teeth as she leaned forward and blew at her cake. The small flames of the candles vanished into smoke as the parents cheered. Her mother stood up and pulled the cake away. Stepping into the kitchen, she reached for the knife. The blade shined in her hand. The birthday girl licked her lips as her mother began cutting into the cake.

"What did you wish for, pumpkin?" The father asked, sitting down next to her at the   small dining room table.

"I can't tell you or it won't come true, daddy!" She giggled.

"Oh, of course! Silly me! Well, I hope it comes true for you!"

The father chuckled as the mother handed him a plate with cake on it, "Here you go, honey." She turned her attention to her child seated at the end of the table. A wide smile grew across her face as her mother handed her a large slice of cake. She licked her frosting covered finger as she handed the girl her fork, "There ya go, birthday girl! And with extra frosting, just for you!" She tapped her finger on the girl's nose, leaving a dot of red frosting behind. She always loved her mother's homemade cakes and pastries. It was only ever saved for special occasions and the child savored every bite. She would always claim that, "I could never bake a dessert that was as sweet as my little girl!"

This little girl was named Rose. Today was her sixth birthday—October seventeenth, nineteen twenty-nine. One week before "Black Thursday" and the beginning of The Great Depression. After scarfing down every bite of the sugary slice of cake, the daughter was handed a gift from her mother. It was a large box, wrapped in paper and twine that was tied into a bow on top. Rose's eyes grew wide in anticipation. Her imagination raced, thinking of all the possibilities hidden under that wrapping paper. Bits of frosting still stuck to the girl's red cheeks. Her mother grabbed a napkin and quickly wiped her face clean, before sitting back with her husband. Smiling, she pointed to the gift.

"Go on, sweetie! Open up your present!"

The five-year-old, barely containing her excitement, quickly unwrapped the large box. As the colorful paper was torn away, Rose revealed a new doll in her hands. It was a porcelain china doll. She wore a lovely paisley floral dress with a cloche hat. The little brown hat covered the doll's curly blonde hair and rosy-red cheeks. Rose admired the doll's dress and light blue eyes. She thought that the doll looked very much like herself, but a grown-up version of Rose—even though it was only nineteen inches tall—with bright red lipstick and fancy clothes. She was instantly enamored with the doll. The parents watched as their little girl was looking over the gift in silence. Her eyes said it all, and the mother and father's hearts melted.

"Do you like her, birthday girl?" Squeezing her husband's hand, she never took her eyes off of her daughter, biting her lip with anticipation. The father glanced back and forth at his two girls. It had been a rough week for him. His back ached and his hands were covered in bruises and cuts. The work was exhausting and the hours kept him from home, but it was all worth it to see his daughter so happy.

Rose smiled, "I love her! Thank you mommy and daddy!"

The cheerful child stood up from her chair and charged towards the parents. She hugged her parents as tightly as a six-year-old girl could. With the doll still in her hand, she turned and carried it with her to sit over by the fireplace. Jumping onto the couch, she played with her dolly, already starting to brush and stylize the doll's hair with her tiny fingers. Mom and dad watched from the small dining room table, still holding hands. Elsa was a loving mother, who wanted to give her daughter the world. Elsa and her husband, Victor Bradley, were hard workers like many others, just trying to survive in the ever-busy and ever-growing New York City.

Victor was an all American blue-collar worker. His grandparents moved to the states from Germany four decades earlier. Meanwhile, Elsa's family tree had ties to America since before the country was even founded. He was a bulky man, with muscular, sunburnt arms. His shirt was form fitting with suspenders that wrapped across his broad shoulders. His black hair was slicked back while his pale eyes glowed from under his stern, dark brow. Victor worked in a weapons factory where he assembled firearms and ammunition. The hours were long and grueling, but the pay was decent enough. Victor would work anywhere, he didn't care. He would do whatever it took to care for his family.

Elsa Bradley, who was already thinking of new outfits she could sew for her daughter's new doll, was a seamstress and good with her hands. She was a crafty, petite woman with large brown eyes and freckles that danced across her cheeks and down her arms. She had short and wavy dirty blonde hair and wore a matching faded yellow dress. Elsa was a vibrant and kind woman, who wasn't materialistic. She preferred crafting her own dresses, rather than spending fortunes at the shops. Victor loved that about her, yet it always made shopping for her Christmas gifts a nightmare. The one thing she always wanted was a family.

"Isn't she beautiful?" Elsa whispered as she rested her head on Victor's shoulder. She wrapped her around his bicep as his hand caressed her knee.

"The most beautiful thing in this world." He grinned, "But you're a close runner-up, darling." She looked up at him and he smirked. Before he could say another word, she kissed him and pinched his cheek, "You always know how to make a lady feel special." This world had not gone easy on the Bradley family, but they had each other, and that was all that mattered to them in the end.

"I'm going to call her...Violet!"

"Why, that's a fine name, Rose!" Victor nodded.

"Yes, Violet. What a lovely name!" Elsa added as she rose to her feet. She collected the plates and trash before washing the silverware off in the kitchen sink. Victor walked over to the couch and sat down, pulling out the newspaper of the day. As he read, he would peek over the papers, keeping an eye on the birthday girl. *She was growing up so fast.* He thought to himself, *Next thing we know, she'll be off on dates with high school boys.* Turning back to spot his wife in the kitchen, she was leaning against the wall—with the same look in her eyes. It was days like these that they would remind themselves to cherish every moment. These days were few and far between, and there weren't many more left for the Bradleys.

The fire was dying when Victor gently picked his sleeping daughter up from off of the couch. Elsa grabbed the new doll and followed her husband to Rose's bedroom.

"I told you she'd love the doll." Elsa whispered, softly rubbing the large man's back. Victor placed the girl in bed before Elsa tucked her in. The little girl snored and giggled in her sleep as her mother placed the doll on the bed next to her. Elsa took a moment, watching Rose sleeping in her small bed, before kissing the young girl's forehead and whispering, "Sweet dreams."

The parents quietly shut the door behind them and made their way down the hall. Elsa grabbed hold of her husband's hand and kissed it. He looked down as her soft eyes looked back up at him. Victor quickly picked her up in his arms and carried his wife to bed as she tried to stifle her own childish giggling. Their baby's birthday was a success. It was a day they would never forget. The glowing embers of the fireplace slowly faded away as darkness took over the home.

———

The following week, on Black Thursday, the stock market crashed eleven percent. A few days later, on Black Monday, it crashed another twelve, and the following day it dropped even more. "Thousands of investors ruined! Billions of dollars lost! The unemployment rate has nearly risen to twenty-five percent." The news reporter exclaimed. Hunched over in his chair, Victor listened to the radio intently, the morning newspaper crumpled in his fist.

"Any good news?" Elsa whispered as she stepped towards her husband. Rose was still asleep in her bed as the sun began rising. Victor grumbled, "Three out of four people are still working in places like shipyards, construction, schools, theaters, and factories like myself. The problem, however, is that they're still cutting costs, shedding dead weight, and laying off dozens, if not hundreds, of American workers." Elsa put her hand on his tense shoulder.

"There's already been a handful of people fired at my work. My buddy, Mac, was kicked to the curb last week. He's got three kids and a sick mother to take care of…and they do that to him. Things are ruthless right now, honey." He wouldn't say it, but she knew he was scared. She knelt down and hugged her husband.

————

Peering out through the window, Victor saw an endless gray sky reaching across the horizon. Clouds of smoke bellowed from rooftops across the city skyline. The man-made structures were just as dull and lifeless as the sky above. The world was losing its warmth.

Sensing something in the room, the father looked back over his shoulder. It was Violet. The doll's striking blue eyes stared at him from across the living room. *Vibrant but empty*, he thought. What was it doing looking at him? Clearly, the burly man was never a fan of dolls growing up. Besides knowing that they were toys for girls, he found dolls to be just a bit unsettling. This doll was no different. When it wasn't in the arms of his little girl, it had a coldness to it. Those chilling eyes never blinked. Victor took a step toward the doll when his daughter skipped down the hall. She smiled her bright smile, "Hi daddy!"

The girl rushed over and hugged him. Her father could smell lavender as his hand ran across her soft hair. Her tiny body was warm and welcoming. It thawed his bones on this cold winter day. Stepping back, he held her small hand. "What are you up to, Rosie?"

"I'm playing with Violet. We're going to dance, and maybe read my book together later."

"That sounds grand, Sweetie. I can put on some music for you." Victor turned the knob, silencing the dreadful news reporter. Once he found a station that she liked, Rose spun around in circles, giggling and swaying her doll. Victor sat in his chair, gleefully watching his little girl play.

After dancing to a few songs, Rose carried Violet down the hall to her room. A smile lingered on Victor's face as he watched her skip away. Hastily reached for the radio, he turned the dial back to the news station. Moments later and his smile was gone.

Sitting on her bed, Rose ran her fingertips along the fabric of Violet's dress. The floral pattern reminded her of the flowers a man was selling on the corner near their home. She could smell the flowers just by looking at it. Rose admired the simplistic beauty of the doll, hoping to look as elegant as Violet when she grew up. She dreamed of the days where she could wear fabulous dresses and sparkling shoes. As the weeks passed by, Rose would ask her mother to help brush her own hair and style it like the doll.

Victor loomed over their radio as he listened to the news station. Elsa entered the room and lingered behind him. The grainy voice on the radio boomed, "Agriculture hit the hardest! Farms across the country are going bankrupt. A mass-migration of jobless farmers were moving from the Great Plains to the coasts!"

Victor chuckled, annoyed, knowing that this would only make things worse. Endless waves of people were coming to the ever-growing shantytowns and slums of the major cities. This would only add more pressure to an already crowded New York City. He clutched the radio with his large hand and threw it across the room. Hitting the wall, it shattered into pieces that scattered along the kitchen floor. Elsa shuddered and stepped back. His hands balled into fists. Victor turned back to see his frightened wife. A slow exhale and his strained body loosened. He stepped towards her and held her hands, "I'm sorry."

Victor and his family were tired. Every month, following that terrible week in October, only made life harsher. He thought back to the colorful cake that Elsa baked for Rose. He could still taste the frosting. He remembered bits of it stuck to his daughter's cheeks. He remembered her smile. He saw how happy she was holding her gift. She loved her doll. Violet was expensive, but worth every penny.

―――――

"Good morning, sweetie!" Elsa gleamed as she stepped into Rose's bedroom. The warm glow of the morning sun passed through her window. Outside, the birds sang and car horns screeched, creating a symphony of peace and chaos. Elsa looked down at her messy-haired little girl. She yawned and stretched her tiny arms with Violet at her side in bed. Her vision still fuzzy, Rose noticed her mother was hiding something behind her back.

"What's that behind you, mommy?"

Elsa whipped her arm around, holding the surprise before her. Rose couldn't believe her eyes. It was a dress, just like Violet's, but it was fit for her. It laid out in her arms, sparkling in the sunlight. It was as if the angels themselves delivered her this dress. Still struck silent, Rose felt the material of her dress. Elsa watched as a smile grew across Rose's face. The little girl was transfixed with the outfit.

"You like it? I made you your own dress to match with Violet! I know just how much you love your doll."

Rose jumped up and hugged her mother. A warm silence filled the room. For just a moment the world was gone, and everything was peaceful. Elsa's arms gripped her baby tight before letting go. Quickly rubbing tears away from her eyes, Elsa sniffled and smiled.

"I love it! I love it so much, mommy! It's so pretty!" Rose joyfully exclaimed.

"I'm glad you like the dress, honey!" Elsa grinned. She held it up against her daughter. "Now let's help you put it on!"

"Okay!" Rose cheered.

After adjusting the dress, Elsa stepped back, waving her arms, "Ta-da! You look like a princess!" Rose watched herself twirl in the mirror. The dress fit her perfectly as it glistened in the sun. Rose grabbed Violet, now in matching outfits, and swung her around in circles. The smiling mother held back tears as she watched her daughter dance. Rose's smile warmed her heart. It took Elsa days to make it, making sure to always keep it hidden. She loved surprising her family with gifts whenever she could. *With the way things are going, this might be the last gift Rose gets for a while.* Elsa pushed that thought away and focused on the present, watching her giggling daughter jump around like a clumsy ballerina.

That evening the Bradleys took a trip to a movie theater. The theater was showing the new horror picture, *Nosferatu*. Hollywood was one of the few places that was able to thrive during this time. Millions of Americans across the country were lost and hopeless, in desperate need of some kind of entertainment. The family sat back and enjoyed their popcorn as they were transported into the black and white world of vampires. Rose's eyes flashed under the flickering light of the projector. The aroma of butter and sweets filled the dark room. Chill-inducing music was performed by a live organist as the film played. For ninety minutes Victor, Elsa, and Rose escaped the noise of the bleak city. It felt as if they were entering a warm dream. Of course, Rose brought along Violet, who was seated on her own theater chair next to the girl. Rose even covered Violet's eyes, along with her own, when the film was too scary. She told her parents that she loved the motion picture. However, Rose went on to have nightmares of Nosferatu crawling into her room for weeks after that trip to the theater. She told herself that Violet would protect her. Nothing bad could happen when she had her friend at her side.

As winter faded away and spring blossomed, the family continued selling whatever they could. Eventually, their once cozy apartment was nearly empty. Tables and chairs, the couch, and picture frames that hung from the wall were all gone. Some sold to neighbors, others to thrift shops. There was even a wealthy looking man in a dark suit who came by to purchase some of their items. What he was doing there, Victor had no clue, but he wasn't going to turn away money these days. The parents slept on their old mattress, which was now sprawled out on the floor with only one blanket. They even resorted to selling off their pillows.

Elsa cooked whatever she could, attempting to preserve whatever was possible. Victor would come home exhausted. Some days he barely spoke. He just sat there, staring down at his plate. Elsa could see the world weighing down on him. He was getting crushed like so many others. She reached out, grasping his hand at the dinner table. She saw a little sparkle in his eye as he looked back at her. A subtle smirk rose on his face. He gripped her hand tighter, staying silent. After a moment, Victor picked up his fork and went back to eating his dinner.

Like many other mothers, Elsa struggled dealing with food and clothing in this new environment. They began to rely on cheap foods like soups, beans, and noodles. She would purchase the cheapest cuts of meat—sometimes even horse meat—and recycled the roasts into sandwiches and soups. She was always sewing and patching up the family's clothing. Neighbors even traded outfits amongst each other as their children outgrew clothing. She also created quilts out of various cheap materials, as they grew accustomed to living in colder homes. Elsa worked outside the home as well, doing laundry and sewing for cash with others in her community. Her hands were sore and tired, but she didn't stop. She couldn't. Without Rose at her side, Elsa believed that she never would have made it this far.

Rose always found peace with Violet as the world crumbled around her. The Bradleys fought through the Depression, almost losing themselves to it. Watching their daughter handle it all so well, to act as though everything was right as rain, was the fuel that kept them going. Victor and Elsa promised each other that they would do whatever they could to keep their baby girl as happy and as innocent as they could in this ruthlessly harsh reality.

The sun was setting at the end of another relentless week. Elsa watched the sky grow dark as the city blushed into a neon nightmare. Even in the sunlight, her skin was cold. Her husband loomed behind her, leaning against the faded blue couch. He rubbed at his temple with one hand, while holding a glass of bourbon in the other. She watched him in the reflection of the window. He stood there with his head down, looking at the floor. *What was he thinking?* She thought to herself. She was beginning to see what kind of man he was becoming. Or was this who he really was all along? Victor had grown cold and brash. He wouldn't talk to her much, and when he did speak it was harsh and loveless.

There were still moments where he would regret his actions and go to comfort her. There were attempts, at least. He would hold her in his arms. His body was warm, but it wouldn't comfort her like the way it had before. *Why am I doing this? Why can't I love him anymore?* Elsa knew the amount of stress he was under. The fear of failing his family. The fear of losing everything. Why was there this barrier? Was she the cause of the rift? She turned and walked over to him, wrapping her arm around him, closing her eyes and leaning her head against his shoulder. She could feel him turn his head to look at her. His hand grabbed hers gently as the other hand still held the drink. They didn't say a word, but they didn't have to. Elsa knew that those feelings were gone. They were changing. The world was changing and they couldn't keep up with it. She feared what would become of them in the future. She was scared of what the world would hit them with next. Could they survive it?

———

It was nearly Rose's sixth birthday when the family finally lost their home. Unable to afford the rent, they were kicked to the curb, like so many others. Soon after, they found themselves with nowhere left to go, but a "Hooverville." Hoovervilles were shanty towns built by millions of homeless people across the country. They were named after president Hoover, who was largely blamed for the Depression. The Bradley's shanty town was located in the lower east side of Manhattan, near Chinatown and Little Italy. Dozens of families had already made up the ever-growing field of homes made from scraps. The Bradley's believed that life couldn't get any worse. They still hoped for a light at the end of the tunnel. Unfortunately, this was just the beginning.

One gloomy evening, as winter grew closer, Victor stammered through the Hooverville, passing his homeless neighbors. Some young, others old. There were families, small and large, and then there were people that were all on their own. Ex-factory workers, like himself, living next to salesmen, cooks, and veterans. All without hope. Everywhere he looked, there was misery. With what little spirit he had left in him, he put on a smile for his girls. Elsa, and especially little Rose, did not deserve this life. He wanted to do better for them. He was willing to do anything to make them smile. Their laughter meant the world to him. It was more valuable than gold.

Victor tripped over rocks along the dirt road. Kicking up dust, he sneezed. He rubbed his dirty, wrinkled sleeve across his scruffy face. Beads of sweat dripped down his clammy skin. As the nights grew colder, he knew he was getting sick, which Victor would not accept. He didn't have the time or the money for such endeavors. Coughing and spitting phlegm onto the road, he raised his other arm, with a bottle of Jack, to his wet lips. As the bottle was finished, he chucked it across the field where it crashed into a brick wall. There was a man in a dark suit leaning against that wall, staring back at Victor from the shadows. Victor shrugged and put his hands up, to motion that he was sorry. As he continued walking he thought to himself, *where have I seen that man before? What was he doing down here in a nice suit like that?*

Up ahead was their rickety little home. His stomach churned just looking at it, ashamed of their living situation. *Or was that the alcohol's doing?* That's when his daughter came running out of the doorway and right towards him. He smiled and lifted her up over his head before hugging her tightly in his bulky, bruised arms. "How's my little princess doing tonight?" He pinched her cheek and she giggled.

"I was playing hide and seek with momma, but now I want to play outside with Violet!"

"Don't cause too much trouble!" The father chuckled as he set her down. Tapping her on the head, he stepped forward and entered the shack as the girl spun around in circles with her doll. Her golden hair glowed in the evening sun. Rose and Violet wore matching blue dresses. They were the last outfits her mother was able to make.

I wish she played with her friends more than that toy. All these other kids around here and she'd rather dance with a doll. Victor groaned as he dropped down onto the worn out mattress. The old springs moaned with every movement. He laid his head back and closed his eyes, wanting nothing more than to sleep. Sleep away until the world was back to normal. The nightmare had to end soon. It had to.

"Hi sweetheart." Elsa called out as she was looking through an old beat up cabinet they stored their food in. "I'm figuring out what's for dinner tonight." She tilted her head up to look over at Victor, who was still on the mattress with his eyes closed. She gave a faint smile and a nod before peering back down into the cabinet. "Not a lot of options tonight."

"Not like there were many options last night. Or the night before." He mumbled under his intoxicated breath.

"Were you out drinking again, Victor?" She quietly asked, already knowing the answer.

Sitting up, he scowled, "Yeah, what's it to ya, darling?"

"I was just asking." Elsa said sheepishly. She hesitated to speak again. A light sigh left her lips, "Victor. Honey. We need to save what little money we have left. I won't let my baby girl starve. We can't afford you drin—"

"I can spend my money how I want! I know things are tight! I won't let that happen to her!" He growled, "If we're so desperate, maybe we should sell that stupid doll."

"You know we can't do that, Victor." Elsa asserted.

"We've sold everything else that we can, honey." Victor grumbled. "With me outta work, and you barely able to scrounge up some cash…we need to sell it. We have no other options!"

"No, damnit! Victor, that doll is the one sliver of happiness that our little girl has left!" Elsa pleaded. "The world is crumbling around us. We're falling apart, but that doll is her world. We give that away and she'll never be the same little girl we raised. We can't let the world take away her innocence so soon. She has such a vivid imagination, darling! She—"

"I think she'll be a lot worse off if she starves to death, Elsa!" He angrily interrupted. He loosened the tie around his neck. Sweat stained his chest and under his arms. His hair was disheveled and his eyes gloomy. The patriarch of the household was circling the drain. He turned and stormed out of their small home. Elsa followed to the doorway, calling out, "Where are you going now?"

"To get a drink."

———

Things only got worse for the family as autumn grew near. Many nights ended with the parents fighting. Rose would watch from under the covers of her bed as mother and father screamed. Elsa would cry and crawl into bed as her father shambled outside into the cool night air. Victor would take in the sounds of the suffering city. Across the dirt lot, a dozen men bundled up in raggedy clothes stood around a burning barrel. Their eyes glowed in the dark, contrasting with their dirty faces. Most of the men remained silent, glaring into the fire, their minds a million miles away. Victor saw one of the guys pass a bottle to another. Victor walked closer to the scrawny man with the bottle. He looked to be in his early sixties. Victor was sure that this man, like many others, was screwed over and laid off just before he could retire. The older man's apple bounced along his throat as he drank his liquor in the cold. Circular cracked glasses hung off the small man's nose. A librarian or a teacher, Victor assumed. Perhaps a lawyer, although he looked too weak to handle the courts. The trouble was, everyone looked weak these days.

Victor gently held his hand out, signaling to the small man. He looked up at Victor through his round glasses, attempting a weak smile, as he handed him the bottle. Victor threw his head back and took a long swig. It tasted like freedom. Another momentary escape. Victor opened his eyes and looked back down at the bottle. It was nearly empty when he handed it back to the older man. He licked at his lips, enjoying every last drop of the hooch.

"What's your name?" Asked the thin man, "I don't think I've seen you here before? You new to this part of town?"

The father chuckled, "Bradley. Victor Bradley. Yourself?"

"Nice to meet you, Vic, I'm Orville Scott. I used to work in marketing. My office was actually down the road a bit, but they went bankrupt a few months ago. That was, after laying a bunch of us old-timers off last year. Kicking me to the curb saved them a few pennies, but in the end the ship still sank anyways. Ain't that the way?"

The man with glasses quickly stashed the alcohol under his coat. Victor saw a look of panic flush the man's scruffy face. A police officer on patrol wandered along the border of the Hooverville. He looked down at the men with a sympathetic, but guarded glare. The officer appeared tired under his dark mustache and thick brows. A gaunt man in a baggy uniform, with pale skin that grew dark around his eyes. Even someone as authoritative as a cop appeared beaten by the world. Victor was tired too.

———

Victor's eyes raged red with anger and exhaustion. Drops of alcohol ran down his stubbled chin. Veins protruded along the man's forehead as he screamed at his wife, "After dealing with prohibition for all these years… Having to hide in basements, sneak 'em around the cops, such a waste! Now I'm catching up on all that lost time!"

Victor shouted, throwing his head back and drinking more from his bottle. Elsa stood before the doorway, blocking him from entering their home. He wiped his lips and pointed at his wife, "I'm not stopping 'til I'm bent as a rummy! This stuff better knock me out before I knock you out, doll!"

"Victor, please! Rose is asleep inside! You're going to wake her and you're going to scare her! Our little girl! You need to be a good example for her!" He froze. She slowly exhaled. Victor flipped around with his finger pointing at her face, barking, "*Me*, the good example? Have I not already been that? Are *you* embarrassed by me? Stuck with a husband that can't pay the bills and can't even raise his own daughter right? You—you don't know what you're talking about!"

Holding back tears, he cried, "What did we do to deserve this?!" Mr. Bradley looked up at the stars. "I go to church. I take care of my wife and daughter. We—we're good people!" He threw the bottle at their home, crashing like a gunshot, sending shards of glass through the air. Elsa watched helplessly as he stormed off behind the home.

"P—Please stop!" She begged, unable to follow him. Her legs were shaking, barely able to stand. He came back around to the front of their home. His angry fists tightly gripped their old wooden ax.

"You want to lose this house too?! Sure! We've got nothing else, darlin'! Why not tear this down, too!" His burly arms brought the ax crashing down into the wooden boards. Elsa stepped towards him, tears running down her face.

"Victor!" She choked, "Stop this madness!"

His eyes radiated red from tears and fury. The violent drunk staggered toward his wife, "Sweetheart.

There is nothing left, but this madness!" He spun, pointing the ax along the horizon around them, "We're swimming in it!" He chuckled, swinging the ax up over his head, ready to deal another blow to their shanty home. With all of his muscle, he brought the steel down, slicing through the weak wooden structure once more. Elsa ran over to her husband—pleading, "Vic—Victor! You don't need to do this! We'll figure something—"

"Shut up!" He shouted, backhanding her jaw. Her head snapped back harshly. She stumbled—catching herself. Blood dripped from her lip as she rubbed her cheek. Elsa looked in horror at the man she loved. Pulling the ax out, he reached in and broke off a board with his hands, before chucking it across the road. "One piece at a time! Just like everything else life has taken from us! One piece at a time! Stretching out the misery for as long as it can!" He kicked at the rickety house as his eyes glared down at his sobbing wife. "Well, I'm done! I'm getting the hard part over with myself! Tonight we lose it all!"

Sweat dripped down his face. His hair was long and disorderly with strands stuck to his skin. The dirty clothes he wore were littered with holes and stains. Victor's face was gaunt and pale. Around his grim eyes were dark pits. The bottle was the match and the fire was raging. Her husband was gone. He was dead and now this corpse walked the Earth.

"You just couldn't let me sell the damn doll!" He groaned, lifting the ax over his head once again. Else charged her husband, grabbing at the weapon. He lost his balance as she pulled back at it.

"Stop it, Victor! That's enough!"

He fought back, growling through his teeth, and yanked it forward. The couple pulled and shoved. Victor stumbled, bashing his shoulder into the crooked door frame. Elsa nearly had the ax free of his hands when he pulled back at it again. The sweaty drunk lost his grip and the ax came back to Elsa. She too, lost her balance, falling back and crashing face first into the house.

"Hon—Honey… Jesus!" Victor gasped. He dropped to his knees and reached for the still woman. He rolled her onto her back, putting his hand under her head, attempting to relieve her twitching body. The rusty ax stuck out from Elsa's red chest. It jittered in place as she coughed up strands of blood. Her wheezing throat gurgled crimson. The smell of copper flooded Victor's nostrils. In shock, he tried to assess her injury, but words never came to his lips. He couldn't speak. A million thoughts flew through her mind as she looked up at her husband. The man she loved for years. The man she wanted to spend the rest of her life with—which she did. Elsa died that night in his arms. Victor's tear-drenched face shuddered. Holding her body close, he trembled uncontrollably as he cried into her shoulder. He tried to scream, but nothing came out.

A sudden sharp crash came from around the corner. Victor's bloodshot eyes darted up, searching for whatever it was. He couldn't be seen. He couldn't be punished for his sins, he wouldn't be. He clenched the ax in his hand as it still remained in Elsa's ribs. A moment later a scruffy raccoon skittered across the road, vanishing into the shadows of another dirty alley. Victor let out a heavy sigh of relief. He spotted a trash can knocked over near the road where the raccoon was feasting. The father looked around once more, as he rubbed his tears away with his blood-spattered sleeve. He could grieve later. Victor knew he had to act quickly, before he was discovered by the police and put away for life, or worse, executed. He couldn't let that happen. He couldn't let

Rose…Right! Rose—his little girl. She couldn't lose him as well as her mother. He refused to make her an orphan.

The drunk stumbled as he rose to his feet, now standing over her head. The lower half of her corpse still remained outside, glowing under the spotlight of the moon. Bending down, he grabbed under her arms and pulled her back into their crumbling home. His wild eyes darted around, in search of any witnesses. *It's a miracle we didn't wake Rose.* He thought, as his heart burned with regret. *She must have gotten used to our constant shouting. I'm so sorry baby.* Sweat dripped into his eye, stinging as more blood oozed from Elsa's mouth. Passing through the front door, the tired father lay Elsa's corpse sprawled across the floor. He sat down on his mattress, exhausted and trembling as he looked down at her. Her half open pale eyes lingered on her killer.

Mr. Bradley gazed upon the room, spotting blood splattered over the walls and furniture.
The room was painted like a dark red nightmare. His eyes followed specks of crimson dripping from family photos, and dark spots coating flimsy cabinets and tattered chairs. He tracked the blood trails that ran from Elsa's cold body until finally resting his eyes on Violet. The doll was sitting at the foot of Rose's bed—staring at him. A witness to the murder. Her lifeless eyes glared at the shivering father. Small drops of blood were spattered across the doll's dress and face. Victor crouched down at the end of the bed and inspected the toy. Grabbing a towel, he attempted to clean it. No matter how hard he scrubbed Violet's clothes or her porcelain face, the red would not budge. It was embedded into the doll for good. *What am I going to tell Rose?* His heart rattled as panic began to take over. He even noticed a thin trail of blood that ran down from the doll's eye like a tear drop.

"Rough night?" A voice whispered behind him.

Victor jolted, nearly screaming. Losing his footing, he fell back onto the hard floor next to Elsa's corpse. Breathing heavy, his wide eyes caught a glimpse of a man standing in the dark corner. For just a moment, Victor swore that the man's eyes glowed in the shadows. He loomed over Rose, still asleep in her bed. Victor's heart sank, sobering the man up. His muscles tensed as he prepared to fight this stranger.

"Who are—Get out of my home!" Victor growled, clenching his teeth, trying to keep quiet. The man chuckled and stepped forward into the light. He was a tall, lean man, with dark slicked-back hair and a smart suit. He looked rich, especially in those days. The mysterious man spoke eloquently with the cadence of a wealthy upbringing. He closed his silver pocket watch shut before sliding it back into his coat pocket. A burning cigar hung in his other hand. The smell filled the room, reminding Victor Bradley of better days.

"Don't you worry, Mr. Bradley. I'm not here for trouble. Not at all. Actually, I'm here to help. I may have just the solution to your... predicament." He glanced down at Elsa, smiling.

Victor slowly rose to his feet, still unsure of this stranger in his home. The rich man noticed and continued his sales pitch. He waved his arms, pointing down at the body and around the decrepit home. "All of your problems—all of this—will go away."

"H-How? Who are you?" Victor asked, never taking his eyes off of the stranger. "Why are you here anyway?!" Moving in closer, he stood between Rose and this stranger. The thin man slowly walked across the room, keeping the same distance between them.

"I am a man with many resources. All I want is to make you a proposition. Seeing as your situation is not ideal, I believe that you would be in the position to make a deal. A good deal, at that!" The stranger grinned, waiting for Victor's response. The silent father stood there, watching the man as he strolled around the room.

"You see, the deal I am proposing would not only rid you of this crime, it would rid you of your pain. You could go back to how things were before any of this lovely mess began. No more suffering. No more fighting. A family reunited with nothing that could pull them apart."

Victor scratched his stubbled chin, smearing blood from his hands across his face. "You're telling me, you can bring back... my wife?" He asked while looking down at his wife's body which swam in a pool of her own blood. It was already beginning to dry and coat the flooring. Victor was in no mood for this game.

"Get out of my home. Now." Grunted the husband, his hateful eyes now back on the man. The stranger stood under the moonlight, casting sinister shadows across his face. He raised his hands up in a friendly gesture, shrugging.

"I know I must sound absurd, but I can make that wish come true. All you must do is—"

"I said GET OUT!" Victor growled through his gritting teeth, fighting the urge to scream. The man in the suit sighed and stepped toward the door.

"I'm sorry your daughter will grow up without a mother. Most likely without a father, as well. Once the police track you down, that is."

"Are you threatening me? This a hustle? Blackmail?!" Victor was fuming. His white knuckled fists shook at his sides.

"No. I'm simply warning you. I've seen things like this before. They always go sideways. I don't want that for you. Not for your daughter, either. I want your family to be happy. I can do that." The stranger stepped closer to Mr. Bradley. The ax still stood, embedded in Elsa's blood-soaked ribs. Victor hesitated. He didn't trust this swindler, but he was desperate. Rose let out a sigh and moved in her sleep. A silent moment passed as Victor held his breath. Slowly exhaling, he returned his attention to the stranger. He could smell his little girl's hair as he guarded her. He listened to her gentle breathing and the random sounds she would always make in her sleep. It gave Victor the smallest moment of peace in an otherwise miserable night. He never wanted it to end. *What am I going to do, Rose?* He somberly thought, knowing that his little girl would never forgive him for what he had done.

"Step outside with me, Mr. Bradley. We don't want to wake your little girl now, would we?" He waved his arm, gesturing for the father to follow him. Victor cautiously stepped through the doorway, now standing under the pale moonlight. The world was quiet. Victor whispered.

"What do you want?" His eyes locked onto the rich stranger, ready to kill again, if he was left with no other option. His gut stirred, uneasy standing near this dark figure. He wanted him gone. The thin man's eyes lit up as a grin stretched along his jaw.

"I want the doll."

Victor blinked. A moment passed before he asked, "What? The ...doll?"

"Yes. Your daughter's doll. The very thing you killed your wife over." He pointed his long finger at the dark interior of their shanty home. The metal of the ax gleamed in the shadows. His wife's pale, empty eyes looked back up at the men. The trail of a tear had dried along her cheek. Victor couldn't believe what was happening. So much in one evening. His life was about to change. One way or another, no matter if he took the deal or not. *Not like I have much of a choice.*

"...and Rose and I...we'll be back with my wife, her mother, Elsa? I need my family back together. I—I can't lose her too!"

"Trust me. You will all be reunited sooner than you think!"

Victor paced, his dirty hands rubbed at his tired eyes. The father looked back over at his sleeping daughter. The doll was wrapped in her arms, slowly rising and falling with every silent breath. Such an innocent and kind thing, his little girl was. He had been so bitter. So unlike himself since everything had started. He wanted a good life for her. A better life. Now it was all gone. Wasted. *This was our last chance. Her last chance.* Victor thought. This was his moment to save her life. Their lives. He wanted more than anything to undo his choices. His mistakes. He had dug himself a grave, and one for Rose, as well. He clenched his fists. His nails dug into the skin of his palms. Victor's blood froze in his veins, even as he felt his heart thumping in his skull. The world seemed to be frozen. As if Victor had stepped out of time—out from reality. *This had to be a dream. A nightmare.* He wanted to wake up and he only saw one solution. The answer was easy.

"It's a deal then?"

The shadowy figure removed his glove and stuck out his right hand. It was pink and deformed. The melted and misshapen skin on his hand continued up his arm, hidden underneath his sharp suit. The stranger must have been badly burned in some kind of fire. His other hand remained gloved. Victor assumed it was just as badly damaged. The father hesitated for a brief moment, before leaning forward and shaking the man's hand.

The pale figure's smile gleamed from within the shadows. His face was smooth, almost too smooth. Even as Victor was sobering up, he couldn't spot any blemishes or imperfections in his skin, not even any pores. Yet his hand felt slimy. The damaged and disfigured fingers clung onto his hand like talons. He could feel the man's bones disproportionally moving under the melting flesh. Victor's skin crawled as he pulled away. The deal was made and the stranger slid his dark glove back over his hell-ish fingers.

"Have a good life, Mr. Bradley. I promise you that all of this will be gone before you know it!" He waved as he walked off into the night. "I'll see you soon!"

The drunken father fell to his knees. His stomach churned and boiled before he violently vomited onto the cold soil. The shuddering husband staggered to his feet to see that the stranger was gone—and so was his wife! Her body, the blood, everything was gone. It appeared as though it never happened. The old ax was even gone. *This wasn't possible.* No one could have cleaned that up in such an instant. This didn't feel real. Victor didn't know what to trust anymore. His eyes and stomach were going against him. Perhaps his mind was as well.

Mr. Bradley did not sleep that night. He spent the late hours laying in bed, watching his sleeping daughter. Her arms outstretched, searching for her missing doll. She tossed and turned, but never woke up. Elsa was gone, but the room still smelled like copper. The air was thicker. It was as if the murder had tainted the home. The shadow of the crime still lingered over him. Victor watched as the sunrise peered in through the broken window. The sky was warming to a golden orange, filled with clouds and birds that chirped in harmony. A lovely day was beginning after leaving behind such a dark night.

The father spent the day nervously pacing inside their home. Her body was gone. The deal was made. All he could do was wait and see. Wait and see if that well-dressed stranger was telling the truth or pulling his arm. Was it a dream? Had he lost his mind? It had to be true. It had to be real. Why else would he want the doll and nothing else? A doll to cover a murder? *Maybe it really was all a dream.* Little Rose walked up to her tired father and asked,

"Where's momma at, dad? Where'd she go?"

Her father swallowed. His throat was dry and hoarse. He ran his hand through his hair, attempting to appear in a better state. Victor bent down and softly placed his hands on her shoulders. Her bright blue eyes pierced through his heart. Struggling to stay calm, he slowly exhaled, before his shaky voice let out, "Mommy just had to run to the doctors. She wasn't feeling well, but she'll be back soon, darling. Don't worry."

The small child could see that something was wrong, but she trusted her father and nodded. It must have been grown up problems. She knew that her mother would be back eventually, never expecting that she could suddenly be gone forever. Rose walked back to her small bed and tilted her head. The bed was empty. As was the floor around it. She bent down and peeked under the bed to find nothing there either. Where was her doll? Violet was missing too. The little girl's heart fluttered as panic set in. She couldn't lose her doll too. She tried to stay strong for her daddy. Even though she couldn't grasp what was wrong, she knew that her parents were tired. She knew they needed her to act grown up. Rose felt grown up when she took care of her doll, just like how her mommy took care of her.

"Daddy… Where's Violet? My friend is missing!"

Victor watched as his child waddled around the small room, still searching for the doll. His heart couldn't take much more. "I think mommy took Violet with her to the doctors."

"Why?" Rose asked, her eyes watered, ready for tears.

"Mommy…didn't want to go to the doctor's office alone. You know how scary it can be. I had to stay behind to watch you, so mommy took Violet with to keep her safe." The father bent down and hugged his child. He lifted her up, holding her tight, and wiped a tear from under her eye. "They'll both be back soon, baby, I promise."

Sniffling, Rose nodded. "Okay, daddy…"

That night, just after midnight, the crickets stopped chirping. Everything was silent, until a woman screamed out in the distance. More voices soon joined her. Screams of chaos and terror rattled across the sky. The Hooverville erupted in panic, like an earthquake, disrupting the peace of the night. Victor had finally fallen asleep when he heard the commotion. He jumped up from his bed and stepped outside. Several people sprinted past him. One woman crashed into his shoulder, nearly knocking the both of them down to the ground. He grabbed her arm and helped her back to her feet.

"You alright? What's going on here?!"

He asked as she stared back at him, horror in her eyes. A baby cried in her arms as the woman shouted something in Italian, but Victor couldn't understand her. She hesitated for a moment before running off into the night. More people stumbled out of their derelict homes, searching the area for any kind of answer. That's when Victor saw it in the distance. Fire.

Rose awakened to the sounds of the screaming crowds outside. She tilted her small body up in bed, sweating from the unusually warm night air, and turned to hang her feet off the side. Her vision was foggy as she felt around in her bed. It was empty. Her doll was still missing. Violet was still gone.

"Daddy?" She called out. The small home was quiet, while the sounds of panic grew outside. An orange glow flickered through the windows in an otherwise empty, dark world. Squinting, she could see that her father's bed was empty. The little girl's eyes grew wide. She jumped to her feet and frantically searched the room. Her mother was still gone and now her father was missing. Her best friend was lost and the people outside were crying. It sounded like everyone in town was having bad dreams. Rose didn't know what to think. She had never felt so lost before. Up ahead, the front door was cracked open. More of the warm light splashed through the gap, dancing as shadows ran by. Clouds of smoke pooled in from outside through the windows and holes in the walls. Her dry throat started coughing as she inched her way forward, pushing the door open.

Chaos rang out before her. Everyone was running and shouting. The adults were crying and pushing each other. Some of her neighbors' homes were on fire. The raging flames quickly spread, taking over the small crumbling structures. Rose stepped forward as people ran in all directions. The dark smoke filled the land, giving her nothing to see but dancing shadows in the copper gray horizon. Her lungs wheezed as she continued to cough— now more violently.

"Mommy?! Daddy?" Her dry voice cried out, before tripping over a glass bottle that lay hidden in the dirt. Rose dropped to the ground, her little hands stung as they landed in the rocky soil. Strands of disheveled blonde hair clung to her sweating face. Tears rolled down her cheeks, cutting through the ash that began coating her skin.

"Where are you, mommy!? I'm scared!" She screamed. The crowds had grown quieter in the distance. Rose didn't know where she was going. She couldn't see anything anymore. She quickened her pace, as her heart raced, wanting nothing more than to be held by her parents again. She knew that if she found Violet, somehow, everything would be okay. Rose kept walking forward, disappearing into the smoke forever.

"Daddy! Please, help me!"

Victor Bradley was busy pulling a neighbor, the elderly Mr. Scott, out from under the burning wreckage of his home. He spotted the shack burning in the distance before hearing the man's screams follow. Without thinking, Victor ran to his aide. Tossing aside wood and sizzling scraps, he dragged Scott out from under the wreckage. The older man's back and neck were badly burnt. The skin bubbled and ran like a melting candle. His leg was bleeding, but he was able to walk. Gripping his boney fingers, Victor helped him to his feet. Mr. Scott limped forward, fighting the tears that dripped down face.

"Thank you, sir! Thank God for you!" He cried, in between thunderous coughing. "If you didn't find me, I'd be toast."

Bradley, with his arm around the man's slender frame, stated, "We aren't out of this mess yet. I'll help you go as far as I can, but I think I heard someone else screaming for help. I swear I heard—"

"Help me, daddy! I'm scared!"

Victor froze as his sweat-soaked skin ran cold. Within all of the chaos of the crowds he could hear his little girl. He left her behind. "I'm coming Rose! I'll get you sweetie!" He turned back to Mrs. Scott, "Are you able to walk?"

"Yes, now go!" Scott ordered.

Victor's aching body limped across the dusty dirt path. *What was I thinking!? What kind of a father am I?!* His gut sank. A million thoughts coursed through his mind as he ran towards his daughter's screams. The flames were growing. The heat intensified from all around him. The world was an unwavering war zone, as the fire destroyed everything in its path.

"Keep calling out baby! I've got you, Rose!"

Almost there! Spotting their home in the distance, he pushed himself harder, picking up speed as he neared the front door. Burning boards fell behind him as he snuck through the crackling doorway. His tired body burned with a fever, unlike anything he felt before, aching as though he was being stung by hornets. That's when he noticed the fire was closing in. No—*he* was on fire! Victor rapidly patted away at the small flames that sparked along his sleeve. Coughing harder, he forced out, "Baby! I'm here! Where are you?"

Her distant cries turned to coughing. She could hardly breathe and neither could he. His ash covered face was riddled with the trails of teardrops. "Don't worry, baby! I'm going to find you!" *Please, God, let me find her!* He prayed. His heart beat pounded in his chest, like an over-run engine ready to blow.

The structure creaked and snapped above him, sending a large beam crashing down onto his back. His beaten body was slammed down onto the hard floor. Rose screamed out for her father, crying in the distance. He coughed and spit, as his face was pressed against the warm wooden floor. Screaming through his clenched teeth, he tried pushing himself back up. The burning beam still loomed over him, too heavy to move. Soaked in sweat, Mr. Bradley tried once more to move. The weight of the debris was only increasing. He couldn't move. Attempting to pull himself free, he clawed at their small table, only for it to be just out of reach. Victor pushed and kicked and screamed, never budging an inch.

"Rose!" He cried, snot and tears running down his miserable face. "Rose! Where are you baby!? Daddy needs help!" His daughter never answered. Rose never called out. She was gone. "Rose, please!" Victor screamed. The heavy debris pressed further down on his ribs as smoke filled his lungs. Victor struggled to speak—he could barely even breathe. A dark figure appeared in the burning red room, slowly stepping through smoke and ash as it neared the father. Through his crying eyes, he saw someone standing ahead.

Looming over him was the corpse of his wife. Elsa looked down at the miserable man. Her skin was pale and her tattered dress fluttered in heated breeze. Black blood oozed from out of her chest and dripped down from her dark lips. Ghostly white eyes peered through a mess of strands and knotted dark hair. Hanging from her pale white fingers was the bloody porcelain doll, Violet. Its small eyes cried blood as it glared into the man's soul. Victor couldn't believe it. He was losing his mind. His phantom wife never moved. She never spoke. Never blinked. She simply glared at her suffering husband. Soon, he would join her.

"I'm sorry!" He cried out. "I'm so sorry! I ne— never wanted this!" Victor reached out for her hand, "Please, please help me!"

The flaming roof of the structure finally caved in. Chunks of sizzling debris smashed down onto the father. Victor Bradley was killed in an eruption of dust and flames. The crowds around the Hooverville were an orchestra of panic and screams. No one heard his cries for help. No one came to the rescue of the father or the child. The Bradleys were far from the only casualties of that night. The blaze covered several acres, destroying everything and everyone in its path. Dozens of lives, possibly more, were lost in just under an hour that fateful night. Rose Bradley was never found. The New York fire and police found multiple charred bodies, including three children, most of which were unidentified. Many of the victims of this fire were on their own, without any family or support to run to. With no other options, these strangers gathered in this lot like an island of misfit toys. No one was looking for Rose or her parents. The Bradleys were gone, and life went on.

The man in the dark suit watched the fire burn on in the distance. A smile crept across his face. In his disfigured, red-ish right hand, he held the small doll. The specs of blood scattered across the doll's dress had dried and darkened. The porcelain girl hung from his claw-like fingers as flames consumed the horizon. The man glanced down at the doll in his hand once more. So simple. So fragile. Just like the brittle family he watched over. It didn't take much to get what he wanted in a world of desperate beggars. Stepping forward, he released the doll, where it met the ground with a splatter. Violet was left stranded in a gutter, littered with trash, as ashes rained down from above like snowflakes. The doll was alone in a cold world. Its family was gone.

After eradicating dozens of lives and destroying several buildings, the fire was finally extinguished. Work was soon underway to create a potter's field on the decimated land. It was a mass grave site created for the burial of several unknown bodies. The world was covered in sites like these dating back to the earliest days of man. These tragic places even have a biblical origin referring to "Akeldama," meaning *field of blood* in Aramaic, even tying back to Judas and the blood money he received for his betrayal.

This potter's field in New York City was lined with nearly one hundred unnamed grave markers for the victims of the fire. No one was ever certain of every individual who had died. In the early years of the Depression, death had taken over the city with a range of illnesses, murders, and suicides. The city struggled to keep track of the endless tragedies. The Bradleys did not have much for extended family. Any living relatives they had were located in other parts of the country. It wasn't until much later that they would discover the fate of the family. Victor, Elsa, and Rose Bradley were amongst the several lost souls buried in that field. In that soil, the family remained together forever, just as he was promised. As time went on and the city continued to grow, that land was converted into a public park, like many other potter's fields across the nation. In the years since, the victims were all but forgotten. All that remained was the little girl's doll—the catalyst in a long string of misery and loss.

Years passed by, becoming decades. The doll survived. It was carried on through time by different owners. People would clean her and repair her where they could, but the blood never came off. The darkness of those deaths were etched into that doll forever, and wherever Violet found herself next—misery soon followed. Much like Rose and her parents, anyone else who came in contact with the doll were struck with misfortune and death. The doll itself, with her golden hair and bright blue eyes, was not evil. At least, that's what the people thought, before they too, were lost to time.

The question now is—where will Violet end up next? Will the new owners face the same fate as the others? Or will the bloodshed finally cease when the doll finds itself engulfed in flames like Rose all those years ago? Ashes in the wind, like a forgotten dream. Nothing left but a ghost story.

HIGH MOON

The hot desert winds blew through town, as if the gates of Hell had opened. The wooden structures creaked as they roasted under the boiling sun. Just over a dozen buildings lined the street of the quiet town of Baker. The tombstones scattered across boot hill in the distance outnumbered the living residents almost ten to one. Life was short and painful in the west. It was a violent frontier, yet people persisted to answer the call of adventure. Baker was practically a ghost town at this time and it wasn't getting any better.

The most popular spot in town was, of course, the saloon. The barkeep stood behind his counter, wiping it down with an old dirty rag, before using that same rag to wipe the sweat from his brow. The middle-aged man sported a glorious blonde mustache that made up for the lack of hair on his head. Bart Landis was the owner of this establishment. He moved into town right as it was founded—back when business was booming from the gold rush. Landis built the saloon from scratch himself, with the financial aid of many drunken travelers who came in search of fortune. Over the years the crowds faded, as did the gold. Spending many of his years on the move, Landis finally found a home for himself in Baker.

Next to Landis, stood the painted lady of Baker; Miss Selina White. Leaning against the bar, she fanned herself, mentally counting down the days until Autumn would arrive. Strands of her dark hair danced across her face. Radiating confidence in a rich, red dress, the young woman's dark eyes glimmered in the sunlight. This beauty was protected by Landis, although he never had to step in. After stabbing a drunken delinquent below the belt, word spread quickly that she was not a woman to take advantage of.

The sound of heavy boots walked up to the saloon doors that morning. A tall figure passed through the doors and stepped up to the counter. With tan skin like jerky, his features were sharp and rugged. He was dressed in black with long dark hair and eyes that glowed from under the brim of his hat. A sense of uneasiness filled the room as the stranger stood at the bar. Everything was still and silent, as if the world was waiting for him to speak.

"Whiskey." He ordered with a gravelly voice, like a barrel full of sand and stone.

Landis cleared his throat, "Yessir. Coming right up." Beads of sweat continued to roll down the server's head as he poured the drink. *It's hotter than the devil's horns outside, yet this man, dressed head to toe in black leather, looked ice cold.* The stranger drank. White and Landis watched. The stranger didn't notice, or if he did, he didn't care. He put the glass down and looked up at the bartender with a glare stating that he wanted more. Landis poured another, and as he did so, the sheriff came walking in.

Douglas Roth was his name. The sheriff was an older man with a grand salt-and-peppered beard, dark hair, and a hard brow with soft eyes. His badge glistened in the sun as he walked across the saloon. He was a big man, but this stranger made him look as small as Miss White. Sheriff Roth leaned up against the counter, his right hand at his holster, eyes on the man in black.

"Howdy, stranger. What brings you to our little town of Baker?" The stranger didn't answer. Landis and White stood by, glued to the conversation. "Pour me some Bourbon, Landis." Roth asked with a smile, never taking his eyes off the stranger. "Now I'm asking nicely, sir. If I have to ask again, I won't be too friendly, ya hear?" The man in black exhaled, begrudgingly turning to look at the sheriff.

"I'm just here for a drink."

"I can see that. Any other business you have here? You on your own?" The sheriff asked. The stranger had the slightest smirk. Roth didn't like that.

"As a matter of fact, I have a group of fellow travelers with me. They should be here any moment. I got a head start on 'em this morning. We're all hungover as hell from a good time last night. I'm sure you wouldn't know what that's like, sheriff…?"

"Roth." He answered, now irritated by this man, "I didn't catch your name?"

"Jedidiah Hollow."

A gust of wind blew the saloon doors open with a bang. What followed was a tornado of men. They were all dressed in dark colors, matching the leader of their pack. They were loud, rambunctious and cocky, acting as if they owned the town that they just entered. Stumbling up to the bar, the rowdy men surrounded Hollow and Roth. The sheriff and the stranger never took their eyes off each other.

"How's it going boys? I see you all found the alcohol." Hollow laughed.

"Of course, boss! Why else would we stop in a shit-hole like this?" The mangy man shouted, then turned his attention to Miss White, "Well, well... I might have found more than one reason to visit. Wouldn't mind spending a few nights here." He smiled, revealing his gnarly yellow teeth as he looked her up and down. She grimaced and backed away from the men. Landis was nervous, but kept his eyes on the men. He knew a bad crowd when he saw one and predicted that this would escalate quickly.

"So how long do you plan on staying here in my town, Hollow?" Sheriff Roth asked. Hollow took another drink.

"I'm getting tired of these questions." Don't you have anything better to do on such a miserable day, sheriff?"

Roth kept his hand on his holster, "No sir, I'm right where I need to be."

"Sheriff!" A voice boomed from outside. A large man with thick brows and hairy arms stomped into the saloon. Sweat stained his clothes and shimmered off his shiny balding head. It was David Porter, the blacksmith of the town. Mentally, he was on the slower side, but a good man that Roth had known for years.

"Getting crowded in here!" One of the cowboys laughed.

"What is it, David?" Roth asked, glancing back and forth between his friend and the man in black before him.

"I need you to come and take a look at something." Porter asked nervously, which was out of character for the large man.

Roth followed him out of the saloon, and the two walked down the dirt road to the blacksmith's business and home. The town was just as quiet as ever, outside of the saloon, which was now the loudest it had been in weeks. The coffin maker, Mr. Gurr, was working on his carpentry next door, while Mr. Chan, the local tailor, was sweeping the front porch of his business. The few children in town were all sitting inside the small school house that resided at the end of the road. "It was just like any other Thursday. Not anymore." Roth muttered under his breath.

Entering the business, Roth put his hands at his hips, "What seems to be the problem here, Dave? I've got trouble in town with these men..." David rubbed his bald head, tears forming in his eyes, "My dogs." He pointed down at the ground, behind his business. "Something... got them. I've never seen an animal do this. This is something else. Something...vile."

Roth stepped forward to inspect the remains of the two dogs. They were torn open, with their remains scattered across the dirt. Blood was smeared across the walls of the shop. David was right, whatever did this was vile. Something wasn't right here, and he had a feeling that the strange men in town had something to do with it.

"I'm so sorry, David." Roth put an arm around the sad blacksmith, "I'm going to find out what happened here. Take the day off, mourn and if you need a drink or two, give me the bill."

The sheriff walked back down the dirt road towards the saloon. *These men needed to go.* He was too old to deal with thugs like these. The saloon window shattered as a body came soaring through it. Landis hit the dirt, tumbling into the street. His head was bleeding, but he was alive. Roth ran over, extending his arm, and helped the bartender to his feet.

"Those men are going to ruin me!" Landis muttered, "I tried to stop them, but they're animals! Oh no, Miss White!" Roth didn't hesitate, running up to the saloon doors. Inside, the now disheveled saloon, some of the men had cornered Miss White behind the bar counter. The woman wielded a broken bottle with her trembling arm.

"Back off you monsters! I'm not afraid to kill you! I've made many men bleed for what they've done!" The loudest member of the gang, Kenny, snickered as he pulled out his revolver and pointed it at her.

"I've killed a lot of women. You ain't no different, sweetheart. Now we can do this the easy way or the violent way, which I much prefer. So please, Miss, give me the best you've got!" Roth slammed the doors open as he entered.

"Listen up, all of you! I want you out of my town in the next five minutes or I will personally throw you all in a cell or in a shallow grave! Either way, we have the room!"

The saloon went silent. All eyes were on Roth. He counted at least a dozen men. They were dirty, with clothes torn and stained, and they smelled worse than they looked. All of them were armed and Roth knew that this was not their first rodeo. The long silence was broken when the scoundrels burst out laughing. Roth was furious.

"I said get! I swear to the heavenly father that I will send you all to Hell if you don't get moving!"

"I don't think you have enough bullets, Sheriff."

Roth jumped. Standing in the doorway behind him, Hollow towered over the sheriff. Roth could smell his rotting breath as he spoke. As the two men locked eyes, Roth felt that something was wrong with the man. Something off. His skin began to crawl when he noticed that his eyes were an off-white, almost yellow, glowing in the dark pits of his sockets.

"Even if you did, they wouldn't work."

Puzzled, but angry, Roth raised his revolver. "Final warning!"

The gang just kept on laughing as they drank. Three of the men turned their backs to Roth and closed in on Miss White in the corner. Holding back tears, she swung her bottle at the attackers. Roth's finger rested over the trigger. *There's too many of them. I can kill the ones by Selina, but the others will be on me in seconds. I pray our men can stop them. This is it. I can—*

"That's enough!" Hollow barked. The room fell silent. All eyes were on the man in black. "Let's get going, boys."

The boisterous men moaned.

"I said—that's enough!" The dozen men went silent. Each of them slowly rose to their feet and walked out of the saloon. Kenny winked and blew Miss White a kiss before leaving. Hollow stood by the doorway, keeping an eye on each of the men as they left.

"Sorry for the mess." The leader grumbled, before following his gang outside. Stopping before the swinging saloon doors, he looked over his shoulder at Roth, "I'm sure we'll see you around again real soon." The sheriff stood tall with fire raging in his eyes. Hollow knew exactly what he was thinking without ever saying a word. He took a final glance over at White and Landis, who shuddered behind the bar.

"Y'all have a good day now, ya hear? The night may not be so kind." With that, the man in black stepped outside. The pack of devious men followed him down the road and off into the blazing frontier. The three left standing in the saloon, slowly exhaled, letting out a collective sigh of relief. *It was over.* Landis collapsed into a chair and Selina wiped away the tears that began running down her face. The sheriff stepped closer to the doorway, watching them go. Roth's heart skipped a beat when he noticed something strange.

"None of them had any horses. They walked into town. There isn't any sign of life outside Baker for fifty miles!"

That evening, Sheriff Roth helped Landis and White clean up the saloon and repair what they could. In the short time that those men had disturbed this establishment, they broke; two chairs, a table, several bottles, and the window that Landis was tossed through.

"I'm sorry that I didn't get those scoundrels out of here sooner..." Roth started.

"Don't you go apologizing, Sheriff. Not on behalf of those beasts. I'm an old man, same as you, and I've seen my fair share of tussles. Not the first time I've had customers toss up my place...However, that was the first time I was tossed out of a window!" Landis chuckled as he wiped down the tables. One hand was busy cleaning, while the other held a towel to his bleeding head. Catching his reflection, he noticed that his pristine curly mustache was now a mess across his face. Twirling it between his fingers, he turned to Miss White, who was sweeping up the broken glass. "Selina, go ahead and get yourself cleaned up! You've done enough down here, thank you."

She wiped her forehead and sighed, "Alright, if you don't need any help...?"

"Yes, dear, everything is alright. You go get some rest now." He waved his hand, gesturing toward the stairs.

She smiled softly, before making her way upstairs. As the sun was setting, the vibrant colors of the town and its surroundings were fading and began to glow pale under the moonlight. With the fading colors, Landis climbed the stairs and crawled into his bed. The school children had all been sent home to their families who were sharing supper. The blacksmith stood over the two graves of his dogs. Still holding his shovel, the large man cried behind his home. Mr. Chan was locking up his front door when Roth came walking his way.

"Howdy, Chan, how was your day? That gang give you any trouble?" Edward Chan was a young man who had moved to town last year. He was raised as a tailor, like his father before him. They lived in New York, but after his father's passing the young man ventured west until stumbling upon the small town of Baker, where he met his wife and set up shop. He was always seen wearing a sharp suit with his dark slicked-back hair and small bifocals that lingered on his nose.

"No. No problem here, Sheriff. Those men came out of nowhere and left just the same. Only visited the saloon as far as I could see. You alright, Mr. Roth?"

A wolf howl boomed across the desert. The sudden loud noise caused both men to jump. "Never heard a wolf around here before." Chan stated.

"No. I've never heard one before either." Roth added. "Have a goodnight, Mr. Chan. Hopefully we've seen the last of those bandits." As Roth walked down the main street, along the creaking wooden porches, he waved to Mr. Gurr, the town's undertaker, who was also turning in for the night.

Up ahead the town's teacher, Mrs. Taylor, was crossing the road. She was an old woman, with no children of her own, and had been alone ever since her husband's passing three years earlier. Roth knew her to be a sweet woman, with a kind voice, and more patience than anyone else in this town had combined. She had grown frail and gaunt since the loss of her partner, but she carried on teaching the young minds of their town.

"I don't know how you deal with all those kids day in and out." Roth laughed, "But I guess my job ain't too different, babysitting a bunch of people and putting them in time-out when they misbehave."

"Oh, the children aren't too bad. You make them out to be little demons!" Taylor smiled, "Speaking of bad, what did you have to do to get rid of those mongrels today?"

Roth exhaled, "You saw them too? They bother you and the kids?"

"No, not at all. Just heard the ruckus is all. I kept the children at their desks, while I went to take a peek. I saw you got them all to walk out of here pretty quickly. You earned your badge is all that I can say!"

"Thank you, Ma'am. Have a good night."

Roth titled his hat and gave her a smile, when more wolves howled in the distance. His eyes left her gaze and looked up to see a full moon in the sky at the edge of town. Dark figures stood on the horizon. He couldn't tell what they were. *Were the men back? Where are all of the wolves?*

A woman's blood curdling scream shattered Roth's eardrums. Startled, he turned to see where it was coming from. There was a loud crash that came from within the town's bank. *Must be Mrs. Kilmer locking up for the night.* Roth thought as he ran towards the noise.

His eyes darted, watching for suspects around the bank, but it was quiet. He stepped up to the building and burst through the doors to find Carrie Kilmer dead on the bank floor. She was torn to shreds. Her dress was soaked in blood and her eyes wide, staring right back at the Sheriff who stood frozen in horror and disgust.

"What on God's green earth could have done..." Another loud crash interrupted Roth, followed by more screams from townsfolk. Roth staggered out to see Mr. Kilmer running and shooting his revolver at an alleyway across the road.

"Die, you devil!" His shaky voice screamed out.

"What's going on?!" Roth shouted, but Kilmer couldn't hear a thing. Before Roth could move, Kilmer reloaded his gun and ran into the dark alleyway. Another few shots went off, before the man screamed out in agony. Roth could hear the growling sounds of a giant beast in the dark. *That doesn't sound like any kind of wolf I've ever heard before.* Blood splattered across the dirt from out of the shadows. Roth slowly stepped forward out into the road, his gun drawn, as he moved closer to the alley. He could barely make out two eyes reflecting the moonlight, like cats eyes in the dark. He fired his gun three times at whatever killed the Kilmers, but in a flash the eyes were gone. Silence.

More wolves howled from across the street. One creature sounded like it came from behind the saloon. One down by the school house, and more on the other end of town. Finally, a loud wolf howl boomed from the dark alley that he stood before. Mr. Janisse, another employee of the bank, walked up to Roth.

"What's going on Sheriff?"

Roth looked back and forth surveying the main street. Landis, White, Gurr, and several other residents, stood frozen in place. They all shared the same terrified expression.

"I don't know...the Kilmers are...dead. Is everyone else alri—"

A large figure burst out from the dark alley, grabbing Mr. Janisse and taking him into the bank. Janisse screamed as Roth shot his gun off, sending three more bullets through the bank doors at whatever was attacking them. Several people screamed. Porter and Landis drew their guns and began shooting at the bank along with the sheriff. Janisse's screams quickly fell silent. Another creature ran out from the dark and grabbed Ms. Shelley, one of the painted ladies that worked with White.

These things were huge. Tall and covered in scruffy fur. They appeared almost human. Roth couldn't comprehend what they were dealing with anymore. More gunfire rang out as the men in town frantically pulled out their weapons. Shelley's severed head rolled down the slanted roof and bounced across the dirt road below. Nearby children screamed and another woman fainted. Roth noticed the smell of smoke in the air. Something was burning. Down the road, a fire had started in the town's bank.

"Damnation! Fire!" Roth looked to Gurr and Chan, "Help me put this out! Get some water!" Smoke billowed from out of the building as the fire rapidly spread.

"Let's go, hurry, before it spreads to the courtroom next door!" Chan and Gurr ran over, carrying pails of water, and threw them at the bank with no avail. The fire was already too large. They had to act quickly before the whole town would be nothing but ash and ember by sunrise.

"Everyone! Help us put this fire out! Grab anything you can!" Suddenly Roth froze when he spotted a large figure standing in the doorway of the blazing building. Its eyes glowed as bright as the raging fire behind it. It stepped forward, through the dark smoke and onto the dirt road. It was humanoid, but covered in dark thick hair and tattered clothes. It had sharp claws that came from its hands and feet. Legs arched like a dog, but fingers like a man. Razor sharp fangs protruded from under its lips. *The face neither resembled a wolf nor a man, but a devil*, Roth thought. Evil had come to his town.

The wolf-man stood there, its large shadow hung over the sheriff as the two locked eyes. The burning bank building began to collapse in on itself behind the monster. The wolf howled and more followed. Howling now came from all around them. Roth looked around to see more of these werewolves stepping out from the shadows. There were at least a dozen of them surrounding his people. Guns were raised and aimed at these things, but no one fired, as if waiting for their sheriff to make the first move. He had no idea what to do now.

"This is our town now, sheriff." The wolf growled. Its voice was deep and cold, ragged like an old razor. It sent chills down Roth's spine. His hand trembled as he aimed his gun at the wolf.

"You can not kill us. If you try, you will all die. One by one..." Roth fired six more bullets into the chest of the beast. No one else moved. All eyes were on Roth. The beast never took his fiery eyes off of the sheriff. The wolf simply whistled. Another werewolf across the road grabbed Mrs. Taylor and tore into her throat with his teeth. The old woman's screams quickly turned into gurgles as she spat out blood and her body shivered as the wolf ate her flesh. The wolf dropped the dead teacher's corpse onto the dirt.

The crowd gasped, collectively holding their breath. The red spread across the soil. Her disfigured corpse stared up at the sky. Roth prayed for her peace. Desperately hoping that she would see her husband again. She deserved a happy ending. Not to be torn apart, alone and scared in the middle of the road. Many of the women and children burst out crying. Their legs quivering as another painted lady fainted against the saloon steps.

"What did I just say, sheriff?" The wolf boomed. Roth stood there, shaking. Sweat dripped into his eyes as he silently prayed. The sheriff finally dropped his revolver, flinching when it hit the ground.

"Drop them! Drop your weapons everyone! You heard him…" He choked. The defeated eyes of the town remained glued to their leader. Hopeless and lost.

"Good boy." The wolf laughed. He grabbed Roth by the collar and flung him across the road, smacking his head against a wall. Roth was soon unconscious. The last thing he heard were the screams of his people and the crackle of the growing fire.

———

Slowly opening his eyes, Roth spotted blurry figures that loomed over him growing closer. He realized he was inside the saloon where Ms. White and Landis watched over him. Roth groaned as he pushed himself up. "What happened…?"

Selina placed her hand on his chest, stopping him, "Take it easy, lay back down for a minute."

"You were rattled, Sheriff. That thing tossed you across the road face first into a wall. Lucky to be waking up, I say." Landis nervously rubbed the back of his head as he spoke.

"What happened?" Roth asked, rubbing his fingers over his eyelids. As his vision and his mind came into focus, frustration began to set in. A silent moment passed. White spoke.

"They killed so many."

"Twelve of us. Dead. We found five of the bodies torn to shreds." Landis closed his eyes, trying to forget what he had seen, "The others are missing. I think they took what was left of them…saving them for a later meal. The Kilmers, Janisse, Ms. Shelley, the Reynolds family, David Jackson and Mrs. Taylor. All of them—gone—just like that. I just wish we could have done something… I should have…"

"There was nothing any of us could have done." Roth muttered as he rose to his feet. "Your bullets. They did nothing? Did they go through the beast like he was a ghost? What could do such a thing?"

Landis panicked. "I shot the damned thing. The bullets went right into his chest. Nothing. I might as well have thrown pebbles at the monster!"

"Like I said, nothing we could have done." Roth paused and looked around. "How long was I out? What happened to the fire?!" Roth ran for the door, losing his balance and crashing into a table. He was muttering curses as Selina walked over to him.

"Be careful. I just finished bandaging your head. You've been asleep for just over two hours, sheriff."

"We got the fire out, Roth. The bank is lost. The shop next door was also damaged, but not completely burned down. We stopped the fire after they left."

"They…Where did those things go?" Roth grimaced as he stood by the window, looking across the road at the burned remains.

"They left the same way they came." David Porter grumbled, stepping into the saloon. The blacksmith was drenched in sweat and dirt after putting out the fire. "After they knocked you out, the leader gathered his gang and headed west, out of town, and towards the moon." Grabbing his side in pain, Porter sat down at a table, "Chan, Gurr, and some of the other men helped with the fire, while the women gathered the children and took count of everyone in town. Landis and White dragged you in here and patched you up. Now Gurr is off collecting the bodies of the ones we lost. Father Gramm is with him, blessing them or whatever, before the funerals begin."

Roth limped over, putting a hand on the burly man's sweat-soaked shoulder, "Thank you, David."

"The sun's rising. We should be safe for now...but come nightfall—I think those monsters will be back." Porter stated, his eyes locked onto Roth's, "What are we going to do?"

The four of them stood in silence. Their eyes wandered as they searched for ideas. Selina noticed a hopeless glaze over the bartender's face. She reached out, grabbing his hand and holding onto him tightly. His sad eyes looked down at hers. A subtle smile crept onto his face. Selina wasn't sure if she could do the same.

Finally, Roth spoke. His voice boomed against the silence of the room. "We need to hold a town meeting. Spread the word around town—courthouse at noon. We'll devise a plan. For now, let's let everyone rest a moment. It's going to be a long day." Roth exited the saloon and limped his way home, leaving behind his nervous friends.

———

Panicked voices shouted over one another. The courtroom was in chaos. The main doors flew open, rumbling like thunder. With eyes wide, the people turned to see what blew into town. It was a stranger. He was a tall man who wore a dark leather trench coat. A crossbow hung from his back, straps and belts across his chest and around his legs, hidden beneath the coat. The man's face was hidden under the large brim of his hat. His spurs rattled as he made his way down the walk way towards the sheriff. Everyone sat in silence as they took in this strange newcomer. He appeared to be a walking arsenal and commanded the room without even saying a word. As he approached Roth, who was standing at the podium, the stranger reached out his hand,

"Name's Krave. I do believe I have a solution to your town's predicament."

Momentarily stunned, Roth went to shake the man's hand, "…and what is that solution, Mr. Krave?"

"Me." The stranger said, turning to face the rest of the townsfolk, "I am what some call a hunter. I track down and slaughter things that go bump in the night. Much like those werewolves that attacked you last night. I've been tracking them for days. They slaughtered an entire town about sixty miles south of here last month, and now they've come to your sweet little town of Baker."

"We shot those things last night! Nothing could kill them! How do you plan on taking them out?" Mr. Chan asked as he stood up from the second row of the courtroom. Krave pulled out one of his pistols and removed a bullet. He held it up for all to see.

"Silver. Silver is the only thing on God's green earth that can kill these creatures. I've read everything there is to know on these things. I've talked to other hunters over the years from all over the world—the one and only thing we know of that can send those beasts back to Hell—is silver! You can beat them with silver rods, impale them with silver tipped arrows, stab them with swords, but nothing beats a silver bullet, folks."

The town whispered and awed as their new savior spoke. He was a grizzled and rough, but still handsome, man in his thirties, with a long scar across the right side of his face. The hunter loaded the bullet back into his revolver. He rotated the loaded cylinder, and spun his gun before bringing it back down into its holster. Roth still had his reserves on this mysterious stranger—but in times like these—he had no better options.

"I've killed nearly a dozen wolves in my time. All dirty, barbaric creatures. Their deaths were only a drop when compared to the amounts of innocent blood that they shed." Krave paced the front of the courthouse, his eyes scanned across the citizens of Baker. "I have strategies in mind to battle these monsters. We can take them on tonight if you are willing to join me in the fight. If you'll allow me, that is. This is your home." He glanced over at Roth. After a moment the sheriff nodded.

"Yes, of course. We could use any help that we could get. You seem to know quite a good deal on these things."

Krave nodded, looking back at his audience, "Does anyone have any questions?"

The blacksmith stood up amongst the crowd, "What do we do first?"

"Everyone! Bring us any silver you can find! We need every bit you've got to fight the wolves!" Roth declared as he walked along the main street. Drenched in sweat and filth, Porter was at work in his forge, melting down silver items into his crucible. The people gathered outside of his business carrying jewelry, coins, mirrors, knives and other utensils. Sheriff Roth looked around and smiled. He had hope.

This town wasn't going down without a fight.

As the sun was setting, Roth circled the town once more. Father Gramm rang the church bell, signaling to get indoors. Everyone made their way towards the saloon. All of the women and children shuffled inside as they finished barricading the windows and doors. The continuous ringing of the church bell echoed across the valley.

The blacksmith handed Krave more silver bullets as he made his way over to Roth, "Alrighty sheriff, you, Krave, and I have all of the silver bullets. I was able to make forty-eight bullets from all of the silver we had in town." The large man was breathing heavily. He was scared."I wish I had more time. I could have made us more. I could have searched for more silver in town. I co —"

"It's not much, but it'll get the job done. Thank you, Mr. Porter." Roth put his arm out and the blacksmith went to shake it. Porter's skin was coated in sweat and grime. His hand was still warm from the fires of the forge. Roth loaded his revolver with six of the bullets, stashing the others in his pocket.

"That's nineteen grams of solid silver in each bullet. They won't know what hit 'em." Krave said as he twirled the bullet between his finger tips. "Mighty fine job, blacksmith. Thank you." He loaded the bullet into his colt with a grin. "After this is over I could use your—"

A wolf's howl slashed through the stars in the sky. Every head in town turned to look down the road, where the wolves had come from the day before. Nothing. Another howl came from behind them, at the opposite end of the road. Another from behind the burnt remains of the bank. Another to the right. Another and another. The wolves were everywhere and they were closing in on them. Yellow eyes began to glimmer from within the shadows. Growls rumbled through the streets as they moved in on the townsfolk.

The hunter walked out into the center of the dirt road. The sheriff followed, stepping out in front of the saloon. Porter, Landis, Chan and the other men joined them in the street. All behind Krave.

Hollow, the wolf leader, walked out from behind the school house. The wolf man was smiling. His glowing copper eyes never blinked while he walked up to Krave. Without taking his eyes off of the hunter, he asked Roth, "So you found yourself some backup?"

Roth didn't answer.

"I told you—all of you—that this town was ours!" Hollow declared. "All you had to do was sit back and let us have our fun. You didn't listen. For that, you will all suffer. We would have made it quick. None of you get that luxury anymore. Well, perhaps some of the ladies will…if they can make it up to us."

The wolves laughed through jagged teeth. Their devilish voices rumbled like thunder as they stepped out from the shadows and onto the road. Roth's heart trembled. *Looks like there's even more of them than before!*

Several wolves stood amongst the rooftops and balconies along the length of the town's main street. They were all large, with tense muscles hidden under their scraggly fur. Ancient warriors of the underworld. They didn't kill for survival. They simply hunted for the thrill. Death was simply fun and games to these monsters. Roth knew it. They all knew. The men behind Krave were scared. Their fingers jittered, hovering over their pistols. Roth wanted desperately to tell his men to run. To leave while they had the chance, but there was nothing else they could do. They had to fight for their home. *Or die trying.*

Krave stepped closer to Hollow. "I've been following you and your pack for weeks. I've killed monsters like you before. Dirty rancid werewolves." He spit at the wolf's feet. "This will be the last full moon you ever see. There will be no more blood on your hands!"

Two of the massive wolves jumped down from the rooftops, running up from behind the hunter. Krave spun around, pulling out his two pistols and firing. One silver bullet was sent straight through the wolf's skull. The beast's body dropped, skidding across the dirt road, stirring up dust in its trail. The other bullet was embedded in the second wolf's gut. That monster cried and dropped to the ground. It convulsed and rolled on the ground, screaming in pain. Dark blood spewed from its foaming jaws, coating the matted fur of the beast. A moment later it was dead. Krave kept his guns raised—ready to kill more of them.

A large wolf hand grabbed the back of his neck. Krave screamed in agony. Blood dripped down his shoulders and back. He flung his body back and forth, cursing at the creature, with no hope of escape. Hollow's sharp claws dug down deeper, piercing his skin like shredded paper, before ripping his head off of his jittering body. Blood glistened as it splattered in the moonlight. The hunter's body jolted and danced before collapsing on the dirt. The wolf leader held the hunter's blood-soaked head high up in the air. Hollow howled into the night before throwing the skull to his side.

Just like that, the town's best hope was gone. Roth's heart sank as he wielded his revolver. He fired his shot at the wolf closest to him. The werewolf lunged at the sheriff as the silver sliced through his neck. The black blood soaked the earth as the creature's limp body slid across the dirt road. It cried out and rolled to its side, struggling to breathe, before finally resting still. The sheriff stood over the corpse of the beast. *I killed one.*

Gunshots popped like fireworks around Roth, snapping him out of his trance. He turned his attention to more of the wolves ahead. Hollow had disappeared in the chaos. *It's fine, I'll kill him last.*

Chan and Landis fired their guns and dove for cover as the wolves came for them. The sheriff came around the corner of the school house, firing at the monsters. One of the wolves, bulky with reddish clumpy hair, came hobbling up behind him. A bloody knife was lodged in its ribs and its right leg appeared to be healing from a large gash taken out of it. The wolf cursed to itself as it outstretched it claws, closing in on the unaware officer.

The blacksmith charged at the red wolf from across the road. The man howled as he brought the ax down into the back of the wolf's neck. It screamed and shambled, falling back against the school house wall. Roth leapt back, now realizing what had happened. The wolf attempted to crawl away with the weapon still lodged into its bleeding spine.

"Finish it, sheriff!" Porter spoke. His throat was raspy and worn. In an instant, his friend pulled the trigger. With a bang, the silver bullet passed through the temple of the creature's skull. Roth turned to the blacksmith as the wolf's body hit the dirt.

"Thanks, pal."

After a strain of rough, wheezing coughs, Porter spoke, "You're welcome." He spat at the dirt and cleared his throat, "I don't recommend getting a cold before having to fight a pack of werewolves."

Roth chuckled, "Let's keep at it, partner! We're not out of this mess yet!"

The two men ran around the building, ready to attack their next monster. As the gunfire continued, screams were silenced. Bodies from both sides began to litter the street. Blood was everywhere, and they had only just begun.

Several wolves surrounded the saloon. They clawed into the doors and windows, pulling back at the barriers. Their guttural growls rattled the building. Inside, the women armed themselves with pitchforks, broken bottles and knives. They kept the children hidden behind them as several sharp claws pierced through the wooden barricades. Blood and drool dripped down from their jaws. Their fiery eyes glowed in the shadows. The young children cried as they all backed into the corner.

One woman shoved her blade through a broken window, slicing the wolf's hand. It screamed in pain. She stabbed at him again, but this time he grabbed her wrist. She pulled back resisting, but before she could even scream, the wolf brought his teeth down into her skin. The monster tore off her hand and swallowed it whole. Her bones crunched between his teeth as she dropped to the floor, crying out in anguish. Two young women, Beth and Barbara, ran to her aid. The one handed lady's blood was gushing everywhere. Soaking into the wooden floor, she left dark stains all around her. Beth tore off a piece of her dress, wrapping the fabric around the stump of her arm.

While they took care of her, Porter came running up behind the wolf that had just consumed the woman's hand. The creature licked its crimson teeth as it began to crawl its way through a broken window. The large man carried blood-soaked tools in his hands as a raging fire glowed behind his dark eyes. Out of silver bullets, he swung his hammer, bringing it crashing down into the wolf's skull. The bones in its head and neck shattered. It let out a high-pitch cry and dropped to the ground. The creature shuffled and whimpered along the floor, waiting for itself to heal. Without hesitation, the wheezing blacksmith brought his hammer down again and again. Soon there was nothing left of the wolf, but a red paste that littered the front porch of the bar.

"You ladies okay in there? Are the children safe?" Porter called out, "We're gonna beat them! We're—" A sudden sharp pain filled the man's lungs. He struggled to breathe. His throat locked up. A soft warmth slowly spread throughout his body—and then a chill. The blacksmith gazed down at a furry, bloody fist protruding from a hole in his chest. The wolf's fist held his still-beating heart. Porter let out a gasp as blood filled his mouth. The wolf pulled its hand back through the man and kicked the blacksmith down to his knees. The large man looked up at Selina in the window. She was crying. He wished she wasn't crying. The blacksmith collapsed. With his bleeding face pressed against the ground, he struggled to take his final breath. Blood pooled around him as he died. The wolf licked at his bloody hand after eating Porter's heart.

"No! Porter!" Roth screamed in a rage. Raising his pistol, he staggered towards the saloon. The feasting wolf turned, with blood and guts dangling from his chin, now spotting the sheriff charging ahead. Before it could pounce, the sheriff fired off two more bullets. One missed before the second sliced through the monster's eye socket. The bloody wolf moaned before it came crashing down to the ground next to the blacksmith. The pale sheriff looked down at his dead friend. He could hear Selina's cries besides him, standing on the other side of the broken window. The two shared a glance before hearing another scream. It was another woman in the saloon. It was Jane —Mr. Chan's wife.

Another monster had broken in through the back door. The scruffy creature grabbed her by the waist, dragging her back outside. Roth raised his pistol, but refrained from pulling the trigger, in fear of hitting the children that stood in the line of fire. Another young woman, Katherine, grabbed hold of Jane's arm. Roth ran around the building to catch the monster at the back door. By the time he made it around the corner, the wolf had dug its claws into Jane's stomach. It tore through the skin like paper, releasing her steaming intestines out into the cold night air. Jane's guts dangled down to her feet, covering her vibrant blue dress in crimson. The killer was biting at her hip, swallowing chunks of warm flesh with glee. Jane's jaw was dropped limply as her eyes were frozen wide with no life left in them.

Two more shots of silver rang off in the night. Both cut through the monster's lungs. It choked on its own blood as it dropped Jane's dead body. The wolf collapsed, sliding back against the saloon wall. Trails of blood followed down to the ground where the wolf finally died. Silver bullets jittered in Roth's shaking hands while he reloaded his revolver. Ammo was dwindling in his pockets. Many wolves still ransacked the streets. *I'm sorry, Jane.*

While the sheriff aided the women and children inside, Mr. Chan was in the midst of battle across the road. His bullets weren't silver, but at least they slowed the wolves down. Chan spotted Krave's still bleeding corpse in the dirt road. The hunter's guns lingered in his dead hands, still loaded with silver ammunition. Quickly, the tailor dived towards the body, grabbing the dead man's pistols. One of the werewolves spotted him, and charged at Chan on all fours.

"You're a dead man!" Its demonic voice roared. Chan could feel the hatred and the pain spewing from every syllable that came from its mouth. Rapidly aiming the gun, he fired. The bullet hit the wolf's right shoulder, sending the beast rolling. Missing Chan by inches, the wolf—with his razor sharp claws, tumbled and crashed into the horse's water trough. Gallons of water erupted into the night air, soaking the dirt road.

For a moment Chan thought it was over, but the wet wolf was still alive. It shambled its way towards Chan, cursing through gritted teeth, as blood rained down from its shoulder. Wet strands of fur danced across the wolf's golden eyes. *The devil smells even worse than before*, Chan noted. The nervous tailor backed up, tripping over the front steps of his business. The bleeding wolf grew closer as Chan crawled backwards, kicking dirt at the creature's face.

"Don't bother running!" It hissed with a smile. The wolf raised its right claw, ready to kill. Chan finally fired off once more, sending a bullet through the killer's rancid throat. Chunks of skin and bone erupted from the back of its skull. Blood oozed out, into the wolf's fur and down its muscular back. The twitching body collapsed at Chan's feet. Dust filled the air as Chan laid his head back in the dirt, exhaling a sigh of relief.

"Still alive." He muttered when the undertaker, Mr. Gurr, ran over to Chan.

"You alright?"

Chan nodded. Gurr put his hand out, "Toss me one of those pistols! We got work to do!"

The tailor rose to his feet, handing the second gun to the older man. Gurr was a lean man, in his late fifties, with barely any hair left on his head. To most, he appeared as a frail figure, and nothing more, but he was once a general of the civil war. Stories whispered amongst drinks at the bar, claiming that Gurr had witnessed more bloodshed and death   than the devil, himself. There was a reason why Gurr was talented in the craft of coffin making.

Side by side, the two men fired at attacking wolves. One monster was shot in the knee cap, sending it face down into the dirt. It screamed and cursed at the men before Gurr kicked the wolf's teeth in. Chan shot at another wolf that clawed at the roof of the saloon. Red mist flew through the air before it stumbled back, falling over the ledge, and hitting the ground with a loud splat.

"They won't let us in!" Growled one of the wolves. Another beast's scowl slowly formed into a sinister smile, "...Why don't we make them come out to us!"

The wolf grabbed a lit lantern that hung near the front door, slamming it against the saloon's broken window. Flames erupted, rapidly spreading across the wooden structure. In the distance, the wolves began howling one after another. The cries passed through the town like a harsh winter's winds. Soon, the army of monsters began running towards the saloon carrying lanterns and torches. The wolves tossed their torches and burning lanterns at the structure. Some came crashing through the windows, nearly hitting the families inside. Surrounded by flames, the dozen young children started to scream. Sweat dripped down Selina's brow as she searched for an escape. Dark smoke was beginning to fill the boiling structure. In no time, their vision would be gone, and their oxygen soon after.

"Aim for the bottles inside!" One werewolf called out, "Get it burning faster!"

"Let's burn this town to the ground!" Another beast screamed, followed by cheers and howls from the vile gang.

Rapidly rising, the raging fire spread across the beams and ceiling. Mr. Landis ran towards his burning business, searching for a way inside. All while Jedidiah Hollow stood in the street, watching the chaos unravel. His fangs glistened in the night as a smile stretched across his harsh face.

Roth appeared from the shadows between vandalized buildings, sneaking up behind Hollow. He cocked his gun, ready to fire, when Hollow's ear twitched. His head snapped back, locking onto the sheriff. In an instant the monster crossed the road, towering over the man with the badge.

He grabbed hold of the sheriff, digging his claws into his skin. Burning pain shot through Roth's body. He grit his teeth as he fought free of the wolf, kicking and punching the beast to no avail. Baring his sharp teeth, the wolf brought them down into Roth's shoulder. Blood cascaded down the sheriff's body as he cried out in agony. The fangs dug deeper into his muscles and scraped along his bones. The wolf whipped his head back, taking chunks of Roth's skin with him.

"You taste bitter, old man!" His gravelly voice boomed. He swallowed the bloody bits of skin before licking his lips. "But I've had worse."

"Choke on it!" Roth spat.

The wolfman moved in for the kill, when Selina rushed around the corner, jumping onto the monster's back. Swiftly swinging her knife, the blade sliced through Hollow's right eye. The wolf screamed violently and flung Selina off of his back, sending her crashing into the wooden beam of the tailor's shop. Selina wheezed, spitting up blood, as she rolled over on the ground. Her vision blurred as she spotted a wolf—no, wolves— walking towards her. She struggled to stand, dizzy and weak. Her legs wobbled before dropping to her knees, and she laughed.

"Do your worst. I've dealt with monsters like you before. You're nothing!"

Hollow slowly slid the knife from out of his eye socket. Bits of tissue and blood dripped down his face. The eye was already slowly healing when he tossed the blade aside. He grimaced before snorting, "Just wait and see, miss. We'll make you soon regret those words!"

Boris, the largest of the wolves, picked the woman up and threw her over his shoulder. She kicked and punched at the large wolfman, even though she knew that there was no hope of escape. Hollow rubbed his head as he growled, "Get a move on—but remember she's mine! Take whatever else you want now! Guns, women, alcohol...well shoot, looks like that's all up in smoke!"

The wolves laughed as the flames consumed the saloon. Like a plague, the monsters had passed though their home, destroying everything in sight. The fire had spread to the other buildings. Dark smoke filled the skies and the sound of the burning wood crackled in the night. "We've done enough for one night. We'll be back for the leftovers tomorrow! Now get going!" Hollow ordered.

The surviving wolves howled and cheered as they galloped down the road, vanishing along the dark horizon of the desert once more. For a moment the town fell silent. The cries of the night winds filled the air as the survivors stood trembling under the cursed moonlight. Women screamed and ran to the savaged bodies of the husbands strung out along the dirt road. Mrs. Lombard collapsed, holding her husband's shredded body. The couple ran their bakery together that resided at the end of their small town. Roth had known them for as long as he lived in Baker. His heart felt cold as ice as it thumped behind his fractured ribs. His weeping friend, Carol Lombard, was pregnant with a baby on the way. *A baby that would never know their father.*

The dead werewolves—now naked, brutalized bodies of men—were scattered across town. Their transformations were complete, leaving no trace of the monsters behind. Roth limped across the road, passing the corpses of his friends and enemies. These demons were all sent back to hell, and the bodies, much like their spirits, would soon burn.

Landis stumbled towards Roth. His distraught face only grew worse as he noticed the carnage across the sheriff's shoulder. "Dear Lord…you were bitten by one of those beasts!" Looking around nervously, the bartender lowered his voice, "Th-that—doesn't that mean… you're going to become a werewolf, as well?"

"I don't know." Roth looked coldly into his eyes. "I really don't know. But I've got one silver bullet that I'm holding onto just in case. If I can't control what I become… I'll use every last ounce of will power left to pull that trigger and send me off to Hell. After all of this, that's where I truly belong anyway."

Landis somberly looked Roth over. After a moment of silence, he stuck his hand out. "Whatever happens, I'll have your back, sheriff." Roth grabbed it and the men shook hands. "This is our home. It's worth fighting for. Selina believed the same."

The Sheriff closed his eyes. "I watched them take off with her. I don't think they would have killed her. She must still be alive. There's a chance we could save her. I'll do whatever I can to bring her back."

"As will I." Landis nodded.

As the sun began to rise, survivors gathered in the street. What was once a vibrant small town, was now an empty shell. The few buildings left standing were torn apart and vandalized with blood, now husks of what they once were. The rest were burnt to the ground, leaving behind only ash and despair. Businesses, schools, homes, all gone. The population of Baker was made up of just over one hundred and fifty people. Over the last two nights it was cut down to a measly twenty-six souls.

"We lost, sheriff. We need to get out of here!" A woman called out from the crowd. Her eyes glowed red with despair. Several others nodded in agreement. Roth licked his lip, both nervous and exhausted. His heart ached, ready to give up.

"We all should have left before dark yesterday." Katherine cried, tears still staining her cheeks. "All of our friends, our family…they didn't need to die! Not like this!"

"My wife and kids are gone…I have nothing left! I'm leaving this cursed place before you get me killed too!" Shouted the patriarch of the Wellings family. The pale father sat hunched over in the middle of the road, still holding the corpse of one of his children. His clothes and skin were stained with their blood. The father's eyes were the darkest, bleakest eyes Roth had ever seen. The man's soul was crushed, blown out like a candle in the dark. Roth wanted to speak, but knew of no words that could help him.

"I aint got nothing left either." Gurr started, stepping up to Roth. "So I'm staying and fighting! Gonna kill as many of those damned things as I can if it's the last thing I do!" Landis and Chan followed and stood by their sheriff.

"We send these monsters back to hell. Tonight!" Chan roared.

———

Roth and the others went around collecting all of the bodies. Their friends were buried at the base of boot hill. Porter, Jane Chan, Mrs. Taylor, and so many others, all gone. A service for the fallen friends was led by the town's preacher. Roth and the other men were soaked in sweat from digging so many graves under the intensity of the blazing sun.

"I could have done a better job. I'm sorry." Gurr whispered to the sheriff as they stood before the graves. The clouds passed overhead, offering a moment of relief from the brutal heat wave. Roth looked over at the man and patted his back.

"You made as many coffins as you possibly could have. You did a good job. All of our friends are looking down at us—at you—thankful for what you did." Roth reassured the older man.

"Thank you." He muttered. "I've seen my share of bloodshed. I know that I will most likely die tonight. I am prepared for that. Those monsters need to die. I'll tear down as many as I can with my dying breath. I don't need a casket like the others. You can burn my body with the wolves. The wood and supplies should be saved for the others. The families and—God, help us—the children." His jaw trembled as a tear ran down his cheek, "I'm sorry. The violence, the blood—it's so much. I thought I was ready for more, but I wasn't." Gurr exhaled slowly.

Before Roth could speak, Gurr whispered, "Don't worry about me. Just make sure you kill as many of those demons as you can. We are not letting them take our home."

The old soldier walked off, back to his workshop. Gurr spent the rest of the daylight crafting more caskets for his neighbors. More blood would soon be shed. How much? God only knew.

Sheriff Roth, Chan, Landis, and the others, dragged the rotting corpses of the wolf men to the edge of town. When all was done, they piled eleven dead men on top of each other in the dirt. A fire was started and soon the blue sky was filled with black smoke. The men walked away, leaving the sheriff alone to stare into the blaze. *Tomorrow, I will join them. Burning in the dirt, naked and soulless. Tonight, I become one of them. A werewolf. A monster.*

———

The sun was beginning to set as night approached. The few remaining citizens ran around boarding up windows and gathering weapons. Families, including the Hoopers, the Greenwood couple, and the Wahls, had gathered up their belongings and headed west. Roth prayed for God to watch over them, and to keep them safe on their travels. He couldn't have their blood on his hands as well. They were smart enough to leave. Roth desperately wanted the same—to turn and run, and never look back—but the sheriff knew that if he didn't do something, the wolves would never stop killing. They would simply move on to the next settlement. Another ghost town in a trail of bodies. Who knew how many innocent people these monsters had killed. Who knew how many families they tore apart. How many children suffered. *That ends tonight.*

The final full moon glowed in a sea of endless stars that danced above them. Like clockwork, the wolves' howls echoed through the land.

"You really were stupid enough to stick around! I must commend you on that, folks!" Hollow bellowed followed with a hearty laugh."And *you*!" He pointed at Roth. The Sheriff stood in the middle of the road, with his friends behind. "You look to be very much alive, and still human! I thought by now you'd be dead...or improved." Hollow stepped closer and Roth did the same. The two leaders faced off in the center of town, their armies standing ready in the distance.

"Sometime's people can't handle the power. It tears them apart. Others...take some extra time for it to finally kick in. Can't wait to see what you do, Roth. Until then..."

In an instant, Hollow charged the sheriff. His razor sharp claw swung down, tearing through the leather of Roth's belt, nearly slicing open the man's gut. The pistols fell to the ground, moments before Roth could grip them in his hands. Hollow was already ahead of him and gripping the sheriff's throat. Lifting the man up off his feet, Hollow kicked the guns aside, out of the sheriff's reach.

"You won't be needing those. What are you doing using those pesky silver bullets and ruining our fun?" Hollow turned back to his men, "Borris! Diego! You two, over here! Help me keep our friend...seated for the event." The two large wolves marched over as Hollow lowered the sheriff down. As his feet touched the dirt, the two wolves kicked the back of his legs, sending Roth to his knees. The sheriff grimaced, helplessly. They were no match for these monsters. They had been toying with them all this time. Tonight they weren't holding back anymore.

"You're gonna love this next part, sheriff! The night is just getting started!" The werewolf looked back at his pack and roared.

"Kill them all!"

The two wolves held Roth down as the rest attacked the survivors. Their nails dug deeper into the sheriff's shoulders. He cursed at Hollow, but was drowned out by the sound of screams and gunfire. The wolves moved like blurs in the shadows. Their eyes glowed like demons, and their growls like thunder, as they slashed their claws at Roth's friends.

Chan shot at the lean wolf they called Kenny, tearing through his ear. The dog cried and swung his mangled arm, backhanding Chan. His gun went flying and landed out of reach. Chan quickly backed up, dodging the wolf's attacks. Chan dove into his dark shop. The raging werewolf followed, sending a wooden barrel crashing through the shop's glass window.

"You're dead! You're dead, little man!" Barked the wolfman, "I can't wait to peel your skin off and lick the bones dry! You're gonna die screaming, just like your wife! She tasted so sweet, little man!"

Chan crawled across the carpeted floor, hidden by shelves and displays, as he neared the register. A mannequin was hurdled through the air, shattering the glass counter display. The fear had passed as Chan was fueled by his anger. He was going to kill this wolf. His wife's killer was not walking away. He slunk behind the counter, where he found his old rifle. No silver bullets— but it was better than nothing. Sniffing the air, the wolf searched the small room for the tailor.

"Come out here you yellow-belly coward! Double yellow, you chicken! Let me kill ya like a real man! I'm hungry ton–"

Before Kenny could finish, Chan rose to his feet and fired off a round into his ribs. The scrawny beast stumbled back against the wall, cracking the brittle wood behind him. The bleeding wolf pressed against his rubs, groaning through the passing pain. Furious, the wolf was ready to end this game. Chan reloaded, firing again. The bullet cut through the monster's throat. With his hand over his throat, the angry wolf kept coming.

As gunshots rang out from the tailor's shop, two wolves followed Gurr who ran behind the roasted blacksmith's forge. Gurr got two shots off. One missed both targets, and the other cut through the taller wolf's gut. The beast held his stomach, trying to stop the bleeding, as he stumbled back against the burnt building. Gurr kept running, knowing that he needed to circle back and finish the wolf off. The other werewolf who dodged his bullet was closing in on the older man.

"You won't be the freshest meal, but nothing tastes better than killing the food that fights back!" The creature chuckled. Its eyes flickered in the dark as it reached out for the undertaker.

The smell of gunpowder lingered in the night air as the battle carried on. Landis led the last wolf inside the burnt remains of his saloon. The ground crunched with every step. His home was taken from him. The massive werewolf crashed through the brittle frame of the doorway. Part of the ceiling collapsed next to him. Landis turned and fired three rapid shots. Two missed, as one cut through the wolf's kneecap. The werewolf cried out as he crashed down to his knees. Landing on the bloody wound, he cursed out in a blood curdling howl.

"I'm gonna kill you…you stupid peasant! Just a… weak human! You'll be shredded…like bacon, and stuck between my teeth by morning!" He hissed out between grinding teeth. Landis stepped near the injured wolf. He had three bullets left, when he looked around his home. The fragile framing was ready to collapse. He spotted a crispy beam of wood in the corner, near the beast. Landis stepped closer, tears built up in his eyes as he looked down at the wolf.

"You took everything from me–from us! My home. My friends. Everything!" He pointed the gun down at the monster's head. As Landis pulled the trigger, the wolf grabbed the bartender's leg, sweeping him up, before the man came crashing down onto the crispy wooden floor. The wolf laughed, pulling Landis closer, with his claws still hooked into the man's dusty pants. Landis reached out for his gun, but it was lost in the debris. Without much time to think, he saw the wooden beam ahead. With all his muscle, he kicked down at the support. The wolf's teeth grew near as the frame of the saloon's second floor came crashing down.

As the dust settled on what was left of the main street, a loud crash came from the tailor's shop. A body was thrown through the broken glass window and sent tumbling across the dirt road. It was Chan. He was covered in blood and glass as he struggled to slowly raise his head up. Roth and the bloody man locked eyes for a moment while the scrawny werewolf stomped out of the shop and towards the defeated tailor. The monster clenched a handful of Chan's dark hair in his fist. Pulling the man up to his knees, the scrawny wolf laughed as Roth was held down, unable to help his friend.

"It's gonna be okay, Chan! We're gonna get outta this! I promise–" Roth began as the wolf pulled Chan's head back and bit down onto his throat. Chan choked as blood spewed from his lips. The werewolf twisted and tugged as he dug his fangs into the man's neck. Roth trembled as he could do nothing but watch as his friend was murdered. The wolf violently ripped away from his throat. Blood dripped down the body and into the dirt as strings of flesh and muscle dangled from the beast's sharp teeth. Chan's body slowly swayed in the night air before collapsing face first in the dirt. The killer stood over the bloody corpse of his friend, howling up at the moon. The other wolves joined in, celebrating the bloodshed.

"You monsters!" Roth screamed.

A deep burning pain shot through Roth's weathered body like a lightning bolt. He shuddered and convulsed. The wolves struggled to hold him still as the sheriff screamed out in absolute horror and pain. His muscles ached and pulled as the bones underneath shifted and transformed. A sinister smile grew on Hollow's bitter face as he walked up to the screaming sheriff.

"Looks like you are one of us after all. Sometimes it takes a minute for the blood to really kick in. You think it hurts now, just wait!" Hollow laughed.

Roth's fingers cracked as they bent, extending into claws. His jaw bent and cracked. His teeth slowly sharpened into fangs. Everything burned like a fire was cooking him from the inside out. Fur rapidly grew from out of his skin, covering his body. He could feel his legs changing form as he began to rip through his tightening pants and shoes. Roth fell to his hands and knees, unable to control himself. Tears ran down his cheeks, dripping onto the cold dirt. His screams began to change as his voice grew deeper and harsher. His cries turned to roars that rumbled like a thunderstorm. Roth's skull erupted in pain, enraging him, driving him to fight—urging him to kill. He threw his head back and howled at the moon. The transformation was complete. The sheriff was a werewolf.

"Now it's a party, sheriff! Should we let you go and see how many of your friends you maul? Or perhaps we'll just keep you restrained to watch them all die, knowing that you can't do anything about it?" Hollow grabbed him by the jaw, forcing Roth to look up at him. Roth hated his vile yellow eyes.

"You...and these people...killed twelve of my men. Twelve. Some of those men I've known for decades. And on top of everything, you burned them. Treated them like trash! Why should your people deserve anything better than that?"

Hollow dug his claws deeper into Roth's jaw, kneeling down to him, face to face. "I will shower this town in every last drop of blood you all have to offer. Your bones will be scattered across this desert, and your structures turned to ash, leaving no memory of you whatsoever. A meaningless existence. Your death will be the most meaningful thing you've ever done when we feast on your flesh!"

In a flash of fury, Roth pushed himself up, breaking free of the two wolves and knocking Hollow back onto the dirt road. The sheriff swung his razor sharp claws, slicing through the neck of the wolf to his right. That monster staggered back and collapsed to one knee, struggling to contain the strands of flesh dangling from his throat.

Roth turned around as the bigger wolf rushed towards him. The jaws of the beast were inches away as the smell of copper and rot invaded his senses. The sheriff braced himself for impact, when a gunshot rang out. A bullet cut through the furry chest of the large wolf. The monster cried out, leaving a trail of dark blood behind him as he stumbled past Roth, crashing into the burnt remains of the town's bank.

The sheriff spotted his friend, Mr. Gurr, in the distance. Soaked in blood, the undertaker held his smoking gun. He gave his sheriff one final nod before closing his eyes and passing on, sprawled across the front steps of his business.

Something large tackled Roth, knocking the wind out of his lungs as his back hit the dirt road. Hollow was over him in an instant, biting at his face. The sheriff pushed back at the monster with his forearm against its throat, using the other arm to punch it repeatedly in the gut. The wolf whimpered while Roth knocked him over and took control.

The two tussled in the bloody dirt as the rest of the wolves gathered around them. They snickered and barked as they fought. Roth kicked at Hollow and bit down into his arm. Punches were thrown and claws slashed through each other's flesh. Their rapid healing kept the fight going.

The two leaders, both huffing and puffing, struggled as they rose to their feet. Blood gurgled in their throats and filled their damaged lungs as they fought for oxygen. One of Hollow's ears had been bitten off, and the sheriff was missing two fingers. His right arm was dislocated and six of his ribs rattled broken. Hollow spit out blood-soaked teeth and rubbed at the large gashes taken out of his leg. The two were tired, but they kept on fighting.

Roth wanted this night to end. Hollow wasn't standing down. He would fight on until the bitter end. His men cheered him on and cursed at the old sheriff. Roth spat blood at their feet and roared as he struck their alpha, tearing chunks of skin from his face. Bits of red cheek and neck dangled below Jedidiah's furious blood-shot eyes. Roth braced himself as the wolfman charged him.

The wolf stumbled as the sheriff dodged him. In a flash, Roth wrapped his claws around Hollow's head. The werewolf fought, twisting his head and biting at Roth's fingers and face. Drool and blood splattered across his face as he held the madman back. The sheriff pressed his thumbs up against the wolf leader's eyes. Pressing down against the vile yellow eyes, the wolfman screamed. Roth's claws stabbed into his dark eye sockets. Blood and puss poured out from his skull. Hollow cursed and cried out in agony as the sheriff pressed deeper. His legs finally gave out, bringing Hollow to his knees.

"Please! God, please! I'll let you all live! I'll leave! I'm begging y—" With all of his might, Roth clenched the screaming skull in his hands, and tore the wolf's head apart. The skin under his fur ripped and peeled. Blood and brain matter cascaded down Hollow's neck and chest. The black blood dripped from Roth's beastly hands.

Their leader was dead.

Roth tossed the two halves of the monster's head at the feet of the wolves that surrounded them. Jedidiah Hollow's butchered wolf body trembled on its knees before collapsing on the dirt below.

Surrounding the sheriff, the pack of surviving wolves stood frozen in disbelief, unsure of what to do next. Roth growled, revealing his bloody jagged teeth. Drool dripped down from his jaws. The shaggy gray hair along his body rose as goosebumps spread across his skin. Standing under the pale moonlight, the wolfman regenerated. The deep cuts in his flesh came together, bones reset, fingers grown back and teeth repaired. *This curse was a miracle.* Roth had never felt better in his life. He felt unstoppable. He felt like a god.

His booming voice sent the wolves stepping back. Some even flinched in fear. Roth smiled. The sheriff took a step forward and two of the wolves took off running. Trails of dust followed the beasts off into the darkness. The rest of the pack swiveled their heads back and forth, still too frightened to move.

"You can either stay where you stand, or run off and hide in any of the dark corners you can find along this earth. No matter what you do, no matter how far you run —you will die. I will not stop until each and every one of your skulls are mounted on my wall!" Roth roared. The remaining wolves turned and ran, desperate to catch up to the others. Not one of them said a word. Roth thought he even heard a whimper.

The wolfman was surrounded by pools of blood and dismembered bodies. Bullet holes lodged through skulls and teeth marks along peoples ribs and necks. The bloodshed was over. *Was it worth it?* Baker–his home, their home–was destroyed. It's buildings, its people, its life—gone. It truly was a ghost town.

"You did it!" Landis cheered, almost in disbelief, as he limped towards his werewolf friend. "You really did it, sheriff! How...do you feel?"

The sheriff looked down at his monstrous figure. The tattered remains of his clothes still clung to his muscular form. Injuries from battle were already healing themselves. Cuts and gashes sealed up as fractured bones snapped back into place. In mere minutes he would be back to his peak performance. The wolf exhaled, his body was fine, but his mind was— "Tired. But there's still work to do."

The bartender looked around, "I'll handle this. I will bury our friends and neighbors. After that, I'll make sure to destroy these monsters once and for all." Landis looked up at the sheriff, "You just worry about saving our friends. They need you now more than ever."

The wolf looked up at the ghostly-white moon. It radiated a warmth that he had never felt before. "Only have a few more hours 'til the sun comes up. I'll see what I can get done before then." He raised his bloody arm, extending his clawed hand toward his friend. Landis cautiously shook it.

"I'll find them. We'll see our friends again soon." He paused, "I'm gathering every silver bullet we have left and lodging them inside each and every wolf's heart.

Spotting one of his pistols under a body in the dirt road, he stepped towards it. A trail of blood dripped down from the gun as he retrieved it. The sheriff turned back to the corpse of Jedidiah Hollow. The body had already begun its metamorphosis. Its hair was shedding and the bone structure of the beast was slowly reforming. Soon he would be nothing but a human again. In the distance, Roth watched as the separate chunks of his head began transforming back into the man he spoke to at the bar two days ago. Roth aimed the gun down and fired, sending a silver bullet through the dead wolf's dark heart.

"Just to be safe."

STORY NOTES & ACKNOWLEDGMENTS

BLOOD IN THE DARK

I wrote this story when I heard of a contest for short stories that took place on Halloween night. *Blood In The Dark* ended up being one of the stories selected, and you can find it in the horror anthology, *Doors of Darkness II: Trick or Treat*. My love of exploring caves across the country on road trips with my family has never left me. One night, while watching a scary movie screening inside Cherokee Caverns in Tennessee, I came up with the story of a giant bat creature terrorizing kids that entered its lair on one fateful Halloween night. I combined that with a mysterious haunted house on a quiet suburban street which resulted in this titular story of my first horror anthology!

SCARECROW

This was one of the first stories I came up with that was always meant for this anthology book. I've always been fascinated by cornfields and the creepy scarecrows looming over them. Wether it's the Batman villain or the *Jeepers Creepers* monster, scarecrows have always been something creepy that I love. Corn mazes can be frightening as well. Endless seas of crops where anyone can easily get lost, and in some cases, never make it out alive. That chilling thought alone gave me the idea for a horror short about kids being hunted down by a cursed scarecrow hiding in the cornfields. During long road trips, fall festivals, and even spending a summer trip on a relative's farm, I would look at the fields and imagine wandering through it at night, thinking how scary it would be to feel lost in there. Then imagine how much worse it would feel if you knew there was something else in there with you. Following you.

THE WIDOW

The core of this story was always about a savior that was secretly a monster. I wanted to create a character that had brought in people before this protagonist. Someone that killed them all for some reason. That ended up being a widow that was desperately searching for someone to fill the void that their husband had left in their life. She was searching for that perfect replacement, but no man ever lived up to him. She couldn't just let them go. She did whatever she could think of to change them and make it work, but nothing did. So then the widow would release that anger and frustration onto these poor men. I never wanted to clarify what exactly happened to her husband. I leave that up to the readers to decide.

UNMASKED

I've always been fascinated by Halloween masks

and horror makeup. I love the craftsmanship and the story-telling artists can create all through the look on a disfigured face. R. L. Stine's *The Haunted Mask* was always my favorite of his books. It creeped me out when I was a kid. That claustrophobic feeling of being suffocated under a latex mask has always stuck with me. I had my own idea for a mask that was a living thing. Something we didn't fully understand. It wasn't here to possess you or control you. It was simply a hungry creature that consumed the poor souls that wore it. For something so strange I thought it must be from another world or another galaxy. Then I thought of the protagonist. Someone who knows that something is wrong with this mask, but doesn't think anyone else would believe him. Throw in a noir crime mystery setting, with a cosmic evil being, and you get yourself a freaky little Halloween story.

DADDY'S HOME

Believe it or not, this story isn't far off from reality. My grandparents would tell me the story of when my mother had similar senses at two or three years old. She would randomly know whenever her dad was coming home from work. My grandparents were shocked by this. Then one day my grandpa falls off a ladder and hurts himself at work, and much like in this story, my mother knew and said that daddy was all gone. Fortunately for her parents, her dad was okay and sent home, and my grandmother lived to tell the tale. It was always such a shocking true story, that I couldn't help but write it as a short scary story in my book!

MONSTER

This was another story inspired by my family. Growing up, I'd spend nights with my sister and cousins at our grandparents house, where we would watch scary movies and play our monster game. It was like hide & seek, but we could run and hide somewhere else before the person playing the monster could tag us. One night writing, I thought, what would we have done if a real monster showed up and tried to get us? The monster in this wasn't always a werewolf either. At first it was a shapeshifter, that the readers would never get a real sense of what it was. It was just something evil that was after these kids. I also originally had the brother sacrifice himself in the end, while grandpa was killed by the wolf much earlier on in the early drafts. My grandpa's favorite monster has always been the wolfman and I decided, to keep the story simpler and the monster less abstract, to make it one big bag hungry wolf.

THE MAD HOUSE

This was actually the first short story I ever submitted for a contest. It was a new horror anthology series called *Doors of Darkness*. Unfortunately, it was not selected for that book. However, my submission for their second book was chosen and that story was *Blood In The Dark*. This story was slightly changed and edited since that first submission, but the core and the spirit of that mad house stayed intact. Thanks to that contest, it really lit a fire in me to finally write and publish my own anthology book I've had on my mind for years.

BLOODY EGGNOG

I wanted to write a vampire story that centered

around Christmas. From there, I thought of a vampire using the disguise of Santa Claus to get closer to people, and hunt down his prey without suspicion. For the protagonist of that story, there was no option better to fight such an evil being than a priest on the holiest of holidays!

THE CRIMSON CANVAS

Heists are always fun movies and stories. My love of art and horror combined to make one of my most gruesome stories yet. I wanted to see a story where the team of criminals had no idea what they were getting into. I wanted to write a story where the item they stole fought back. My mind went to Ed Gein and other mad men throughout history that created art through carnage. What if there was something created that was so vile that the thing itself passed on these acts of cruelty and violence that birthed it in the first place? That's how you end up with *The Crimson Canvas.*

DARK RIDE

I've always loved old carnival dark rides and visiting the piers along the coast of California growing up. Later in life, when my family took a drive up to *The Lost Boys* pier in Santa Cruz, I thought of a story where the haunted dark ride was actually filled with spirits and monsters. That idea eventually morphed into this story of a boy working on the ride that was terrorized by a vengeful spirit lurking inside.

MINES OF MADNESS

I thought of a story where a film crew gets lost in some old haunted building and discovers a secret place buried underneath it that was somehow even worse than what they had originally come to see. I thought back to something ancient and otherworldly like the monsters of Lovecraftian tales. This was the story of an every day film shoot turning into an apocalyptic nightmare.

DESPERATE TIMES

I wanted to write a story about a creepy doll, but I didn't want to just do the stereotypical possessed doll that we've all seen a million times. I wanted something more emotional. A doll that has an evil aura around it that somehow corrupts the people it comes in contact with. I thought of Talking Tina from *The Twilight Zone* and the turmoil that doll stirs up between the members of that family. I also thought of Christmas shopping and the struggle of simply buying loved ones gifts. How everything seems to cost an arm and a leg these days. I wanted money problems and real world issues to also cause the drama and disdain to thrive inside this home. What better time for that than the Great Depression? Throw in a demon and some supernatural flare, and you end up with this story.

HIGH MOON

I love werewolves. I love Westerns. I realized that no one has ever really mixed those two together. That's how I ended up writing this story. You've got your typical gang of criminals that roll into a small town in the old west and terrorize the locals, but this time throw in the supernatural. Instead of the more animalistic version of a werewolf that I wrote in the short story, *Monster*, I wanted to create wolves that were closer in appearance to the classic Lon Chaney Jr. *Wolf Man*. However, the wolves in this story are smarter, more human, and able to speak. I wanted to show just how evil these monsters were, in control of their vile actions with incredible powers. These guys weren't sympathetic victims of the curse like Larry Talbot and David Kessler. These wolves liked it.

This book, *Blood In The Dark*, never would have been made possible without the love and support of my friends and family. I want to thank my grandparents, especially Linda Petzoldt, who first got me into creative writing. We would bond over reading scary stories like the *Goosebumps* series by R. L. Stine, and books by Stephen King, Darren Shan, and Edgar Allan Poe!

I've been blessed to be surrounded by such caring friends, cousins, aunts and uncles, and of course my parents, Ted and Angie Joneson. They have always had my back when pursuing any of my artistic endeavors. I wouldn't be where I am today without them. I can't wait to get to work on my next projects. I hope to publish more books, create more cartoons, and perhaps even venture into new territories in story-telling and entertainment! I love playing in this world of make-believe, and hope you all have enjoyed riding along with me through these dark tales of chaos and mystery!

ABOUT THE AUTHOR

Tucker Joneson is a writer, artist, and filmmaker. He is the author and illustrator of the children's book, *The Soldier Bear.* He has created several animated short films including the film festival awarded *Hide & Shriek, Hero,* and *Pinhead.* Born in Burbank, California, Tucker currently enjoys living among the Great Smoky Mountains in East Tennessee.